THE CAT
CAME BACK

The 9 Lives Cozy Mystery Series
Book One

Louise Clark

Book and Cover design by eBook Prep
www.ebookprep.com

September, 2016
ISBN: 978-1-61417-858-3

ePublishing Works!
www.epublishingworks.com

CHAPTER 1

━━━◆━━━

"I have to throw *that* out too?" *That* was a stuffed kangaroo sent to Noelle all the way from Australia.

"We aren't throwing anything out. We're giving the toys you've outgrown to a charity," Christy Jamieson said patiently. Since she and her daughter were moving from a big house to a very small one, everything had to be assessed before it went into one of the 'keeper' boxes. There just wasn't enough room for all the material goods that had been part of their lives in the rambling mansion.

The kangaroo was one of dozens of stuffies that Noelle hadn't played with for a year or more. Convincing her daughter to give up each toy, no matter how ignored, was a struggle. So far there were more toys in the 'donate' box than in the 'keeper' box, so Christy was winning out. She wasn't sure how much longer her run of luck would continue.

Noelle picked up the kangaroo. "Gerry gave it to me."

He had indeed. Christy could remember when the courier had delivered the small, red-brown stuffie. Frank, her husband and—if she could ever find him—soon to be ex, had looked at it, then commented that Gerry Fisher had probably written it off as an expense against the Jamieson Trust. Christy didn't believe that for an instant. She knew there had been conflict between Gerry and Frank through the years, but she'd always considered Gerry the best of the close-knit group who ran the Jamieson Trust.

"If you want to keep it, put it in the packing box. Remember, you're only allowed two big boxes. We're moving to a townhouse, so there's a lot less storage than there is here."

Christy rubbed the back of her neck. The afternoon was unusually hot and humid for Vancouver, British Columbia. The trustees had demanded Christy cut the air conditioning as a cost saving measure, so the windows were open to catch a breeze. So far, all they'd let in was more heavy, humid air. She wished it would rain and let the temperature return to more normal levels.

Noelle stared at the kangaroo. "I don't see why we have to move."

"This house has been sold, and we had to find a smaller place to live," Christy said. She could hear the edge in her voice, but this was the twentieth time Noelle had asked the question in the last fifteen minutes. She thought she was doing a pretty good job keeping her patience.

"I don't want to move!"

"I know that, honey."

Noelle took one last, scowling look at the kangaroo, then threw it into the donations box.

Christy breathed a sigh of relief. Noelle was acting out, angry at the absence of the father she adored and grieving the loss of Stormy the Cat, the family pet who had not returned since the night he'd walked out of the house behind Frank. Her everyday world was changing too. With the house sold and the liquid assets of the trust gone, the trustees were finding jobs for the servants. Maria Elena, the nanny Noelle known since birth, had headed off to a new job in Calgary. Yesterday had been the last day for their housekeeper, Mrs. Grimes. With important adults disappearing from her life, it was no wonder that Noelle was clinging to objects with the least little symbolic meaning.

Noelle went over to a floating wall shelf opposite her bed. She reached up and grabbed the soft baby doll that held pride of place there. "I suppose you want me to throw out *this* too!" She added a disgruntled look of scrunched up eyes and a sour smirk for impact.

Christy stared at the shapeless doll in her daughter's hand. Frank had given it to Noelle on her third birthday. It had been her favorite toy for years, until Frank started being absent more and more often. Then she had put it up in a special spot where it was safe and she could see it. "No, of course not, Noelle! Look, kiddo, you keep the important things and give away the stuff that doesn't matter."

"Yeah, right," Noelle muttered as she turned away.

Christy sighed as her daughter carefully placed the doll into the 'keeper' box. The last few months had been hard. When news got out that Frank had flown off to Mexico with a big chunk of the assets of the Jamieson Trust, the Vancouver media had descended on the mansion like a cloud of locusts. Christy hated being the focus of all the attention. Though the staff had fielded the phone calls, Christy was grateful when Gerry Fisher advised her the Trust would handle the media.

Even so, she was still surrounded by photographers and reporters every time she left the protection of the mansion's gates. At first she was hopeful that interest would fade quickly, but throughout June and into July the case took on new twists and turns. The media was delighted. Frank Jamieson's disappearance and the troubles at the Jamieson Trust became a staple.

Altogether, it had been a tough summer for her and Noelle. And it was not looking as if the fall would be much better.

For a time Christy and Noelle worked together in silence. Christy sorted through a pile of clothes Noelle had outgrown, saving more than she put into the donations box, while Noelle did something similar with her smaller toys.

"Mom! What are you doing with my school uniform?"

"You aren't going to need it anymore and it barely fits. If you were still going to be attending VRA I'd keep it, but since you're not..."

"I could still use it."

"Noelle, it's a gray skirt, a navy blue sweater, and a white shirt. It's a uniform. It looks like a uniform. Why would you want to keep it?"

Noelle's eyes filled and her lower lip quivered. "I won't be able to see my friends anymore."

"Oh, kiddo, come have a hug." As she wrapped her sniffling daughter in her arms, Christy cursed her wandering husband. Not only had Frank stolen away the liquid assets of the Jamieson Trust, but he'd also sold their home for a fraction of its real worth and left hefty debts behind him that the Trust had been obligated to pay by selling core assets like shares in Jamieson Ice Cream.

Since the Trust was required to provide for the heir and his family, some kind of accommodation had to be found for Christy and Noelle. To protect what was left of the Jamieson stock, the decision had been made to buy a townhouse in the suburbs. Noelle would go to the local public school. Vancouver Royal Academy, the pricy private institution she had attended since pre-school, and the place where all of her friends also went, was no longer an option.

"We'll take your uniform," Christy muttered over her daughter's head as she hugged her tight. "We'll take anything you want to. Oh, baby, don't cry."

Noelle cried harder.

Christy rocked her, making soothing sounds that didn't do a lot of good. Her daughter's tears tore at her soul. Noelle was Christy's life, her reason for being, but like Noelle, she was facing a painful restructuring. The fat allowance that came from the fruitful Jamieson Trust each quarter was now little more than a small stipend. Christy knew that once she was certain Noelle was settled in their new life, she was going to have to get a job if she wanted to give her daughter more than the basics of life. That meant she'd be gone all day and would need after school daycare, since they could no longer afford a nanny. She'd be new in the job, so she wouldn't be available to participate in class field trips or help out in the classroom as she had at VRA.

And what kind of job could she get with no university degree and the reputation of being a society woman who had helped her husband embezzle his trust fund?

She wasn't going to think about how the media had played up the rumor that she'd been the one to arrange to have the trust's liquid assets transferred to a bank account in Indonesia, an account in her name only. She still got angry about the way the media had made her the public face of everything that had gone wrong at the Jamieson Trust.

Christy's cell rang. Still holding a sniffling Noelle, she pulled it out of the pocket of her shorts and checked the screen. "The guy from the auction house is at the door, Noelle. I've got to go let him in."

Still sniffling, Noelle pulled out of Christy's arms. She rubbed the tears out of her eyes and dried her cheeks as she settled glumly in front of her box. She was a Jamieson, after all, and Jamiesons didn't show their emotions when outsiders were around.

Christy headed downstairs. The Trust wanted to auction off all of the household furnishings that Christy wasn't taking with her to the townhouse. The appraiser was coming to start the process. With the staff gone, from the security people to Mrs. Grimes, the housekeeper, Christy was now opening her own front door for the first time in years.

She ran down the broad curving staircase and crossed the golden travertine marble tiles in the front hall, then peeked out one of the glass panels that flanked the mahogany double doors. The man waiting on the porch was wearing a dark suit, white shirt, and a silk tie the blue of a cloudless Vancouver sky. His black leather shoes had a high shine, and his thick, black hair was carefully combed. Reassured this was the appraiser, and not a scruffy reporter, Christy opened the door.

"Good afternoon." She smiled politely. His job might be sanctioned by the Trust, but she didn't like what he was going to be doing in her house, and she didn't have to be friendly while he was at it.

His gray eyes assessed her thoughtfully. "I'd like to speak to Christy Jamieson. Is she at home?"

She frowned. What kind of question was that? She had an appointment with this guy. "You know the answer to that."

The gray eyes lit with a sudden spark that shot right through her. "You're Christy Jamieson, aren't you? I didn't recognize you at first."

Not surprising, since she'd cut off her long, golden hair and died it back to her original red-brown color in an act of defiance and despair when confirmation had come through that the mansion had been sold. She looked into those way-too-perceptive eyes, which she noticed were fringed with thick black lashes that most women would kill for. She'd expected the appraiser to be impersonal, almost clinical. This guy wasn't.

Time to show him she didn't intend to be bullied, even if it was the Trust, and not her, who had arranged the contract with the auction house. "I'd like to see your ID," she said coolly.

He reached in his hip pocket, pulling his jacket open and showing that the crisp, white shirt fit very nicely over his broad chest. Once he had his wallet free, he dug out a business card.

Her stomach sank to her knees and her mouth flattened into a hard line as she read the card. "You're a reporter." For form, she added, "How did you get on to the grounds?"

"Your gate was open," he said, raising arched, black brows.

Very aware that Noelle could erupt from her room at any moment to see what was going on, she stepped out onto the porch with the reporter. As she shut the door behind her, he scrutinized her in a way that told her he would analyze every word. How was she going to get rid of him?

She lifted her chin and tried for haughty. "My security people will hear about this!"

He smiled faintly, not in the least intimidated. "You ought to can the head guy." He nodded in an amiable way, as if he discussed hiring and firing servants every day. "If you haven't already."

Haughty had never worked for her and now this reporter—she glanced at his card and read Quinn Armstrong—had caught her out. She swallowed hard and hoped Armstrong wouldn't notice the note of desperation in her voice. "What are you talking about?"

Quinn Armstrong shrugged. His gray eyes assessed her. Christy felt as if he was digging through her thoughts, sifting the rubble, looking for a rich nugget of truth. "It's no secret that this estate has been sold. Or that your husband has been playing fast and loose with his trust fund, victimizing you in the process. I'm guessing that you've come down on hard times, Mrs. Jamieson."

This man was dangerous. "I have no comment to make. Please leave." She stepped back, put her hand on the door handle, ready to slip inside then slam the door in his face— as she should have done in the first place.

"I'm a journalist, not a reporter, Mrs. Jamieson. I'm writing a series of articles on the heirs of the establishment. I want to profile Frank Jamieson's case, and I want my readers to be clear about your part in it."

Christy stared at him, this man who was as good-looking as an angel, but who represented the devil to her. "I don't talk to the press."

"I would like an interview. An exclusive—the Christy Jamieson story."

"No."

He nodded at the card in her hand. "Think about it. I can help you, if you'll let me."

She looked down at the business card. She would never give Quinn Armstrong an interview. "No."

"I'll call you tomorrow to see if you've changed your mind."

He'd pester her, he was a reporter. They never let go. He'd be after her until he wore her down and she finally agreed to an interview. Then he'd promise not to print anything she wouldn't like so he could coax out all her secrets. The article, when it was written, would twist every word she'd said. She wasn't just being paranoid, or absurdly private. It had happened to her before.

"No, don't call. It would be pointless, a waste of time." He raised black brows and she hurried on, explaining herself when she didn't have to. "I have family visiting, and I'll be showing them the sights. Call me in three weeks."

She held her breath while he considered this outright lie.

Finally, he nodded. "Okay, Mrs. Jamieson. I'll be back on September ninth. We'll do the interview then."

She nodded, then watched as he climbed back into his practical subcompact car.

On September ninth she'd have moved from this fine, old house into her neat, little Burnaby townhouse. She hoped he wouldn't be rude to the new owners.

Quinn Armstrong backed, then turned the car, aware of Christy Jamieson's eyes on him. He smiled cynically. Who did she think she was fooling? Call her in three weeks and she'd give him the interview. Yeah, sure.

At the end of the drive he paused before turning left. She might have been telling the truth about family visiting. It was August after all, prime tourist time in British Columbia, but the bit about showing family the sights was way out there. In Quinn's experience, you couldn't sightsee for more than half a day before burnout happened. Christy Jamieson had plenty of time to give him an interview—if she wanted to.

Which she didn't.

The Jamieson mansion was located on a quiet, treed circle in the heart of Vancouver's west side. Traffic was light, but it did exist. While Quinn waited for a solitary car to pass, he pulled off his tie and loosened the top button of his shirt. The car slid past. With the road clear he made a left off the mansion's grounds.

He'd give Christy a couple of weeks, then he'd be back at her door. In the meantime, he would use the time to do more research on her.

He accelerated out of his turn. Christy Jamieson was not what he'd expected. When reading the published material on her, he'd formed an impression of a beautiful, self-absorbed woman who had married money for money's sake. The accompanying photographs showed a woman groomed to the point of perfection, the kind who froze out everyone but the best social contacts. Yet the woman who answered the door wore wrinkled shorts that showed a lot of leg and a T-shirt that hugged her breasts and was faded from the wash, hardly the costume of an avid, social-climbing bimbo. Not that she didn't look great, she did, but—

A gray animal with black stripes burst from the hedging bordering the property on Quinn's side of the road. From the sounds of deep-throated barking coming from behind the bushes, the creature—a cat—was probably being chased by a very large dog.

The cat darted onto the sidewalk. If it kept on moving at the rate it was going, it would end up right in the path of his on-coming car. Quinn hit the breaks and his horn at the same time.

The cat, caught mid-leap, landed on the road in front of his car and froze. Quinn spun his wheel and ended up sliding into the opposite lane, just as a car rounded the curve and headed toward him. Quinn braced himself for impact, desperately hoping the cat had had the sense to jump back onto the sidewalk or to stay put. Tires squealed as they burned over pavement, but there was no shriek of metal impacting on metal. Quinn breathed a sigh of relief.

The other car drove slowly around him, the driver pausing long enough to shout, "Idiot! What the hell do you think you were doing? You could have killed us both!"

Quinn didn't bother to shout back. He figured the guy had the right to vent. Quinn had almost wrecked his and someone else's car, and potentially caused them both bodily injury for a small animal that didn't provide anything useful to society, except perhaps the capture of a mouse or two and a lot of love and affection for its owner.

But then there were plenty of rapists and drug dealers who didn't do a lot for society either. He figured that if they had a right to life, so too did dogs, cats, and all the other animals that walked the earth. He backed the car into his lane again and pulled it off to the side of the road, then he got out to see if the cat was okay.

At first he thought it had disappeared, then he saw that it had made it to the opposite side of the road after the other car had gone on its way. The cat was limping badly, dragging itself along as if it was on the edge of exhaustion. He checked for traffic, then sprinted across. Crouching near the cat he spoke quietly, "Hey, puss. Let me help you."

Tiger-striped, the creature was one of the largest cats Quinn had ever seen. It stared at him balefully, hunched into a tense, compact shape. Quinn crept closer. The cat swished its tail, but it didn't run.

"There's a pretty lady beyond that fence. I bet she'd help you."

The cat eyed him cautiously, still tense, ready to bolt.

"That's it, kitty." Quinn kept his voice soothing as he stretched out his hand toward the cat. "I imagine you're hungry." He stroked the cat's head gently. Its eyes watched him and its tail continued to twitch, but it didn't bolt. "Let me pick you up and help you out. There, that's a good kitty." He caught it under its belly and scooped it up.

The cat allowed him to inspect its wounds, although its tail lashed back and forth with annoyance. Its fur was missing in places and it was skinny. There was a nasty cut on one of its back legs that looked as if it had happened some time before and hadn't healed properly. There were also a variety of lesser injuries.

From its appearance, the cat was a stray. Quinn nipped back across the road and put the animal in his car. "Hang on," he said, "and we'll get you some help." He could have sworn he heard the cat sigh as it curled into a ball on the passenger seat, but he dismissed that as his imagination.

He certainly couldn't dismiss the cat's uninhibited outrage when he took it into the emergency animal hospital on Boundary Road. It clearly did not want to be there, fighting with claws and teeth, but then, that was no surprise. He'd never found an animal that enjoyed a visit to the vet.

It took Quinn, the vet, the vet's assistant, and the antiseptic steel of the examining table to convince the cat that resistance was pointless. The vet worked quickly, though in a competent and careful way. He cleaned the cat's wounds, stitched the worst of them, and advised Quinn on how to get rid of the animal's fleas and care for the injuries. Quinn put the now subdued cat back in the car and headed for home.

He'd give the cat to his father to take care of since the old man was as big a sucker for animals as Quinn was. Roy Armstrong had needed someone to look after since his wife Vivien, Quinn's mom and the practical hand that held their family together, had died two years before. Taking care of the cat would give him focus and maybe drag him out of the melancholy that never quite went away.

Then, maybe, Quinn could get back to his own life.

Maybe.

CHAPTER 2

Roy Armstrong draped his long, lanky length along the black leather sofa, then struck a match. The flame hissed as it touched the end of the joint he'd just rolled. A rich, aromatic scent wafted through the spacious living room.

Roy sucked in, drawing smoke deep into his lungs with an almost sensual pleasure. It was nine forty-five in the morning, a bit early to be smoking a joint, but if he burned a little incense the smell would be out of the room by the time Quinn got back.

He took another drag and considered the situation. Living with his son was a pain in the ass, he thought, not for the first time. The boy meant well, but he tended to treat his old man as if he was teetering on the edge of senility. In fact, Roy was strong and healthy and at the peak of his creative powers—if he could be bothered to set his fingers to a computer keyboard.

Roy took another puff. His thoughts drifted off into his current work in progress. It wasn't going well and he couldn't quite pinpoint what was wrong.

The cat Quinn had brought home bounded up onto his chest. It was a brute of an animal, big as a small dog and heavy boned. He called it his house tiger because of the restless way it prowled through the rooms, almost as if it was exercising to gain strength in its healing muscles. He scratched behind the cat's ears absently and the beast settled in on his chest, purring in a satisfying, soothing way.

What if he made the brother into a sister? Would that change the dynamics enough to disrupt a fictional family that he'd decided was incredibly boring, even to himself, its creator?

God, that smells good.

Roy contemplated the glowing tip of the joint. "It does, doesn't it?"

I wish I could join you, but I can't.

The voice was clear and seemed to reverberate inside his head. Roy glanced around the room, but the cat was the only other occupant. He looked at the joint and said, "Oh, man," and started to butt it out. The cat tapped the back of his hand with its paw, claws in.

Don't do that on my account.

Roy looked at the joint again. "Are you going to stop talking to me if I put it out?"

No.

"Far out." Roy smoked in silence for a minute, while the cat breathed in his fumes. "So why are we having this conversation? You've been living here for over two weeks and we haven't spoken before. Why start now?"

I've been trying to get through to you for days. I have to go. I wanted to say good-bye and thank you.

Roy considered that. "Why do you have to go? Don't you like living here?"

The cat likes it just fine. He wants to stay. I can't.

That was interesting. "So there are two of you living in the cat's body?"

You might say we're roomies for now. Until I've completed my mission.

"And you talk to each other?"

We share thoughts, just as I am sharing my thoughts with you. Restless, the cat leapt onto the floor, then prowled to the top of the stairs that led down from the living room to the front door. His movements were lithe, controlled, decisive. Big and powerful, he was clearly a male in his prime, a male with a mission.

Roy believed in possibilities. He'd built his life visioning what couldn't be and making it happen. He liked to keep an open mind, but this was really pushing his limits. A cat on a mission, who was communicating with him telepathically. Yeah, sure. He contemplated the smoke rising lazily from the glowing tip of the joint. Maybe it was time to quit.

The gray and black tabby shot him a look that could only be described as disapproving. *I thought you would understand.*

A happy idea brightened Roy's mood. Maybe this conversation was his writer's imagination going out of control. His characters tended to take over the creative process once he knew them well. Maybe one had decided to give him a poke and let him know how he could sort out the problems in his current project. They were such a dull bunch, though. He would never have pegged one of them for being a talking cat. For that matter, even thinking up the idea of a talking cat. If he added a talking cat, how would he work it into the plot? Maybe...

The vision of a narrow alley, closed at one end, plugged at the other by a beat-up car that had once been someone's luxury ride, rose in his mind. He was there in the alley, huddled in the shadow of a dumpster that stank of rotting food. Someone was with him, someone he trusted. While his nose twitched with distaste, his eyes focused on the small, sealed plastic bag the other person was holding. The bag was filled with pills that were a rainbow of colors. Need, intense, powerful, demanding, slammed into him. He wanted that bag. Now.

His hand shook as he reached into his pocket for the ready cash he always kept on him. He should quit—and he would, when he was ready. For now he'd enjoy the rush that would take away the guilt over the mess he'd made of his life.

He had the bills in his hand when he sensed movement nearby. He lifted his head to look, but before he could see who was behind him something hit him, connecting with his skull with a vicious crunch. Agonizing pain shot through his head. He staggered forward, disoriented.

He heard a voice say, "I've got him. You grab his other arm."

Hands took hold of him, keeping him upright, forcing him to stagger forward. Each step was agony. The inside of his head felt as if a maniac wielding an ice pick was slamming it repeatedly. He concentrated on keeping his head still to minimize the jarring, but it was an impossible task. His vision wavered, dancing in a sickening way that distorted everything. He glanced at one of the people helping him. All he could see was hair the same blond color as his own above a pale, narrow face that was nothing more than a blur.

As he stumbled forward, he was pretty sure they were leading him out of the alley. Relief coursed through him. They were taking him out onto the main drag where they could signal for help. That was great. Still, it would have been better if they'd let him slump onto the ground where he could lie until rescued. Maybe he should suggest that.

"Here we are. Okay, ready now. Do it!"

The hands released him. As he swayed unsteadily, relieved he didn't have to plow forward anymore, his blurred vision showed him a car trunk gaping open before him. Confused, he looked around. He only had a moment to realize that rescue was not in his future, before he was hit from behind with another blow that sent him sprawling.

Darkness closed around him.

Gradually, the vision merged with reality. The dark, smelly alley became a suburban living room in a modern townhouse development. Shaken, Roy squished the joint into the ashtray. This was getting too weird. His imagination didn't need any help from the weed.

He sat up so he could put the ashtray on the coffee table. A sense of what he thought might be compassion wrapped itself around him. The cat came over and rubbed against his leg, purring loudly. *I'm sorry. I thought I was losing you. I had to show you to make you accept me.*

Roy sighed as he reached down to scratch the cat behind its ears. "I can't deny you shook me up," he said. "That was what happened to you? How did it end? Did you die?"

Yes. I'll spare you the details. They aren't pretty.

The voice was wry, filled with a self-depreciating amusement that was oddly touching. Roy picked up the cat to give it a hug. It rested for a moment before it wriggled away, jumping off his lap onto the carpet, where it sat and carefully cleaned a paw. "How did you come to be living in the cat?" he asked, respecting the creature's need for independence.

There was a heavy sigh in his mind. *I went home, to tell my family where I was, but I couldn't reach them. Only the cat seemed to accept me. He invited me in.*

"Interesting," Roy said. "If you can't communicate with your family why can you talk to me?"

I've been practicing. That's why I need to go. I can talk to them now, explain what happened. Help them heal.

An image of his late wife Vivien popped into Roy's mind. His throat closed, and he had to push back tears. He wouldn't have made it through those first few days after Vivien's passing if Quinn hadn't been with him, irritating him, making him deal with the details of death, keeping him away from the misery of being alone. "Okay," he said. "I'll get the door for you."

He levered himself to his feet. The cat twined around his legs once, then bounded down the stairs. Roy followed him at a more dignified pace. "So do you have far to travel?"

I had almost reached my destination when your son kidnapped me.

The cat's disgruntlement made Roy grin. "Quinn's a good boy, but he tends to interfere, like his mother, bless her. Never met a cause she didn't like. That's why she became a lawyer, and a damn good one, I might add." He opened the door. The cat leapt through, then paused on the other side, almost as if he'd stopped to shake hands before leaving.

"Look, if you ever need any help, come back. Okay?"

Thank you. The cat hesitated a moment more, then it bounded away into the bright sunlight and the dangers that any feral animal faced in dealing with a mechanized world.

"Good luck," Roy said, then he went back to burn incense and air out the living room.

Christy turned onto the street on which her townhouse was located. She had just dropped Noelle at the local public school a few minutes' walk away. The principal had been warm and friendly, making Noelle welcome and quickly putting her at ease. By the time Christy left the school, Noelle had been assigned to a grade three class and was the focus of attention from the other kids. With her child safe and in a good situation, Christy enjoyed her walk home. For the first time she looked around at her surroundings.

Just over a year old, the complex was well kept, with flower borders that showed the loving care of house-proud owners and gave the complex personality. Although her unit was one of the last built and over six months old, it had never been lived in. Bought originally for a corporate relocation that never happened, it had come on the market again about the same time the sale of the Jamieson mansion closed. The previous owners agreed to sell the house to the Trust at cost, a good deal that appealed to Samuel Macklin, an accountant and one of the Jamieson trustees. Christy hadn't been asked if she wanted to live in Burnaby, a generally working-class suburb east of Vancouver. The deal had been done and the address given to the moving company. She'd had her first glimpse of the place when she arrived to tell the movers where to place the furniture and unpack the boxes.

As she neared her house she could see a man standing beside the planter box that separated the front walks of two of the townhouses. Head bent, deep in concentration, he appeared to be pulling deadheads off the annuals that grew in lush profusion in the box.

Since she'd not yet had the opportunity to meet any of her new neighbors, and the man seemed to belong to the house two doors down from hers, she decided to take a few minutes away from her unpacking chores to introduce herself. Besides, she had to pass him to get to her place.

He looked up at the sound of her footsteps—a good-looking man on his way out of middle age into his senior years. His eyes were an intense gray fringed with black lashes. Sharp and clear, they inspected her without apology. Christy smiled at him, not at all put out because she was inspecting him in much the same way.

He was wearing jeans and a T-shirt, and his silver hair, still shot through with black in places, was worn long and tied back in a ponytail. Between his gardening and his clothes she guessed he must be retired, able to do and dress as he pleased.

"Hi," she said, holding out her hand. "I'm Christy, your new neighbor two houses down."

His handshake was little more than a brush of skin touching skin, then it was over. Strange, she thought. That was a woman's handshake. "Roy Armstrong," he said.

"Nice to meet you." She looked around her and gestured vaguely. "What a lovely complex this is."

Roy looked around too, his expression rather critical. "Modern and suburban," he said. "Good for bringing up kids. You have one, I'm told."

Christy stifled a little gasp. "Boy, news travels quickly around here."

Roy grinned. "If you know the right people. Now, our on-site manager lives in that house over there—" He pointed to a townhouse across the road from where they were standing. "—and he likes to share his news whenever he gets it. Since I'm on the neighborhood watch and usually around, I tend to be the first person he fills in."

"Oh," Christy said, feeling rather overwhelmed.

Roy noticed a decaying blossom and plucked it off of the

tangle of Shasta daisies that were growing with wild abandon in his planter box. He grinned at the dubious note in her voice. "We're a small complex, so we tend to know each other pretty well. You'll get used to it."

"I suppose so." Wanting to get his enquiring mind away from her, who she was, and what her aspirations for the future were, she searched for a new topic of conversation. "Armstrong. You know, that name sounds familiar."

He shrugged in a nonchalant way, but she could have sworn that he tensed. "It's a common enough name."

"That's true, but I'm sure I've heard it fairly recently. Armstrong, now where—" She broke off to look at him more closely. He met her gaze levelly, but with a trace of resignation in his expression. "Your face seems familiar too." She laughed in a self-depreciating way, aware that she was making him uncomfortable. "I'm sorry, don't mind me. I have the most lamentable memory. I've probably seen you at the grocery store and not realized it."

He raised one still-dark brow. A faint smile curled his firm lips.

There was something about that smile, something Christy couldn't pinpoint, an amusement that said he knew where she'd seen him, but he wasn't telling. "Well, I guess I should be going. I've still got loads of unpacking to do. This is Noelle's—she's my daughter, in case you need some info for the on-site super—first day of school so I want to make good use of my quiet time before she gets home."

Roy nodded and smiled. "Nice to meet you, Christy."

"And you too." It came to her suddenly where she'd seen his face and why she knew his name. "Oh!" she said, smiling with excited pleasure. "You're Roy Armstrong, the writer! I've seen your picture on the dust jackets of your books."

"You caught me," said Roy.

He smiled in what she guessed was his I'll-be-polite-to-fans smile and she decided she'd wait until she got to know him better before she started asking him what it was like to be a Scotiabank Giller Prize-winning author. But she couldn't go without expressing how much she enjoyed his writing. "I really love your books, Mr. Armstrong. It's a privilege meeting you."

"Thank you," he said in a dignified voice. The door to his townhouse opened and a man stepped out. Roy looked over, frowning. Much younger than Roy Armstrong, the man held a bowl in one hand and a bag of dry cat food in the other. On the porch he crouched down to put the bowl at the edge of the top stair. He was concentrating on his task and apparently didn't notice Christy and his father standing on the sidewalk chatting.

But Christy noticed him. Oh boy, did she notice him. She stood frozen in place, goggling at him with complete horror.

"My son," Roy Armstrong said to Christy. "Quinn," he said to his son, "I told you, the cat isn't coming back. There's no sense in putting out food for him. You'll just attract every stray in the neighborhood."

"The cat will come back," Quinn said, dogged determination in his voice. "He's used to coming to us for his food. He'll be hungry. He'll be back." He shook food into the bowl.

Roy advanced to the porch, shaking his head. "Quinn, listen to me. He's on a mission. He's not coming back."

Quinn made a disgusted sound in his throat. "Come off it, Dad. Cats don't go on missions. They chase mice and climb trees and eat packaged cat food when it's offered, then they find a warm place to sleep because they like their comfort." He looked up at Roy. "He'll be back—Well, well, well. Who is this?" he said in a tone that was somewhere between gleeful and smug.

Roy glanced from his son to Christy. He frowned as he made the introductions. "Quinn Armstrong, this is our new neighbor, Christy...I'm sorry, I didn't catch your last name."

Quinn started down the porch stairs. "It's Jamieson, Dad. Christy Jamieson."

His use of her name released Christy from her horrified trance. "Nice to meet you," she said. "Gotta go. See you!"

She sprinted for the relative safety of her townhouse feeling Quinn Armstrong's eyes burning into her back every step of the way.

CHAPTER 3

At two thirty Christy wiped her hand over her sweaty forehead and blew out an exhausted sigh. She'd been unpacking since she'd run from Quinn Armstrong hours earlier. Her clothes were put away and Noelle's toys arranged in the family room off the kitchen. The kitchen itself was still a mess, but she'd leave that until tomorrow. For now she'd done a terrific job and it was time to quit so she could go over to the school to pick up Noelle.

She changed out of the shorts she'd worn while she worked into a pair of vivid blue cropped pants that were cool, but a little more respectable than the comfortable cut-off shorts. She quickly brushed her hair, then, satisfied she looked neat, but not overdressed for an excursion to the school, she ran lightly down two flights of stairs to the door. There she paused long enough to put on her sandals before she headed out.

And stopped dead.

Quinn Armstrong was sitting on her porch steps, peeling the bark off a stick. He didn't look up when she emerged, but he said, "Nice trick you pulled, telling me you weren't available, expecting me to respect your privacy, then moving out of your home without leaving a forwarding address."

Standing behind him, Christy was unable to judge his expression. She could see his long fingers as they tore at the bark, though. They were beautiful fingers, narrow and agile. She wondered if his relentless peeling of the twig was a satisfying way for him to rid himself of the frustration her actions must have caused. "I didn't—don't!—want to talk to you."

"Yeah," he said, tossing the twig aside. "I kind of got that one."

She tried to brush by him. "Excuse me, I have to—" He caught her ankle in one hand, stopping her cold. "Let go."

"Not so fast, sweetheart. We've got a conversation to finish."

She tugged cautiously, testing his hold. Those long, surprisingly strong fingers tightened, keeping her still. "I have to pick up my daughter."

He looked up at her, his expression thoughtful.

Her breath caught as their gazes met. His dark gray eyes, fringed by black lashes and marked by arched, black brows, set off the hard angles of his face. Shaken, she ripped her gaze away and tugged her leg again. Quinn Armstrong was a good-looking man, but he was a reporter, a member of a profession she disliked on principle. She could not—would not!—be attracted to him.

Quinn released her and stood in one fluid motion. "I'll come with you," he said. "We can talk as we walk."

Christy squared her shoulders, avoiding his eyes as she brushed past him. "I told you I don't want to talk to you. I'm not giving you an interview."

"Sure you are," he said, falling into step.

Incensed, she looked over at him. He was smiling at her, the jerk. She tossed her head in defiance and denial. "No, I am not."

"Like I said, sure you are. You just don't know you are. Yet."

In the ten years she'd been married to Frank Jamieson, Christy had learned a few survival skills that she'd never needed as plain, ordinary Christy Yeager. One of them was how to ignore people who would hound a person for a cause, for help on a committee or two, or for the endorsement of an event or a product. Worthy people, nice people, decent people, all demanding more than one individual could give, because all of them assumed they were the only ones who wanted something.

Sometimes an explanation that her time was fully committed or she didn't do endorsements, or that the Jamieson Trust handled all of the charitable donations worked and she'd be left alone. Other times a polite explanation just wasn't enough. Then she'd learned to walk with her head high and pretend the person harassing her wasn't there yapping at her like a small dog endowed with too much testosterone.

That's what she did to Quinn now, marching along with eyes straight ahead, arms swinging by her sides as if she was walking over to the school all on her own.

"You might as well talk to me," Quinn said in a conversational way.

Christy pretended to ignore him, even though she couldn't shut him out. She was very much aware of his big body beside hers as they walked and she could feel his eyes watching her.

"I'm not going to stop pestering you until I get an interview."

Christy glanced at her watch. She was in good time to get to the school before classes were dismissed. She did not want to be late picking Noelle up on her first day.

"I can do it, you know."

Christy paused at a crosswalk, waited until the crossing guard indicated it was safe to walk, then headed onto the road. The school was within sight now. She had two or three more minutes of pretending she was alone and then she'd be at her destination.

"I know where you live."

Quinn's final thrust bit cleanly, threatened danger. No, *promised* danger. Her sanctuary was being violated, the new home where she planned to sort out her life, where she assumed she would be just another suburban mom, invisible to intrusive reporters like Quinn Armstrong.

On the far side of the street she stopped. As she faced him, she once again reacted to the impact of those intense gray eyes. She pushed the shiver of awareness aside. "What you are describing is harassment," she said crisply. "Try it and I'll have my lawyer slap a restraining order on you so you won't be able to come within five hundred feet of me." She whirled away to continue at her previous brisk pace.

He followed. "You won't get an order like that. You'd be evicting me from my own house. Think of the kind of damage this could do to neighborhood relations."

Christy heard amusement in Quinn's voice as he made the last statement. It was almost her undoing. She wanted to laugh at the rueful comment, but she knew she couldn't. If she did, Quinn Armstrong would consider it a crack in her defenses and he'd slither inside before she could stop him. "Like I care about neighbor relations when one of the neighbors is the reporter who's harassing me," she said, shooting him her 'Stern Mom Disciplining Rowdy Child' expression.

"You wouldn't be sorry if you talked to me. I've got lots of dope on Frank Jamieson. I know that he's the one who embezzled from the trust, which makes you a victim of his crime, not his accomplice. I'd write the article with that point of view."

Just outside the door to the school, Christy stopped again. "Mr. Armstrong, please allow me to be clear. I do not trust reporters. I do not want to be profiled in the media. What my husband is doing and has done is his business, possibly mine, but certainly not yours. I will not be giving you an interview, now or in the future. Please accept that and save us both a lot of trouble." She turned away without waiting for his reply.

As she pulled the door open, he said, "Not a hope, sweetheart."

The only indication she gave that she'd heard him was the faintest of pauses and the tremor that ran through her body. She entered the school, childishly pleased when the door slammed behind her with the finality of a shotgun blast.

Later that afternoon, the phone rang. Noelle was sitting in the breakfast nook, reluctantly coloring in a nameplate for her desk at school. The handset rested on the counter nearby.

Christy eyed the phone warily and let it ring. She half expected the caller to be Quinn Armstrong with another pitch for an interview, and she wasn't prepared to discuss the issue with him.

Noelle looked up. "Are you going to get the phone, Mom?"

A month ago she would have let one of the staff answer. Then, she didn't have to worry about fending off pushy reporters or aggressive sales pitches. She hadn't realized how pampered she had become until now when the support of a household of servants was gone.

She and Noelle stared, fascinated, as the phone rang again. "Mom?"

The phone had call display. She picked up the handset, but the number wasn't one she knew. It was a local number, though. What if it was Quinn Armstrong calling to pester her about an interview?

"You're going to let it go to voicemail?" Noelle said. "Cool! I get to pick up the message."

They hardly ever got phone calls, so voicemail was still a fascinating novelty for Noelle. What if Quinn Armstrong left a message and mentioned Frank? Noelle would ask questions. Questions Christy didn't want to answer.

She punched the answer button and caught the call before voicemail clicked in.

"Am I speaking to Christy Jamieson?"

The voice belonged to a woman, not Quinn Armstrong. She knew those tones, but couldn't quite identify whom they belonged to. "Who's calling, please?"

"It's Detective Billie Patterson of the Vancouver Police

Department. I have further questions regarding your husband's disappearance, which I'd prefer to discuss in person. Will you be home in the next hour or so?"

Christy thought about dinner routines and Noelle coloring at the kitchen table. If Billie Patterson came over now dinner would be late. Already cranky about her new school, Noelle would be looking for negatives. Their townhouse was fairly large, but it was a townhouse, not a mansion. If Noelle wanted to listen in on what her mother and their visitor said, she could, no problem. She'd hear every question Patterson asked, whether it related to her dad or attempted to implicate her mom. That was a trauma Christy wasn't prepared to have her eight-year-old daughter endure.

Then she thought about Billie Patterson's car, parked out in front of her house. Most of her new neighbors might not guess that it was a police vehicle, but she'd bet Quinn Armstrong would. He'd take one look then he'd start to ask questions. She had a sneaking feeling that she'd crack before he would.

She didn't want to give him any more ammunition.

Altogether it would be better to take the meeting elsewhere, even though she was desperate to know the latest on Frank's disappearance.

"Now's not a good time," Christy said. Her voice was husky, filled with emotion she knew would keep her awake most of the night. "Can we get together tomorrow morning?"

The meeting place was a coffee shop near the police station. Christy figured that was good, that Patterson didn't intend to haul her off to jail—right now, anyway. Still, she was nervous as she stood in the doorway of the bare-bones café looking for Billie Patterson.

The main police station was located in the downtown east side, an area of prostitutes, runaway kids, drug dealers, and decent people struggling to make a living and bring up families in the poorest section of the city. The café reflected the reality of an area where life was lived on the edge of survival and there wasn't any extra for pretty nothings. The walls were painted a glossy green that had faded to a mere shadow of color. A row of booths lined one wall, while practical Formica tables and chairs with cold, steel frames and tired leatherette seats filled the center of the small room. Two waitresses buzzed through the maze of tables with a competence born of experience.

Packed with large men and tough-looking women drinking coffee, eating meals full of greasy protein, or buying takeout coffee and donuts, the place was doing non-stop business. Just inside the door was a counter where a burly man with sharp, inquisitive eyes manned the till and organized the take-out orders. As she hesitated in the doorway, scanning the room for Billie Patterson, he looked her over.

Christy could feel herself blushing. Even though her outfit was gray, lightweight pants, a blue shell, and a black cloth jacket, the fabrics were finely woven and the garments were designer. Together, she guessed the clothes had cost as much as most of these people earned in a month. She worried her bottom lip. This was not her kind of place and everyone in the café knew it.

Still, the man said politely, "Would you like a table?"

Christy swallowed hard, fighting down panic born of worry and anticipation. "I'm here to see someone."

The cashier's eyes narrowed, then he shrugged. "You're welcome to take a look. Grab a seat if your meet isn't here yet."

Christy swallowed, smiled. "Thanks." Cautiously, she penetrated deeper into the room, scanning it. She had chickened out of parking nearby. She couldn't afford to have her new GM car stolen or vandalized while she talked to Billie Patterson, so she'd parked closer to the center of town and walked. Now she was five minutes late.

She saw Patterson seated in a booth at the far end of the room. She slipped through the close-packed tables, ignoring the looks she could feel burning through her. It was a cop's job to notice and observe. She just wished they wouldn't observe her.

Sitting with her back to the wall, facing the doorway, Billie Patterson didn't move as she watched Christy thread her way through the tightly packed tables. She nodded when Christy reached the booth. "Thanks for coming."

Christy sat down. A waitress flew by. "Coffee?" she asked, dropping a menu on the table.

Christy nodded. The waitress disappeared. Christy pushed the menu aside. "You wanted to talk to me?"

Patterson nodded, sipped her coffee. Christy clasped her hands in front of her and pretended a calm she wasn't feeling.

Patterson held the mug for a minute more, watching Christy over the rim. Her look was assessing, narrow-eyed, and critical. Christy resisted the urge to tug at the lapels of her jacket. She learned long ago how not to squirm when she was nervous thanks to the worst of Frank's trustees, Samuel Macklin and Edward Bidwell. Never let them see you sweat, Frank had advised when Bidwell accused her of marrying Frank for his money and she'd started to cry. They'd still been close then, passionately in love and protective of each other.

Patterson put her cup on the lime-green tabletop, then rubbed her thumb over a scar that followed the line of her jaw. She was a tall woman, long-legged and lean. Somehow that made up for the wide mouth and full lips, made to smile, and the short, upturned nose that turned a pleasant face cute. When Christy had first met Detective Billie Patterson, two days after she'd last seen Frank, she'd underestimated the policewoman. Those big, brown eyes, the glossy brown hair, tied back in a French braid, said woman, not cop. Christy assumed the police department wasn't taking Frank's disappearance seriously.

It was only later that she realized she'd lucked out. Billie Patterson was smart. She was also curious. She questioned everything. Even more, she was stubborn. She didn't like puzzles with pieces that didn't fit. And Frank's

disappearance didn't fit. Sure he was a drug addict and a
playboy who was screwing around on his wife, but he came
home every night, even if sometimes it was four in the
morning before he reached his front door. His
disappearance didn't fit his pattern, so Billie went to work
asking questions.

The waitress plunked a mug of coffee on the table in
front of Christy, then scooped up the menu with a sniff.
Billie sighed and rubbed her scar again. "Mrs. Jamieson,
has your husband contacted you recently?"

Six weeks ago Frank was seen in Mexico with a blond by
the name of Brianne Lymbourn on his arm. The witness
was a respectable man, the owner of an up-and-coming
electronics company who knew Frank well enough for his
identification to be considered credible. He hadn't spoken
to Frank or Brianne—they had slipped away when he tried
to greet them—but he was quite sure it had been them.
With Frank's whereabouts confirmed, everything changed.
He was no longer considered a missing person. Now he
was wanted for questioning for the embezzlement of funds
from the Jamieson Trust.

"No, he hasn't." Christy took a gulp of coffee, felt it burn
through her, momentarily chasing away some of the cold
the tension had caused. "Why?"

"I believe he will. When he does I would like you to get
in touch with me."

This was not what Christy had expected. "Well, okay, but
zero plus zero equals nothing."

Patterson fiddled with the cup, but she kept her assessing
gaze on Christy. "You don't think he will attempt to
contact you in any way?"

A memory of his promise that he would always look after
her and Noelle added a painful edge to Christy's reply.
"Frank's been gone three months. He hasn't phoned. He
hasn't e-mailed. He hasn't written a letter. Frank may be
living somewhere deep in the Mexican countryside, but
things are not so different down there that he couldn't have

sent me a message if he wanted to. No, Detective, I do not think he will contact me."

Patterson's eyes were steady on her. "What would you say if I told you he was back in Vancouver?"

Christy drew her breath in a quick hiss. "I'd want to know where he is so I could find out what the hell he's playing at."

"So would I," Patterson said. She sat back and drank her coffee, and watched Christy over the rim of her cup.

"You're not making any sense."

"Two days ago Mr. Jamieson arrived at the Vancouver Airport on a flight from Mexico City. He filled in a customs declaration, went through the primary customs checkpoint. There, a customs agent read his declaration, then asked him a few questions. The agent said he seemed nervous and his answers didn't ring true, so he coded Jamieson's card so the guard at the exit door would send him for a baggage search, but there was a huge crowd. A half-a-dozen jumbos arrived one after the other and there were line-ups halfway to the arrivals gates, passengers jostling other passengers, people getting annoyed. Somehow, Frank figured out his card didn't have the right coding and he managed to switch."

"How?"

Patterson played with her coffee cup, watching Christy in silence.

Trying to decide how much she can tell me. Evidently, Detective Patterson didn't quite trust her. She stared back, annoyed and amused and damned if she was going to accept the blame for Frank's misdeeds yet again.

A slow smile crept into Patterson's eyes and her mouth curved up into a rueful smile. "Customs wasn't particularly helpful. All they would tell me was that Frank had made it through and a German male, blond and about your husband's height, traveling on a flight that landed ten minutes before the Mexico City flight, was discovered to have Mr. Jamieson's declaration when he was sent for a baggage search. The German's declaration was later found with a stack of cards taken at the exit doors. A search was made for your husband, but he couldn't be found." For the first time Patterson showed annoyance. "He probably walked out the door and grabbed a cab into town."

None of this sounded like Frank. "How would he switch a customs declaration card without another person's knowledge?"

"The German had tucked his card into the outside pocket of a carry-on, which was slung over his shoulder. The baggage area was crowded. It would have been easy enough for Frank to slip the German's card out and stuff his own in its place."

Before Patterson had finished, Christy was shaking her head. "No. No, something is wrong. Frank doesn't necessarily think the law applies to him, but he's not a criminal. He doesn't know how to pick pockets. Nor is he the kind of guy who would victimize a stranger visiting from abroad."

Patterson watched her narrowly. "How well do you know your husband, Mrs. Jamieson?"

CHAPTER 4

Christy sighed, then sipped some coffee. "You've asked me that before, Detective. Before Frank disappeared, I would have said pretty well. Now I'm not so sure. Why would Frank be worried about a baggage search? Detective Patterson, he's rich. He's always been rich. He'd laugh off a few thousand dollars in customs charges, and how would he know that his luggage was likely to be searched anyway?"

Patterson rubbed her scar. "I wondered about that too, although I suppose it isn't that hard to tell. When I checked the air manifest I found he was traveling with a woman."

Christy looked up, jarred by the sympathetic note to the detective's voice. Billie Patterson thought Frank was cheating on her. Well, maybe he was. There hadn't been much to their marriage before Frank disappeared. She said carefully, "Brianne Lymbourn."

Patterson nodded. "I believe they compared codes once they were both through customs. Lymbourn may even have checked hers against other, innocent looking people, made an assumption that she'd received a green light code, then tipped off Mr. Jamieson. He then made sure he acquired a similar one."

Patterson paused. Christy said, "Brianne Lymbourn has slept with half the men in Frank's crowd. Not surprisingly, I don't know her very well, but she made no secret of her desire to marry money or her opinion that the bedroom was the way to reach her goal. Still, I don't believe that Frank is one of her lovers, Detective."

Billie Patterson sighed. "That's your right, Mrs. Jamieson."

Christy blushed. She knew the cop thought she was being blindly faithful to her husband. In fact, her assumption was based on Frank's loyalty to his daughter. Any relationship Frank formed would have to have Noelle as a central part, and he'd said more than once that he couldn't imagine Brianne being a step-mom to Noelle. "Okay, let's get back to the customs mess. You're telling me that Frank and Brianne are back in town."

Patterson nodded.

Christy picked up the cup to take a sip. She was surprised to find that her hands were shaking. "So now what? Do you arrest Frank for theft?"

The embezzlement of the liquid assets of the Jamieson Trust had come to light three weeks after Frank disappeared and the day before the sale of the mansion had been confirmed. Funds from both the embezzlement and the sale had been transferred into an account in Christy's name. The money had then been quickly wired to an overseas account in Indonesia, this time to an account in Frank's name. From there the money was sent to Brazil where it was deposited into the account of a numbered company. Since Brazil refused to identify the principals in the numbered company or to release bank account information, there the trail ended.

For a time Christy was implicated in the embezzlement, but there was enough ambiguity in the case for Patterson to question whether or not Christy was involved. With Frank on the run with another woman, she had become an abandoned wife, and her participation considered unlikely. Still, she was a suspect. She would always be a suspect until Frank was apprehended.

Billie rubbed the scar again, clearly uncomfortable. "At the present I only wish to speak to Mr. Jamieson to discuss his case."

Christy held the cup in both hands, just below her chin, and looked at the detective over it. "So what do you want from me? Are you're asking me to report to you if he comes home? Is that it?"

Billie took a deep breath. "Not quite. You will remember, Mrs. Jamieson, that initially we were looking for your husband because he was a missing person. Given the size of the Jamieson Trust there was a good possibility he had been kidnapped and would be held for ransom. Then it came out that his disappearance was the result of his own actions. Further, he'd diverted funds from the trust for his private use. Now that's embezzlement, Mrs. Jamieson, and embezzlement is a crime. But stealing money from his own trust fund could be considered a victimless crime by some people. Who gets hurt? Frank Jamieson mainly."

Outrage raced through Christy. "His daughter, for one! She's had to move from the only home she's ever known, change schools, find new friends…"

Patterson put her mug down on the table with a deliberate *thump* that cut through Christy's tirade. "She's got a mom who loves her, a clean house in a nice neighborhood, food to fill her belly, and a decent school where the teachers can concentrate on making sure the kids are learning, rather than surviving. She's doing pretty well, Mrs. Jamieson. Not having a few million bucks behind her isn't going to hurt her any."

Billie Patterson was undoubtedly right. Though Noelle complained about her teacher, she had begun to talk about one little girl in her class, and she was entranced at being able to walk to a neighbor's door, ring the bell, and ask a friend out to play instead of arranging a play date through a nanny or parent and being driven to another child's mansion. "Okay, Frank and his family are the only ones who see the result of his crime. What does that mean?"

Patterson drew circles on the tabletop with her mug. "It means that we would like to speak with him to ensure that he chose to leave the country and was not forced to do so by others. We will question him about his knowledge of the embezzlement of his trust fund, again to ensure that he was not being coerced by a third party. Then we will decide if laying charges is warranted. We would like to be able to close his case."

Christy gaped at her. Of all the things she had imagined she'd hear from Billie Patterson today, closing Frank's case was not one of them. Patterson drew more nervous circles on the tabletop, then caught herself and stilled the movement abruptly. She drank some coffee, then put the mug down with a *thunk* that spoke of finality. Bewildered, Christy said, "Frank may have returned to the area, but he hasn't contacted me. Who's seen him? Have you talked to any of the trustees? If he hasn't called me, surely he must have spoken to one of them?"

"I talked to Gerald Fisher, the chairman of the trust, and Edward Bidwell, the legal counsel. Neither had seen or heard from Mr. Jamieson."

"How about Brianne Lymbourn's friends? Have you talked to them?"

"Ms. Lymbourn's friends appear to be mainly male. A large number of them are aware she has returned to Vancouver. They have also heard that she's flush with cash and looking for fun." The derision in Billie Patterson's tone was clear. She thought Brianne Lymbourn was two-timing Frank and she didn't approve.

"Don't you think it's a little strange that Brianne is announcing her presence, but Frank isn't?"

"Yes, I do. I've spoken to Ms. Lymbourn, but she claims she's no longer with Frank."

"And you accepted that?"

"Look, Mrs. Jamieson, there's nothing further I can do." There was resentment in Patterson's voice. "The department is confident your husband was not the victim of a kidnapping. Further, he is no longer a missing person.

Lymbourn checked into the hotel as a party of two, but since then she's been acting as if she's solo. People do split. That's probably what happened here. The department doesn't have the resources to waste on a case that's basically been solved. Frank Jamieson is back and what you do about it now is your problem. Sorry to be blunt, but that's how it is."

That's how it is. *Sorry, lady, your husband is cheating on you with a woman who's cheating on him. Don't like it? Figure it out and deal with it. I'm not involved.* "You want me to confirm your assumptions," Christy said slowly.

Patterson leaned forward. There was resignation and a certain lurking concern in her expression. "I want you to contact me if you hear anything, Mrs. Jamieson. Anything at all."

"Do you have an address for Brianne Lymbourn? She probably knows how to reach Frank. I'll start with her."

As if Billie Patterson realized how much that even tone and reasonable statement had cost Christy, she nodded without comment. She pulled a notebook from her pocket, quickly wrote an address. "She's registered at a third rate hotel downtown." She underlined the name of the hotel and frowned. "Unusual choice for a woman like that." She took a deep breath, then ripped the sheet from the book and handed it to Christy. "Start there."

As Christy walked back to her car she was largely oblivious to the rundown neighborhood around her. Instead, she was trying to puzzle through the information Patterson had just given her.

Frank's behavior didn't fit. Oh sure, it seemed to fit. The rich self-indulgent playboy straying from his marriage vows, using drugs, and doing whatever he needed to get the funds to pay for an expensive lifestyle.

That wasn't the Frank Christy knew, though. The Frank she knew was self-indulgent, sure, but he was also devoted to his daughter and he had a deep commitment to her well-being. And for Frank, the definition of well-being for a child meant that the child would be loved and cared for by two parents. It was a legacy from his own problematic childhood, and it was rooted deep within him.

She thought back to the last time she had seen him. The argument they'd had that night, and the promises he'd made, lingered in her mind and made her shake her head as she walked.

Patterson was wrong. Frank couldn't be back in Vancouver.

The final evening had begun as evenings always did in the last few years of their marriage, with getting Noelle to bed.

"Hey, kiddo, you've gotta do what Mommy says." Frank smiled as he hugged Noelle, but the smile was gone when he looked over his shoulder at Christy.

Christy ignored the annoyance on his face. Frank was as much a kid as Noelle was and, if allowed to get away with it, he'd play with her until she collapsed with exhaustion. The trouble was, Noelle faced a full day of school the next day. Though the child was only eight years old, academic expectations were high at the exclusive private school she attended. If she was tired, she wouldn't be able to keep up.

The annoyance disappeared from Frank's face as he once again focused on his daughter. He held out his hand. "Let's go upstairs, poppet. I'll put you to bed tonight."

"Will you read with me, Daddy?" Noelle asked, looking up at him with adoring eyes.

Frank pretended to consider this, although it was actually a done deal and they all knew it. "Depends what's on the reading list."

"Harry Potter," Noelle said. A perennial favorite.

Frank frowned, apparently considering.

Noelle giggled. She widened blue eyes the color of her father's and tilted her head to look up at him, spilling thick blond hair over her shoulders. "If you don't like Harry Potter, there are other books we could read."

Christy had to stifle a laugh. At eight, Noelle was already

a conniving female, though still wrapped up in a little girl package. She understood how to manipulate the daddy she loved. Frank realized Noelle could twist him anyway she wanted, but he didn't care. He loved her with the same intensity she loved him. For Christy it was her husband's best characteristic, and the one that kept her in a marriage where love had dwindled into familiarity.

"Hm," Frank said, a serious expression on his golden boy features. "Let's discuss this when you're ready for bed. How's that?"

"Okay," Noelle said happily.

"Lights out in a half hour, guys."

"Aw, Mom!"

"It's a school night, Noelle. I'll be up in a half hour to say good night."

Noelle looked up at her father, making effective use of those lovely blue eyes of hers. "Daddy, do I have to?"

Frank looked down. Christy could tell he was torn. Though he knew Noelle wasn't above playing one parent off against the other to get her way, he would happily have read longer. Still, he never contradicted Christy in front of their daughter. It was one of the few parenting strategies they had talked out and agreed upon that they still carried through.

"You heard what Mommy said. A half hour is all we've got, kiddo. Come on, we'd better make the best of it."

They went off at a trot, Noelle giggling as they slid across the travertine marble tiles in the hallway and Frank hooting as he pretended that he'd nearly lost his balance on the slippery surface. Then they were charging up the broad, curving staircase to the second floor.

Christy smiled, but it was a bleak expression, not a happy one. On the surface she had a pretty good life. She was married to one of the wealthiest young men in the province of British Columbia, and they lived in a huge mansion on an exclusive, tree-lined crescent in an old, established part of Vancouver. Servants did the cooking and cleaning, and she didn't have to go to an office to toil at a boring nine-to-five clerical job. Best of all, her daughter was smart and healthy, blessedly free of the emotional burdens that warring parents could load onto their young.

That was the essence of the problem, though. Over the course of their ten-year marriage, she and Frank had evolved from passionate lovers, through a stage as parents who were lovers, to parents who were friends and allies in an important job.

They'd been content. Or she thought they had. She turned away from the staircase, chewing her lip. Ellen Jamieson, Frank's aunt and one of the trustees, had called that morning. She wanted to know why Frank had been talking to offshore investors about selling the mansion.

Ellen Jamieson wasn't Christy's favorite person, but she understood the anger and frustration she'd heard in the woman's voice and sympathized. The mansion was Ellen's family home too, even if she hadn't lived here for years.

Though Frank hadn't said anything about selling the mansion to her, Christy wondered if the information Ellen had obtained could be right. About a year and a half ago something happened to Frank. His social patterns changed. There were times when he seemed to be filled with energy and others when he was so lethargic Christy feared for his health. She began to hear rumors of a girlfriend, coupled with snide sideways looks or pitying condescending ones.

Though their marriage was melting down, their relationship with their daughter, together and separately, remained stable. Frank might go out every night, but he did it after Noelle was in bed. And if he came in at four in the morning and slept through breakfast, he always made a big fuss of her when she returned from school. Christy might be the responsible parent, but Frank was, without a doubt, the most beloved.

With a sigh, Christy checked her watch. Time to break up the party.

At the door to Noelle's room she paused, smiling at the scene. The room was pink, the bed canopied in white ruffles. Favorite stuffies, including a cinnamon-colored bear and a goofy-looking horse, had been settled at the footboard to make room for Frank. Noelle was sitting up, her legs crossed, her elbows on her knees, holding the thick hardcover with both hands. Frank lay beside her, resting against the walnut headboard, propped up by Noelle's pillows. In his lap was the family cat, a twenty-pound monster with the heavy stripes, bulky build, and blocky muscles of a tiger. When Stormy moved it was with the same kind of powerful grace as that big cat. Right now though, he was stretched on his back, purring noisily as Frank rubbed his belly while he read over Noelle's shoulder, correcting her pronunciation from time to time.

It was a beautiful scene, one that spoke of love, contentment, and security. Tears caught in Christy's throat. She wished she had some way of capturing this moment and freezing it so it would be there for them—for her—forever.

She must have made a sound, or perhaps Frank was still attuned to her, the way he had been when their marriage was a romance. He looked up. Feeling his attention drift away from her, Noelle looked up too. So did the cat. They all glared at her. "Lights out time," Christy said with an inward sigh.

"Aw, Mom. Just a bit longer. Please!"

"Sorry, sweetheart. It's bedtime."

"You heard your mother," Frank said. He shifted and the cat leapt from his lap. As Stormy stalked past Christy she could have sworn he hissed at her. She may have imagined it, but she doubted it. The cat was Frank's pal first, Noelle's second, then way below, on about the same level as field mice and birds, was Christy.

Noelle was a good sleeper. Once she'd accepted that she wasn't going to be able to coax another hour or two out of her parents, she settled in. She was almost asleep before Christy and Frank left her bedroom.

They made it to the top of the broad curve of the staircase before the argument started.

"God, you're such a nag," Frank said.

Christy didn't respond to the taunt. Instead she said, "Is it true you want to sell the mansion?" She headed down the stairs, looking forward, very aware of his presence beside her.

"Are you kidding? Why would I want to sell this place? It's my home."

"Money."

He snorted. "Get real, Chris. I'm loaded, remember? Money's not an issue."

They reached the bottom of the staircase. She turned to face him. "It is according to Aunt Ellen."

Frank's blue eyes narrowed. "What's she been saying now?"

"That you've been running through our income from the trust before the end of the quarter. To get around it, you've been borrowing against your inheritance." Christy's voice faltered. Frank's face was set in a hard, impassive mask, but fury blazed from the blue ice of his eyes. She swallowed hard. Ellen's call had been eating at her all day. Ellen had brought Frank up after his parents had been killed. That didn't mean there was any love between them, though. Frank loathed her. Now Christy wanted to hear Frank's side. She continued on, less angrily than before. "Ellen says the Trust won't honor your debts anymore, so you've decided to offload the mansion so you can squander the cash."

"My dear Aunt Ellen is so full of crap I'm surprised she doesn't explode," Frank said. Christy winced at his choice of words. Frank ignored her as he pulled a light jacket out of a cupboard cleverly hidden beneath and behind the stairs.

Christy crossed her arms as she watched him shrug on the jacket. Part of her wanted to reach out to him, to ask him to stay, to tell him they could work it out. To reassure him that she believed him, in him. Part of her knew it was a wasted effort. "So you're not talking to brokers about selling our home?"

He put his hands on her shoulders, then shook her lightly, gently. "Look, Chris, I know we don't have much of a marriage anymore, but do you think that I'd do that to you and Noelle?"

As she looked up at him, meeting his eyes, he cupped her cheek with his palm in a remembered caress from better times. When she searched his face the anger was gone. In its place were regret and the rueful honesty that had once captured her heart. "No. I don't agree with a lot of the things you are doing, Frank, but I believe you will always take care of Noelle and me."

"Damn straight," he said. He bent to drop a light, chaste kiss on her lips. One final, gentle caress and he was sauntering toward the front door.

Christy watched him with regret. They'd loved each other once, enough for Frank to defy his trustees and marry a professor's daughter from small-town Ontario. Enough for her to abandon her goals, quit university before graduation, and brave the bitterness of his guardians. Their love might have passed the first test, but it hadn't survived the everyday struggle of their lives together. "Frank."

He paused at the door, his hand on the latch, his brows raised in question. "Stay home tonight. Take that assistant's job at the company Gerry Fisher mentioned a couple of weeks ago. Go to bed before eleven so you can make an early start in the morning. Begin again."

His expression was incredulous. "Take a trainee job at my own company? Are you kidding?" Stormy the Cat appeared out of nowhere, twinning around his ankles. He bent to pick up the animal. Idly he rubbed behind the cat's ears. Stormy began to purr loudly. "Face it, Chris, I'm the Ice Cream King's tragic son, the face of Jamieson Ice Cream. Nothing more."

She made an inarticulate sound of denial in her throat.

He put the cat down on the marble floor. "I have," he said.

When Frank went out the door, the cat went with him. Christy followed them to the porch where she stood and watched as Frank slid into the two-seater Porsche convertible. As he revved the engine, the cat leapt onto the back of the car and dove into the narrow space between the seats and the small trunk.

Christy stepped forward, waving to catch Frank's attention to let him know that the cat was hitching a ride. Frank ignored her, or perhaps he didn't notice her. He gunned the engine and roared down the drive.

The last Christy saw of either of them was the red of the car's taillights as Frank checked for traffic, before turning onto the street and disappearing from view.

CHAPTER 5

Quinn Armstrong was waiting. He was lucky. It wasn't raining. He tipped his face to the mid-afternoon sunlight. There had been times when he'd staked out a quarry that he'd had to stand for hours in the cold, enduring a downpour that was closer to sleet than rain. Others when the sun had been so hot that he could feel his body dehydrate as sweat poured off him.

Today, though, the weather was gorgeous. The golden September afternoon made him remember why he loved the Pacific coast. He stretched in a leisurely way, enjoying the opportunity to sit on his own front porch, wearing a T-shirt and jean shorts, and still be at work. It wasn't often that he could combine a stakeout with a coffee and a relaxed reading of research materials on his intended quarry. He knew, though, that his subject—his newest neighbor, Christy Jamieson—couldn't get past him, so he was free to flip through the raft of notes and photocopies he'd gathered, looking for the kind of details that would make sense of often contradictory information.

Christy's arrival a week ago at the vacant unit two doors down had been a surprise, to say the least. A townhouse complex in suburban Burnaby was the last place he would have expected to find a woman rumored to demand the best in big quantities. That had made him wonder about a lot of the other information that swirled around Christy Jamieson. Was it fact or innuendo?

He considered what he knew of his new neighbor down the street. Her hair was brown with red highlights, cut in a sophisticated, layered style that shouted expensive. It framed a face that was pretty in a delicate, heart-shaped way and accented brown eyes that were deep-set and mysterious. Unless, he thought, she was annoyed.

He chuckled aloud at that. Christy Jamieson always seemed to be annoyed when she was around him, which wasn't surprising considering the way the media had hounded her after Frank Jamieson disappeared. Or the accusatory tone of the articles that appeared after the embezzlement from the Jamieson Trust was discovered. He had to admit that he liked watching her dark eyes flash with fury, animating her face.

He'd pegged her as a capable, intelligent woman whose lifestyle had been radically changed, leaving her a single mom with tremendous responsibilities. It wasn't surprising that she reacted with hostility at times.

Quinn was surprised at himself for the empathy he was feeling for Christy. Where did it come from? Since an assignment in Africa, when he'd stood in an encampment and stared at the slaughtered and defaced bodies of Dr. Tamara Ahern and her team, he hadn't allowed himself to feel anything for the subjects of his articles. So what was it about Christy Jamieson that made her different? Her looks? No doubt she was attractive, but he'd met good-looking women before and been unmoved. Was it her reputation as a gold digger and bimbo, a reputation that appeared to be undeserved? That was intriguing, but more of an intellectual puzzle than an emotional one. The vulnerability he sensed beneath the strength she showed the world? He visualized her. Could be. She had a wide, generous mouth, made to smile, but he'd only seen her use the expression on her pretty daughter.

He thought it would be nice to see her smile at him that way once in a while, not that he wanted her to like him, but because she had beautiful lips, full and sensual. There were moments when she'd pouted at him, thrusting out her lovely lower lip, that he'd wondered what it would be like to kiss her. He laughed silently at himself. Not a good idea. If he ever tried she'd probably give him a bite that would leave scars. He suspected, from the jut of her pretty, pointed little chin that she was blessed with a personality that was stubborn, to say the least, controlling at worst.

Some reports in the local press hinted that her desire for control had pushed the charming and very likable Frank Jamieson off the righteous path of good behavior into the decadent world of indulgence, drugs, and crime.

Were the reports right? Had Christy helped her husband steal from the trust? Had she used the sexual prowess promised in those dark eyes and full, pouty lips to tempt him into the darkness of drugs and deception?

The sound of kids' voices floated over from the nearby school. Quinn stood and stretched, then leaned against the beam that supported the roof over the porch and waited.

They walked down the street hand in hand, Christy Jamieson and her pretty little daughter. The bond between them was clear, though the pout on the girl's mouth indicated storms a-brewing. Quinn couldn't help but smile. He doubted Frank Jamieson's daughter was accustomed to life as one of the common horde.

He ambled down the shallow steps and perched on the planter in front of his house. Christy would have to pass him to get to her place. He was just letting her know he was there. He was waiting.

He could afford to wait.

"Hello," he said as she passed. "Lovely afternoon, isn't it?"

Christy cast him a sideways look as she nodded stiffly.

The little girl, Noelle, peered at him cautiously. She'd obviously been taught to be wary of strangers. He grinned at her. She drew back, startled, her expression horrified.

"How was school today?" he said to her in a conversational way.

"You don't have to speak to him, Noelle," Christy said. She shot Quinn a sharp look. "He's just a reporter."

"He also lives two doors down," Quinn drawled. "And is a card-carrying member of the local neighborhood watch." That wasn't precisely true, his father was the member, but he wanted to shake Christy out of her self-righteous attitude about reporters and let her know they weren't all bad. At least, he wasn't.

"Yeah, right," Christy said. "Come inside, Noelle, and tell me about your day."

"Have a nice afternoon," Quinn said. "I'll see you later."

For a moment Christy's footsteps faltered, then she continued on without acknowledging his remark. But Quinn was certain he'd hit his mark. He'd let her know that this time she couldn't shake him off the way she'd done before. She didn't live in her gated mansion with servants to cover for her. She lived in a townhouse now, with neighbors crowding close. She was accessible, and he was after her story. All she could control was how long she'd make him wait to get it.

"Martin Burford is a jerk."

"Which one is he, Noelle?"

"The boy with the yellow hair."

There were four boys with blond hair in Noelle's grade three class. As far as Christy could tell they all irritated her daughter to some extent. "What's he done now?"

"He took my brown pencil crayon and it's the only brown one I have!" Noelle's full lips were pulled down in a scowl. Christy turned her back to her daughter and grinned. She couldn't help it. As a newcomer to the school, all the kids in her class were showing interest in Noelle. The girls were asking her about her clothes, what books she liked, and where she lived. The boys were seeking her attention by wrestling in front of her, or 'borrowing' things from her as the unfortunate Martin had. All this did, of course, was annoy her, since Noelle wasn't in the least interested in the little boys in question.

"Then he scribbled on my picture and said I was supposed to be drawing a summer picture not a creepy old house for Halloween."

Christy's smile faltered and died. "Was it a Halloween picture?

"No!" Noelle said hotly. "The teacher told us to draw a picture that described our summer, so I did a picture of our house and Daddy leaving. It wasn't creepy. It was real. Martin Burford doesn't know what he's talking about. He's stupid!"

"No name calling, Noelle," Christy said as she considered how best to deal with the issue Noelle had just raised. Sitting down, she took Noelle in her arms.

Noelle sniffed. After a minute she crawled up into Christy's lap. "I miss Daddy."

"Me too, kiddo," Christy said, rocking back and forth.

"Why did he have to go?"

Christy sighed. "Not because of anything you did, Noelle." She hugged her daughter more tightly. "It was Daddy doing something he needed to do. One of these days he'll come home and the first person he'll want to see is you."

Noelle raised her head. Her big, blue eyes were luminous with tears shed and unshed. She brushed her wet cheeks with the back of her hands. "Promise?"

Christy smoothed the hair away from her daughter's face. The unhappiness she saw there twisted inside her. "Promise," she said, though she knew the word was a lie. She would do anything to keep her daughter safe and happy.

Noelle sighed, cuddled close for a moment, then slipped back to her chair. "Mary Petrofsky is nice," she said in a conversational way. "We borrowed skipping ropes from the gym and played together at lunch."

"Great." Christy headed for the fridge to organize a snack for Noelle. The sudden switch from distraught daughter to socially adept Jamieson was disconcerting, but a relief. She didn't want to discuss Frank with Noelle until she knew why he hadn't contacted them when he returned to Vancouver.

His words to her on the night he disappeared kept coming back to her—his promise that he would always look after her and Noelle. She'd believed him then. Part of her still believed him, mainly because she knew how deeply he loved Noelle. How could he have done this to her? It didn't fit.

"She lives down the street, beside that man's house."

Christy pulled an apple from the fridge. With the water running as she washed the fruit, she said, "I didn't catch that, pumpkin. Who were you talking about?"

"The man who spoke to us when we came home. The friendly one."

Christy turned off the water with a snap. Quinn Armstrong, reporter. Oh, man, what was she going to say to Noelle? She didn't want her near any reporters, but this one was their neighbor. How did she handle it?

When Frank first disappeared, before he showed up in Mexico with his bimbo, the trustees and the police had believed he'd been kidnapped. Noelle had been ferried to and from school with an unobtrusive police escort. During recess and lunch she'd been forced to stay inside where she could be adequately monitored. Noelle knew about security and the dangers of strangers. And she had no reason to like reporters who had hounded the mansion and lain in wait for her at the school gates.

Still, this reporter was a neighbor. How could she convince Noelle that not all neighbors were the kind you were friendly with without scaring her and making her into some kind of tortured introvert now that she had to live in the real world?

Take the easy road. Focus on Mary Petrofsky until you can figure out how to handle the Quinn Armstrong issue. "Have you thought about asking Mary to play outside with you after school?"

"Maybe, but not today. She's in daycare today, cuz her mom works part-time." Noelle paused to eat one of the apple slices Christy had put on the table. "Mary says her mom's an admin assistant. What's that, Mom?"

In the discussion about the duties of an administrative assistant, Noelle forgot about Quinn Armstrong. Christy didn't. While her daughter worked on her homework, Christy fussed around the kitchen, emptying the dishwasher, wiping the counters, picking up bits and pieces of things that were out of place, and generally perfecting an already tidy environment. While she worked, she wrestled with her problem. Her thoughts weren't pleasant.

Quinn Armstrong wasn't going away. She couldn't escape him by disappearing this time. He was going to put himself in her face, constantly reminding her that he was there and that he wanted an interview. When she was just going through the daily motions of life, that was a bother, but she didn't want an intrusive reporter following her around while she sought out Frank.

Her imagination conjured up a scene any reporter would delight in—the curvy blond Brianne wound around Frank, who was pretending to be innocent while his wife tore a strip off of him. Yeah, a reporter would love that one, she thought, particularly if they could capture it all on tape for the six o'clock news. It was the kind of notoriety of which nightmares were made. Her nightmares, at least.

She brushed away the image. Finding Frank would not be easy. Detective Patterson couldn't do it. What made her think that she would be able to?

She would check out the address Patterson had given her, the Strand Manor, an inexpensive tourist hotel. She didn't think Frank was staying with Brianne Lymbourn—the Strand wasn't his usual style—but she could talk to Brianne. Maybe Brianne would open up to her. Unlikely, but worth a try.

She leaned against the clean counter and watched Noelle work diligently at a page of addition problems. She needed to find Frank before he hurt Noelle any further. Her research skills were limited, though. If Frank didn't want to be found, she'd probably discover more dead ends than open pathways.

She thought about that as she helped Noelle with one of the math problems. Why would Frank want to hide from her and Noelle? She could understand him avoiding the trustees. He would be pretty certain that Samuel Macklin, the Trust's accountant, or Edward Bidwell, the legal arm, would turn him in if they caught wind of his being in town. He might even figure that his Aunt Ellen would be ready to disown him for his embezzlement, since she had more invested in it than the other trustees.

When the Jamieson Trust was set up, Frank had been a baby. Frank senior had expected to live to an old age and to father more children, but there had always been the chance he would die young or that his baby might not survive childhood. So a second beneficiary was chosen to ensure that the Jamieson fortune would stay in the family. Should Frank junior, or his heirs, die before they inherited, Ellen Jamieson would be the recipient of the Jamieson fortune.

Christy had always suspected that the possibility she might one day inherit her brother's fortune had been why Ellen had hated her so much. Frank's marriage meant that there was a potential for kids, and Christy had fulfilled that fairly quickly. Noelle's arrival was one more reason why Ellen, though wealthy, would never be as rich as her annoying nephew.

But what about Gerry Fisher, who had been Frank's mentor and father figure? Wouldn't Frank want Gerry to know he was safe, that he was home again?

Noelle put the math sheet away, drawing Christy's attention. "What's next, kiddo?"

"Handwriting." Noelle drew out a lined sheet of paper. "I have to practice the letter *g*."

"Why *g*?"

"Because it's hard to do." With painstaking slowness and infinite concentration, Noelle shakily drew the letter on the page.

Christy watched, fascinated. Her daughter was absolutely right. The only way to learn was in the doing. She could stand here for hours thinking about finding Frank, or she could do something about it.

She sat down beside Noelle at the kitchen table and wrote down all the places Frank might go if he had returned to Vancouver. It included all the top hotels in town, much more Frank's style than the economy-grade Strand Manor.

Then there were the people he would want to see—or not see. Top of that list was Noelle. Just below was his best friend, Aaron DeBolt, another wealthy young man with too much time on his hands and more than enough money to spend wasting it. At the bottom were the trustees.

By the time she finished she'd filled a page and she was completely overwhelmed.

"What's that, Mommy?" Noelle asked, taking a breather from her handwriting practice to rest her hand.

"It's a list of stuff I have to do, honey," Christy said, frowning at the paper.

Noelle frowned too. "There's lots on that list. It looks like the ones you used to make for my school."

When she had been president of the Parents Advisory Council at VRA. "That was different, honey."

"Yeah," Noelle said with a sigh, "it was."

Christy faltered, then continued on with nothing more than a little shake in her voice. "I had a bunch of people helping me. All I had to do was figure out what needed to be done, then give the jobs to the people best suited to handling them."

Noelle nodded. "Then why don't you find someone to do all that stuff for you?" Conversation over, Noelle went back to her careful practice writing the letter *g*. Christy stared at her daughter as if she'd just announced that the world was round at a meeting of the flat earth society.

Noelle was totally right. What Christy needed was a professional to find Frank, a detective like Billie Patterson, only the private kind, not one on the public payroll. *How did you go about hiring a detective?*

For that matter, did she have the funds to pay one?

She mentally reviewed her income and decided, reluctantly, that she didn't. She could approach the trustees and ask that the cost be borne as a direct expense of the trust, but that would mean selling more Jamieson stock. Even if Macklin and Bidwell agreed to it, dear Aunt Ellen certainly would not.

That put her back where she began. She'd have to do the digging herself, because she didn't know any professionals who'd provide her with a free research service…

Or did she? Reporters researched their stories. Quinn Armstrong was a reporter. Quinn Armstrong wanted an interview with her. What if she offered to give him an exclusive? In exchange he would have to help her find Frank. The idea of involving Quinn Armstrong had her stomach clenching and her hands shaking, but there was a certain seductive quality to it.

Over the years she'd learned to manage people, but was she good enough to handle Quinn Armstrong? There was only one way to find out. She'd have to put her proposal to him and set the process in motion.

The doorbell rang. She went to answer it with Noelle hot on her heels. A dark-haired girl stood on the porch. "Can Noelle come out to play?"

"Hi, Mary," Noelle said. "Can I, Mom? This is Mary Petrofsky. I told you about her. She's in my class."

"And I live down the street in the end house," Mary added.

"I thought Mary was in daycare," Christy said.

Mary grinned, revealing a gap where an eyetooth had once been. "I am. Mom picks me up at four thirty. I'm off tomorrow though. Maybe Noelle and I can play together then, too."

Christy looked at Mary, but she thought about Quinn Armstrong. If she followed Noelle outside, she could keep an eye on the kids and ring the Armstrongs' doorbell at the same time.

"Okay. Put away your homework first, Noelle. Then you can go out."

"Thanks, Mom!"

Noelle rushed away. Christy took a deep breath and stepped outside. Time to put the process in motion.

Roy Armstrong answered the door. He was holding a cup of coffee and there was a distracted look in his eyes, as if his body was here, but his brain was somewhere else. But he smiled when he saw Christy and opened the door wider.

"Hi, Roy," Christy said. Dressed in tie-dyed T-shirt and jeans with holes in them, he didn't look like a famous author. There was more than a passing resemblance to his son, though. She heard her voice shake as she added, "I'm Christy Jam—"

"I know you," Roy said. "I do. Quinn!" he bellowed over his shoulder. "Shake a leg. Christy, our new neighbor, is at the door." He smiled at Christy again. "Since meeting you, Quinn's been jumpier than that cat he took in a while back. Be kind to him, and give his old man some peace, would you?"

Christy's eyes opened wide. "It's not like that, er, Roy! It's…it's business."

His eyes lit up. "You don't say."

Footsteps sounded, then Quinn Armstrong appeared. The layout of the Armstrong house appeared to be exactly the same as Christy's. The front door opened into a small landing from which stairs ran up and down. At the top of the up flight was the living room-dining room combination, which opened into the kitchen. Further stairs led up to the bedrooms. The other set of stairs went directly down to a large family room.

Christy watched Quinn descend, her nerves tightening with each step.

On the last step he paused and surveyed her. "Mrs. Jamieson."

"A mite formal, aren't you, boy?" Roy said, cocking a brow. He observed his son over the rim of the cup before taking a sip.

Quinn shot him a look. "Until this moment, Mrs. Jamieson was hardly willing to acknowledge my existence. Formality seems appropriate in the circumstances."

"Is that a fact." There was laughter in Roy's eyes as he looked from his son's cool expression to Christy's reddening cheeks.

"Until this moment, I had no reason to agree to your request, Quinn," she said, deliberately using his first name.

His brows snapped together. He stepped down that last stair to the landing, a movement of lithe grace and loose-limbed elegance.

Christy watched him with an enjoyment she didn't want to acknowledge. Quinn Armstrong was a pleasure to look at, and she had a suspicion that he could be defined as 'hot.' He was, however, a member of a profession she loathed. She had also decided he was going to be an employee, of sorts. That alone should be a reminder to keep her eyes to herself.

"Christy, why don't you come in? Dad, don't you have something you need to do? Like work on that book?"

"You nag me worse than your mother did, boy," Roy said amicably. He sipped coffee as he locked eyes with his son.

Christy said, "I can't. Come in, that is. Quinn, would you mind talking to me out on the porch while I keep an eye on my daughter and her friend?"

"Solves that problem," Quinn said, shouldering past his father.

"Work, work, work. That's all the boy thinks about," Roy muttered to no one in particular. "Okay, you two, have fun." His eyes danced as Quinn glowered at him, then he firmly shut the door, leaving Christy and Quinn facing each other on the small porch.

Quinn shoved his hands in his pockets and leaned against the doorframe. "What made you decide to do the interview?"

"You get straight to the point, don't you?"

He shrugged.

She drew a deep breath, told herself she was doing the right thing, then put the process in motion. "I haven't agreed to do the interview—yet."

He didn't move, but Christy could have sworn that he stiffened. "So you've got terms? Most people in your situation do. I don't write promo pieces. I do my research. If what I discover differs from the spin you're putting on the information, I write the story the way I feel it should be told."

"I'm glad to hear that. It's your research skills that prompted me to agree to your request."

"Checked me out, did you?"

Christy laughed. It wasn't a happy sound, but one aimed directly at herself. "Oh no. I wouldn't know where to start. That's my problem, I don't know how to find information on people."

He studied her, his brows drawn together in that little frown that was surprisingly sexy. "You're losing me."

"I have someone I need to find."

"Your husband."

"Yes. I have a place to begin the search, but I don't know how to proceed from there. I need help."

"My help."

She nodded. "What I'm proposing is that you help me find Frank, and I'll agree to give you an interview."

Straightening, he said, "Everything we find out I can use."

"Agreed."

"Once we find him, I get an interview with Frank Jamieson, as well as the one with you."

"Agreed," Christy said without hesitation. It was the least the rat could do after deserting her and Noelle.

Quinn shot out his hand. "Okay, we've got a deal. Tell me what you've got, and we'll start from there."

Christy slowly put her hand in his. His palm was warm and a little rough. As his hand closed around hers she had a sense of strength and protection that was immensely reassuring.

There was no going back. She was committed.

CHAPTER 6

"This is not Frank's sort of place."

Christy had doubted that Frank would stay at a hotel like the Strand Manor from the moment Billie Patterson gave her the scrap of paper with his location written on it. Standing here now, she was quite sure it wasn't possible.

At Christy's comment, Quinn glanced around the small lobby, then he cocked her a questioning look. "His tastes run to luxurious, do they?"

Lit by bright white overhead fluorescents, the lobby branded the hotel as cheap but clean. It featured a seating area to one side of the reception desk and in front of the elevators. The furniture consisted of an overstuffed sofa with square, blocky arms covered in durable leatherette with two matching chairs opposite. A potted fern drooped dispiritedly at one end of the couch. There was nothing welcoming about the little area. This was minimal seating, to be used while a guest waited for a taxi. It was not there to encourage leisurely chats.

The Strand Manor was clearly a pit stop for travelers looking for a place to crash and little else. It was not the kind of place she and Frank patronized when they traveled. Not only was the Strand a bottom feeder hotel, but it was located on Pender Street, in a shabby area on the edge of the Vancouver's downtown east side, the poorest area of any city in Canada.

"Frank has always had money. The cost of a night's stay was never an issue. It isn't an issue now, either, since he has access to the money he embezzled. He likes nice surroundings and he likes people to be there to see to his needs." She looked dubiously at the clerk at the reservation desk. The woman was dressed neatly, but without a uniform. A further sweep noted that there was no bellman in sight and the lobby didn't feature a concierge desk.

Quinn considered her comments thoughtfully as he assessed their surroundings. "So Frank staying at this hotel is out of character."

"Yes. I'd say it's also out of character for Brianne Lymbourn. I only met her a few times, but I got the impression that money and luxury were big issues for her." Christy stopped, hearing the sneer in her voice and mentally cursing herself for expressing her feelings for Brianne all to clearly.

"As in she was looking for a male with lots of the former so she could spend it on the latter?"

Christy laughed, relieved that Quinn had not commented on her situation or the emotions that were so clear in her comment. That showed a respect for her feelings she hadn't expected to find in a reporter. "Yeah, something like that."

At the desk, the reservation clerk finished checking out a guest. Quinn nudged Christy. "Do you have the picture of Frank ready?"

Christy nodded.

"Okay, let's see what we can find out."

He approached the desk with Christy one step behind. She watched his mouth curl in a smile that would melt the hardest female heart. The clerk, a woman in her mid-twenties, smiled back warmly.

"Hi, Selma," Quinn said, reading the woman's nametag.

"Good morning. How can I help you, sir?" She tilted her head just the slightest degree. Her smile grew wider.

Christy held the picture of Frank by its edges so the nervous sweat from her fingertips wouldn't ruin the image. She had spent a lot of time choosing the photo they would use for their search. On Quinn's advice, she'd found a clear snap of Frank showing his torso and head. He was staring directly into the camera, only the faintest of smiles on his mouth. The shirt he was wearing was the casual, open necked and short-sleeved kind she would expect him to travel in.

Quinn leaned against the desk. He appeared to be a man with all the time in the world to flirt with a pretty woman. He got straight to business. "We're here to visit an old friend who is staying at this hotel."

"Not a problem, sir. If you give me his name, I'll key it in and ring his room for you."

"Frank Jamieson." They waited while the clerk typed and frowned.

"Are you sure he is staying here?" She looked up apologetically. "I don't have a Jamieson registered."

Quinn shot her a small, rueful smile. "Would you try his girlfriend, then? Maybe they registered under her name. It's Brianne Lymbourn."

The clerk keyed in the name then watched the screen. "Ah, here she is. Brianne Lymbourn, party of two." She frowned. "I'm sorry, sir. She checked out an hour ago. You just missed them, I'm afraid."

"Did Brianne leave a forwarding address?"

The clerk played with some keys then shook her head. "She gave her home address as a city in Mexico, but that's all I have."

Quinn looked at Christy. He was frowning now. His eyes told her he wanted her to play along with him. "If that isn't Brianne at her worst!" he said. "Does that woman ever stop to think? We've all been planning this for weeks!"

"Now come on, Quinn! She's not that bad," Christy said. "Maybe Frank got restless and wanted to move on. You know what he's like when he travels." She turned to Selma the desk clerk with a smile.

Selma smiled back, more interested in the conversation than whatever other duties she had.

Christy dropped the photo of Frank on the desktop. "Frank's problem," she said in a confidential way to the desk clerk, "is that he's a nice guy. He's also good looking. The result is that women indulge him."

Selma glanced at the picture and smiled. "Yeah, I can see that."

Christy glanced at Quinn. He was watching her with the hint of a smile on his lips and amusement in his eyes. Enjoying herself, Christy continued on. "So he does pretty well whatever he wants. If he decided it was time to head off to Calgary, Brianne wouldn't have much of a choice. She'd just have to pack up and go with him."

Selma frowned. By the time Christy had finished speaking she was shaking her head. "I don't think your friend was with Ms. Lymbourn. I may have seen this man before, but not with Ms. Lymbourn. And not at this hotel. Maybe our other front desk clerk can help."

But the other clerk shook his head when shown Frank's picture and they also had no luck with the waitresses in the hotel's tiny coffee bar. No one could remember seeing Frank, with or without an attractive blond on his arm.

"So now what?" Christy asked when they were back on the sidewalk.

Quinn stared thoughtfully at the old, low-rise buildings that lined Pender. Cars packed the four-lane avenue, crawling slowly along, just shy of gridlock, even though it was mid-morning, not rush hour. Pedestrians bustled down the sidewalks. As they flowed around the stationary Quinn and Christy, she had a feeling that Quinn was looking more inside his head than at the scene around them.

Suddenly his gaze sharpened. "We check the eating places in this area, particularly the ones that serve breakfast. People don't usually go far without their morning coffee."

Sounded reasonable. An hour later, they were several blocks away from the hotel and had received too many headshakes to count. Christy looked around the tiny storefront café that served fresh-made wraps. The place smelled of fragrant Mediterranean spices and was doing a brisk business in takeout, even though it was not yet noon.

"Okay, no one has seen Frank, but we don't know if Brianne has used any of the restaurants we checked because we don't have a picture of her." Christy's stomach grumbled. She blushed, but ignored it. "Do we keep on looking? Or do we try to get a photo of Brianne and start over?"

Quinn frowned. "First we find something to eat. While we're fueling up we figure out our next step." He indicated the counter at the back of the room. "Want to eat here? The sandwiches look pretty good."

The café had three tiny round tables, two chairs at each. None were in use. "Sure."

Quinn nodded briskly. "Why don't you snag a table? I'll get the food. What would you like?"

Christy scanned the menu chalked on a blackboard. The flowing script was complemented with drawings of scantily clad creatures that might have been mermaids. "Mediterranean Chicken with extra sauce." She chose a table near the plate glass window and sat down with a sigh. She hadn't expected a search for Frank to be easy, but she hadn't expected it to be so physically exhausting either. Or so frustrating. It was as if Frank was invisible. Surely someone had seen him!

Quinn came over carrying a tray crammed with two large, waxed paper glasses and two paper plates holding wraps. The enticing scent wafting from the food made Christy's stomach grumble again. Quinn's lips twitched as he handed her one of the plates.

"Thanks." Christy took a bite. The sauce oozed over the edge of the wrap. The chicken was moist and juicy. She closed her eyes as she savored the taste and texture of veggies and sauce sliding over her tongue. It was wonderful. She sighed with satisfaction.

When she opened her eyes again she found that Quinn had placed a waxed paper glass filled with a soft drink in front of her. He was biting into his own wrap, but over the sandwich he was watching her with amusement and an appreciation that was frankly sexual. She straightened. Putting the wrap back on the flimsy paper plate, she dabbed at her lips with a napkin. Quinn glanced away, dropping his sandwich on the plate before he picked up his soft drink and sipped. When he looked at her again, the lusty gleam was gone from his eyes. Christy wondered if she had imagined it.

"The first question we have to ask ourselves," he said, "is why a guy like Frank, who likes his comforts and who can afford them, would stay in a place like the Strand Manor?"

"He wouldn't. How much do I owe you?" Christy replied, digging through her purse.

"You don't owe me anything," Quinn said. "That's not an answer. We know Frank was traveling with Brianne. We know Brianne was staying at the Strand. Therefore the natural assumption is that Frank was the unnamed man staying with her at the Strand."

Christy squinted at the menu on the wall beside what served as the kitchen and service counter. She put a five-dollar bill in front Quinn. "That should cover it, I think. What if the natural assumption is wrong? What if Frank decided to use another hotel?"

Quinn pushed the five back to Christy. "There's still the guy staying with Brianne. If he's not Frank, then who is he?"

Christy stared at the five-dollar bill in front of her as she finished chewing a bit of her wrap. She looked at Quinn. "I can't let you buy me lunch."

"Why not?"

"Because we're not friends."

He didn't move. His expression didn't change, but the easy relaxation of a moment before was gone. Tension crackled from him.

Christy regretted her words instantly, but there was no going back. She pushed the money again. "Take it, Quinn. Please."

He picked up the bill, held it between two fingers, stared at it. Then he looked at her deliberately, coolly, before he pocketed it. "I don't think your husband is the man rooming with Brianne."

Christy winced inside at his impersonal tone, emphasized by his reference to her married state. "Okay, how do we prove Brianne has another man on her string if we can't find Brianne herself?"

"We find your husband." He nodded at her. "Come on, eat up. This is guaranteed to take a while."

For the next two hours they checked the better hotels in town, but they had no more luck than they'd had at the Strand Manor. Frank wasn't registered in any of them and no one remembered seeing him, although a few people did recognize his picture.

"Now what?" Christy asked as they emerged from their seventh hotel. She glanced at her watch as they walked. "School is out in an hour, and I've got to be there to pick up Noelle." Her feet were sore, and she was exhausted. If this was typical of Quinn's job, she didn't envy him it.

They were passing a trendy coffee shop. He pulled open the door. "Planning time. Let's have a coffee." Inside they both lined up at the counter. Quinn ordered a regular coffee. Christy chose a Café Vienna. She figured she needed the hit of sugar the chocolate would bring. They each paid for their own drink.

"We've checked most of the top hotels in the downtown core, but not all of them," Quinn said when they were seated at a little wrought iron table on uncomfortable matching chairs. "I'll take the photograph of Frank and continue asking around."

Steam rose from the coffee, bringing with it an aromatic scent that made Christy's mouth water. She blew on it, then took a sip. It burned with satisfying heat, infusing her tired body with renewed energy. "This doesn't feel right, Quinn."

There was an edge in Quinn's voice as he said, "Spending the day together or coffee with me?"

She looked at him, startled. "Neither. I'm talking about Frank just being…well, nowhere. I mean, it doesn't make sense."

Quinn searched her face for a minute, before he glanced down, studying the coffee cup. When he looked up there was no evidence of emotion in his eyes. "No, it doesn't. Though my gut tells me Frank wasn't the guy in Brianne's party of two at the Strand, I'm going to ignore my instincts and assume that he was since we haven't been able to locate him at another hotel."

"But no one recognized him at the Strand!"

"Like the desk clerk said, they see a lot of people, and in a place like that customer service is minimal and the staff aren't expected to notice guests or remember their names. It would be easy for someone to slip through."

Christy wrapped her hands around her cup. "So much for my great lead." She stared moodily into the mocha brown contents. "It's turned out to be a dead end." When Quinn didn't reply a simmering stew of annoyance and impatience bubbled up. So much for planning. He couldn't even be bothered listening to her. A little support would be nice too, even if the man was only an employee.

She looked over at him. His eyes had taken on that same abstracted look he'd had when they first emerged from the Strand Manor, as if he was looking at things, but not seeing them. Her bubbling irritation began to rock the lid that kept her boiling emotional cauldron from overflowing.

Quinn leaned back in his chair, drank some more coffee. "What we need to do is go back a step, and forward one as well."

Shocked, her eyes widened. He *had* been listening to her. Amazing. "You've lost me. Explain."

He gestured with his coffee cup. "We can't locate Frank in town, so we need to go back to the airport, talk to the customs employee who processed Frank's customs declaration. Find out if Frank and Brianne were actually together or just returning on the same plane. Then we go forward to where Frank might have gone if he split with

Brianne after they left the hotel today." Quinn fixed a penetrating gaze on Christy. "They've been in Vancouver for a few days. Who would he contact first when he came back to town?"

There was one person he'd never abandon and who would welcome his return with delight. She said without hesitation, "Noelle. She'd be the first person he would call."

"His daughter," Quinn said.

"Our daughter." There was a snap to her voice that had nothing to do with Quinn. It stemmed from years of dealing with Aunt Ellen who called Noelle the 'youngest and best Jamieson', and the trustees, who referred to her as 'The Jamieson Heir'.

Quinn frowned. There was a thoughtful expression in his eyes. "Has he contacted her?"

Christy shook her head. "No. There have been no calls, no hang-ups, no messages. Nothing."

Quinn leaned forward. "Who else would he go to?"

She sipped her drink as she thought about that. Who would Frank contact? He'd burned a lot of bridges by stealing from his trust fund then running away to Mexico. "I suppose he'd start with the crowd he ran with. There's one person he was close to, Aaron DeBolt. He might call him. Me, I suppose, although after running off with Brianne, he must know I'd be pretty mad at him. His trustees, but again, he'd have to know they'd be angry, and even willing to turn him over to the police."

"Not a lot options," Quinn said. "Let's focus on going back first. Did the police report have the name of the customs agent who processed Frank through?"

Christy thought back to her conversation with Billie Patterson. "I think so. If not I can get it."

"Okay. We'll head out to the airport tomorrow. With luck we'll get a firm identification of Frank. We can move on from there."

Christy nodded. She glanced at her watch. "Yikes! I've got to run. I'll see you tomorrow, Quinn."

She left him sitting, apparently relaxed, with the chair tilted back on two legs, his gaze abstracted, thinking the problem through.

After her first day on the job with Quinn Armstrong, she was impressed.

She didn't want to be.

"Mrs. Jamieson, do you have a moment, please?" Noelle's teacher, Mrs. Morton, was a middle-aged woman with black hair that was fading to iron grey and a brisk, no-nonsense manner.

"Of course. Hey, Noelle, why don't you go hang up your backpack while I talk to your teacher?"

Noelle nodded and gave Christy a hug, completely unconcerned by her teacher's desire to talk to her mother. She was used to her mother being a fixture at the school. She expected it.

Christy, on the other hand, stared at the teacher warily. It was the only the second week of classes, and Noelle had already pegged Mrs. Morton as grouchy and mean. Christy was prepared to be more charitable, but Mrs. Morton's lips were folded into a straight, tight line. She looked scary, to say the least.

The teacher didn't waste any time with pleasantries. "I believe Noelle's father, and your husband, is Frank Jamieson, the embezzler."

Christy blinked. The shot had come out of nowhere. "What happened to innocent until proven guilty?"

Morton dismissed that with an airy wave of her hand. "Noelle is a lovely child, very well-mannered."

"Thank you," Christy said. She waited for the 'but' to follow. With a woman like Morton, she knew there would be one.

"I believe she is repressing strong emotions relating to her father's criminal activities and her mother's—"

Christy straightened, assuming her best Jamieson snooty look. She had the satisfaction of hearing Morton's voice falter and fade. "My daughter is no different from any other child whose parents have split. Furthermore, I would appreciate it if you did not call her father an embezzler. He is not. More importantly, Noelle does not see him that way."

Out of the corner of her eye she could see that the kids were all seated. One girl leaned close to another and said something. Giggles ensued.

Mrs. Morton rallied, tilting up her chin defiantly. "Nevertheless, I am sure she knows something is wrong."

There were more giggles, louder now. Realizing their teacher's attention was elsewhere, the kids were testing authority. Christy smiled blandly at Mrs. Morton. If she didn't spit out what she wanted to say, soon, the class would erupt into pandemonium. That was something Christy would enjoy as much as the eight-year-olds would.

Mrs. Morton frowned, apparently becoming aware of the noise. "Children, please! Get out your math books and pencils. We will be working on page ten in a moment or two." She turned back to Christy. "I want you to know I will be assessing Noelle's behavior. If I believe she needs counseling, I will recommend it."

There was a shriek of painful anger. Mrs. Morton turned to face her classroom. "Children! This is no way to behave!"

"She doesn't need counseling," Christy said.

"We shall see," Mrs. Morton replied, before she steamed off to the front of the classroom. Christy followed her to Noelle's desk in the second row from the front. She gave her daughter a hug and a kiss before she marched out of the classroom. At the door she paused to check her watch. Behind her the chatter and giggles were still at full volume, with Morton's angry voice demanding order. Christy smiled with satisfaction as she hurried down the hallway and out the door of the school.

As the door thumped closed behind her, Christy stopped. Parked in the tow away zone in front of the school was a familiar gray Mercedes. Christy walked slowly down the path that lead from the front door to the street as Edward

Bidwell, one of Frank's trustees, eased his bulk from the driver's seat.

She looked down at her trousers and sandals. With the short-sleeved silk blouse and linen jacket she was wearing, her clothes were proper enough to pass muster with the ultra-conservative Bidwell, who was, like the car he drove, the very essence of respectability. It was a good thing she was going to the airport with Quinn today. Her normal costume of jeans and a tee wouldn't have cut it.

Bidwell was standing on the sidewalk, scrutinizing the school building. The frown on his face said he'd noticed every weed in the lawn, every rust mark on the railings, each place where the paint had rubbed off. "Good morning, Christy. Are you satisfied with Noelle's new school?"

Nice of you to get right down to business, she thought. Edward Bidwell had intimidated her from the time she'd first met him. A partner in a law firm used by the wealthy families in the city, he was a trial lawyer and an expert at catching people out. Christy always minded her words around him. "Noelle seems to be adapting well."

"Seems?" he said.

CHAPTER 7

Christy cursed herself. Give Edward an opening and he'd take it. Now she'd have to face him head on. "Seems, Edward. She says she likes her teacher and she's making friends, but kids don't always know how to express their reservations about a situation, so some issues take a while to come out."

Bidwell nodded. He indicated the luxurious gray car. "May I give you a lift?"

She'd rather walk home, but politeness dictated that she accept. "Sure."

He held the door for her while she slipped inside, then he rounded the car and wedged his bulk into the driver's seat. The extra inches he was packing around the middle pressed against the steering wheel.

"I believe Noelle is very fond of Frank, despite…everything," Edward said, as he pulled away from the curb.

"She loves her daddy," Christy said. "And he is crazy about her." She winced as she heard the fierceness in her voice. She did not want to spar with Edward Bidwell. She would always come out the loser. With a sigh, she added, "Even if it doesn't seem that way since Frank took off."

Bidwell kept his eyes on the road. "Frank's activities have caused many changes in all of our lives. Does Noelle ask for him?"

"Yes." They paused at the crosswalk to allow a woman pushing a stroller to cross. Bidwell's fingers tapped on the steering wheel. Christy continued, "I've read everything I can find about how kids deal with divorce and moving to a new area…"

"Divorce!" The woman reached the other sidewalk and the Mercedes exploded forward. "What are you talking about? Are you planning to sue Frank for divorce?"

The question startled Christy. She had been so caught up in the day-to-day issues of dealing with the press, coping with the move from the mansion, and helping Noelle through her transition to a new school, that she hadn't looked far enough into the future to consider what she ought to do about her straying husband and their empty relationship. She stared out the window at the tidy suburban street and considered the potential of this frightening new vista.

"Well? Christy, I can assure you, divorce would not be a good idea."

"That's between Frank and me," Christy said stiffly. "In the meantime, Frank isn't in Noelle's life anymore, so she's dealing with some of the same issues that children of divorced couples face." She hesitated, shooting Bidwell a considering look. "In fact, that's what I'm up to today. I'm looking for Frank."

"Frank is in Mexico," Edward said.

There was something wrong here. Detective Patterson said she had spoken to the trustees. "The police tracked Frank back to Vancouver, but lost him at the airport. As far as they, or anyone else, knows he's somewhere in the Vancouver area. Isn't that why you came by today? To talk to me about his return?"

They reached an intersection. "Which way do I turn?"

"Left, then left again. My townhouse is near the end of the street."

Bidwell followed her directions. "If the police are looking for Frank you should leave the search to them."

"Normally I would, but in this case, I can't. I've been told his case is non-priority. If he comes their way the police will charge him. If he doesn't, they're not actively looking to catch him. If I want to find him so we can figure out how to handle our future without hurting Noelle, I'll have to do it myself."

Bidwell's bulgy brown eyes narrowed as he glanced at her. "Stay at home where you're needed, Christy. If Frank is back in Vancouver, I'm sure he'll contact the Trust. We'll let you know when it's safe to meet with him."

"Safe? What are you talking about, Edward? Frank isn't dangerous. He just doesn't have a lot of scruples."

Bidwell's hands tightened on the steering wheel, then eased. The movement was so small and quick, Christy might have missed it if she hadn't been staring incredulously him. She'd struck a nerve, she thought with satisfaction. She'd caught him out on his choice of words, then called him on it. Point to her.

Bidwell was not about to be one-upped. He smiled thinly before he said, "You forget that Frank is traveling with another woman. I doubt you would want to meet Frank when he has his girlfriend by his side."

Heat burned in Christy's cheeks. She tramped it down ruthlessly. The way to beat Bidwell was to stay cool and in control—or so Frank had always told her. Of course Frank had never been particularly successful in his dealings with his trustees.

Christy decided that right now a little needling was in order. It would help boost her self-esteem a notch, no matter how it affected Edward. "I don't know about that. It would certainly bring the D word to the surface pretty quick."

She had the pleasure of seeing a flush rise in Bidwell's face. She'd gotten under his skin, and the knowledge made her want to cheer. She stifled a grin and braced herself for the lash back that was sure to come.

"The obligation of finding Frank belongs to the Trust. We can make inquiries more effectively than you. Now that you no longer have staff to handle things for you, I doubt you'd know how to go about searching for Frank."

The comment dug into her past, to the days when she'd first arrived in Vancouver, the newly-made wife of a Jamieson. Frank's Aunt Ellen and the other trustees had considered her a dumb social climber who had married Frank for the Jamieson money. *I doubt you know how to*...had been a constant refrain. *I doubt you know how to* dress for this social event or that. *I doubt you know how to* use the proper cutlery during a four-course banquet. *I doubt you know how to* manage servants. *I doubt you know how to...*

The refrain had never stopped. It had been said less often over the years, but the words always had the power to hurt. Christy took comfort from the scene around her: the rows of tall, narrow townhouses, the Japanese maples still in leaf, the last of the summer blooms. The middle-class neighborhood was much more her style than the fancy mansion had been. This was her turf, not the Trust's.

She raised her brows as she responded to Bidwell, a snarky expression she'd copied from one Frank used in his dealings with his trustees. "You're probably right, Edward. I do need help for this, so I got it." They had reached her street. It would only be a matter of moments now and she'd escape the poisoned atmosphere Edward Bidwell created around him. All she had to do was hold herself together for a few minutes. She could do it.

She would do it.

Bidwell looked at her with what she thought of as his fishy-eyed courtroom look. "You've taken family issues to a stranger?"

She swallowed hard and hung on to the snarky expression. "It's no big deal. I want to find Frank. I know I can't do it alone. So I found someone to work with me."

"How much is it costing you?"

"Nothing, except my time and my cooperation." Bidwell

opened his mouth. Christy knew he was going to question her on what she meant by cooperation. She had no intention of answering. She said hastily, "It's that house, the second to last one on the street. Stop anywhere and I'll hop out."

Bidwell drove her to her door. As he parked he said, "Whatever agreements you have made with this individual, Christy, they are not necessary. The Trust will handle this. We are here to look after the legal and business matters affecting your life so that you can spend your valuable time ensuring that Frank's heir has an excellent childhood and receives the best possible schooling."

Christy didn't like where this was going. Instinct was telling her that Bidwell wasn't as altruistic as he was pretending to be. She held up her hand, palm forward. "The Trust, Edward, is almost broke. When Frank fled to Mexico with all the assets he could get his hands on, he changed all of our lives. The Jamieson Ice Cream shares held in the trust provide dividends that pay for our day-to-day expenses and a few extras and form the basis of a nest egg for Noelle's university tuition. In the meantime, she's going to a public school, because the Trust can no longer afford the private school she's attended since she was four years old. Why would I even consider letting the Trust take on the expense of searching for my embezzling husband?"

She'd lost it. The minute Edward Bidwell had reduced Noelle from a beloved daughter to an obligation as *Frank's heir*, her temper had snapped. This was one of the jerks who had raised Frank to be a scarred, hurting man with too much money and not enough to do. They would not do the same to Noelle. Christy would not allow it.

Bidwell's plump cheeks reddened and those scary brown eyes of his looked like they would pop out of his head. Christy tugged on the door handle, needing to escape. It was locked, controlled by the electronic console at the driver's fingertips.

"Perhaps I have failed to make myself clear," Bidwell said, his voice glacial. "The Trust does not feel that it is acceptable for the guardian of our heir to waste her time on a wild goose chase when she should be focusing on the child's development."

Christy held herself very still. Inside she was quivering with temper and claustrophobia. "What are you talking about, Edward? Noelle is my life and I'd do anything for her! I think we're through. Please unlock my door." They glared at each other for a minute, then Bidwell tapped a button. The lock clicked. Christy flung open the door.

As she pushed out of the car, he leaned toward her. "The Trust will seek out Frank, Christy. You concentrate on Noelle."

She slammed the door, a crack of sound in the morning quiet. Edward would be annoyed—*I doubt you know how to close a car door properly, Christy.* She grinned with satisfaction and hoped his irritation stayed with him all the way back to his posh, downtown office tower.

She stood at the end of her walk and watched as his car turned the corner. What had that really been about? He'd come as a representative of the Trust, but why? Because he'd learned that she'd asked Quinn Armstrong to dig up Frank for her? A likely reason, but there was no way the Trust would have heard about her decision. It was too soon.

Because Frank was in town? Christy didn't have any illusions about the trustees. They'd be delighted to have her gone from Frank's life, but why would they want to keep him from Noelle?

"Who was that and what did he want from you?"

Christy jumped, then turned. Quinn Armstrong was standing a few feet away, a frown on his face. She'd been so deep in her thoughts that she hadn't heard him close his front door or walk down his steps. She pursed her lips. "That was Edward Bidwell, the legal member of the Jamieson Trust. He wants me to stop hunting for Frank."

"Interesting. How did he know that's what you were doing?"

"I told him. He told me that the Trust would do the searching. I'm supposed to stay at home and mind the hearth fires."

Quinn laughed. After a moment, so did Christy.

"So, what do you want to do?" he asked.

She drew a deep breath. "I'm going to keep looking."

"Good, then let's go." Quinn glanced at his watch. "We're wasting time if we want to get you back here for three o'clock."

The doorbell rang. When Christy went to answer it, Noelle followed, still intrigued by the act of answering your own door. She hovered at the top of the staircase. Before Christy could throw the deadbolt and pull open the door, the bell rang again, followed by a determined pounding.

When Noelle saw the visitor was Mary Petrofsky, she ran down the stairs to greet her friend. Christy left them to chat and headed back up to the kitchen.

Moments later Noelle reappeared, followed by the other girl. "Mom, can I go over to Mary's house?"

Christy looked at the can of tomato sauce and the package of hamburger she was planning to turn into spaghetti and meatballs—for the second time that week. "It's almost dinnertime, Noelle, and it's a nice afternoon. Why don't you girls play outside until then?" Christy stifled a sigh at the pout forming on Noelle's mouth. Storms were ahead.

"Christy, can Noelle stay for dinner at my house if she comes over?" Small, with long black hair that danced in time to her quicksilver moves, Mary Petrofsky's sunny temperament was reflected in her bright brown eyes. Right now, her winning smile was an excellent counterpoint to Noelle's glower.

"Yeah, Mom, can I?"

"I don't think so, Noelle." The pout was in evidence again. "It's kind of late to expect Mrs. Petrofsky to get ready for a guest. Perhaps another night."

"Mom!"

"My mom won't mind. I've asked kids to stay over before and she's always said yes."

Then she's a better woman than I am, Christy thought. "Your mom sounds great, Mary, but she doesn't know Noelle, or me for that matter, and—"

"Then I'll go get her so she can meet you!" Mary was already on the move before the last of the words were out of Christy's mouth.

"Mary, that's not—"

"I'll go too!"

"Noelle, wait!"

The girls tore down the stairs. Christy followed, rather more slowly. At the door, she was in time to see her daughter dash down the street behind her new friend. With a sigh, she followed. If the girls were dragging Mrs. Petrofsky from her home so she could be introduced to Christy, then the least Christy could do was meet her halfway.

Rebecca Petrofsky proved to be as cheerful as her daughter. She greeted Christy warmly, welcomed her to the neighborhood, told her how much Mary liked Noelle and how well the girls got along. Then, without prompting, she invited Noelle to dinner that night. Both girls cheered. Christy muttered a few protests, but the enthusiastic children and the laid-back Rebecca overruled her. After five minutes she headed back to the house on her own.

The evening stretched before her, empty.

She hadn't had a night off since the servants had departed. So much had happened, there had been so many changes in her life, that she wasn't sure she knew how to use that free time.

Leaning against the sink, sipping reheated coffee, she considered how she could spend the next few hours. There were books to unpack, then stack onto shelves in the family room. A load of washing needed to be done, and if she was really industrious, she could change the bedding. With Noelle out, her dinner could be something more flavorful than the child-pleaser she'd planned. Once her meal was cooked, she could watch the news while she ate, something strictly forbidden if Noelle was home.

Exciting stuff, she thought, laughing at herself. The phone rang. She set her mug on the counter as she answered.

"Hi, it's Quinn."

Transmitted over the phone line, his voice was lower, with a sexy edge that sent shivers down her spine. "Hi. What's up?"

"I've got some new information about Brianne's traveling companion. I think we ought to get together to discuss it."

Christy's heart began to beat harder. After her argument with Bidwell, their trip to the airport had been anticlimactic, another dead end. The customs agent who checked through Brianne and Frank had provided no new information. He remembered Brianne clearly because of her spectacular, blond good looks, but when shown Frank's picture he had shrugged and said, "Could be." Not a helpful reply.

Quinn continued. "Can you come over tonight? I know it's short notice, but my dad would be happy to entertain your daughter while we talk."

Christy thought about the ponytailed, award-winning author Roy Armstrong babysitting her daughter. Her brain couldn't cope with the image. "Well...uh..."

"He was the parent who stayed home while I was growing up, so he's used to having kids around. And he was great with all my friends."

There was something about that low, very male voice talking about childhood that was seductive. She wished she knew of a way to keep that sound sliding over her nerve endings for hours. She was smiling as she said, "Actually, Noelle is having dinner at the Petrofskys' house, so I'm free till about seven thirty."

"Perfect," Quinn said. "Come over now. We can get started right away."

Christy thought about laundry, book-shelving, and television. There was no contest. "Okay."

A few minutes later, after she'd let Rebecca Petrofsky know where she could be found, she was following Quinn into his kitchen. It was exactly the same as hers, except that the Armstrong kitchen was painted a vivid orange with highlights of cinnamon red and daffodil yellow while Christy's was a basic builder's white.

Quinn grinned when her eyes widened as she entered the glowing room. "My father chose the colors."

Roy Armstrong looked up from the vegetables he was chopping. "I painted the walls too," he said, glancing around him with satisfaction. "There's something about putting your own imprint on a place that's very gratifying."

Pumpkin orange was not a color Christy would have dared put on her walls, but she had to admit that it worked here. The room crackled with energy.

Quinn gestured to a pine table set in an alcove. Papers were strewn over the surface, with no apparent organization. "Have a seat. If you don't mind, I thought we'd include my dad in the discussion. He's pretty good at putting details together to make a story, so I thought he'd be able to help."

Christy laughed as she settled onto one of the ladder-backed chairs. "I'd be delighted to have Roy Armstrong's talents working on my problem. Of course I don't have any objections."

Quinn sat opposite and started rifling through the papers. "This is what we've got," he said, tapping a yellow lined pad, which was covered with bulleted points. "Your husband's passport was used one week ago at the Vancouver airport, but no one can identify his picture. At the airport he was nervous and deliberately avoided having his baggage inspected, not typical behavior for Frank Jamieson. He was known to be traveling with Brianne Lymbourn, who was staying at the Strand Manor downtown. Again, no one at the Strand can identify Frank's picture. Brianne Lymbourn has now checked out of the hotel, leaving no forwarding address, so for the moment we can't question her."

Christy nodded. Since she had been part of the gathering

of this information there was nothing new here. So what about the important discovery Quinn had mentioned on the phone?

"All right, that brings us to what I found out today." He picked up the photocopy of an article and photograph that had appeared in a Vancouver daily tabloid. The page was dated four months ago, shortly before Frank's disappearance.

Christy scanned the article quickly. Sensational in tone, it was a rant about the justice system. Christy frowned a little as she read. Articles like this appeared every time there was a big trial or a gangland murder. There had even been one or two that suggested she ought to have been arrested for conspiring with her husband. She'd learned to ignore them.

The photograph, though, made her read the caption carefully. An unnamed woman was sitting on a dark sofa beside the man identified as Thaddeus 'Crack' Graham. She snuggled in the crook of his arm, her head resting against his shoulder. There was a contented, reflective smile on her lips that spoke of a comfortable, long-term intimacy. Graham himself was laughing at something happening off camera. He was a slim man, with light hair, a long face, and straight nose. Behind them was a wall covered with striped wallpaper. A potted fern had been placed beside the sofa.

The woman was Brianne Lymbourn.

She was wearing an evening dress made of some kind of silky looking fabric, the bodice cut low between her breasts and held up by narrow straps. The man, Thaddeus 'Crack' Graham, was dressed in tight-fitting pants and a long-sleeved shirt, open at the neck. Christy guessed they had been photographed at one of the better downtown hotels, probably when Brianne was attending an event of some kind. The caption suggested that Crack Graham had been there to sell dope to the well-heeled crowd.

"The photo doesn't do her justice," Christy said, staring at the picture.

"Then it is Brianne Lymbourn?"

Christy looked up. The image clearly linked Brianne to Crack Graham, but it raised as many questions as it provided answers. "Yeah, it's Brianne. Who is this guy, Crack Graham? Do you know anything about him, Quinn?"

"As the article says, he's a drug dealer. My sources in the police department tell me he's a middleman between the kingpins and the street sellers. He's known to supply a string of dealers who work the fashionable clubs and neighborhoods in town."

"Hence his link with Brianne," Christy murmured, glancing again at the picture, looking for clues, finding none.

"Could be."

"How long have they known each other, I wonder," Christy said.

"That is a good question." Quinn looked down at his own copy of the photograph. "They appear to be comfortable together."

Roy offered Christy a glass of wine. He glanced over her shoulder at the photo. "Looks like she was two-timing Frank with this guy," he said passing a second glass to Quinn.

"I'm not sure Frank *was* having an affair with Brianne," Christy said. "I had no indication of it until he disappeared and he was reported to have run off with her."

"That fits with what I found out today." Quinn paused and Christy raised her brows in question. "After I dug up this picture I began to wonder about a few things. Take another look, Christy. Is there anything that leaps out at you?"

She stared at the photo. No matter how hard she tried, all she could see was Brianne and Graham, blond, slim, and good-looking, seated together beside a potted fern. "I don't know…"

"If someone asked you to paint a verbal picture of Frank, how would you describe him? Five-two? Brown hair?"

Christy laughed. "Frank was six feet, slim build, blond hair, blue eyes, no distinguishing marks on his features."

Her breath caught. "Are you suggesting that this man could pretend to be Frank?"

Quinn nodded. "His police description has him as six feet tall, blond hair, blue eyes, lean build. Change the picture in Frank's passport and this guy could pass for him."

"Particularly if Brianne was along to vouch for him." Christy frowned at Quinn. "Is this possible?"

Quinn nodded. "I took this photo down to the Strand. The desk clerk and the girl at the coffee bar immediately identified Graham as the guy with Brianne."

"But—does that mean he used Frank's passport?"

"Could be."

"Oh man," Christy said, taking a big gulp of wine. "Then where's Frank?"

CHAPTER 8

The sound of a car door slamming drew Noelle into the kitchen to look out the window instead of getting ready to leave for school. "It's Uncle Gerry!" she squealed. She rushed for the front door.

"Hold it!" Christy yelled. "Shoes and backpack on first. We can meet Uncle Gerry outside."

Noelle tied her shoes in half the time it usually took her, resulting in short bows and trailing laces sure to be snagged loose. She grabbed her backpack from the cupboard and wrenched open the door at the same moment the bell rang. "Uncle Gerry!" She flung herself into the arms of corporate mogul and senior trustee, Gerald Fisher, with an unselfconscious abandon that made Christy smile.

A big man, well over six feet, with a heavy build that he kept toned by working out, Gerry swirled Noelle around as if she weighed nothing at all, then kissed her loudly on the cheek. "How's my girl?" he said, putting her back on her feet. "Do you like your new school?"

Noelle's fearsome pout appeared. "It's okay. It's school, after all."

Gerry and Christy laughed. "Good point," Christy said. "And if we don't get going you'll be late. Gerry, do you have time to walk over to the school with us?"

"With two such lovely ladies as my companions, it will be my pleasure," he said. He extended his hand.

Noelle beamed at him and took hold. "My school's really different, Uncle Gerry. It's in a new building and it doesn't have a fence around it like the VRA did. And I don't have to wear a uniform anymore!"

Gerry Fisher, head of Fisher Disposal, a waste disposal company that had expanded so rapidly in the past fifteen years that it now controlled landfill sites in all ten provinces and over thirty states, smiled at Noelle and said, "That clinches it. Your mother made the right choice taking you out of VRA." He made a point of scrutinizing her clothing. "A T-shirt and pants looks like a very comfortable way to dress for school."

Noelle nodded, oblivious to the edge of sarcasm Christy heard. "My teacher is a real grump. She's always telling us we have to be quiet and listen. But," she added philosophically, "my teachers at VRA used to say that too, so I guess it's part of being a teacher."

Gerry laughed. Christy said, "I guess."

The sidewalk was only wide enough for two people to walk side-by-side, so Christy let Noelle and Gerry go ahead, while she followed, listening to Noelle monopolize the conversation. She was anxious to learn why Gerry had shown up this morning, but she didn't want to ask him in front of Noelle, in case he'd come, like Bidwell, to tell her to stop looking for Frank.

"I have a new friend. She lives down the street. Her name is Mary Petrofsky, and I can go to her house and ring the bell if I want her to come out to play. I went to her house for dinner last night."

Fisher's broad back, covered by an impeccably cut suit without the hint of a wrinkle, straightened, just a little, enough to tell Christy he wasn't pleased by Noelle's new companion. She said hastily, "Mary is a lovely little girl. I checked out her mother before I let Noelle go over. Rebecca Petrofsky is a respectable woman with a job and big heart."

"And what does Mrs. Petrofsky do?" Fisher asked, his tone disapproving.

"She's an executive assistant," Noelle said, stumbling a bit over the multi-syllable words.

"I see," Fisher said, the censure in his voice stronger now.

Noelle shot him a frowning look that said she'd caught the disapproval, but didn't understand why it was there.

"Gerry, she's okay," Christy said, trying to smooth over the rough patch. Before his disappearance, Frank had managed their business affairs, so her interaction with the trustees had been social—Christmas and Noelle's birthday party, the events at which Frank was representing the Jamieson name, and family parties. Gerry's obvious delight in Noelle had touched Christy and turned a pleasant relationship into one of friendship.

Since Frank's disappearance, she had been forced to become involved in the business side of the trust. If she hadn't had Gerry guiding her through, her understanding of the financial mess in which Frank's embezzlement had left the trust would have been much less.

They stopped at the crosswalk to wait for the morning crossing guard to give them the go ahead.

"Mary Petrofsky has a dad," Noelle said. "He ate dinner with us last night." She tilted her head, looked at Gerry with big, wounded, blue eyes. "I miss my daddy, Uncle Gerry. Can you tell him to come home to us?"

The color drained from Gerry's face and for the first time Christy saw him at a loss for words.

The day Frank had been born, his father, Frank Jamieson senior, an aggressive businessman with visions of a corporate empire built on his inherited family money, had set up a trust fund that would ensure his son's future. He'd arranged for his three best friends and his sister to be the trustees. He'd also made those four people his son's guardians, in the unlikely event of his death.

Twelve years later Frank Jamieson had grown his family's successful, but regionalized, dairy into a national corporation that produced dozens of flavors of ice cream. His death in a car crash that also killed his wife left his young son heir to a huge fortune.

Over the years Gerry Fisher had become the senior trustee. He'd assumed the role of father in Frank's life, creating a relationship that was not always a happy one. Noelle looked upon him as a grandfather, a problem-solver who fixed what others couldn't.

"Hey kiddo," Christy said. "Uncle Gerry will do what he can, but Daddy goes his own way. He'll come back to us when he's ready."

Fisher shook his head and moved his shoulders, as if shaking his body would bring his world back into perspective.

The crossing guard held out her red stop sign and blew her whistle, indicating it was safe for them to cross. Gerry forged ahead, striding through the crossing while Noelle trotted along beside him. Christy followed, glad of the interruption.

When they reached the school Gerry insisted he be introduced to the teacher. Mrs. Morton, abrupt and no-nonsense with Christy and the kids, warmed considerably under Gerry's blatant flattery. Somehow, by the time Christy was kissing Noelle good-bye, Mrs. Morton was talking to Gerry Fisher the way she would to a parent. Noelle hugged Gerry, who did his twirling thing again, making her giggle.

Mrs. Morton watched this byplay as she said to Christy, "Men who abandon their families leave a big hole in their children's lives. Noelle is fortunate she has a man like Mr. Fisher looking after her."

Noelle kissed Christy again. Mrs. Morton closed the classroom door, leaving Christy alone with Gerry. He was silent as they left the school. Once outside, he said, "How badly does Noelle miss her father?"

Christy looked at the trees lining the road, another pedestrian on the sidewalk, a car passing, anything to avoid meeting Gerry's probing gray eyes. "She doesn't say a lot.

Frank and Noelle were very close, so I know she's hurting, but I thought she was getting used to the idea that he had left us."

Gerry grunted.

Christy stole a glance at him. He was staring straight ahead, a frown between his brows, as they retraced their steps toward the townhouse.

"Christy, I know Edward spoke to you about Frank's return to Vancouver. Have you told anyone that he's back?"

She had told Quinn and his dad, but they didn't count. "No."

"There's a rumor going about that he has returned. This has caused a number of calls to the Trust. People are phoning to say they won't supply him if he visits their shops. Others are demanding payment for bills I've never heard of before now." He drew a deep breath. "And some calls have been extremely nasty." Christy made a distressed sound in her throat. Gerry nodded. "I don't suppose Frank has contacted you, by any chance?"

"No."

"I can't say I'm surprised. I didn't think he would actually come home."

"Gerry, I talked to the police. There was a nasty situation when he went through Customs, where he stole someone else's declaration and used it to slip through without a baggage check. They know he's in Vancouver."

Gerry shrugged. The perfect suit jacket moved with his body as if it were part of him. "Oh, I don't deny that Frank has returned to Canada. I just don't think he would have the nerve to reestablish his position here."

They reached the crosswalk. A car passed and they moved onto the road. "Frank has plenty of reasons why he would want to do that."

"And plenty why he wouldn't," Gerry said. "But people will believe what they want to believe, and right now, if the rumors are any indication, plenty of people think that Frank is in town. That brings up all kinds of problems. The trust has taken a beating since Frank took off with the bulk of the assets. We've dealt with the worst of the financial fallout, but opening up the issue again will solve nothing and only create more problems."

"What kind of problems?"

"We may have to sell off more of the Jamieson Ice Cream stock."

"No! Jamieson Ice Cream is Noelle's heritage."

"It's also a valuable asset. We need to take the focus away from Frank and put it somewhere more positive." He drew a deep breath. "There's a high-profile charity event this weekend, a fundraiser for the Infant Heart Transplant Foundation. I believe you should make an appearance."

Christy thought her jaw was going to drop. Whatever else she'd expected, this certainly wasn't it. "The IHTF Awards Night always sells out well in advance. I doubt I'd be able to get a ticket."

"My company has bought a table," Gerry said. "I've reserved a ticket for you and a date. Perhaps you could invite one of Frank's friends, someone like Aaron DeBolt. His mother is chair of the IHTF Board."

"Gerry, I don't think the IHTF Awards Night is the best event for me to attend." Christy said. "I was on the board of the IHTF."

"I know," Gerry said. "That's why I thought this would be a good event for you. You'd be amongst friends."

Christy laughed. There was an edge of bitterness to the sound. "Hardly. A month after Frank disappeared, when the press was reporting that he'd embezzled from his own trust fund with my help, I received a letter from the executive director of the foundation noting that positions on the board were for one year only and, as my term was up, thanking me for serving on the board. The letter arrived precisely nine months from the day I was originally appointed."

Gerry was quiet for a minute. As they turned into Christy's complex, he said, "Christy, the Jamieson Trust needs positive press. Having a Jamieson participate in a worthy event like the IHTF Awards Night will give it to us."

"Gerry, I told you…"

He reached into his pocket and pulled out an envelope. "Christy, Noelle is the Jamieson heir, but until she is an adult, you are the figurehead. You need to be seen." He shoved the envelope into her hands. A commanding note entered his voice. "You will come to the dinner."

Her fingers closed around the envelope. She didn't want to go. "Gerry, I don't—"

"I won't take no for an answer," Gerry said with a smile. The hard edge was gone from his voice. "I'll expect to see you there for cocktails at seven o'clock."

Long after he'd gone, Christy sat on her porch staring at the envelope. She didn't want to be the face of the Jamieson fortune. She was lousy at networking and events like this made her nervous. She'd stand in a corner somewhere and spend the night feeling like an outsider.

The awards night was on Thursday evening, two days from now. She'd have to find a babysitter and organize clothes, not to mention a date, since there was no way she'd ever call Aaron DeBolt. Maybe she wouldn't go at all. She'd just call Gerry up on Thursday afternoon and tell him she had the migraine to beat all migraines. He'd be ticked, but what could he do?

That would be a cop-out, though. Gerry would know she'd chickened out. Worse, she'd know. Then the next time she had to do some event for the Trust it would be harder than this. But why should she have to do public appearances? She hated the press. She did her best to avoid them—

"Hey there. What's up?"

Quinn's voice had her looking up with a frown.

"Hell," he said. "You look like someone just died."

That brought her out of her funk. Sure, she didn't want to go to this event, but no one had died. It wasn't that bad. She held up the envelope and said lightly, "I've been invited to a party and I'm supposed to bring a date. Can you imagine that? Me, a date." She shook her head.

Quinn reached out and took the envelope from her hand. He flicked open the flap and took out the tickets, then he whistled. "Some party. Tickets for this event go for a thousand bucks. I heard they sold out a month ago. Where did you get these?"

"Gerry Fisher gave them to me. He says I need to go to counter the rumors that Frank is back in Vancouver."

Quinn frowned at her, then he sat down beside her on the steps. "Fisher was the one who gave you the tickets?"

"Yeah." Christy searched his face. "Do you think it means something?"

"Could be. Probably not." His well-muscled shoulders rose in a shrug. "It may be exactly what he said—the Trust needs to put a positive spin on the Jamieson name and you, Christy, are a much better example of the family than your missing husband is." His lips turned up in a smile that was boyish and heartwarming at the same time.

Christy couldn't help it, she smiled back, even though the thought of the IHTF evening made her stomach churn. "Thanks."

His voice was husky. "No problem."

Her heartbeat accelerated. Her lips parted. Quinn's eyes darkened as they focused on her mouth. Christy thought he was going to kiss her and for one mad moment she wished he would. Then she drew a deep breath and banished feelings that weren't supposed to be there.

Quinn handed her back the tickets. She considered them gloomily. "I still have the problem of a date. Gerry suggested Aaron DeBolt. Yuck."

"Do you think DeBolt is likely to be there?"

"He might be. It's not his favorite kind of event, but his mother is chair of the IHTF Board. I imagine she'll have her whole family there."

Quinn rubbed his chin. "You tried to get hold of DeBolt, but haven't had any luck so far, right?

Something in his tone made Christy's eyes widen. "You think we could corner Aaron at the dinner and interrogate him about Frank's whereabouts?"

"We?"

"Quinn, I don't want to go on my own." Christy tilted her head. She curled her lips into a tempting tease of a smile she'd almost forgotten she knew how to do. "Come on, say you'll be my date." She shot him a sideways look from under her brows. Quinn's breath hissed as he inhaled sharply. Her smile widened just a bit. "Please?"

"Hell," he said. "Do I have a choice?"

CHAPTER 9

Quinn tugged at the jacket of his tux, then touched the ridiculous bow tie at his throat to make sure it was straight. Much more at home in jeans and a sweatshirt, he hated formal wear, but he understood that there were times when it had to be worn—and worn well—in order to achieve an end. His mother, the practical parent, had taught him that. A lawyer, she'd fought for causes big and small, but she'd never wasted her energy battling the little issues, like social custom. Blend in, don't alienate people for no reason, she'd always said. Attack them on the big issues and they'll respect you. Challenge the fabric of their lives and they'll crucify you.

Quinn had taken that pithy wisdom to heart. Over the years he'd found it helped him open doors closed to others, gaining him entry to events like this one and access to people who might otherwise refuse to talk to a reporter. So he mentally morphed the tux into jeans and a tee, told himself that the stupid bowtie wasn't choking him and the damned cummerbund didn't make him look like an idiot, and opened the door for Christy.

As she eased from the car, he admired the way her gown flowed around her. Cut away to expose one shoulder, the sapphire blue silk hugged her breasts in smooth elegance, but flowed in a swirl of diaphanous fabric from the waistline. Her dark hair shimmered with red highlights. She had drawn it up in a severe style that added a touch of haughty elegance to the lovely gown and accented her features. Diamonds dripped from her ears and winked at her throat in the harsh lights of the hotel breezeway.

"You look fabulous."

She flashed him a smile as dazzling as the diamonds adorning her neck. "I feel totally out of place. Give me a moment while I put on my Jamieson princess persona so the sharks at this gathering won't assume I'm the first course."

Quinn laughed. "Can't be that bad."

"After his parents died, Frank lived with his Aunt Ellen."

"Ellen Jamieson," Quinn said.

A harried bellboy appeared. Quinn handed him the keys and received a parking chit in exchange. Quinn took Christy's elbow to help her through the door into the hotel, then debated whether or not to let her go. He'd discovered that he liked being with Christy Jamieson, enjoyed touching her, was proud of her beauty and her warmth of spirit. The evening took on a brighter hue. He thought he might even enjoy himself.

"Yes, Ellen Jamieson, one of his trustees. She'll be here tonight, by the way. I'll introduce you. When we were in Kingston, Frank didn't tell me much about his childhood, so when we moved here I wasn't prepared." She glanced at him. "This is off the record, okay?"

He nodded. He wanted to know where this was going. He'd deal with the off the record clause if he thought the information was important to the article that was drifting further and further away each day.

"Frank's trustees were horrible to me when we arrived. Of all of them, Gerry Fisher—"

"Of Fisher Disposal?"

"Yes, do you know him?"

Quinn grinned. "In a way. Go on."

"Gerry was the only one who welcomed me. The rest made it clear that they believed Frank had married below him. Edward Bidwell, the lawyer, was absolutely furious there was no prenuptial agreement. Not my fault! Samuel Macklin, who is an accountant, told me I'd better watch my spending and that he was going to keep a close eye on the books. Aunt Ellen Jamieson looked me up and down then asked Frank why he'd wasted his name on inferior goods."

"Ouch." They were almost at the end of the long hallway that led from the breezeway to the lobby. "You and Frank were married for a number of years. Did it ever get any better?"

"I learned to hide my feelings. They backed off. The more Frank and I drifted apart, the friendlier his trustees became. I think in the beginning they were afraid I'd change him. When that didn't happen it was easier for them to be polite." They reached the foyer. She took a deep breath. "Okay. Time to become the Jamieson princess."

The transformation was subtle but startling. She was still a beautiful young woman wearing a gown that made the best of a gorgeous figure, but now her spine was a little straighter and she held her head tilted to an imperious angle. Her smile was warm, but impersonal, her eyes watchful. Even her walk was different, her steps smaller, a hint of arrogance in the movement.

She put her hand on his arm. Quinn could feel the tremor and knew how much she disliked this kind of event and understood how heavy the Jamieson princess persona was.

They neared a knot of people waiting for the elevator. "The dinner is in the main ballroom on the mezzanine."

A woman whose eyes were a mass of black makeup cut herself free of the group to come over. "Christy, darling! I didn't expect to see you here tonight. We didn't deliver any tickets to the mansion—" Lips the color of dried blood curled up in a snarl that pretended to be a smile. "Oh, I forgot. You had to vacate. So sorry to hear, darling. Lovely to see you." She kissed the air on either side of Christy's head in an age-old parody of affection.

Christy did her own pair of air kisses. "It's been too long, Natalie. May I introduce my friend, Quinn Armstrong? Quinn, Natalie DeBolt. Natalie is the chair of the IHTF Board."

"Hello, Natalie." So this nasty creature was Aaron DeBolt's mother. He studied her with frank interest and noted that she was observing him with equal curiosity.

"Well, Christy," she said, a sneer in her voice. "I had no idea you were so daring." There was a suggestive gleam in her eyes as she looked Quinn up and down. "Somehow, I wouldn't have thought it of you."

Christy blushed, but she smiled and her tone was musical with laughter. "Why, Natalie, you've always had a very clever imagination."

Natalie bared her teeth again as she lifted her hand in a dismissive wave. "I'd always pictured you as a—a homebody!—darling. I had no idea you would find a lovely male so quickly after Frank deserted—" The doors to the elevators pinged, then opened. Natalie blew a kiss. "Must go, darling. I'll see you up there." She oozed away, chattering effusively to some other poor soul.

Christy and Quinn waited for the next car. "Lovely woman," Quinn said. He clamped down on emotions he didn't have the right to feel, so hard a muscle twitched in his cheek. He wished he had the right to deal with Natalie and all the others like her Christy would have to face tonight, but he didn't.

Christy laughed. There was an edge of gritted teeth and restrained anger in the sound. "She's not so bad, really. She works hard for this charity."

"Events my dad attends can attract people like Natalie DeBolt. They'd often try those little games out on my mom."

Christy took his hand and squeezed it. Quinn realized with considerable astonishment that *she* was comforting *him*.

"How did your mom handle it?" The doors to the elevator opened. Quinn and Christy boarded with a few others.

Quinn grinned. "My mom always said they were jealous, acting like a leashed dog, barking and lunging at a loose one. Put that way the meanness didn't matter much. My father, on the other hand, fumed." He looked down at Christy. Understanding came quickly and unexpectedly. "I used to think my mother had it right. I just got my father's point of view."

Christy's lips parted. The elevator doors slid open. She shot him a blinding smile that could only be a thank you, straightened her shoulders, then swept out, her head high. Quinn followed, his mood considerably lighter.

The foyer was awash with elegantly dressed people, drinking a variety of beverages from sparkling glasses. There was a steady flow of bodies as people moved from one little knot to another, schmoozing. Their chatting echoed loudly in the contained space.

"Aaron DeBolt usually hangs out with the younger crowd," Christy said. "If we can locate them, we'll find Aaron."

"In the meantime we have to thread our way through the snake pit." Quinn looked about with a sinking feeling. There were a lot of people in a confined space. It wasn't going to be easy to find one man in this mob.

Christy laughed. "The foundation will be happy. They've held a hugely successful event. Okay. Let's see what we can do."

She headed off. Quinn followed. There was an interesting mix of local celebrities, city dignitaries, business people and socialites. Christy seemed to know many of them. She stopped to chat frequently, always with that friendly, impersonal smile and detached warmth, but they had no luck finding Aaron DeBolt before the announcement of dinner had the crowd flowing into the ballroom.

As they made their way to the table assigned to Fisher Disposal, Christy continued to stop and chat. She introduced Quinn, each time carefully adding a description of how the person fit into her life.

"Quinn, this is Edward Bidwell, a lawyer sitting on the board of the Jamieson Trust. Edward, this is my friend, Quinn Armstrong."

Bidwell was tall and running to fat. His bulgy brown eyes observed Christy the way a scientist might look at a frog he was about to dissect. "You're wearing the Jamieson diamonds. I thought Frank sold them."

Christy went white, but her smile didn't falter. Quinn whispered in her ear, "Want me to deck him now or after dinner?"

She laughed out loud. Bidwell frowned. Quinn grinned, feeling considerably better.

"Edward, thank you for your concern! These were in the vault at the bank, so they were quite safe. Have a good evening."

They moved on. "Nice guy," Quinn said sardonically, but he realized soon after that Samuel Macklin, the accountant trustee, was just as bad.

Christy did her introductions.

Macklin nodded, not really paying attention. He pointed to her sapphire gown. "That's a pretty expensive dress."

"Yes, it was, Samuel. Two years ago."

Macklin frowned.

"I think she means the dress was purchased a while ago," Quinn said helpfully. "Pretty thrifty, isn't she? It's not every woman who can recycle a dress and still make it look good."

Macklin glared at Quinn. He smiled back, enjoying himself.

Christy gripped his wrist. Time to move on.

Their next stop was Ellen Jamieson. Quinn didn't think it was possible, but she was even worse than the first two trustees.

"Aunt Ellen, this is Quinn Armstrong, a friend of mine. Quinn, this is Ellen Jamieson. Ellen raised Frank after his parents died."

Ellen Jamieson was positively quivering with indignation. From the pictures he'd seen, she had the same body type and facial bone structure as her nephew, but deep grooves bracketed her mouth and frown lines marked her forehead and eyes.

"What are you thinking of, Christy? Everyone here knows you, knows the story of Frank's disappearance. You were invited tonight to stop the rumors. Instead you're making them! What are you doing with this man?"

The hand on Quinn's wrist shook, but Christy said calmly enough, "Aunt Ellen, Gerry told me to bring a date. So I asked Quinn."

"You were supposed to come with Aaron DeBolt. He knows everyone, and they know him." She swept Quinn with a disdainful, all encompassing glance. "This one is a nobody. There will be questions."

Quinn favored her with raised brows and his own version of cool. "Wrong on two counts, Ellen. I know lots of people, and they know me." He pointed to the publisher of one of the city's daily papers, followed by the manager of the network TV outlet and the multi-millionaire owner of a chain of grocery stores. "He knows me. He knows me. He knows me. I'll introduce you, if you'd like."

"That will not be necessary," Ellen said. She looked as if she was trying to puzzle out how he could possibly have met these men.

Christy tugged on his wrist. Time to go again, before Ellen decided to start another bitchy conversation.

As they threaded their way through the mass of tables, Quinn searched for something to say to Christy that would minimize the behavior of the trustees. He figured she must be pretty upset by now. "You know, I don't blame Frank for running off to Mexico. His trustees certainly are a nasty bunch of people. I think if they were mine, I'd probably do anything I could to escape them."

Christy stopped. She turned to him, laughter and gratitude on her face. "Thank you," she said. She put her hands on his shoulders, stood on her tiptoes and kissed him.

It was on the cheek, but she did kiss him, there, in the middle of a hotel ballroom set for five hundred people. His spirits soared. He put his hands on her waist, wishing he could turn his face so his lips could meet hers. That would be going too far, though, so he contented himself with whispering in her ear, "My pleasure. Am I going to have to square off against anyone else?"

She laughed again as she drew away. "Probably. If we ever find Aaron DeBolt you'll discover that he makes Aunt Ellen look polite by comparison."

"Terrific," Quinn said. He frowned as he looked at her. She glowed as she stood before him. Her eyes were bright with spirit, her face alive with the small victories of the moment. She had the look of a woman who hadn't felt this positive in a long, long time and was relishing every second. If she were his, he'd do everything in his power to ensure she always kept that vibrant joy alive. "Why did Frank hang out with people like this guy DeBolt? I can understand the trustees. He was stuck with them, but why DeBolt?"

"Habit." Her face clouded briefly, then she smiled again and took his hand. "Come on, let's find our table."

Their table was in a prime position. A tall, heavy-set man whose tux did a great deal to minimize mid-life bulges stood to one side of the round table greeting people.

"That's Gerry Fisher. He's the senior trustee. You mentioned earlier that you knew him. Did you interview him at some point?"

Quinn laughed. "No. I protested against one of the dump sites his company had chosen."

Christy stared at him, her expression incredulous. "Protested? You mean with picket signs and people chaining themselves to trees?"

"Yeah." Quinn chuckled. "Is that so hard to believe?"

"No, I suppose not. But…when and how?"

"Years ago. Fisher Disposal was just becoming a force in the area and they were expanding rapidly. They had a reputation of being lax about following proper sealing procedures for their landfills. They'd bought a site in the Valley, near a salmon stream that fed into the Fraser River.

My parents were both involved in the protest. My dad used his celebrity to draw attention to the issue, while my mom managed the media links."

"You must have been young. Fisher Disposal has been a model corporation for as long as I've lived here."

"I was in the seventh grade." He'd been full of raw black and white passions, and the opportunity to skip school to aid in the protection of the environment had been irresistible for an idealistic twelve-year-old. "My father marched in more than one demonstration against the company. I was proud to tag along and carry a picket sign too."

"Amazing," Christy said. "Your protest obviously worked. Gerry got the message and turned his company around."

Not before he had threatened to bankrupt the leaders of the protest and had even had his lawyers issue a lawsuit against them. Quinn could still remember the smile on his mother's face when she heard what Fisher had done and the satisfaction in her voice as she said that Fisher Disposal didn't have a case and she would be the one to ensure Gerry Fisher knew it.

Quinn wasn't going to tell Christy about that, though. It was old news now and people changed. Sometimes.

He looked at Gerry Fisher, twenty years older, heavier, with less hair. There was still a cold calculation in his eyes that reminded Quinn of the man who had announced to the press that he'd make sure none of the demonstrators ever worked again.

"My dear Christy," Fisher said, "has anyone told you that you look lovely tonight?" He took both of Christy's hands in his and smiled at her in an avuncular way.

"I did," Quinn said. "You're the first of the trustees to mention it, though."

Fisher stiffened, then looked Quinn up and down, his gray and brown mustache fairly bristling with disapproval.

Christy rolled her eyes at Quinn, making him laugh. "Gerry, this is my friend, Quinn Armstrong. I'm afraid the other trustees haven't made a good impression."

Fisher's thin lips disappeared into a frown. "I didn't realize they were expected to." He looked at Quinn. "Armstrong. The name is familiar, but I can't quite place it."

"I've been helping Christy look for Frank. Or you may have heard of my father, Roy Armstrong."

Something flickered in Fisher's eyes, something dark and interesting. Quinn couldn't decide what it was, but his gut was telling him it would be a good idea to be careful of Gerry Fisher.

The emotion disappeared, ruthlessly suppressed by the cold calculation of before. "I'm afraid I'm drawing a blank. Now, Christy, I've put you between Eve and me as you didn't let me know you would be bringing a...date. Quinn, there's an empty place beside Stan Czernaki."

Color washed up into Christy's cheeks and her eyes flashed. "Gerry, Quinn is with me!"

For the second time that evening Quinn's spirits soared. He squeezed her arm. "It's okay."

Christy smiled at him, relief on her lips, concern in her eyes. At that moment he wanted very much to put his lips on hers and kiss away the distress.

Hold it! Back off, Armstrong. Wrong place, wrong time.

Gerry's long, almost ascetic features folded themselves into disapproving lines, but he introduced Quinn to his wife, Eve, and the rest of the people at the table, all of whom apparently worked for Fisher Disposal. Quinn discovered Stan Czernaki was the vice president of sales. On his other side was the vice president of product development. He settled in for an unproductive evening.

Dinner was more interesting than he'd expected. Stan and the other VP apparently thought Quinn was an uncritical audience and talked a little too freely. He heard about Fisher Disposal's extensive business in garbage removal and recycling collection, the dump sites in British Columbia and Alberta and five western states, and the company's current thrust toward expanding its business into the production of animal feed from waste products. That fired up Quinn's animal rights beliefs, but he held his tongue and let the earnest gentlemen talk. He stored the data they provided away in a memory file marked 'potential story.'

Dinner was a grade above rubber chicken and the speeches went on interminably, as they always did at this kind of function. Finally, the evening ended. People smiled and said good night to those around them. Quinn abandoned the vice presidents in favor of Christy.

"My dear, I am so glad you came tonight," Fisher said, ignoring Quinn. He'd taken both of Christy's hands in his and was smiling at her in that avuncular way.

Christy leaned forward and kissed his cheek. "Thank you, Gerry. Come by and visit Noelle again soon, okay? She always enjoys seeing you."

He smiled. "I will." His gaze sharpened at he looked at Quinn. "Armstrong, a pleasure meeting you. I do recall your father now. It was several years ago we had cause to meet, was it not?"

"It was," Quinn said, holding the other man's gaze.

"Yes." Fisher's eyes went flat and cold. "Your family tends to seek out causes. I hope you have not decided Christy is one of them."

Quinn touched Christy's shoulder in an intimate way, a reckless answer to Fisher's challenge. "Christy needs help, and I'm giving it to her because no one else around her will."

Before Fisher could respond, Christy squeezed his hands, drawing the man's eyes back to her. "Gerry, thank you for inviting me tonight, but I've got to get home. It's late, and Noelle will be up early, demanding to hear everything that happened on Mom's night out. I need to get my sleep!"

"Of course, my dear." He kissed her cheek, then Christy and Quinn eased away, joining the stream of people leaving the ballroom.

Christy groaned. "What a night. And we still have to find Aaron DeBolt. He was sitting at his mother's table near the podium. I saw him move away as soon as the awards finished, but he's probably still in the hotel." The area in front of the bank of elevators was crammed. "Come on, let's try some of the corridors, or the stairs. Maybe we can still catch up to him."

CHAPTER 10

Quinn took her hand to guide her through the packed bodies waiting for the elevators. Christy let him. It made sense, really. There were so many people crowded into such a small space, and she didn't want to lose Quinn. He didn't let go, though, when they broke through the pack into the relatively people-free foyer from which the stairs to the main floor descended. Now was the time to pull her hand free, but she was cautiously enjoying the firm grip of his fingers around hers, not to mention the lovely fantasy of being on a date with a very desirable man.

She wasn't on a date, of course, but that was what made fantasies so much fun—you could pretend that your life wasn't full of unanswered questions and that your emotions weren't quivering in confusion because you were overloaded with problems you didn't know how to handle alone.

They reached the top of the stairs. The treads were marble, the posts black wrought iron, the banister rail polished walnut. Christy eyed the creamy marble, shot through with veins of rose pink. "It will take me hours to make it down this staircase."

Quinn looked over the railing to the floor below. "Why? It's probably no more than twenty-five or thirty stairs."

She pointed to the steps. "They're pretty, aren't they?" Quinn nodded, looking baffled. Christy almost laughed. "Shiny and smooth, like the leather soles of my very expensive Italian shoes." Quinn was looking at her as if she'd drunk way too much wine and was talking from the bottom of the bottle. She said patiently, "If I try to hurry down those stairs wearing four-inch heels, I'll lose my balance and tumble to the bottom, where I'll land in an untidy heap. Then we'll never catch Aaron DeBolt before he leaves the hotel."

He looked at the stairs again, then over the railing to the marble floor below. "Not the best plan in the world." He tapped his fingers on the walnut railing as he looked back at the still crowded elevators. "We'll just have to take it slow."

Christy looked at the staircase again. As she leaned over the top of the railing, she saw a man with the brown hair and slim build of Aaron DeBolt on the floor below, walking toward a corridor that led to one of the exits. "Damn! He's down there. I can see him." Still holding Quinn's hand, she reached down with her other to pull off her expensive four-inch Italian heels. Lifting the shoes and the hem of her dress, she tugged at his hand. "Come on!"

His eyes opened wide, but he laughed when Christy shot him an 'I dare you' look and tugged again. They ran down the flight of stairs with the abandon of exuberant kids, laughing all the way. At the bottom they stopped to regroup, both of them panting, both still filled with the exhilaration of the defiant. Christy pointed to the place she'd seen DeBolt. "There. Let's go!" She tugged Quinn's hand again. This time he resisted.

"Don't you think we're a little conspicuous with you holding your dress up around your knees and waving your shoes in the air? Not," he added thoughtfully, "that you don't have great legs."

Heat flooded Christy, rushing through her burning hot, leaving pleasure and shock behind. "I..." She took refuge in looking around her. There were people descending the stairs behind them, others wandering the marble elegance of the hotel's main floor. No one was gawking, but she was quite certain they had all taken at least one look. She colored again, this time from embarrassment. "Blast!" She dropped the hem of her gown, then leaned on Quinn while she slipped her shoes back on. When she straightened she discovered that he was watching her, a half smile on his lips, amusement in his eyes. She sighed and shot him a rueful look.

Quinn laughed as they started to move again, walking, not running after Aaron DeBolt. Meeting rooms lined the corridor he'd taken. They stopped at one so Quinn could check inside, but the door was locked. The others were the same. Wherever Aaron had gone, it wasn't inside one of the rooms.

The hallway turned, leading to double plate glass doors that opened onto a terrace. Ornamental trees in wooden planters and flowering annuals in ceramic pots decorated the gray concrete, softening the hard edge of the man-made material. At the far end a staircase led down to the sidewalk.

Aaron DeBolt was huddled in a corner, near a five-foot camellia with glossy green leaves. Two attractive young women dressed in body-revealing evening gowns hovered by him. They seemed to be passing something between them, but Christy couldn't be certain exactly what. She had her suspicions though.

Her hand tightened on Quinn's. "He's over there. I think he's doing some kind of drug, so he may not be much help, but we don't have any other option." She looked up at Quinn and smiled faintly. "He's a jerk, so be prepared."

When they approached one of the girls squealed, "Oh, look who it is. Frankie's discard." She zeroed in on the diamonds at Christy's throat and ears. "Faux jewels and an out-of-style dress. It's no wonder Frank took off on you."

"Lovely woman," Quinn muttered beside her.

Christy could hear the contempt in his voice and knew he was annoyed on her behalf. That warmed her, providing emotional armor. She shot him a smile. She could get used to having a man on her side.

Wraithlike, Aaron leaned against the wall and watched Christy through narrowed eyes. He was a graceful young man who wore evening clothes with the lazy elegance of one who enjoyed getting dressed up. His hair was brown, thin and cut long from a center part. "Well, well, well, if it isn't Christy Jamieson. What did it take to make you crawl out of your boring suburban hole?" His full lips twisted into a pouty sneer.

Christy was proud of the way she was able to look at him without flinching. "Hello, Aaron. It's good to see you too."

DeBolt's sneer deepened. Quinn moved closer, then took Christy's hand in his in a possessive gesture that had her heart thumping.

It also focused DeBolt's attention on Quinn. His gaze sharpened. "And who would this be? I swear, Christy, you have the manners of a peasant. Introduce us." One of the girls giggled. Another made a derisive sound in her throat.

Quinn was utterly still, then his hand squeezed Christy's. She welcomed his support, but she didn't need it. Aaron DeBolt had never liked her, and he'd been taking potshots at her from the moment Frank had introduced them. She loathed him and avoided him where she could, but she refused to allow his spiteful comments to hurt her, even if he hit a soft spot.

Quinn released her hand. Christy was absurdly bereft considering that he was a reporter and she ought to tell him to go away so this nasty little scene wouldn't show up in the morning paper. She didn't want Quinn to go, though. She wanted his hand warming hers, promising strength and support and the caring found in a relat—

He moved with the speed and grace of a big cat capturing prey. One minute Aaron DeBolt was standing negligently, a sneer on his face, the hand holding a joint raised so he could take a puff, then he was pinned to the wall of the building with Quinn's hands curled around the lapels of his elegant tux and an expression of horror on his thin, sharp features.

One of the girls screamed. The other picked up the joint that Aaron had dropped. She took a drag and watched thoughtfully as Aaron said, "Let go of me!"

Christy stared at Quinn in amazement. Frank had never made any attempt to defend her from Aaron's sharp tongue beyond telling her to ignore whatever Aaron said, that it was just his way. It would never have occurred to Frank to tell his friend to stop baiting his wife.

"My name," Quinn said to Aaron, "is Quinn Armstrong, and you have a nasty way of using your words, DeBolt. I don't like it. It's time for you to clean up your act."

Christy would have been less than human if a part of her didn't revel in the look of abject terror on Aaron's face. He was a mean-spirited creature who had deliberately hurt her time and again over the years. To see him at Quinn's mercy was a balm to old wounds. She knew Aaron DeBolt well, though. Once Quinn let him go, he'd find some way to get revenge. She didn't want to see Quinn hurt, so she put her hand on his arm and said, "You met his mother, Quinn. He can't help it."

"Maybe not," Quinn said, keeping his gaze locked on DeBolt's. "All the same, he'll apologize."

Aaron's face twisted with resentment. His gaze skittered wildly from one face to the other. The brunette holding the joint took a last drag then dropped it on the concrete floor and ground out the butt with her shoe. The other woman was staring at Quinn with an avid expression on her face. Neither was going anywhere.

Aaron's voice squeaked as he caved in to a strength he couldn't undermine. "Sorry, Christy. I was out of line."

Quinn released him. While DeBolt tried to smooth the wrinkles from his lapels, Quinn brushed his hands together as if to dislodge something foul.

Christy nodded a silent acceptance of the apology. Then, as if nothing had happened, she said, "Aaron, have you heard that Frank is back in town?"

Already pale, Aaron went white. The hand on his lapel faltered and fell as his eyes opened wide. "No! That can't be." He wetted his lips. "Frank's in Mexico."

Christy studied him for a moment. Something was wrong here. "You haven't seen him then?"

Aaron drew a deep breath. It seemed to Christy that he had to make a deliberate effort to revert back to his usual insolent manner. "Would I bother telling you if I had?"

"Yes," Quinn said, quietly.

Aaron jumped.

Christy laughed. She couldn't help it. "You know, Aaron, you don't have to protect Frank from me. I'm not after him for the money he embezzled or to rag on him about running off with Brianne. I just want to find out what his plans are so I can tell our daughter when Daddy is going to see her next."

"He loved that kid of his," Aaron muttered. "He'd talk about her like she was the only eight-year-old on the planet." He shot Christy an under-brow glance. "Look, if he contacts me, I'll tell him what you said, but don't get the kid's hopes up. He's gone south for good. I don't think he'd be stupid enough to come back."

"Maybe, maybe not," Christy said.

A car horn honked on the street below. Aaron jumped again. "I've got to go." He pushed away from the wall in a movement that was jerky and out of character. His duo of curvy belles went with him, though the brunette rubbed suggestively against Quinn as she passed.

"That was not particularly useful," Christy said later, when they were back in Burnaby. Quinn had parked the car in his garage, and, as he walked her to her door, he was tugging on the bowtie at his neck.

"I don't know," he said. The tie came loose. He left it dangling, a stark black contrast to the snowy white of the formal shirt. "I learned a great deal about Fisher Disposal that I didn't know. The VPs I was sitting between seemed to think I was one of Gerry's anointed. They tripped over themselves to give me the inside scoop."

"You didn't like him." Quinn had the top button of his shirt open now. Christy's mouth dried.

"Who? Gerry Fisher?"

She nodded.

"Not much. I liked him a heck of a lot better than Aaron DeBolt and his mom, though. Do you think DeBolt has seen Frank? He looked like he was hiding something to me, but you know him better than I do."

"He's always like that. He takes potshots at everybody." They reached her front steps. "By the way, thanks for defending me. It's not something I'm used to."

"You're welcome." Quinn smiled at her.

Christy's heart did an unexpected flip-flop. "Why did you do it?"

A moody frown replaced the lazy smile. "I don't know…because you took off your shoes and ran down the stairs in your stocking feet without thinking twice about it? Because his mother kicked you off the board of her pet charity? Because I didn't like his face, or his manner? Who knows?"

"Because people like Aaron and Natalie DeBolt would have been the type to try to put down your mother?" Christy said softly. It was easier to attribute his behavior to cleansing an old wound than accepting that he'd defended her for no reason other than she deserved his protection.

His expression was enigmatic as he looked down at her. "Maybe. Maybe not."

Christy shook her head. "You shouldn't have pushed Aaron. He'll try to hurt you. I know he will."

Quinn smiled at her. "Guys like him don't scare me." He reached up to brush a strand of hair away from her face. "I wonder why DeBolt is so certain that Frank wouldn't return from Mexico."

"Good question." Quinn's touch, gentle, almost tender, brought her nerve endings to life. Panicked, she dug in her purse for her key. "Maybe they talked about what it would be like to go to prison. I've heard Aaron deals drugs to his friends. He may worry what would happen if he got caught."

"Not that spineless little worm," Quinn said. "He'd just get Mommy the barracuda to attack the legal system and force it to set him free."

Christy laughed. "Yeah. Sounds like Aaron." She held up her key. "I should go in. I wasn't kidding when I told Gerry that I'll have an early morning. Thank you for tonight, even if it was a waste of your time."

He stared at her for a minute. The look on his face made her breath catch and her lips part. He took a step toward her, put the edge of his palm under her chin, and tilted it up. Christy moistened her lips, knowing she was enticing him, but unable to stop.

When his mouth touched hers, she wasn't ready. He tasted of wine and dinner and something else, something essentially himself. Her senses kicked into overdrive as his lips brushed hers, with just the tickle of a touch by his tongue.

She wanted to melt into him, to take that kiss to a more passionate level where their tongues could mate as their hands played. Instead, he pulled away, leaving her dazed. He took her key, bounded lightly up the stairs, and unlocked her door.

If she hadn't been bemused by her body's unexpected reaction to his kiss, she'd have been annoyed at his presumption that he could just take over her key that way. Sure, it was probably a gentlemanly thing to do, maybe, but no one had ever done it for her before, including Frank. Of course, Frank wouldn't have thought of it, because he'd always had servants to open doors for him. But still...

Roy Armstrong appeared in the doorway. He had a laptop under his arm and a rather impatient expression on his face. "You're back?"

"Yup," Quinn said, stepping out of the way.

He clearly knew his father. "Good," Roy said, as he dove out the door. "I've got to go."

"How was Noelle?" Christy asked as he flew past her. "Was everything okay?"

"She's great," Roy said over his shoulder. "Get her to show you the epic she wrote for her composition assignment." He disappeared up his steps.

"Sure," Christy said, staring at where he'd just been. She heard his door slam behind him. Shaking her head, she turned back to her own front door and found Quinn laughing quietly. "What?"

"We must have arrived when he was in the middle of a scene. My father is like a snake. He doesn't write little bits on a regular basis, he gorges himself on immense writing binges that are intense and demand his concentration for hours. He'll write thirty or more pages in one session, then he'll rest for days. When he's in one of these binges, he allows nothing to break his focus."

Christy's brow furrowed as she climbed the steps to the door. "I hope Noelle's okay."

Quinn smiled. Standing in the light, he looked like a fallen angel, his formal—respectable—clothing casually loosened, a lock of black hair on his forehead, a half smile on his face. To gain the sanctuary of her home, she would have to pass the seductive temptation he offered. If he reached out to her, she would go to him. She knew that, even as she knew that she should not.

She was working with Quinn Armstrong. She'd hired him to help her achieve a goal. He was an employee, paid in a different currency, but an employee nonetheless. Allowing her hormones to rule her head was not a good idea.

She mounted the first step, then the second. Quinn watched her silently, waiting for her to come to him. Christy's heart pounded.

The third step. The fourth, then the landing. He reached out his hand. She caught it and he drew her close.

"Noelle will have been fine," he said. "Something she said or they did together set my dad's imagination flying. When I was a kid that often happened. We'd be doing an activity together, throwing a ball maybe, and suddenly this dreamy look would come into his eyes. He'd be there with me, on top of things, making sure everything was okay, but his mind would be working on two levels. When my mom got home, or I was busy on my own, he'd disappear with a pad and pen, eventually his computer. We'd see him again much, much later."

The way his lips formed the words was driving her crazy. He had beautiful lips. She wanted them. She wanted him. God, what was she going to do about this?

He held her hand between both of his. His fingers played with hers for a minute, then he raised her hand to his mouth and slowly, deliberately, kissed each knuckle.

Fire shot down her arm and throbbed through her torso. She wanted to fling herself against him. She wanted to open up and luxuriate in the sensations he could provide.

Drawing her hand from his took every ounce of resolution she possessed. She smiled shakily. "I have to go. Good night, Quinn."

He smiled that knowing, dark angel smile back at her. "Good night, Christy."

Inside the house she closed the door, then leaned against it. As she summoned the will to move, she could hear him humming as he walked away.

CHAPTER 11

Saturday Noelle was up and on the move early, into weekend cartoons on TV. She was still full of questions about the fundraising evening, even though it had happened two days before, but when Mary Petrofsky came to the door asking her out to play, she abandoned Christy without a second thought. Christy laughed, told her daughter to have fun, then worried about the end to her evening, just as she had the previous day.

She wasn't sure why Quinn had kissed her. She wanted to believe it was the result of their shared experience that night, looking to each other for support against the nastiness of Frank's trustees and friends, plus a potent dose of sexual attraction tossed in for good measure.

Quinn Armstrong was a reporter, though, and her experience with reporters had taught her that they would do anything for a story, no matter what lies they had to tell.

Was the emotion she'd sensed in him that evening real? She hadn't seen him since Thursday evening, so she couldn't even guess. As she loaded the dishwasher she told herself she should stay away from him. That was what a sensible woman would do.

She dumped in the soap and slammed the door so it locked. Clearly, she was not a sensible woman, because she had no intention of driving Quinn Armstrong from her life. She set the dial and got the machine running and then she headed upstairs for a load of laundry.

She had the vacuum out and on when she thought she heard the doorbell ring. She flicked the switch to turn off the machine then, hot, she rubbed her arm over her forehead. She was wondering if her imagination had played a trick on her when the bell rang again. Her heart leapt. Was it Quinn? She glanced down at herself. Were the jeans she was wearing okay? Her top was a royal blue, lightweight sweater she'd bought because it brought out the red highlights in her dark hair, but what if the blue made her made her look sallow? What if...

Answer the door.

The people in the doorway were not who she expected.

"Hello, Christy," Gerry Fisher said. "May we come in?"

Christy stepped back. "Of course." All thoughts of sweater colors went out of her head. Gerry Fisher had visited before, and she'd asked him to come again, but Ellen Jamieson rarely had anything to do with them even though Noelle was her niece. So why was she here today?

Ellen and Gerry crowded into her narrow foyer. Christy gestured toward the stairs. "Come up to the living room. Would you like a coffee?"

While Gerry accepted the offer of a coffee, Ellen opted for tea. Christy prepared both, wondering with some trepidation why two of the trustees had arrived on her doorstep two days after a social event she'd attended with Quinn Armstrong. Were they here because of Quinn? Or—

Heavens, had they heard about the run in with Aaron DeBolt? As rude as Aaron and his mother were, the DeBolt family was a power in the city. It didn't do to cross them, especially if you wielded no financial power yourself.

Was it possible they had brought news of Frank? Then why not phone? People imparted good news on the phone. They came in person when it was really nasty. What kind of bad news could they bring? That Frank was in

Vancouver but refused to see Noelle? That he'd been arrested and would be in jail until he could be bailed out? Were they here to tell her they were going to have to sell Jamieson Ice Cream shares to set him free?

She had to tame her frantic thoughts or they would show on her face when she returned to the living room. *Think about setting up a tea tray. Don't use the everyday china. Use the pretty things that signified a social event. Pretend the PAC committee heads had come for a meeting. Deep breathe. Remember you're the hostess.*

She headed into the living room holding the tray before her like an offering. She'd put the coffee for herself and Gerry into the cups—proper cups with saucers—but she'd brought a teapot for Ellen, as well as creamer, sugar bowl, and silver spoons for all of them.

As she poured, Ellen said, "That tea set came from the mansion."

Christy nodded. "Would you like some cream?" The tea set was gorgeous. Hand-made in the nineteenth century, the china was eggshell thin. Delicately rendered cornflowers, daisies, geraniums, and other flowers adorned the surface. Though the set was very valuable, its attraction for Christy was that it had been a tenth anniversary present to Frank's parents.

"That should have been put in the auction with the rest of the valuables from the mansion," Ellen said.

Christy's calm began to crack. Ellen had a way of making her feel clumsy and never quite good enough. Her hand shook as she put the creamer back on the tray. "No," she said. "It is part of Noelle's heritage. She has a right to know who her family is and where she came from. The few hundred dollars the tea set might have fetched isn't worth stealing away a visible part of her background."

"A few thousand," Ellen said, contemplating the teacup. "It is quite lovely."

Christy put her palms flat on her thighs and pressed hard to hide her shaking. She didn't know why Ellen was on the attack—perhaps the woman was just in a mood—but it frightened her, badly. "I'm sure you didn't come to discuss a tea set."

"No," Gerry said quickly. He appeared uncomfortable, but resigned.

Christy wondered if he and Ellen were playing good cop, bad cop. If they were, something big was up. She began to sweat.

Gerry drank his coffee, in no hurry despite his hasty reply. Ellen said impatiently, "We are both very worried about you, Christy."

"Worried?"

"Natalie DeBolt called me last evening," Ellen said.

"She did?"

"She told me you harassed Aaron at the IHTF fundraiser."

Gerry frowned, as if he wasn't comfortable with what Ellen was saying, but was willing to go along with it for the moment.

Ellen put the fragile cup and saucer on the coffee table with a careless snap. "She claims that your date—what was his name?" She waved her hand in dismissal even as she asked the question. "Doesn't matter. She said he attacked Aaron. Is this true, Christy?"

Christy groaned silently. When she'd told Quinn that Aaron would find a way to get him, she hadn't expected it would be through her. "I'm sure Natalie took great pleasure in complaining about me."

"Natalie DeBolt is one of my dearest friends!" Ellen said hotly. "She wasn't complaining. She was advising me of a serious problem."

Gerry said, "The man's behavior shows a considerable lack of judgment, Christy."

Ellen clasped her hands in her lap. "To say nothing of poor manners."

Christy dug her teeth into her lower lip. "Aaron was being vile to me, calling me names, making insinuations."

"Nonsense," Ellen said. "Aaron DeBolt is your husband's best friend. I doubt he likes you—few of Frank's friends do—but he would not allow that to influence his behavior. You should at least be civil to him."

Christy stared at Ellen. This was unbelievable. She was being called to account because Quinn had defended her against a nasty, spoiled brat of a man whose idea of fun was insulting people. What happened to loyalty to family? Except the trustees weren't family, or, at least, Gerry wasn't. There was no excuse for Ellen. "Aaron and I have never gotten along. I don't defend Quinn's actions—"

"I'm glad to hear that, Christy," Gerry said heartily. "Aaron DeBolt's parents are important people. His father is the CEO of the largest lumber company in the province. His mother sits on a dozen charitable boards and chairs three of them." He hesitated. Disappointment crept into his voice and onto his face. "I would seriously question your suitability as a guardian for Noelle if I believed that you had any part in Armstrong's violent action."

This was worse than anything Christy could have imagined. "Come again?"

Ellen made a sneering sound in her throat. She stood up impatiently. "I think you understand, Christy. As Noelle's trustees, we have an obligation to ensure that she receives the best care possible during her formative years."

"She is receiving the best, Ellen." Christy rose too. Her hands bunched into fists.

Ellen looked pointedly at them, her brows raised. Christy blushed and straightened her fingers. Ellen said haughtily, "As her aunt I believe Noelle has a duty to the Jamieson name. She needs to be brought up understanding the expectations and responsibilities of her heritage."

"This is outrageous!" Christy cried. "Are you suggesting that I'm trying to turn Noelle away from her family?"

Even Gerry Fisher was standing now. He patted her on the shoulder. "I know you love Noelle, Christy—"

"But you're not a Jamieson," Ellen said. "And you can't show her how a Jamieson should behave. You proved that on Thursday night."

"Because my date was rough with Aaron?"

"Because you chose Quinn Armstrong to be your date," Gerry said, his voice hard.

"Quinn is helping me find Frank. I asked him to the fundraiser so we could talk to some of Frank's friends to see if they'd heard from him."

"Ah. Another example of your lack of judgment," Ellen said, sniffing.

"I told you, Christy, you shouldn't bother with that investigation nonsense." Gerry said. "The trustees will deal with the rumors that Frank has returned."

Christy wiped sweaty palms on her pant legs and hoped neither Gerry or Ellen would notice. No such luck. After a pointed look Ellen pursed her lips and sighed. Christy swallowed hard. "Noelle asks about her daddy. She worries about why he left. She wants to know when he's coming home. I don't have the luxury of waiting for Frank to show up, or hoping someone else will find him. I need to reassure my daughter. I need to find my husband." She gestured toward the stairs. Enough was enough. "Thank you for coming. I'll consider what you said." She followed them down to the door.

Outside, standing beside the sleek gray car, Gerry said, "Christy, I know you won't take this personally—"

"How can I not? Come on, Gerry."

"Is that Roy Armstrong?" Ellen asked, excitement—no *awe*—making her voice squeak.

Christy frowned. She looked over in the direction Ellen was pointing. A smile twitched her lips. "Yes, it is."

Roy was standing in front of his spacious planter box. One hand was wrapped firmly around the trunk of a thin bush that looked like a rose of some kind. In the other was a spade. He was contemplating the box with the same intensity she'd seen when he charged from her townhouse on Thursday evening. From the rumpled look of his jeans and checked, western-style shirt, not to mention the way strands of gray hair had escaped from his ponytail, it looked as though he'd recently emerged from his self-imposed writing retreat.

"Oh, I love his books. I've read every one," Ellen said, reverence in her tone. "Armstrong. Weren't we just talking about an Armstrong?"

"Quinn is his son," Christy said.

There was a moment when shocked disbelief widened Ellen's eyes, then a calculating look snuck into her gaze. "You know Roy Armstrong?"

She sounded like a teenager who had just been told she could meet her favorite pop idol.

"He's a social activist who uses his dubious celebrity to destroy legitimate businesses," Gerry said.

"I love his work! He writes such beautiful stories. His words are almost poetry. Perhaps we've been too hasty in condemning his son's behavior."

"Absolutely not! Quinn Armstrong is no better than his father." Gerry fixed cold blue eyes on Christy. "Quinn Armstrong is not the only one at fault. It goes without saying that as a married woman you should not be dating."

"I'm not dating Quinn."

Roy made use of the spade to dig a shallow hole before he folded himself down onto his knees. He plopped the bush into the hole, then scooped the earth around it with his hands.

"I'm glad to hear that, Christy," Gerry said, his eyes cold, the hint of a threat in his icy tone. He opened the car door for Ellen.

Roy patted down the softened earth.

"Come, Ellen," Gerry said. "I think we've done all we need to here."

Roy stood. Ellen, who had been watching him avidly while he gardened, ignored Gerry. She turned to Christy. "Can I meet him?"

Christy didn't have to ask whom.

"Thank you for talking to Frank's aunt, Roy."

Roy poured water on his rose bush. "Not a problem."

Christy sighed. "Watching her was painful. Is it always

like that? Do people usually gush the way Ellen did when they meet you?"

Roy laughed. "Not always. Sometimes they critique my work and tell me how they think my books should be written. Frankly, I like the Ellens of the world much better."

Christy shuddered. She rubbed her arms to chase away a cold that had settled on her at Ellen's name.

Roy frowned. "What's the matter?"

"Ellen likes you a whole bunch more than she likes me. She doesn't think I'm a good mother."

Roy snorted. "So Ms. Jamieson is the voice of experience, is she? I wouldn't have thought it."

Christy rubbed harder. "She has opinions about everything."

Roy studied Christy for a moment, then he plopped down on to his porch stairs and patted the space beside him. Christy sat, cradling her chin in hands, feeling glum.

"Is that why the two of them stopped by?" he asked.

Christy nodded. "They wanted me to know that they would take Noelle from me if they chose to."

"Ridiculous. You're her mother." He rubbed his chin. "I don't trust Gerry Fisher, though he claims to be a reformed character. Did they suggest why they'd take such a radical step?"

"They claim it's because Quinn roughed up Aaron DeBolt on Thursday night—"

"Quinn? My Quinn?" Roy sat up straight.

Christy might have laughed at the startled expression on his face, if she wasn't so very frightened.

"Quinn doesn't rough up people. He pries their secrets out of them, then lets them have it with words if they're not so nice. What did this guy, DeBolt, do that fired him up?"

"He was insulting to me."

Roy regarded her for a long, silent minute. "Really."

Christy nodded. Roy was staring at her with a puzzled expression on his face. He looked like a man who had been given the answer, but couldn't quite fit the clues together to get the result he knew was correct.

"I can't let them take Noelle away from me…"

Christy heard a loud yawn. A sense of hunger and a definite desire for food immediately followed. Christy frowned. She was staring at Roy Armstrong, who *wasn't* yawning, and he was the only other person around.

He raised bushy white brows. "Breakfast time," he said.

Damn straight, old man.

Christy's eyes widened. She'd heard Roy Armstrong speaking. His voice had been normal, coming from outside her head. The second voice, the one that had yawned, seemed to be inside her mind, but that wasn't possible.

"Breakfast will have to wait," Roy said. "I've got more important things to do."

"If you want to go in for breakfast, please go ahead," Christy said.

"I don't want breakfast," Roy said. "I ate hours ago. Somewhere around three a.m., I think. No, it's the cat who wants breakfast."

"The cat."

"Yeah. A stray Quinn picked up a few weeks ago. He took off on a quest, but now he's back. Cat," he added, addressing the doorway. "Come out and meet Miss Christy."

Christy laughed. She didn't know if Roy was trying to cheer her up, but there was something delightfully absurd in the way he addressed an animal that was just a pet, as if the creature was a person. She remembered Quinn saying his father was an animal activist and guessed that conversations with cats were probably pretty normal in the Armstrong household.

A sense of annoyance washed over her. Not her own annoyance—she was feeling scared and upset, with a little overlay of hope—but a generally pissed off feeling, as if the owner of the emotion had been forced to do a great deal of useless activity for absolutely no reward.

And now he had to wait for breakfast.

Where were those thoughts and emotions coming from? Christy asked herself. She'd had breakfast; Roy said he'd had breakfast. Who was so anxious to get his breakfast?

You want me to wait? I haven't eaten in two days, and my last meal was a crummy little mouse with a grasshopper chaser. Yuck. Give me canned tuna any day.

Christy shivered. She was so stressed her mind was playing tricks on her. The voice in her head had graduated from sounds to actual words that created really nasty images in her brain.

"I don't have any canned tuna," Roy said. "Stop grumbling and come out here, will you?"

Christy stared at him. She wanted to ask him if he was hearing the voice in his head too, but she couldn't. That would mean admitting her anxiety had pushed her over the edge. She wasn't ready for that.

A cat appeared on the porch, moving with the lithe grace of a tiger. "Would you look at that? It could be Stormy," Christy said.

"Stormy?" said Roy.

"Our cat. Actually, my husband and daughter's cat. He never took to me. Stormy was gray and black with tabby stripes. He looked a lot like this cat."

That's because he is this cat.

"Well, that solves that problem," Roy said.

You moved. Why did you move?

The voice was annoyed and critical, the tone complaining. Christy blinked at Roy. "Excuse me?"

"The cat was on a quest to find his owners. He said he couldn't."

"You...you're talking to the cat?"

So are you. This time the voice was amused.

"Really?" Roy regarded her in an interested way. "I thought the pot had opened up my mind so I was able to hear his voice. Seems I was wrong."

Speaking of pot, I could use a few puffs. After breakfast.

"There's no tuna," Roy said.

"I have a can," Christy said. She wanted to escape into her kitchen and hide until she'd dealt with the stress that put this hallucination into her brain.

Don't go, Chris, the voice said. *It's taken me long enough to find you. I don't want to lose you again.*

As she stood up, Christy looked down. Roy's eyes were bright, his expression keenly interested. The cat was staring at her intently, jade green eyes demanding, body tense, ready to spring. "I'm only going into my house." She turned away from those insistent green eyes and headed for her home.

The cat followed.

Roy said, "I might as well come too."

The cat bounded up the stairs after Christy, but he stopped just inside the front door. *It's the same as your place, old man.*

"The carpet's a different color," Roy said.

You sold the mansion so you could move into this? I can't believe you'd do that. Why?

Halfway up the stairs, Christy stopped. She stared down at the cat who stared back at her. There was a challenge in his eyes, or at least Christy thought there was a challenge. This was a first for her. She didn't usually attribute human characteristics to animals. Clearly the stress was warping her mind.

It was my home, and you dumped it as soon as I was gone. How callous is that?

"Frank?" Christy and Roy said at exactly the same moment.

CHAPTER 12

"The cat can't be Frank," Quinn said. He was glaring at Stormy who was busy chasing a ball Noelle had thrown. Noelle was squealing happily, delighted at the return of her beloved pet.

"Why not?" Roy said amicably.

They were sitting out on the patio behind Christy's house, sharing a pre-dinner glass of wine. Stormy pounced on the ball, grabbed it in his front paws, and rolled with it. His strong back legs jerked, his claws catching the edge of the ball and shredding it. Christy shivered. If the ball had been a bird or a mouse, it wouldn't have had much of a chance.

Laughing and chiding the cat, Noelle charged up to grab the ball for another throw. There was a moment when Stormy glared at her, then he surrendered the toy. Standing up, his tail twitching, the cat stood tensed, waiting for the next throw.

Quinn watched this scene moodily. "Because he's a cat, Dad! He can't be a person too."

"Why not?" Roy said again.

"Come on, Dad! People don't suddenly turn into cats."

A lot he knows.

Roy laughed.

Christy sighed. Frank had been making snarky comments about Quinn since he'd first started communicating with her that morning.

"What?" Quinn said.

"Stormy disagrees," Christy said. "He says he's Frank and that Frank's human body is dead."

"Frank is probably still in Mexico, very much alive, but minus his passport. He's just lying low." Quinn's jaw was set and his voice was firm. He'd made his decision and he wasn't prepared to back down.

"You're too rigid, boy. That's why you're the only one who can't hear the cat talking. You're closed to the infinite possibilities of the cosmos." Roy gestured with his wine glass. "Relax. Go with the flow. Open your mind. Let him in."

Quinn shot his father an impatient look. He jumped to his feet and began to pace, like a lion locked in a holding pen. He certainly didn't look like a man prepared to relax any time soon. "Okay, Dad. I've opened my mind. There's nothing out there. The cat is just a cat."

Stormy, busy eviscerating the ball, laughed. So did Christy and Roy.

Quinn's jaw flexed. "This is stupid." He sat down again and drank some wine.

His father topped up his glass.

Christy decided that Quinn Armstrong was a very sexy man. Not only did he move with the easy grace of a big cat, but he had a way of narrowing his eyes and looking straight into a situation. Physical control tied together with a quick intelligence was a potent combination that she needed to ignore. She'd already shown him that she responded to his kisses. She didn't want him thinking she was mooning over him every minute they were together. Not only was she still married to Frank, but she was very much aware that Quinn was a successful journalist. Everything she said would eventually find its way into the media, including her belief that her husband was living inside Stormy the Cat. Wouldn't that look great in big black type on white newsprint? *Embezzler's Wife Decides Husband Is a Cat.*

Time to follow Quinn's lead and solve this puzzle in a logical way. "Let's step back and see what we've got so far. We know Frank's passport was used by a person traveling to and from Mexico. That individual fit Frank's physical description. He could have been Frank, or someone else. Last week, the person using Frank's passport returned to Canada along with Brianne Lymbourn, the woman Frank was reported to be with in Mexico. On arrival in Vancouver, Brianne took a room at the Strand Manor. The man with her did not register, but apparently stayed in the hotel. Both of them have now disappeared. In fact, no one has seen Frank or spoken to him in months."

"No one here." Quinn was now slouched in a lawn chair, one long jean-clad leg propped on the other. His hand was wrapped around the goblet of his wineglass, which he'd just raised to his lips.

Christy remembered the way those lips had felt on hers and heat sizzled through her. She swallowed hard. "Okay. Let's look at that. What proof do we have that Frank was ever in Mexico? News stories. That's it."

"And the embezzlement," Quinn said.

"As reported in the press." Roy waved his glass. Red wine sloshed dangerously close to the edge before it receded. "If I were writing a story about this, I'd point out that none of the trustees have confirmed any details of the embezzlement to Christy."

That's because I didn't do it. I didn't go to the Caribbean and someone else ripped off all my money. I wish this guy would get with the program.

"Patience, man," Roy said. "I'm on it."

"I hate to ask, Dad, but what are you on?"

Roy ignored him. He waved the wineglass again, with another near miss for a spill. "Now listen, all we know about the embezzlement is that the money is gone. Not who did the actual transfer or where they transferred the money. If you read the newspaper reports, they're pretty vague. In fact, they all sound the same."

"That's a good point." Christy watched her daughter and the cat. Noelle had been delighted when she saw Stormy. She and the cat had been inseparable ever since. They'd given up on the ball. The cat was now crouched in the garden, eyeing a bird perched on a tree branch. Noelle was rummaging in a box of toys for the next game. "It's like they all came from a single source."

Quinn swirled the wine in his glass absently. The motion was neat and precise. The wine climbed a scant millimeter or two up the side of the glass. "I noticed the similarity in the reports too, so I checked around last week."

Oblivious to the danger of the nearby cat, the bird fluttered from its secure place on the tree to a low branch on a bush dangerously close to the cat.

"It seems the source was a reporter named Greg Barret. We had a beer together yesterday afternoon. Hey!" Quinn jumped up. The wine in his glass went flying as he charged toward the bush. The bird fluttered away.

Stormy turned with a hiss and a lashing tail. *Jerk! The cat almost had it.*

"Not in front of Noelle!" Christy said tartly.

"What happened, Mom?" Noelle said, coming over to Christy for a hug, her eyes wide.

"Nothing much, honey." Christy cuddled her daughter for a moment. "The cat spotted a bird and was about to pounce on it when Quinn shouted to make the bird fly away."

Noelle's eyes opened wide. "He was going to eat a bird? Yuck. Stormy! You can't do that!" She headed over to the cat, her finger wagging. The adults laughed.

That's right, make me look bad in front of my daughter when I'm just doing what cats do. Thanks, Chris! The cat sat in front of Noelle and licked his paw while she gave him a lecture about respecting all life.

Quinn observed this with a grin. Christy figured that while he might not consciously accept that Frank's body was dead and his essence was living in Stormy the Cat, part of Quinn had tuned into the idea, and that part of him was enjoying the sight of Noelle lecturing her father.

Drawing his gaze away, Quinn refilled his glass. "Barret claims he received a series of anonymous letters detailing everything Frank did, starting with his flight to Mexico. Each letter was postmarked Vancouver, but there was no return address on the envelope, and the letters weren't signed. They arrived at intervals, and each time Barret received one, he was able to find evidence that backed up the allegations he'd been sent. Barret has never found out who his source is, but I don't think he's tried too hard. He latched onto the Jamieson name and flogged the story to any outlet that would pay for it. This has been a real moneymaker for him."

"And when it became big news all the others copied off the original story, adding their own bits of hype," Roy said.

Quinn sipped again, then nodded. "That's about it."

"Okay," Christy said. "So what do we know then?"

That I'm dead and I did not transfer most of my trust fund to some bank in a two-bit third world country. Do you think I'd do that to you and Noelle?

Roy rubbed his chin. Christy said hotly, "I don't know what to think, Frank!" Quinn groaned. She ignored him. "Three months ago you walked out our front door and didn't come back. Then you show up this morning and tell me that you're dead and your essence is living inside a cat. A cat who hated me when we lived in the mansion! Right now I'm having a hard time adjusting to having a voice that isn't mine talking inside my head."

"I think it's cool," Roy said. "The first time Frank spoke to me I thought I was having a bad trip. When he got in this morning, just after I'd finished breakfast, I wasn't prepared. He had to shout so I'd open the door for him."

"He meowed, Dad, and threw his body against the door. He was so loud he woke me up too. Letting him in is not proof that the cat was talking to you. Or that he's Frank."

I would have been back sooner if he, the cat looked at Quinn and hissed, *hadn't kidnapped me!*

"Whatever." Christy waved her hand impatiently. "The money is gone. If you didn't take it, then who did?"

Beats me. Ouch! Hey, kiddo, careful where you put your feet. The tail's off limits.

Noelle immediately picked up the cat. She stroked him gently and issued apologies. Stormy began to purr.

Christy drew a deep breath. "So what's our next step?"

Find out who stole my money.

"We find Frank," Quinn said, sounding grim. "And get him to explain what is going on."

The voice laughed. *Good luck.*

"Quinn, what if we have found Frank? Or I should say, Frank has found us?" Christy asked. "All we've discovered so far is that Frank wasn't the man who traveled to Vancouver with Brianne. Maybe Frank really is dead."

Quinn swirled his wineglass again. The wine slid up the sides, higher than before, though there was never any danger of it sloshing over the edge. "I don't buy Frank living inside the cat, but you and my father do. The cat claims Frank never left Vancouver. That means all the reports of Frank in Mexico would have to be reports of Crack Graham's activities there. We need proof of that. We also have to eliminate the possibility that Frank was ever in Mexico and that he's not down there right now. I say we take the hunt to Frank. We go to Mexico."

The reported sightings of Frank had taken place in an area of Mexico known as the Mexican Riviera. Located in southeastern Mexico, it encompassed the resort towns of Cancun, Playa del Carmen, and Tulum. Wide, white sand beaches faced an azure Caribbean sea and enjoyed soft sea breezes with endless sunshine. Away from the coast, a lush jungle that hid ancient Mayan ruins begging to be explored and marveled over covered the land.

The gateway to the Mexican Riviera was Cancun. To fly to Cancun from Vancouver, without a layover in an American city, there were two options—via Toronto or Mexico City. Since the flight that Brianne and her companion had used had been through Mexico City, Quinn and Christy booked seats on that route as well.

"Do you think we'll have any more luck with customs here than we did in Mexico City?" Christy asked as they stood waiting for their luggage to be delivered on the slowly rotating carousel at the Cancun airport. When they passed through customs in Mexico City they had interviewed the supervisor on duty. He had no memory of Frank, either his recent departure from the country, or his earlier arrival. He had been apologetic but firm. Three months was too long to remember any one individual.

"I think the odds are low." A suitcase came down the ramp, slid onto the carousel, and bounced against the protective edge. "This is a major international airport. We can try, though. We might get lucky."

The suitcase was black. Quinn stepped forward to check it out, then shook his head. Not surprising. All the luggage on the carousel was rectangular and black. Figuring out what belonged to whom in the busy Cancun airport was a nightmare. Quinn already had his case. He'd found it immediately because he had marked it with a bright neon green tag. Christy hadn't been so organized, or experienced.

Christy looked around her. The Cancun airport was large, modern, and packed with people in holiday mode. "Quinn, I—" He lunged for another suitcase, then stepped back when it wasn't Christy's. "This trip is costing a huge amount. I mean, Frank wouldn't hear of Aunt Ellen looking after Noelle, so I had to get my mom to come in from Kingston. Then there's the ticket price and the hotel. I'll be living off my credit card for the next few months. The trustees have already told me not to look for Frank in Vancouver. They'll go nuts if they hear I've flown to Cancun for the weekend. What happens if we don't—"

Quinn pounced on another suitcase. Christy resisted annoyance. She knew he was listening to her, but it would be nice if he showed her that he was by staying put and looking her way. "Especially if we don't get some answers out of it."

He released the bag, then watched the carousel moodily. "Stick with me, Christy. It's early days, yet." Another suitcase came down. He moved forward, checked the luggage tag, and grabbed the rectangular, black case. "Got it." He grinned at Christy. "Come on, let's check in with local customs and see if their memories are any better than those guys in Mexico City."

They weren't. The customs supervisor shook his head. "I have told you all I can, *señor*. In the high season, eight hundred thousand people pass through our airport each month. Many of them will be using our customs facilities. I'm sure you can see why it is impossible to remember one face from another." The man was very polite, very earnest and very proud of the success of this tourist region. Christy had the feeling that if he could have helped, he would have.

Quinn had rented a car and booked them into one of the more moderately priced hotels, a low-rise complex along the strip of sand facing the Caribbean. Once they had checked in they went through the same procedure they'd used in Vancouver, visiting each hotel in the area, talking to front desk staff, the concierge, bellmen, and waiters and hostesses in the restaurants.

At the first hotel, they entered through revolving doors that sealed in the cool, air conditioned air. "This is certainly Frank's style," Christy said, looking around the enormous lobby, open up to the third floor. There was marble everywhere, and enough seating for several busloads of visitors. Beach access and a fancy beach bar added up to a room rate that was considerably higher than the economy hotel Christy and Quinn had chosen.

Quinn looked around him thoughtfully. "Not exactly low profile. Would a man on the run choose a ritzy place like this one?"

"If the man really was Frank Jamieson, you bet." Christy headed for the reservations desk. "He'd know how to fit in.

No one would notice him, because he'd wear the right clothes and act the right way in every situation."

"Then we have our work cut out for us."

Christy looked over her shoulder and made a face at Quinn. She knew he was right, but oh how she wished he wasn't.

Questioning everyone who might have remembered Frank was exhausting, painstaking work, made more difficult because there were dozens of hotels along the peninsula that made up Cancun's beach resort area.

A few people remembered Brianne. Attractive, leggy blonds stood out, and spoiled, willful blonds stood out even more. They found one restaurant where Brianne had thrown a hissy fit about the doneness of her steak. At a clothing store they remembered her because she had tried on a stack of sun dresses, complained about the quality and sizing, then flounced out, buying nothing, leaving all the items on the floor of the changing room. But every time they flashed the picture of Frank, all they received were headshakes and denials. The longer they searched the more likely it became that Frank had never been in the area at all.

They had dinner at a restaurant in one of the hotels they visited. The prices were extraordinary, but Christy's entrée, an octopus dish in a cream sauce flavored with a hint of mustard and Mexico, hit every taste bud in just the right way. As they drank their coffee, she checked her watch. It was eight o'clock. Three time zones away Noelle would be finishing up her homework, while Christy's mom would be prepping dinner.

She fished her cell phone out of her purse and held it up. "Do you mind? I thought I'd call Noelle and see how her day went."

Quinn leaned back in his chair and shook his head. He was smiling, and there was something about him—warmness perhaps?—that spoke of approval. "Go ahead. I figured after dinner we'd hit some of the nightspots. I imagine Brianne is a big-time party girl."

In the midst of dialing her home number, Christy nodded. "I don't know her well, but I'd have to agree, on the surface, that's Brianne. There may be more to her..." Voicemail clicked on. She heard her own voice repeat the phone number. Disappointed, she left a cheery mom-type message for Noelle and told her she'd try to call again before bed.

Quinn raised his brows. "No luck?"

"Voicemail. Noelle is probably outside with Mary Petrofsky, and knowing my mom she's probably out there too, scoping out the neighborhood."

"Or maybe they're over at my place for dinner. Before we left my dad mentioned something about keeping an eye on them both."

"My mother will enjoy that." Christy fiddled with her coffee cup. "Quinn, this isn't working. We've found proof that Brianne was here, but nobody seems to remember the man she was with, so we're no further ahead. Was she with Frank or Graham? Who knows? We know Crack Graham was in Mexico, but I don't think Frank was ever here."

Quinn put his cup in the saucer, then reached across the table to take Christy's hand. "We know Crack used Frank's passport when he returned to Vancouver. If Frank was ever in Cancun then he's here in Mexico, without a passport. You don't require a passport to enter Mexico, but you do need one to fly across US airspace. That means Frank can't return home. If he's here, we'll find him."

"But if we confirm Brianne was with Graham then it's unlikely that Frank is here now, or ever was here. All the sightings put the two of them together."

Quinn squeezed Christy's hand and smiled. "That's speculation. We're here to find facts. Let's keep going. The worst thing about digging is how much you have to do before you find the treasure."

They hit a dozen bars and several nightclubs in the fashionable hotels, all without success. Brianne might be remembered, but was always solo or with Crack Graham, and always flirting with trouble.

Their second day was a reprise of the first, except longer. They finished with the top hotels and moved on to the second tier ones. Still no sightings of Frank.

Their real breakthrough came late on the third day they were there. They had checked out of their hotel in Cancun and planned to move on to Tulum, where they had reservations for that evening. In the meantime they would visit the least expensive hotels, then check out the town of Cancun.

In an effort to cover as much ground as possible, Christy and Quinn split up. Christy didn't feel comfortable driving the rental car, so Quinn dropped her in town. They agreed on a time and place to meet, then Christy was on her own. She had fun poking into the shops, talking to the friendly merchants, but she ran into the same answers over and over again—shrugs and headshakes and pleasant, but firm, negatives.

By mid-afternoon Christy had strayed into a less well-heeled area where tourists were a rarity. Fewer people spoke English here, and the architecture was plain and functional. This wasn't Frank's kind of venue, and she didn't think it really shouted 'Brianne' either. She was exhausted, frustrated, and feeling the pressure of moving on without having accomplished their goal. As she headed toward the meeting place she'd arranged with Quinn, she saw a small, but attractive, cantina that appeared welcoming and prosperous.

She paused, considering the place. The stucco wall was painted a pretty peach, not unlike many other buildings in the area, and a profusion of flowers cascaded from the boxes hanging from the darkened windows. She wondered if she should go inside. It was not happy hour yet, and the place didn't look open. Moreover, it didn't look like the kind of establishment either Brianne or Frank would frequent. Still, there was always the possibility someone inside had seen them.

The interior lighting of the cantina was dim. A mahogany bar stretched the length of one wall. Round mahogany tables filled the center of the room. The place was completely empty.

Christy was tired, hot, and her feet hurt. A drink would go down very well right now. She bit her lip as she cautiously threaded her way through the tables, pushing deeper into the room. "Hello? Is anyone here?"

There was no answer. She wondered if she should sit down at one of the tables and see what happened or if she should wander back out to the street and go on her way.

Wavering, she continued her inspection of the room. To one side of the bar she saw an unmarked door. Curious, she headed over to it. Her hand was on the knob, ready to turn it, when the door swung open of its own accord. She jumped back. A good-looking man of Mayan ancestry stood in the doorway. Stocky in build, with a round face and broad features, his skin was swarthy and his eyes black. He wasn't much taller than Christy was, but with his muscular build he seemed to loom over her.

"*Buenos días*," Christy said, her heart still pounding.

"*Buenas tardes, señorita.*" He added in accented English, "We are closed. We do not open until eight."

"Oh, that's too bad."

"Is there some way I can be helpful?" He sounded apologetic. The Mayans were a friendly, hospitable people. They didn't like saying no to visitors, no matter how outrageous the request.

Christy immediately felt guilty and backed up a step. She would have liked to leave right away so this poor man could go back to whatever he'd been doing, but she'd already realized that hospitality thwarted was as bad as hospitality not offered. "I came in because I'm looking for someone, my husband. Would you have a moment to answer some questions?"

The man frowned, then gestured to one of the tables. "Sit down. Would you like a soft drink?"

"That would be great," Christy said. He retreated inside the door, then returned with two cans of pop, already dripping with sweat from contact with the hot Caribbean air. He placed them on the table as he sat down, then handed her a straw. "I am Miguel, the manager here. Why are you are looking for your *esposo*?" The can hissed as he popped the top.

Christy cracked open her can, inserted the straw, took a long sip of soft drink and sighed. "He's left me and I need to find him for my daughter's sake. I have his picture if you'd be kind enough to take a look at it."

Miguel studied Frank's photo for what seemed to be a long time, then he shook his head. "I remember a man who looked similar to this one. He had blond hair and the same shape of face, but I do not think he was your *esposo*. He was with a blond woman, tall with—how do you say it?— a...a provocative way of dressing. She was beautiful to look at, but had no manners. I was forced to ask them to leave my cantina."

"What happened?"

Miguel shrugged. "The woman drank too much. She started to fight with the man. To argue, you know? Their voices became very loud. She kept saying he did not understand the good life and that she deserved better." Miguel fingered the picture of Frank. "Her voice was not pleasant and her words were demeaning. The man, he hit her, on her face with the back of his hand. She did not deserve that. No woman does."

Christy slipped the grainy photocopy of the newspaper photo of Crack Graham and Brianne from her purse. She handed it to Miguel. "Would this be the man and woman?"

Miguel looked back and forth between the pictures, then he nodded. "*Si*. The photo is not clear, but that is certainly the woman. I am not sure about the man..." He peered again, nodded emphatically. "*Si*, that is the man who was with her." He cocked a brow, looking from the picture of Brianne and Graham to Frank and back again. "Your *esposo* is this woman's lover?"

Christy smiled wearily. "Amongst other things."

"He is a fool. This woman and the man she is with—" He gestured to the photo of Brianne and Graham. "—are bad people. When he comes back to you, you must tell him to stay away from them."

"Why are they bad people, Miguel?" Christy watched as his face twisted from some internal battle. Conscience at war with the desire to please, perhaps.

Conscience apparently won. "This man, he is dangerous, *si*? He comes into my cantina with a man who is known to sell drugs to the American *turista* who come to our city. He also sends it to the United States by using *turista* to carry it in their baggage. One day, the day the blond man hit the woman, I hear them talking, the blond man and the *Mexicano*. They make a deal. The *Mexicano* offers to pay him much money to bring a shipment of cocaine to your country. The blond man, he agrees. The woman, she does not. She says they are to stay in *México* and he cannot go back to—how do you say it?"

"Vancouver?"

"*Si*, that was the name. Vancouver. This man, he should not return to Vancouver. He tells her he will go back if he chooses. She shouts at him that he made a deal, that they were paid much money to come to Cancun, and to stay here until they were told it was time to return. That is when he hit her, and that is when I told them all that they must leave my *cantina*."

As she put away the photos, Christy's mind was racing. It made sense. Heaven help her, it made perfect sense. "I appreciate your help, Miguel. This may not have been exactly what I wanted to hear, but at least I know a bit more than I did when I walked in here." She brought out a US fifty dollar bill and set it on the table. "Thanks for the drink. *Gracias.*"

He put his hand over hers. "Keep your money, *señora*. You have enough trouble chasing you. The drink—and the information—were freely given. Now, I must work. Please stay and enjoy the rest of your soft drink."

He left through the door that apparently led to the kitchens. Christy was left in the dim quiet to enjoy her refreshment and consider the implications of what he'd told her.

CHAPTER 13

On the drive from Cancun to Tulum they thrashed over what Christy had learned. "We knew Graham was a drug dealer," Quinn said. The road wove along the coastline, jungle on one side, the sea visible on the other. Quinn switched off the air conditioning and opened his window to the breeze. "Looks like he decided to arrange a new supplier while he was here."

"And Brianne didn't like it." The wind ruffled Quinn's dark hair, blowing it across his forehead. Christy wanted to reach over and smooth it back, just for the pleasure of feeling his skin beneath her fingertips and the silk of his hair on her hand.

"Yeah. That's very interesting." He checked in his mirror, then pulled out to pass the ancient pickup chugging along ahead of them. "Brianne wasn't upset because he was running drugs, but because he intended to return to Vancouver."

"She talked about a deal. I wonder who actually made that deal? Crack Graham? Or was it Brianne?"

Quinn passed the old truck, then eased back into his lane. "Good catch! Okay, let's do some speculating. Why would anybody want to send Brianne and a two-bit drug dealer to Mexico on their dime?"

"Simple. Graham looks like Frank. Brianne was supposed to be Frank's girlfriend. Put the two of them together and you get assumptions."

"What kind of assumptions?"

"That Frank has fled the country because of his crimes, but he's got plenty of money, so the place he's chosen is one with luxury resorts and beautiful surroundings."

"And he's taken along his current squeeze to play with while he's here." Quinn glanced at her. There was an apology in his eyes.

"So, if this is a scam, it turns around Brianne, because she's the one who is real," Christy said, cheered by the Quinn's concern for her.

He nodded. "Most people who go on the lam are discovered because someone from their former life sees them where they are not supposed to be. That person tells someone else, who tells a neighbor, who tells a friend, and suddenly lots of people have heard that so-and-so is in Mexico, even though he's supposed to be in Montreal. If Frank really wanted to disappear he would have used some of that huge pile of cash he stole to buy himself a secluded beach house on a tiny island no one has ever heard of."

"But he didn't. Instead he chose to go to a place where lots of people vacation. With him, he brings a woman who stands out, partly because of her looks and the way she dresses, and partly because of her behavior."

"So she'd be noticed, no matter what." Quinn tapped the steering wheel.

"Miguel in the *cantina* said they were paid to be down here. Maybe they were also paid to be noticed."

"So it's unlikely Frank was in Cancun." The road turned away from the coast, diving into the gloom of dense jungle. The fresh sea breeze was replaced with the fetid odor of rotting vegetation. Quinn closed the window and turned on the air conditioning. "The question is, was Frank the person who paid Graham and Brianne?"

"Why would he do that?" Christy asked.

Quinn took his eyes off the road for a moment. He rubbed his hand over hers in a soothing way. She guessed that he wasn't happy about what he was intending to say. "Because he did buy that secluded beach house on the nowhere island and he doesn't want anyone looking for it, or finding him."

Quinn's hand was warm on hers. She kept her hand still, comforted by his compassion, afraid to show her distress. "I don't believe that. It's not Frank. He needs people around him. He'd go crazy in secluded place. We always vacationed in cities—San Francisco, New York, Toronto. Places where Frank knew people. He doesn't like being alone."

Quinn was quiet for a moment, then he gave her hand a quick squeeze. "Okay. Let's speculate from the other direction. Frank was murdered. Whoever killed him asked Brianne to find someone who looked like Frank to act as a decoy. Who would know that Brianne was Frank's girlfriend?"

"But she wasn't!"

"Christy, I know this is tough, but—"

"No! Listen, Quinn, Frank told me that Brianne was after him, but he wasn't interested."

There was another silence. Quinn shot Christy a compassionate look that made her clench her fingers, because at that moment she wanted to hit him. "You think I'm wrong. You think Frank lied to me."

"The thought has occurred." He watched the road, his mouth set in a grim line.

Christy drew a shaky breath. "So we agree to disagree. We're dealing in perceptions here, anyway. Brianne wanted people to think she was Frank's girlfriend. Who would believe that? One of his friends?"

"Aaron DeBolt?"

"Probably not. Aaron always claimed that Frank told him everything. He'd know that Frank wasn't interested in a relationship with Brianne."

The Cat Came Back   145

"But he'd also know that Brianne was after Frank and that her behavior was making it seem that she was Frank's lover. Rumors have a way of gaining acceptance, even if they're totally untrue. If Aaron wanted people to think Frank and Brianne were lovers, all he'd have to do was tell a few close friends that Frank had told him Brianne was awesome in bed. The connection would be made. Suddenly, everyone is thinking Frank and Brianne are deep in an intense relationship."

Christy chewed her lip. The vegetation thinned, chopped back from the road to allow a cluster of houses and a few fields to take root. "Aunt Ellen thought they were lovers."

"And the rest of the trustees, I'd bet," Quinn said, slowing down as they drove past the village.

"Natalie DeBolt believed it, even before Frank disappeared. The board of the IHTF was meeting about a month before it all happened. She said something about Frank and pretty blonds and women who let themselves go after their kids were born. I didn't pay any attention at the time, but after the rumors started that Frank and Brianne had come down here together, I wondered."

Quinn looked over at her and grinned. "Lady, if that's what you look like after you've let yourself go, I'd be happy to have a dozen kids with you."

The words echoed through the car. Christy's eyes widened. Quinn realized what he'd said and muttered, "That is, any man would, because you look great. Sexy, I mean. Oh, hell. Take your foot out of your mouth, Armstrong, and shut up."

Christy laughed, feeling considerably better.

Tulum was the site of the impressive remains of a Mayan city. As they drove past on their way to the resort where they were registered for the night, Christy looked wistfully at the site, wishing she had the energy to tour the ruins, but a day spent tromping around Cancun had left her footsore and ready to do nothing but eat and relax.

The resort was located on a pristine arc of white sand beach bordering an azure ocean. Waves lapped gently, but the water was crystal clear. Palm trees edged the sand and even now, toward evening, the sky was a deep, rich blue. Christy couldn't help thinking that as a place of exile, the Mexican Riviera was not much of a hardship.

The resort was a couple of stars up from the place they had stayed at in Cancun. Christy's room was lovely. Dominated by a huge four-poster bed, cool white walls, and tiled floors, it opened to a terrace that looked out onto the heart-stopping beauty of the beach.

They ate dinner in a restaurant with walls as fresh and white as those in the rooms, but accented with the vibrant colors of flowering oleander and orchids. The food was fusion cuisine, an intriguing mix of French and the local Mayan specialties. While they ate they talked about Frank's non-appearance, tossing out ideas, breaking them down, trying out new ones. In the end they kept coming back to the loose relationship between Brianne and Crack Graham and the lack of evidence that there had ever been one between her and Frank.

When Christy phoned home that evening, she called from the comfort of a wicker basket chair on the terrace outside her room. The sea was a soothing *swoosh* in the background. The sun was setting to the west, a dark curtain over the brightness of the rich, blue sky. Noelle talked excitedly about her day—Grandma had taken her to school and met Mrs. Morton, Roy had taken them to the chicken place where they'd had a feast, and she was stuffed. Then Christy's mom, Rachael, got on the phone to tell Christy everything was fine and not to worry and how were things going in Mexico?

After Christy ended the call, she thought about that question. How were things going? The truth was that she and Quinn were getting nowhere. Her mom had to be back at work on Monday, so Christy had to return to Burnaby by Sunday night. That meant she should leave tomorrow, because travel back to Vancouver from the east coast of Mexico would take most of the day.

Restless, she turned away from the white sand and enticing ocean beneath the rapidly darkening sky. She'd have a swim, then tell Quinn her decision.

The minute her naked feet touched the soft white sand, still warm from the heat of the day, she felt a kind of peace. This was such a beautiful place. It was a pity she couldn't stay longer. Maybe someday she'd come back for a proper vacation.

She was at the edge of the water, wearing nothing but her bathing suit and an almost transparent wrapper that barely reached her thighs, when she felt Quinn's presence. She looked over as he came up beside her. She smiled, and watched his answering smile light up his attractive features. "Out for a moonlight swim like me?"

"I saw you from my terrace. I hoped you wouldn't mind if I joined you."

She shook her head. "My pleasure."

They walked in silence as Christy waded through surf up to her knees. Dressed in shorts and an open necked shirt, Quinn stayed in shallower water. She stared out into the darkness. "Quinn, we're getting nowhere here."

"I can't agree." He kicked up a spray of water ahead of them. "We've proven that Crack Graham was in this area and identified why he would have returned to Vancouver. We've discovered that Brianne was here and that she was noticed and we've confirmed that Frank knows how to lie low."

"But he doesn't! Frank is used to a pampered life, to being noticed because of how he looks and who he is. Whoever arranged for Brianne and Graham to come down here knew Frank, knew his habits, his expectations. And it wasn't Frank! He would never disappear out of Noelle's life. He loves her too much." She stopped. Wrapping her arms around herself, she stared out at the darkening sky. "He used to say that Noelle would be brought up by her parents, both her parents. He'd had such a rotten childhood, he wasn't going to put his daughter through the same kind of grief."

Quinn stopped beside her. He put his hand on her shoulder, drew his thumb along her jawline. "If he didn't organize this, someone else did. That means Frank is probably dead."

"I know." Christy poked through her feelings, wishing she could grieve at the thought of Frank's death. The only emotion she was feeling, though, was the irritation that had become an everyday part of their relationship. That was partly caused by the cat, of course. Since he'd arrived, she and Frank had slipped into their usual pattern of bickering over every little thing. How could she grieve for her husband when he wouldn't get out of her head and she was always arguing with him? "It all fits, doesn't it?"

Quinn made a strangled sound and flung away. He kicked at the water, sending spray flying. "Don't tell me he's the cat, because I don't buy it!"

Christy laughed and started wading through the lazy surf again. She sympathized with Quinn. The very thought of her husband's consciousness taking up residence in a cat was absurd. "Okay, it's tough for you to accept that he's the cat. And maybe...a little too easy for me. Look, since Frank disappeared things have gone from bad to worse. When Detective Patterson told me Frank had returned I was angry. How could he come back and expect our relationship to be the same after all he'd done to me? But he never showed up. Maybe..." She looked out into the darkness, unable to face Quinn. "Maybe I just want him to be dead."

Quinn stopped. He caught her arm, turning her to face him. He was frowning. "I don't believe that."

Christy sighed. "Our marriage was over long before Frank disappeared. We stayed together for Noelle. She was Frank's heart and soul. He loved her with everything he had. If he could have been an ordinary dad, there for his kid, he would have been." A gentle breeze tugged at the wrap she'd thrown over her bathing suit and played with her hair. "I don't know why I'm telling you all this. I don't want it plastered all over the media when you write your article."

Quinn's expression was somber, yet Christy thought she saw some tenderness there as well. "We're off the record, okay?" When she nodded, he continued. "You've hinted about Frank's problems before. Were they more than too much money and not enough to do?"

"Drugs," she said quietly. "He was hooked, and no matter how hard he tried he couldn't get off them. The trustees were always on his case about quitting, but they couldn't get through to him. Neither could I."

"Let me guess. Aaron DeBolt was his supplier."

Christy looked at him in surprise. She began to walk again, splashing through the deepening water. "Yeah. How did you know?"

"You said something about DeBolt being a dealer when we went to the fundraiser."

"That's some memory you've got!"

He laughed. The sound awakened needs she had no business feeling. "Naw," he said, "I've just got a way of remembering bits and pieces of things. What I'm really good at is putting details together in some sort of pattern."

"Are you seeing a pattern now?"

"Not yet, but I will."

A wavelet broke over her thighs, warm and silky smooth. Christy made a sudden decision. She shrugged out of her wrap. "I'm going for a swim. Want to come?" She didn't wait for Quinn's reply, but ran onto the dry sand to where she dropped the thin silk. Quinn followed. As he tossed his shirt beside hers, his bare chest, covered only by a vee of dark hair that disappeared into the waistline of his shorts, gleamed in the moonlight. Christy's throat dried, and she had to swallow hard.

"Ready?" he said, taking her hand.

When she nodded, he sprinted for the tideline, dragging her along with him. Christy shrieked as the water, feeling much colder now, reached her hips. Then a wave surged up and around her. She sank into the water until she was completely wet, then floated on her back, bobbing on the gentle swells, while Quinn dove into a cresting wave.

He came up beside her, treading water. "There's another possibility we haven't considered."

"And what's that?"

"Frank got so heavily into drugs that he couldn't cope anymore. At some point he had all his ID stolen—his credit cards, his wallet, his passport, the whole lot—and now he's living on the street in a drug induced hell."

Christy stood up. She blamed the shiver that went through her to the cool of the night air on her wet skin. "I don't know which is worse, your scenario or mine."

He reached out, gently brushing back her wet hair. "When someone disappears, there are usually painful reasons behind it. But it's better to know what actually happened to them than to speculate forever."

Liquid trickled down Christy's cheek and she wondered, was it seawater from his touch or her own tears? When he put his arm around her, she sighed and leaned against him. It felt good to be held by a man.

Cocooned by the warm, silky water, she was very aware of his heat as their bodies touched. "I've been in limbo for three months. Three awful months of rumors and wondering. Three months of one bit of bad news after the other. I'm tired, Quinn. I do need closure. If Frank is still alive, he and I have to work out an arrangement that causes Noelle the least pain and gives me the freedom to live my own life. If that means divorce well, it does. If he's not alive…I need to know."

Cupping her head in his hand, Quinn gently stroked her hair with the other. "That's why we are here. We'll find out, Christy, one way or the other."

"Thank you," she whispered.

He nodded, then slowly, giving her time to pull away, he drew her in. Her lips parted. Inches away, he paused.

She said huskily, "Don't stop."

He obeyed her. His lips touched hers, a featherlight caress that was followed by a teasing nibble. Her pulse pounded while her body sang with anticipation. She put her hands on his shoulders, needing his support, wanting to feel the texture of his skin beneath her fingertips. The nibbles firmed into a kiss that took and demanded more.

Christy gave it. She pressed her body against his, scraped her teeth over his lip. Her touch was rough enough for him to feel, soft enough to tantalize. His quick intake of breath brought her pleasure and encouraged her to use the tip of her tongue to caress the place she'd nipped. That roused him to a quick response. His hand pushed through her hair to the back of her head, holding her fast while his mouth hardened over hers and his tongue stroked her lips.

Her blood pounded in her head, chasing away inhibitions. Christy was vaguely aware that she shouldn't allow this to go any further. The cat's claim that Frank was dead aside, she was still married to the man and she'd promised to be faithful to him throughout their lives together. If she allowed the wonderful sensations Quinn was creating to go further, she'd break that promise. Then, as pleasant as the physical act would be, she'd have to deal with the emotional aftermath. Guilt. Recriminations. Regret. Was she ready for that?

He slid his hand up her bare midriff to her bikini top. Her breath caught. He broke the kiss to look into her eyes. "You want me."

"Yes." She wanted him to push the fabric aside, to fondle her breast. She wanted him to kiss her again. And, worst of all, she wanted him to use the erection she could feel hard against her. So what did she do?

Her body was shrieking, *Yes! Yes! Go for it!* But her emotions?

He was a reporter. Yes, he was helping her now, and he'd said something earlier about being off the record, but what about the future? "Quinn…"

He stroked her lips with the pad of his thumb. "I didn't expect this, Christy."

"Neither did I." She groaned, fighting herself. "Quinn," she whispered.

He smiled at her. "Yes?"

He was giving her time to think. To decide. "I...we're on a beach."

"Yes." He kissed the edge of her mouth, that tender, sensitive spot where her lips joined.

"Stop. No, don't stop. Oh! We're in the open. Anyone could walk by and see us."

"It's dark. We're in the water. No one can see us."

She sighed. For a time she allowed herself to fall into the sensation. She wrapped her arms around his neck and kissed him with the pent up need of months of abstinence and a great deal of attraction. It would be so easy to sink into the water together, or walk up the beach to her room. Easy and intensely pleasurable.

Too easy. Completely wrong.

She pulled away. Putting her forehead on his shoulder she said, "I'm sorry. I can't do this."

His body stilled. Catching her chin, he forced her to look up. In the darkness his expression was shadowy, hard to read.

"I'm sorry," she said again. "I...I'm married. I don't fool around, no matter what my husband has done, or is doing. I...I want you, Quinn, but I can't. If we made love now, here or in one of our rooms, I would be angry at myself, guilty I suppose." She untwined her arms and put them on his shoulders to push him away.

He stopped her with a gentle touch on her lips with one finger. "Sh."

They stood like that, still bound by desire but slowly easing apart emotionally. The sea lapped around them, cooling the heat in their bodies. Finally Quinn drew a deep breath and let it out in a long, hard sigh. "It's okay. We're okay. I'm not going to pretend that I don't wish we were ending this differently, but I can't argue with a woman who is faithful to her vows. I will promise you one thing, Christy Jamieson."

"What is that?"

"When this is over, when we've found Frank and you know where you stand, we'll finish this."

"What if Frank and I decide to get back together?"

He kissed her. "Then we'll have to see who is the better match for you, won't we?"

CHAPTER 14

People did stupid things in the heat of the moment. Quinn shifted uncomfortably in his seat as the steward explained safety procedures at the front of the cabin. There'd been a lot of heat in that moment in the surf. Desire, passion, need—they'd all been there, softening him up, providing him with the opportunity to open his mouth and say something reckless.

And, oh man, he'd really done it.

The plane powered up, rushing forward. The nose tilted and, with a great leap, it was airborne. The engines throbbed. The ground fell away below them. Quinn stared out at golden beaches fringing the perfect aquamarine of the sea as the jet circled. Then it headed northwest, over the dark, rich green of the lush vegetation. He'd come to Mexico with Christy intent on finding her husband. He was leaving pretty much convinced that Frank had never been in this part of Mexico or any other of its many regions. Which could leave Christy Jamieson a free woman, a prospect that terrified him.

The plane leveled off. The cabin crew made noises in the galley, and a drinks cart appeared in the aisle. When it reached him, Quinn ordered a scotch. He didn't know which was worse, having Christy off limits because she was married and faithful, or having her free and open to new relationships. Like a relationship with him.

The problem was, Christy was a commitment kind of person, and he was not. Commitment was permanent. Committed relationships lasted a lifetime, like the one his parents had had. Committed relationships meant bending and shaping your life to fit it into someone else's. Commitment meant staying in one place, bonding with one person, sharing their pain, watching them grieve. Commitment meant sacrifice.

Been there, done that.

He swirled the scotch in his glass and turned his attention to the window. They were higher now, flying through gossamer wisps of pure white cloud that probably looked thick and solid from the dark, lush jungles spread out below. It was all about perceptions, wasn't it?

Two years ago his mother had died. At the funeral he'd watched his father stare at her casket, his expression empty. Not vague, not lost in his imaginings, just blank, as if the essence of Roy Armstrong was not at home. In that moment he'd decided he would take a leave of absence so he could stay in Vancouver with Roy, to help him over the first raw pain of his loss. That's how he'd sold it to his father anyway.

What a crock.

The truth was that on assignment in Africa he'd met a woman, a doctor working in a refugee camp, who believed her role in life was to tend to those displaced, dispossessed, and all but destroyed by the savagery of wars they didn't start and couldn't end. Her name was Tamara and she was brilliant, furious, and stubborn. He'd fallen for her passion, for her need to right the wrongs around her. He'd loved the way she fought against the restrictions surrounding her and the intensity with which she protected those she cared for.

He knew her for two months. Two months of fierce lovemaking and heart-stopping moments when the war came to them—or when she went to the battlefields in some quixotic errand of mercy.

And that was how it ended, in a hot, dry place where the necessities of life—food, water, and shelter—were scarce and the rules of war didn't exist. She had been a civilian, a healer, her goal to help, not to harm. That hadn't mattered to the group that ambushed her temporary camp.

He hadn't been with her when she was killed. He regretted that. He wondered if he could have saved her if he'd been there. He would always wonder.

Now, three years later, the questions didn't hurt so much. He'd come to Vancouver to heal his father, to help him grieve. Instead, he'd allowed himself to grieve. Now he was able to look back at what was, rather than what might have been. Tamara had been fierce in her beliefs, exciting to be with, and driven by such passion that she dragged everyone along with her. He doubted she was a commitment kind of person, at least not the kind of commitment that created families, nurtured kids, and lasted into old age. She had lived her life in the moment, intensely, so that every emotion was magnified.

Sex had been great. Fierce and fast, the kind of passion that left marks on the body from rough loving. There was no tenderness between them. Tamara hadn't wanted it, and it had never occurred to him that she would. But tenderness was a facet of loving, part of commitment, something they didn't have.

After her death, he had wanted to believe he would have had a continuing relationship with Tamara had she lived. He'd told himself that as he wrote her story. His words shone a light on a dirty civil war that made children into killers and leached the humanity out of all who were trapped within it. It was her cause and, for a time, his crusade. The article had won him awards, but no satisfaction.

Which brought him back, in a roundabout way, to Christy Jamieson, because he'd met her when he was in pursuit of a story, as he had met Tamara. Six weeks ago this had all been so easy. Frank Jamieson was potential unused, money misused, and relationships based on wealth, not caring. By all accounts his wife was a gold digger who had found her pot and then lost it. Some stories about Christy Jamieson were sympathetic, others downright hostile. All assumed that she only used her head to support her mane of bright blond hair.

There was little to like in that image, and he'd gone to the Jamieson mansion prepared to do a scathing exposé of the highlife gone bad. Instead, he'd found a single mom doing her best to raise her daughter when the world had turned against her. The highlife gone bad was there, but it wasn't Christy who was the example, it was her husband, the charming, well-liked heir of the Ice Cream King.

Quinn had never been one to avoid plunging into the emotional soup of whatever stories he worked on, or causes he believed in. When he committed to something, he believed in becoming actively involved. If a cause was just, it deserved the best each participant could bring to it.

And now his cause was Christy Jamieson and her quest to discover what had happened to her husband. And he had dived right in. Oh yeah, he was right there, emotionally involved and every day he worked with Christy he swam into deeper water. Though she didn't rush off to undeveloped corners of the world to rescue the downtrodden, she was the kind of woman he was attracted to. Strong in the face of adversity, yet loving and gentle with those around her, and passionate and willing to fight for what was important to her.

Quinn downed a slug of scotch, enjoying the burn in his throat. He'd blown it that night on the beach. He should have suggested sex, kept it light, but he'd heard the sadness in her voice when she started talking about her husband being dead, and he'd ached for her. He'd begun with the intention of comforting her, but those feelings he didn't want to admit to grabbed hold, and he allowed himself to make a promise that shouted "relationship!"

So now what? Should he stay away from her once he got back to Vancouver? Cut the connection so he could make sure that a relationship—the committed, family kind of relationship—would never grow between them?

He sipped again, more slowly this time. That wouldn't be fair to Christy. She needed closure. He understood that. She needed his help to find the information that would allow her to achieve that closure. He couldn't cut out on her now.

There he was, he thought wryly, deep in her emotional soup. No objectivity. What he should do was step away. Remember that this was the story that would bring him back into the public eye, net him a posting to one of the hotspots of the world. He didn't have time for relationships, particularly *committed* relationships.

In fact, he'd better stop fretting over his emotional future and get to work. The cabin crew had finished the drinks service and had retreated to the galley to take a break before preparing the flight for landing in Mexico City. He pulled out the pictures of Brianne and Crack Graham on the off chance that this might have been the crew that flew them on the first leg of to their trip back to Vancouver.

He was in luck. One of the attendants remembered Brianne. She'd been flying first class and had had too much to drink. She'd had a fight with the man traveling with her. Loud and nasty, their battle had the other first class passengers groaning and complaining.

When Quinn showed the attendant the picture of Frank and asked if he was the man Brianne was with, the attendant shook her head, but she nodded emphatically at the photo of the small-time hood, Thaddeus 'Crack' Graham. "That was the guy," she said. "About as mean as they come, I'd guess. If they hadn't been in the middle of a crowded cabin, I bet he would have taken a swing at her."

"Anything else you think might help?" Quinn asked.

The attendant stared at the picture thoughtfully. "The guy was pretty mad," she said finally. "At one point he said he was glad this stupid—well, he didn't use that nice a word—but anyway, he was glad this stupid con was almost over because being with her wasn't worth the money." She handed back the photos with a smile.

Quinn took the photos and made a note of the woman's name. A con, the attendant had said. Back in his seat, Quinn closed his eyes to block out his surroundings as he tried to put the pieces together in a pattern.

Frank Jamieson, drug addict, embezzler, missing. Brianne Lymbourn, a woman anxious to become Mrs. Frank Jamieson with little hope of achieving her goal. Crack Graham, a small-time hood with the basic physical attributes of Frank Jamieson. The pattern that was forming was beginning to look pretty clear.

A con to mask Frank Jamieson's disappearance?

Or worse? Murder and a cover up.

"Thank you for meeting with us, Detective Patterson," Christy said.

Patterson shrugged. "What's up?"

Christy drew a deep breath. "Quinn and I have found some disturbing information relating to my husband's case."

They were sitting in the same dingy coffee shop where Billie Patterson had told Christy that Frank was back in Vancouver not so long ago.

"Such as?" Patterson asked. She lifted the thick white coffee mug to her lips and took a sip. Over the rim her eyes were watchful.

"Frank wasn't the one who switched declaration forms at the airport."

That made Patterson sit up. She set the coffee mug down on the table with a clunk. "Run that by me again?"

"Why don't I begin at the beginning?" Christy said. Billie nodded. "After I asked Quinn to help me, we went to the hotel where Brianne was staying. None of the staff were able to identify Frank from the photograph we took with us and he wasn't registered at the hotel."

Patterson sat back. She looked relaxed, but her eyes were alert. "Maybe the people you interviewed didn't recognize him. That's not a big deal. Hotels have lots of people in and out. They can't remember everyone."

"They remembered Brianne." Patterson shrugged again. Christy wrapped her hands around her thick, white mug. "But you're right. There's no guarantee. That's why we checked the other hotels in town. None of them had Frank registered."

"So what did Brianne say when you tracked her down?"

"We didn't," Quinn said. He was sitting beside Christy, angled into the corner of the booth. His voice sent a shiver of awareness down her spine. Why was she so attracted to him? He was an associate, a reporter. Out of bounds!

Billie Patterson sat up. "Let me get this straight. You found Brianne Lymbourn, but she wouldn't talk to you. Nor would the man she was with. Is that correct?"

Quinn leaned forward in a lazy, fluid movement that had all of Christy's nerve endings tingling. "We never found Brianne. By the time we got to the hotel she'd already checked out, with no forwarding address. So we looked for her. I checked the places she used to go and talked to some, though not all, of her friends. A couple said they'd seen her at The Rainmaker Club and she bragged about having no money problems. No one I talked to knew where she was staying or had her new phone number."

Billie took refuge behind the coffee cup again. "Lots of people move around and don't let their friends know their new address. So Ms. Lymbourn doesn't want to get back with her old crowd. Maybe she's changed her lifestyle and no longer has much in common with them."

"Maybe," Quinn said. "But at the hotel, where they remembered Brianne, no one who could ID Frank. What they do remember is a blond guy about the same height, with the same color eyes as Frank."

The waitress showed up to refill their coffee cups. She started to chat, but Billie shot her a smile that held a warning. She finished pouring quickly, then went off to a friendlier table.

Christy opened a folder. "We have a picture of the man we think Brianne was traveling with." She pushed the grainy photocopy across the table to Billie. "He's a drug dealer named Crack Graham. We believe he met Brianne sometime before Frank's disappearance, possibly through the crowd she and Frank ran with. Most of them did drugs and most of them were pretty well off."

"I've heard of him," Billie said. She was frowning over the picture. "I suppose his physical description could be mistaken for Frank Jamieson's. But if he was using your husband's passport the picture would have had to be changed."

"Not such a big deal," Quinn said.

"No. More difficult than it once was, but doable if you have the money to spend." Billie was staring intently at the picture. Finally she put it on the table.

Quinn tapped the photo. "Once I found this picture, I took it down to the Strand Manor. They identified Crack Graham as the man staying with Brianne. That made us wonder whether Frank ever left the country."

"Whoa!" Billie said. "You've done a major leap of logic here. Take me through the steps."

"For the last three months Frank is supposed to have been in Mexico," Christy said as Quinn paused to drink his coffee. "He turned up there about a week after he disappeared."

Billie said, "We hadn't had any ransom demands, so I was starting to wonder if he'd had some kind of accident on his way home from the club."

Christy nodded. "I remember you telling me that I was going to have to consider that possibility. We were in the living room at the mansion. I was sitting on an antique settee that was worth thousands and was the most uncomfortable piece of furniture ever made. The trustees were all there. Samuel Macklin looked relieved that the Trust wasn't going to have to pay out any cash, and Edward Bidwell started talking about Noelle becoming the Jamieson heir. Gerry Fisher was sitting beside me, patting my hand, and Frank's Aunt Ellen didn't say or do a thing. She didn't protest. She didn't cry. She acted like she didn't care. She brought him up, for Pete's sake!"

Quinn put his hand over hers and squeezed it comfortingly. Christy looked over at him. She smiled shakily then looked at Patterson. "Sorry about that."

Billie nodded, her expression unreadable. Christy had a feeling that she'd put up a defensive barrier around herself, one that kept out the emotions of the victims she was trained to help. "Just after that meeting there was a report in the paper, a scoop, that Frank had been seen in Mexico. Then after that the media reported everything—the embezzlement, Frank taking Brianne with him to Mexico."

"Look, Mrs. Jamieson, I know it's hard to accept that your husband has been playing around on you, but—"

"Those stories were planted." As Quinn cut incisively into Billie Patterson's world-weary platitude the expression on his face was dangerous. "They all came from one source, a second-rate stringer who received a series of anonymous tips. Whoever sent them provided the information in the form of a press release. The reporter did a little basic research, then reworked the original material and sold it as his own."

The atmosphere at the table had cooled to frosty. Billie Patterson was sitting up straight in her seat, her hands closed tightly around the coffee mug, while Quinn slouched, apparently relaxed in his chair. Only his narrowed eyes and tight jaw indicated his feelings.

Christy intervened hastily. She needed Billie Patterson's help and support. "Quinn and I went to Mexico, to the Cancun area where the sightings of Frank were made, to find out whether he and Brianne were ever really there. We didn't find anyone who remembered seeing Frank. We did find people who saw Brianne and Crack Graham together."

"That doesn't prove Frank wasn't in the area." Patterson didn't sound or look particularly impressed.

"What do you need as proof, an engraved business card saying 'I was not in Mexico?'" Quinn asked.

Patterson flushed. "Look, I'm a cop. We deal in facts, not speculation. Yeah, you've got proof Crack Graham was in Mexico. So what? Anyone can go to Mexico. They don't need a travel visa. The only reason they need a passport is because they're flying over U.S. air space."

"Crack has a record. He's done time. He couldn't get a passport of his own, and I believe he would face travel restrictions when crossing the border to another country." Quinn's voice was silky smooth.

Billie frowned at him. "Could be."

"And here's another point I can prove. Graham was on the plane seated beside Brianne when she returned to Canada. Frank was not on that plane. I have witnesses."

"Who?"

"The flight crew. Graham and Brianne had a fight on the plane, a very loud, very public argument in which the word 'con' was mentioned."

"So it's fair to assume that Crack Graham was out of the country and using someone else's passport to make him seem like an ordinary Canadian traveling for pleasure," Christy said.

Patterson traced a circle on the table with the base of her mug. "And you think that passport was Frank's."

"I do, but I don't know how Graham got hold of it."

Patterson stared at Christy for a minute, then she put her cup on the Formica table top with a decided *thump*, as if she'd just come to a decision. "I think I can guess. Do you remember the robbery at your home that happened just after Frank disappeared?"

Christy's brow furrowed. "Vividly. Not much was taken, but the safe was opened. The trustees were furious. Gerry Fisher sacked the security guard on duty that night."

"Yeah. The safe was cleared out," Billie said. "You said at the time that Frank only kept a few papers and his passport there. No money or jewels, just his passport, and it was gone."

"That's true." Beside her Christy was aware of Quinn straightening. "I wondered about that at the time, then the reports started to come in that Frank had been seen abroad with Brianne. He would have needed his passport if he wanted to go to Europe or somewhere else in the world, so

I assumed he'd been carrying it with him the night he walked out on me and that I was wrong about it being in the safe."

"So did I," Billie said. She took a pad and a pen from a coat pocket and started to make notes. "Jamieson disappearance. Passport very likely stolen. No evidence Jamieson ever left Vancouver. Evidence a mid-level drug dealer whose physical stats are similar to Frank Jamieson's was using his passport." She looked up. "So here's the big question. Why?"

Quinn leaned forward again. His expression, his body language was intense, a man passionate about the idea he was about to impart. "My guess is that someone offered Graham the opportunity for an all-expenses paid trip to Mexico as part of an elaborate hoax that includes manipulation of the media and a body double to put Frank Jamieson somewhere far away. That meant Graham had to be seen with Brianne Lymbourn from time to time, but otherwise he was free to do whatever he wanted. He chose to make contacts with the local drug crowd and set himself up as a new conduit for drugs coming into Vancouver. When he hopped on that plane a month ago, it was because he had his supply channels set up and now he needed to get back to Vancouver to put them into action."

"You're suggesting that he's now working on his own."

Quinn nodded. "I'll also bet that whoever arranged for him to go down to Mexico is mighty surprised that he's back home again."

"Possibly. I'll look into it, but I still need a reason why someone would want Graham to impersonate Frank Jamieson."

"I believe Frank is dead, Detective Patterson." Beside her Quinn tensed. Christy almost laughed. She'd bet that he was afraid she'd bring up the conversations she had with Stormy the Cat. "I think someone murdered him."

Billie stared at her. "That's a hell of a statement, Mrs. Jamieson. Who would want to kill your husband? And for what possible motive?" She waited a heartbeat, then, when

Christy didn't reply added, "We don't even have a body to prove your allegation."

"Do we need one?" Quinn said impatiently.

Patterson slid Quinn a hard look that spoke volumes. Quinn raised a brow, his expression critical. With the two of them shooting daggers at each other, Christy ruthlessly dragged the discussion back to the basics. "I think someone was stealing from Frank's trust fund. They had to make sure he disappeared forever to cover their tracks."

The waitress appeared again, holding up her coffee beaker. Patterson shook her head. She snapped her notebook closed as the waitress moved away. "All of this— someone other than Frank Jamieson using his ID, his disappearance not being voluntary—hinges on a conspiracy to steal from the Jamieson Trust." She tapped the notebook with her pen, thinking. Quinn watched her intently. Christy fiddled with the handle of her coffee cup. She wasn't sure she wanted to know what exactly was going on. She knew she had to find out.

"Okay. What we need to do is trace the financial dealings." Patterson pointed at Christy with her pen. "You're one of the recipients of the trust. With all the reports of embezzlement going on, you could ask for an audit and no one would be surprised."

Beside her, Christy sensed Quinn stiffening as Patterson laid out her plan. "I could, but I don't know any auditors."

"I do," Billie said. "I'll set up the auditor. You square it with the trustees."

"Wait a second," Quinn said. "Whoever embezzled from Frank's trust fund isn't going to like the idea of an audit. That could put Christy in danger."

Billie looked at Christy. She raised her brows in a question.

A little shakily, Christy said, "I need to know the truth, Quinn." She turned to Patterson. "I'll do it."

CHAPTER 15

"An audit? Christy, why on earth do you want an audit?" Gerry Fisher's voice was puzzled. It had been angry a few minutes ago when she first brought up the subject.

"Gerry, Frank is back in Vancouver. He hasn't come to visit me, he hasn't called, and he hasn't tried to see Noelle. I can't live like this. I need closure. I need to know what is going on." Christy's palms were sweating. She rubbed one hand on her pant leg, then the other. It was a good thing that Gerry, on the other end of the telephone line, couldn't see her face, because he'd know she was telling him some great big whopping lies.

"I can understand your distress, Christy," Gerry said. His tone was sympathetic. "Frank is a good man, but he tends to be careless of people's feelings. I'm sure he'll get in touch with you sooner or later."

Gerry had always been the most supportive of the trustees, but sometimes he treated her as if she was a dimwitted child who would do what she was told. Time to be assertive. Christy wiped those sweaty palms again and took a deep breath. "Gerry, I have my daughter to consider. She has questions about her father and why he never comes home anymore. Questions I can't answer. I think we both need to move on, to take Frank out of the center of our lives and put him on the edge where he clearly wants to be."

"I'm not sure I understand, Christy. What's this got to do with an audit?"

Christy drew a deep breath. Her heart was pounding. This was it. The BIG EXCUSE. She'd worked it out last night, while lying sleepless in bed. It was the reason for the audit, something that would make sense to Gerry Fisher. "I'm going to divorce Frank. He has clearly abandoned us. Once our marriage is over, I'll be able to provide a more stable environment for Noelle."

"Is there a man in your life? Is someone forcing you to do this?" Fisher asked.

"No!"

"Are you sure?" His voice had hardened.

Christy shivered. "I'm sure."

"What about that fellow with the writer father?"

Gerry sounded like a parent grilling his teenage daughter about her boyfriends. Like that teenage daughter, Christy couldn't help the uneasy guilt that colored her voice as she responded. "Gerry, I make my own decisions. I'm doing this because I want the best for Noelle—"

"The best for Noelle is to have her parents living together, with her."

"Agreed. I think you need to have this conversation with Frank, not me."

Gerry laughed at that. The laugh was an ironic chuckle rather than a great sidesplitting guffaw, almost as if he knew that finding Frank was impossible. "Frank will come to us when he's ready."

This gave Christy the opening to drag the conversation away from divorce and back to the audit. "In the meantime, he's got plenty of opportunity to embezzle what remains of the trust."

"He won't, Christy. We're on to him now. We've made sure he can't steal anything more."

Christy's hand was sweating again. She changed the phone from one ear to the other and wiped her palm.

"Gerry, how much did Frank take? When and why? How long did it go on? I need to know these things. Every time the company makes an announcement or launches a new product, there's a story about Frank, the Ice Cream King's embezzling heir. Noelle is eight years old! It won't be long before she starts watching the TV news and reading headlines on her iPad. I have to be able to tell her what is truth and what is fabrication. For her sake, I have to find Frank."

"You're overreacting."

She almost snapped, *Don't patronize me!* but she didn't. She bit her tongue and held her peace, but she gave up on the reasonable discussion approach and headed directly into confrontation. "Gerry, funds have been stolen from the Jamieson Trust. That requires an audit. I don't care if it was my husband who did the stealing. I want an audit, and I'm sending in an auditor today. He should be on his way there now. Please instruct the staff to have the documents ready for him."

"This is incredibly inconvenient!"

"I wish there was another way, but the man I found is in my price range and he's willing to work over the weekend, to reduce the disruption to the office staff."

There was a fuming silence, then, "I can't convince you to change your mind?"

"No."

"All right. I'll set it up. What's the man's name?"

When Christy put down the phone she was trembling. She brewed a cup of coffee to steady herself. Holding the mug in both hands, she went out onto the porch. The sky was cloudless, the temperature cool. The last of Vancouver's summer sunshine before the autumn rains set in. She sat down on the steps and drank the coffee as if that ordinary pleasure could somehow take away the feeling that she'd just sent a snowball rolling down a mountain and started an avalanche.

Quinn's car drove slowly down the street, then turned into his carport. Christy drank more coffee and waited. He came out, saw her sitting on her step, and walked over.

His smile made her shiver again, but in a much nicer way than before.

He sat beside her. "So, did you do it?"

"Yes."

"How did Fisher take it?"

"He wasn't happy. He tried to persuade me to give up the idea, but in the end he caved." She drank more coffee, shook. Quinn put his arm around her shoulder, pulled her against him. It was meant to be a comforting gesture, and it was. It also sent Christy's pulse rate into the stratosphere.

"How did you convince him an audit was necessary?" he said. His breath ruffled her hair and tickled some very sensitive skin near her ear.

She said rather breathlessly, "I told him I wanted a divorce from Frank."

Quinn's arm tightened for a few seconds before he pulled away. "A divorce? Do you think that was wise?"

She shrugged. Even though it was just a hug, she missed the warmth of his body against hers, the strength of his arm holding her secure. "I figured it sounded realistic coming from a woman whose husband deserted her and ran off with another woman." She shot a quick look at him from underneath her lashes. He was a great looking guy, dressed now in jeans and a V-necked sweater that hugged his body and showed off his toned physique. He was frowning, his expression concerned. She smiled at him, but he didn't smile back. Her smile faded.

"Did he ask how long you've been planning this?"

"No. He just told me that Noelle deserved to have both of her parents raising her." She looked down at her feet. "It's a reasonable point of view, but so is the concept of a divorce. Frank was an addict. I wanted him to get treatment, but he wouldn't or couldn't. Frank and I bickered about his drug use for at least a year before he disappeared. I told him his habit was interfering with Noelle's life and mine, and that if he didn't stop, I'd leave him and take Noelle with me."

"But you didn't."

She shook her head, staring, not at Quinn, but at the house across the way. It was painted a different color from hers, but the trim was white, just as it was on her unit. "He kept promising he'd change, and I kept saying if he didn't I'd leave. Every time we argued a little part of my love for him died. Every time Noelle said, 'Where's Daddy tonight, Mommy?' I bled for her and cursed her father, until there was nothing left of what I'd felt when I married him. I suppose on the surface we seemed to have a stable marriage. That's why guys like Gerry Fisher are surprised when I mention divorce."

"Living with a drug addict must be tough."

Quinn's matter-of-fact tone was a balm. She glanced over at him with a smile. Then her heart stopped at the intensity in his eyes.

Hey babe! What's up?

Christy dragged her gaze away from Quinn's intriguing expression to see Stormy the Cat emerge from some bushes and trot up the road. In his mouth was a mouse. A dead mouse. She hoped. "What have you done?"

Quinn frowned, clearly puzzled.

Christy shook her head and pointed. "Not you, Quinn, the cat. What's he got in his mouth?"

His brows snapped together in a frown. "Looks like Stormy is a mouser."

"Frank! Make Stormy take that poor creature back into the bushes and bury it. Immediately."

Stormy reached the bottom of her stairs. He spat out the mouse then sat down and licked each front paw in turn. *The cat is pleased with himself. I don't think burying the mouse is in the cards, Chris.*

"Ugh," Christy said. "Are you going to eat it?"

There was a mental sigh.

"I'll find some tuna," Christy said a little desperately. The cat raised his chin and fixed wide green eyes on her.

"The mention of tuna seems to have struck a chord," Quinn said.

"I think I'm being blackmailed," Christy said. She shook her finger at the cat. "No tuna unless you give that poor creature a proper burial."

The cat stared at her, unblinking.

He's reluctant. He wants the mouse and the tuna too. I'm working on him.

"The deal's off if the mouse isn't buried."

The cat scrutinized her for another minute, then picked up the mouse and trotted off down the road. When it disappeared into the shrubbery Quinn said, "That almost makes me believe the cat is communicating with you."

She smiled. "And if you believe the cat is communicating, will you also believe he's a reincarnation of Frank?"

Quinn's mouth quirked. "A hallucination, maybe."

Christy stood up, ready to fulfill her part of the bargain. "It sure would fit in with his lifestyle."

"My findings are not conclusive, you understand."

Harry Endicott, the auditor supplied by Billie Patterson, was a middle-aged man, overweight and on his way to a big gut. His face was round, and the extra flesh at his jawline sagged into a second chin that jiggled as he talked. His tie was unloosened and he wasn't wearing a jacket, a sensible precaution, for his office was in an old building that featured heritage construction and a furnace that pumped out heat like fuel oil was still at 1950s prices. There was no ventilation system. The old-fashioned sash windows were supposed to be used to supply fresh air, but they had been painted shut long before, and even though it was October the rooms were hot and stuffy.

Endicott brushed his hand over an abundant mustache then continued, "A forensic audit can take months or even years to complete."

"We don't have years," Billie Patterson said. She was sitting, apparently relaxed, in one of the hard chairs that Endicott provided for his visitors. One leg was crossed over the other knee and she slouched a little, as if she had all the time in the world to listen to Endicott's assessment.

Christy did not. It was one fifteen and she had to pick up
Noelle at two forty-five. Since Endicott seemed willing to
chat forever about the philosophy behind auditing, it was
time to cut to the chase and hear what he had to report.
"Did you discover how my husband removed money from
his family trust without the trustees knowing?"

"If he did," Billie said.

Endicott played with his mustache again. "Mrs.
Jamieson, did your husband have any direct access to the
funds, beyond what the trustees dispensed to him?"

Christy shook her head. "That was one of the conflicts
between Frank and the trustees. He thought the trust should
have been wound down years ago. The trustees claimed
that it was his father's choice to end the trust when Frank
was thirty-five, not earlier, and that was that. Frank thought
their decision meant they didn't believe in him. He was
angry and always trying to find ways to poke at them or get
around their rules."

Endicott shook his head. "A sad story, but it fits with my
findings. There were at least three individuals involved in
this embezzlement, but I do not see how your husband
could have been one of them."

Christy sat forward on her hard wooden chair. "After
Frank disappeared and the money was gone, everyone
believed he was the one who took it."

"Possibly because he'd said in front of witnesses, more
than once, that the money was his and he didn't think it was
fair that a bunch of old geezers should be keeping it from
him," Patterson said.

"There can be no doubt that there were an inordinate
number of expensive charges against the trust, run up by
your husband, Mrs. Jamieson. It is my belief that he
deliberately overspent his quarterly allowance and used
credit to acquire the extras he wanted. He knew that the
trust would pay his debts. That is reprehensible, but hardly
illegal. However, unless he is a banker or in the financial
management field, I think it unlikely he would have the

expertise to transfer funds from a bank in this country to one in the Far East."

Christy shifted uneasily in her chair. She wished Harry Endicott had offered her a cup of coffee or a glass of water before they began. She needed something to hold. "Frank was a man full of talent and too much money," she said at last. "I think he would have been happy if he'd been able to manage his father's business—"

"Ah, yes, the Ice Cream King. I have wonderful memories of Jamieson Ice Cream." Endicott sighed reflectively and smiled at no one in particular. "One of their dairies was near my house. On hot summer evenings they would stay open late to serve ice cream. My parents would buy my brother and me triple scoop cones, each scoop a different flavor." Endicott rubbed his ample belly. "I buy Jamieson Ice Cream in the carton now, as a special treat." He beamed at them, energized by the memories.

Christy stared at him, grappling with the image of Harry Endicott as a child. She glanced over at Billie Patterson, who looked as astounded as Christy was feeling. "Okay. Well, as I was saying, Frank wanted to work at Jamiesons, but Gerry Fisher insisted he needed to learn the business from the bottom up because he had no experience. It was an ongoing issue between them. On the day Frank disappeared, Gerry called to say he'd set up an internship. Frank absolutely refused to participate."

"So you're saying Frank was smart enough to have done the money transfers," Patterson said.

Christy nodded.

"That's what the embezzler is counting on us believing." Patterson's tone was decisive, in contrast to her slumped, lazy position. She shook her head. "Hell, it almost worked. If that drug dealer using Jamieson's passport had stayed away, we'd never have considered anyone else."

"Three anyone else's," Harry said. He looked from Patterson to Christy. "There were definitely three minds doing the embezzlement. I could see that in the way the transactions were buried. Detective, I do not believe the

Louise Clark

clerical and secretarial staff are implicated. These transactions were done by people in a position of control."

Billie Patterson sat up straight. "The trustees?"

Harry Endicott's eyes gleamed. Very slowly he tipped his head in a nod.

You're sad.

The cat rubbed against Christy's arm, then pushed his head under her hand. Absently, she scratched behind his ears. A loud purring erupted.

"I'm not sad, not really. I'm upset. I'm worried, but not sad."

The cat beat a circle on her lap, then settled into a comfortable position that allowed continued petting. *Tell me about it, babe. I was never around when you needed me before, but a guy can change.*

Christy laughed. "I hope you are truly in there, Frank, because otherwise I'm telling my troubles to a cat and hoping for an answer."

She heard the ghost of laughter. *It's hard to get used to, isn't it?*

"Oh, yeah." She sighed. Her hand stroked rhythmically along Stormy's back. "Quinn doesn't think you're Frank."

There was a mental snort. *Quinn's a decent guy, but he's focused on the real world. He's closed his mind to things that can't be proven.*

"Maybe that's a good thing." Stroking Stormy seemed to be a good thing too. The cat was purring, filling Christy with an absurd sense of accomplishment and satisfaction. "He's going to freak when I tell him about the auditor's report."

Every one of Stormy's muscles tensed. *It's done? So quickly?*

"Yeah." Christy peered down at the cat. If nothing else, that sudden tightening would have told her Stormy was more than a normal cat. "Harry Endicott, the auditor, hasn't figured everything out yet, but he's found out enough to know that there were three people embezzling from your trust. He can't tell us who, but he's working on it."

Stormy relaxed. He put his head under Christy's hand again, inviting more petting. *Well, yeah. I was blackmailing them.*

Christy surged to her feet, bouncing the cat off her lap. "What?"

Stormy twisted into an elegant arch so he landed on his feet. *Careful!*

"You were blackmailing someone? Someones? Frank!"

The cat turned his back on her and busied himself with cleaning behind his ears by licking one paw then rubbing it over his head.

Christy circled round him, so they were again face-to-face. "Frank, who were you blackmailing? Three people, your trustees? Tell Stormy to stop cleaning himself and talk to me!"

The cat glared at her, but after a final rub, he stopped preening and paid attention.

"That's better. Frank, why didn't you tell me about this before?"

There was a mental shrug, and the answer was laced with defiance. *You would have reacted the same way you did just now. We've been getting on pretty well and I thought…I didn't want you to be upset.*

"Not upset? Frank!"

The telephone rang. Christy looked toward the sound, debating whether she should answer or have this out with Frank now. Stormy decided the issue by heading down the stairs toward his litter box. Christy went for the phone. "Hello?"

"Christy, it's Gerry Fisher."

Oh God, not now, not when she'd just learned that her husband might have been blackmailing the man on the other end of the phone line. "Uh, hi, Gerry. What's up?"

"We, the other trustees and I, need to see you. We expect you at Jamieson Ice Cream in an hour."

"But—"

"Be there." Gerry hung up the phone.

Christy stared at the handset, listening to the buzzing dial
tone, thinking furiously. The Trust had an office in the
Jamieson Ice Cream building on Georgia. This had to be
about the audit, and about the blackmailing. Dear heavens,
Frank was blackmailing three of his trustees. Was it
possible? Which ones?

In the way of cats, Stormy trotted back into the living
room as if nothing untoward had happened. Christy
rounded on him. "Why?"

Frank didn't pretend to misunderstand. *They were
keeping me on a short leash, Chris. Even though I asked,
they wouldn't increase my allowance. I wanted more. I
deserved more. Hell, it was my trust fund! So I made them
give it to me.*

Christy could imagine the charming smile Frank would
have used as he said those words. His rueful, little boy grin
that had helped him avoid far too much in his lifetime. "Not
good enough, Frank! You were blackmailing people.
That's illegal."

It was my trust fund.

The tone was petulant, the excuse self-serving. Christy
had heard that note of self-righteous indignation many
times before, particularly when she criticized Frank for
partying too much or doing drugs. This particular attitude
was a showstopper because not only did it mean that Frank
had no intention of explaining any further, but it also made
her abandon the argument with a growl of frustration. This
time was no exception. She made an irritated sound in her
throat and headed up the stairs.

Stormy followed. *Where are you going?*

"I have to go downtown to see the Trustees."

What? You can't!

Christy stopped in her bedroom doorway and faced her
cat. "I have to. That was Gerry Fisher on the phone and he
summoned me, now."

Don't go!

Thoroughly annoyed at both Frank and Gerry Fisher, Christy said, "Gerry didn't offer me a choice. I have to go."

This is not good, Chris. Ignore him. What can he do to you if you don't show up?

"I don't know! And I don't want to find out." She slammed the door in the cat's face. Stormy whined a few times and scratched on the panel, but inside the room, Christy ignored him as she hastily changed out of her sweatshirt and jeans into a ribbed top and mini-skirt that made her look stylish and feel good about herself. A quick brush of her layered brown hair and a flick with her lipstick and she was ready.

When she came out the hall was empty. That suited her just fine. She checked her watch, saw she had a scant half hour to get to the city and ran down the stairs. Grabbing her purse, she headed outside.

There she found Roy Armstrong, peacefully sitting on her front steps with Stormy beside him. A joint drooped between his fingers. Smoke curled from the glowing end. "The cat doesn't think it's a good idea for you to go to this meeting."

"The cat doesn't have a say."

Roy shot her an amused look as he nodded. He took a drag, savored the smoke, slowly exhaled, then dropped the butt onto the pavement and ground it out with his foot. "I thought you'd say that." He picked up the squashed butt, dug a little hole in the soft earth in the garden box, and buried it. "Still, it seems to me that if you go, you should have back up." He picked up a backpack that was sitting on the steps.

"And that would be you?"

Roy grinned. "That would be me. Armed with my laptop, cell phone, and my dubious celebrity as an award-winning author."

Christy stood stock-still, staring at him. "Come again?"

"Cell phone to connect to Quinn and have him meet us there so we don't just disappear, laptop to remind your trustees that my pen can be lethal, and my fame to convince them that I can hang them out in front of a huge audience."

There was a light in his eyes that Christy could only describe as pleasurable excitement. "You've done this before."

Roy laughed. "What's the good of having power if you don't bother to use it?"

CHAPTER 16

"Who's he?" Indignation laced Edward Bidwell's tone, and his long features were screwed up into a frown as he pointed at Roy Armstrong, who had settled himself on a cream colored leather chair in the sumptuous reception area.

Christy looked at Roy, viewing him through Bidwell's eyes. What she saw was a middle-aged man, pushing senior citizen, dressed in worn jeans, a checked shirt, and running shoes. A leather bomber jacket was casually open over the checked shirt. His face was shaven, but his iron-gray hair hadn't been cut in a long while and was tied back in a ponytail. Though he was clean, he looked far from prosperous and totally out of place against the thick pile carpet and wood-lined walls of the Jamieson Trust office suite in the Jamieson Ice Cream building.

"Edward Bidwell, this is my neighbor and friend, Roy Armstrong. Roy, Edward is one of trustees of the Jamieson Trust." Roy cast Bidwell a long, hard look as he nodded acknowledgement. While Bidwell turned purple with annoyance, Roy rummaged through his backpack, which he'd dumped on the floor beside him. He pulled out a laptop, flipped open the lid, and pressed the power button. The screen flickered, then came alive.

"Roy, how delightful to see you again." Ellen Jamieson advanced with both hands outstretched.

Bidwell snorted. Roy moved the laptop to a nearby table and stood.

Ellen took advantage of the moment to take both of Roy's hands and sneak in a continental greeting. Roy managed to kiss air through the process. Ellen achieved two very real kisses as they brushed cheeks. "Edward, Gerry has met Roy, but I don't think you have had the opportunity. He is a fabulous writer and quite my favorite author. He wins awards and his books are made into the most haunting movies." Ellen beamed at the assembled company. Roy blushed.

"So what is a famous author doing in the Trust's office at exactly the same time as we have a meeting with Christy?" Edward asked, eying Roy through narrowed eyes.

"As Christy mentioned, he's her neighbor," Gerry Fisher said. He made no effort to shake Roy's hand or even greet him directly.

Bidwell glanced from Gerry to Roy, then back to Gerry again. The two men exchanged looks. "I see," Bidwell said, sounding as if he'd just learned the prosecution's star witness had shoplifted as a kid.

"I can work pretty much anywhere." Roy smiled as if he wasn't aware of the tension in the room, or the annoyance. "Christy needed company, and I wanted a fresh perspective, so here we are."

"It's so exciting to see an author at work." It didn't seem to matter to Ellen that Roy wasn't doing anything except talk at the moment. The expression in her eyes really did indicate Roy and his creative process fascinated her. "Do you have a new book coming out soon?"

"I'm working on a family saga of missing relatives, embezzlement, and redemption," Roy said blandly. "I expect to turn it in to my editor in a month or two."

Even the gushing Ellen caught the innuendo in that one. Gerry Fisher said curtly, "We should get started. Christy, I hope you understand your friend cannot be part of this meeting."

Christy's heart thumped with nervousness, then steadied. Roy had coached her in the techniques of civil disobedience all through the drive into the city. *They want to know what you know about the audit. Don't let them scare you. Remember, you don't have to tell them what you know, and they can't do anything to you. Limit the length of time you'll meet with them, then stand by it.* She took a deep breath. "Yes, Gerry, I'm with you." She glanced at her watch. "I can give you half an hour. Where are we meeting? In the conference room?"

"That's right. Sam is already set up there."

Christy nodded. "Right. Roy, I won't be long. If you need me, the conference room is down the hall, the second door on the right."

Roy sent her a thumbs-up and glanced at his watch. "Gotcha. Thirty minutes. See you then." He smiled at Ellen, then raised first one of her hands and then the other to be kissed. "Dear lady, it was delightful seeing you again."

Edward Bidwell's lips pursed. Gerry extended his arm to indicate they should all get moving. Ellen blushed, sighed, then eased her hands away before she followed Christy, Edward, and Gerry down the hallway.

Inside the conference room, Samuel Macklin was working on a laptop. He shut it when the others entered. Gerry gave them all a chance to be seated, then wasted no time in beginning. "Christy, our recent conversation has raised concerns for each of us here."

Was this about the audit or Frank's blackmailing? "Really?"

He nodded. "This will have repercussions for the trust."

It was the audit. Did they realize she already knew that three of the trustees in this room had been embezzling from the trust? Nervousness had her heart thumping so hard she was sure they could all hear it. She remembered more of Roy's advice. *Breath deep, keep calm. They can only threaten, they can't harm.* She inhaled quietly, then let the air out slowly. Her voice was a miracle of control. "Undoubtedly."

Gerry nodded. "We realize that this has been a difficult time for you..."

"But that doesn't excuse your behavior!" Samuel Macklin said, thumping the table as he interrupted. Christy jumped.

Ellen nodded in agreement with Macklin. Bidwell studied Christy through narrowed eyes. Gerry looked pained as he continued. "You must remember, Christy, that *you* now represent the Jamieson name. What you do will affect stock prices for Jamieson Ice Cream and that in turn affects the income of the trust. You must be beyond reproach."

That seemed a little steep, considering the man talking might have a secret bad enough that he would succumb to blackmail and have embezzled the trust itself. "That's difficult for me to accept, Gerry, since it's common knowledge that my husband ran off with his girlfriend after stealing most of his trust fund."

Gerry set his elbows on the table and clasped his hands together as he leaned forward. "All the more reason for you to cultivate a respectable image. Ice cream is a family product. Jamieson Ice Cream is a family company. People look up to the Jamiesons. Frank has tarnished the image, so you need to put it right."

"Gerry, are you trying to make me believe that an audit of the trust's finances is going to affect Jamieson stock prices?"

Samuel Macklin jabbed a finger at her. "No, but your divorce of the Jamieson heir will!"

"What?" Christy stared at him. Macklin liked to shout and intimidate, but he usually made sense. This time she hadn't a clue where he was coming from.

"The audit," Macklin snapped. "You wanted the audit because you plan to divorce Frank. Right?"

Gerry shot Macklin a warning glance. "We are concerned about the public reaction. If you divorce Frank, people will start asking questions."

"People are already asking questions," Edward said.

Christy stared at Gerry, slowly remembering the Big Excuse—divorce from Frank—she'd used when she set up the audit. She looked around the table. "Is that what this is all about? You don't want me to divorce Frank?"

Samuel Macklin said, "Personally, I wish you would. I'd be very happy to see the last of you, but I do not think it is advisable."

Ellen Jamieson's voice was hard as she added her agreement to Macklin's. "You are tearing the Trust apart with your demands for an audit! Sam is right, Frank—all of us—would be better off without you. But as long as Frank is away, the company needs a public face." She stopped, smiled maliciously. "That can be you. Or it could be your daughter."

The shot came out of nowhere. "Excuse me?"

Edward smiled, contempt in the expression, then in his voice. "Noelle is the true heir of Jamieson Ice Cream. As she is a minor, we have been allowing you to assume her responsibilities as well as care for her. However, if you cannot instill the proper respect for family—for her family!—we will have to revisit that arrangement."

Outbursts of fury were not normally part of Christy's make up. At this moment, with the person she cared most for under threat, outrage consumed her. She grabbed on to it, holding it fast, using it to help her through a situation that was a mother's worst nightmare. She looked around the table, glaring at each of the trustees in turn. Finally she settled on Edward. "I am Noelle's mother. There are no arrangements to revisit."

Bidwell seemed to be taken aback by her assertiveness. "Well, there are social responsibilities. You don't do a good job at that."

With Bidwell floundering, Ellen weighed in. "You insisted on withdrawing Noelle from the select private school where she was enrolled in order to place her in the local public school—"

"The Trust couldn't afford the fees at her old school and still have enough left to send her to university! I had a choice. A fancy K to twelve school, or a good university. I chose the university. Noelle won't have the option Frank did of wasting his life in shallow social events. There isn't enough money. Noelle will have to work. She'll need that university degree."

"You've missed my point." Bidwell's voice was strained, his mouth curled down in a frown.

"I don't think so," Christy said. "I think you each care more about your reputations than you do about Noelle. Why else would you be so anxious I remain married to Frank? If I sue Frank for a divorce his assets will have to be assessed. That means a much more extensive audit of the Jamieson Trust."

"Exactly," Gerry said. "We can't have that, Christy. We can't have the negative publicity a divorce will generate. We were all hurt by the reports of Frank's embezzlement. We don't want it brought up again, but the press will jump on it as if it was fresh news. They'll repeat it over and over until your divorce is complete. We're professionals here. We have reputations to protect. Frank is gone! Why do you need to divorce him?"

"I need to get on with my life."

"To run to that fellow you've been consorting with?" Macklin said.

"No! Where do you people get off? I don't need an excuse. My husband is a drug addict who deserted me. That's enough."

Gerry cleared his throat, almost apologetically. "Actually, it isn't, Christy."

"That you would think it was proves to us that you lack a basic understanding of the responsibilities of the Jamieson name," Ellen said.

"If you sue for divorce, the Trust will act on behalf of Frank," Edward said.

Samuel made a disgusted sound as he waved his hand dismissively. "Let the girl divorce Frank. She's showing us the kind of trouble she's capable of with this damned audit. Let her go and good riddance." The others all looked at him in surprise. Macklin grinned. "But we keep the kid. We'll fight her for custody on Frank's behalf."

"And we'll win," said Edward.

Christy was numb as she walked out of the conference room. She would never have imagined that Frank's trustees could turn on her so viciously, and even now she could not comprehend it. She walked down the hallway on autopilot. Her mind absorbed the rich golden patina of the paneling that covered the walls, the thickness of the plush carpet on the floor, the muted sound of keyboards. That was all. She couldn't think. She couldn't feel. If she allowed herself to do either she'd shatter into a million little pieces here in this elegant bastion of moneyed good taste.

When a hand grasped her arm, she jumped. Like a rabbit caught in the jaws of a coyote, she turned huge, bewildered eyes on her predator.

It was Gerry Fisher. "Christy."

She tugged against his hold. He let her go. "Yes, Gerry?" She should have snapped something smart, something rude, something cutting. Heaven knew she wanted to hack and slash.

He studied her, his expression grave. "I think we got carried away in there."

Christy waited silently. There was nothing for her to say. She agreed with him totally.

He drew a deep breath. "The others...I understand how they feel about a divorce. Frank's dad, Frank senior, would have been appalled at the idea of divorce in his family. We were all his friends. Ellen was his sister. We care about his legacy. The others are just trying to make sure it isn't tarnished."

"The others? You hold yourself apart from them?"

"To some extent," he said. "Christy, none of us wants to take your child from you, but extreme actions result in extreme measures. The Jamieson legacy is important and we are the guardians of it. If you forget about a divorce and drop this investigation you've started, including the audit, I think I can safely say that Noelle will remain in your care."

She stared at Fisher's narrow, aesthetic face, into eyes that were the cold gray of hammered iron, and shivered. Was this what blackmail looked like? Or was this the face of compassion and compromise? Whichever it was, she had little choice but to bend and agree. "I would do anything to keep Noelle safe."

Gerry's hard, gray eyes bored into her. Finally he nodded. "I knew you would understand."

Christy swallowed. It galled her to be forced to abandon something she knew was important, but she could not jeopardize Noelle. She gave Fisher a quick, jerky nod of agreement, then turned away. She wanted out of there.

Fisher followed her down the hall. As they neared the reception area she could hear the sound of voices.

"Nice digs." Roy was speaking. He sounded thoughtful. "Opulent. I like the color scheme. That green on the walls, what would you call it?"

"I don't know." Quinn's voice, amused, comfortable. "Dark green."

"Humph. How about forest? Or pine woods?"

"Sounds like an air freshener."

Roy sighed. "Okay, I'll note it down as dark green, with a crisp white chair rail and wood paneling below. What kind of wood do you think it is?"

There was a pause. Christy could visualize Quinn crouching down to give the paneling a closer look.

"Walnut."

"It's mahogany," Gerry said to no one in particular. "Doesn't he know anything? Who the devil do they think they are, dissecting our reception area?"

"Carpet's nice," Roy said. "How would you describe it?"

"Thick," Quinn said.

Roy laughed. "Quinn, boy, what kind of journalist are you anyway? How do you illustrate where an interview takes place, if you don't know basic descriptors?"

"My interviews don't usually take place in fancy reception areas."

"My stories don't either," Roy said, "but I've got something new, something entirely different, boiling around right now and this reception area is just perfect for it."

Gerry grabbed Christy again, whirling her around to face him. His expression was furious, his gray eyes as bleak as a November sky. "He's a reporter?"

"Journalist," Christy said.

Gerry's face flushed then paled. "Bad enough that you've hooked up with a damned environmental activist! But the man supposedly helping you find Frank is a reporter? Are you crazy? Or are you just stupid?"

"Neither." Christy heard her voice. It sounded scared and guilty. It probably sounded the same to Gerry because those cold steel eyes flashed with contempt and he dropped her arm as if she was diseased.

"He's been investigating us, hasn't he?"

There was nothing to say. Christy stared mutely into Fisher's eyes and knew he found this unforgivable.

He drew a deep breath. "We'll talk later, Christy. Now is not the time, not with your snitch here. Good-bye."

He turned and walked away, back to the conference room. Christy knew a kind of fear that was so deep, so powerful, that it consumed her. Gerry Fisher had made his feelings very clear. He saw her search for Frank as a betrayal. If she continued, the trustees would take Noelle from her. This wasn't blackmail. It wasn't spite. It was power, wielded ruthlessly.

She had two options. She could continue with the investigation and hope that she proved Frank was dead. That would straighten all this out. Or she could stay home, pretend her husband was still alive, and wait for him to contact her, just as the trustees demanded.

She knew which she would prefer to do.

She knew what she had to do.

And it wasn't what she'd prefer.

CHAPTER 17

I *cannot believe you allowed that to happen.*

There was disdain in the voice. Roy slanted a glance at the cat. Stormy was prowling the Armstrong living room, his blocky tiger's muscles flexing with fluid grace. Fury and outrage emanated from him, all wrapped up in impotence. Roy knew how he felt. He was pretty pissed at the moment himself.

She says she won't continue the investigation. How could you let them terrify her so badly that she would retreat like that?

Good question. When Christy emerged from that hallway, Roy had taken one look at her pale features and guessed she was about to faint. He'd have done something, but Quinn had leapt to her side as soon as he saw her. Christy had smiled, but shaken her head to his offer of help. She'd walked out of that office on her own. Alone, without help, uttering not a single complaint.

Quinn was prowling the room too, in the opposite direction from the cat. Roy watched them both, two souls needing action. Being forced to do nothing was tearing each of them apart. He waited a few more turns while he assembled his thoughts. Quinn was not going to like what he had to say, but that couldn't be helped. He could only guess how the cat would react.

He sank deeper in his chair, thrusting out his legs. On one side the cat abruptly stopped. Facing him on the other, Quinn stopped too. They both looked at Roy. In their eyes were identical expressions of frustration. He smiled.

"Seems to me that both of you care for Christy." He pointed to his son. "You, Quinn, like her despite yourself, and you're mad as hell that she's being bullied by those cheating trustees." To the cat he said, "Frank, I hope you loved her when you were alive. It's what she deserved. I'll give you the benefit of the doubt and assume you did. Now that you're back, you want to help her, but you can't."

"Give it up with the reincarnation bit, Dad! This is serious!"

He's narrow and arrogant and his mind is closed. What does she see in him?

"You two are bickering like brothers fussing over a shared bedroom. Grow up! Quinn, you're thirty-two. You should know better. Frank, you're dead! You have no more claim on her. We need to work together to make sure that whatever is going on here doesn't harm Christy and Noelle." He glared at each of them in turn, very much the father figure, despite the shabby jeans and long hair tied in a ponytail. "Got that?"

They both glared back at him, pushing the limits, testing his resolve.

The cat caved first. He sat and curled his tail, before carefully cleaning his front paws. *I did love her. And I do love my daughter.*

Roy nodded. "Quinn?"

Quinn looked down at the cat, then at his father. The expression on his face was impatient. "Dad, you're asking a hell of a lot. How am I supposed to believe a cat can talk to people?"

"Because I'm the one talking to the cat," Roy said quietly, his gaze level.

"Have you been smoking anything?"

"Not today."

Too bad. I could use a joint right now.

The cat's voice was wistful. Roy laughed. "Later. Right now we need to strategize."

Quinn sighed and sat down in a deep wing chair that had been his mother's favorite. "What do you think they said to her to make her decide to forget the investigation?"

They must have threatened her. Put her down. Told her she wasn't good enough. They probably yelled at her too. Macklin and Fisher are good at that. Bidwell would freeze her out, then make his point in a soft voice that is really scary. Aunt Ellen would be shrill and sniff a lot.

Roy frowned as he passed the information on to Quinn. "Is that how they were with you when you were growing up?"

"Dad! I can play along with this to a point, but come on!" Quinn said. "We're not here to analyze a dead guy's childhood. What we need to know is the threat they used so we can counter it."

The cat glared at Quinn. *I don't want my childhood analyzed either. Back off!*

Roy sighed. "Let's go at it from another angle. They're probably upset about the audit. What would be the best way to convince Christy she shouldn't continue?"

"They probably told her they would cut off her money," Quinn said. "Having an audit done is costly and they'd assume Christy is paying for it herself."

Good call. There was surprise in the voice. *Every time they wanted me to stop doing something they threatened to withhold my allowance. They couldn't though, because of the terms of the trust.*

"Frank agrees with you. He says that's a typical ploy they use. Now here's the thing, he also says the terms of the trust will not allow them to cut the recipient off. So what we have to do is convince Christy that what they threatened, they can't do."

Well, old man, you're pretty good. So who gets to do the persuading?

"She won't go for it," Quinn said, rather gloomily. "She's too stubborn."

Christy? Nah, she's a pushover. She's into people and emotions. All we've got to do is tell her we'll handle everything and she'll be happy.

Roy looked at the cat as if he'd just produced a fish from his pocket. "You poor man."

"What?" Quinn said.

Stop staring at me like that old man. The voice was defensive.

"You don't know, do you?" Roy turned to Quinn. "Frank thinks Christy will just rollover and do what we tell her."

Quinn laughed. "She's changed, cat." He closed his eyes briefly. "I can't believe I'm having a conversation with a dumb animal." Then a wicked little smile curled his lips. "Or is it a dumb husband I'm talking to?"

The cat stood in a sudden lithe movement. His lips curled back in a snarl and his tail lashed as he glared at Quinn.

Roy interrupted before battle could be joined. "We know quite a lot at this point." He lifted up his hand to tick the items off on his fingers. "To start with, Frank is dead, not disappeared. He did not embezzle from his trust fund— three of his trustees did. Probably because he was blackmailing them." Very much in parental mode, Roy fixed the cat with a disapproving look. "Not the smartest move, Frank."

The cat hunched a shoulder and didn't reply.

Roy continued on. "Frank's friend Aaron is a pusher and is somehow involved in his death. So is Crack Graham, Aaron's dealer. Graham has been impersonating Frank to make it seem that Frank is still alive." He cocked his head toward the cat, who was glaring at Quinn. Neither responded. "The question is, why is it necessary to make it seem that Frank is still alive?"

So the jerk or jerks who ripped off my trust fund could keep on stealing from it until they'd drained it dry.

"Follow the money," Quinn said. "The audit showed that the biggest chunks of cash were moved after the day Frank disappeared. If a man has skipped town with his girlfriend, it's not surprising that he's also going to move his money somewhere he has more access to it."

"Endicott said the money that was embezzled after Frank died was transferred to a bank in the Far East. After that it was sent to a numbered corporation in Brazil and the trail ended there," Roy said.

The cat hunched his back and his hair stood on end, adding an impressive volume to his bulky frame. *That's a lot of money to disappear into the ether. All the cash assets and the proceeds of the sale of the mansion. Whoever did it must have a pretty good understanding of the banking business.*

Roy passed this information on to Quinn, who frowned. "Macklin is the obvious choice."

He likes to bully people, but he's a coward at heart. There was a sneer in the voice. *He's got a good life, and he's afraid of getting caught, so he doesn't stray far from the straight and narrow.*

Roy thought about big chunks of cash. Visualizing the process of money transfer in his mind, he said, "But maybe the trail didn't end. Maybe we're just looking at it the wrong way."

Quinn learned forward. "What do you mean, Dad?"

Roy struggled with the ideas forming in his mind. "What good is money in a bank in Brazil if you're not living it up in Mexico with your bimbo?"

I wouldn't know. The cat stood up and started to prowl. *I never got a chance to find out.*

"Exactly!" Roy said.

"Dad! Stop talking to the cat. Fill me in."

"The money disappeared into the bank account of a company in Brazil. We don't know what happened from there. Everyone has been assuming that Frank has been using it to fund a fancy lifestyle in Mexico, but we know Frank is dead. Further, we know he never got to Mexico. Would anyone who stole millions of dollars be willing to leave it in Brazil forever?"

"You think the money is on the move again?"

Roy nodded. "Back to whoever stole it in the first place."

"What we have to look for is someone who has suddenly come into a lot of money."

Not bad, Armstrong. Finding out where it is now isn't going to be easy, though. But that's your job. You're the one who can do the legwork.

Roy stood up, then went into the kitchen. When he returned, he had a bottle of beer in one hand and a lit joint in the other. He handed the bottle to Quinn before taking a drag of the marijuana. When he exhaled, he blew the smoke the cat's way. "Whoever embezzled the bulk of Frank's estate probably killed him. Before we go any farther, I think we have to ask if we want to find out who that person is. Would Christy want us to?"

Yes! The cat breathed deep, his eyes narrowed in pleasure. There was a sigh of satisfaction in Roy's mind.

Quinn held the bottle to his lips and drank. "If we don't find out, the trustees will hold Christy hostage for the rest of her life."

Roy nodded. "In that case, I think Frank's right, Quinn. You are the one who has to do it."

He didn't mind being the one to do the digging to keep the case alive. Research and investigation was what he did best. He enjoyed asking questions, particularly the ones no one wanted to answer. He lived on the rush that came when the pieces fell together to create a completely new pattern.

He parked his car in an underground lot. Thanks to awards that gave him name recognition and a publisher who respected his international experience and wanted to feature his material, he had access to the research facilities of a major Vancouver daily.

For a moment he remained in the car, staring blindly out the windshield. When he'd come to Vancouver, he'd estimated it would take him about a year—no more than two—to help his father through the worst of his grief. He would sort out the family finances, which his mother had always handled, and make sure Roy would be able to cope, then he'd slip back into his own life.

Now, as he sat behind the wheel of his car, he wondered about his future. Though his father seemed to be adapting to his loss, he truly believed he was talking to a cat. A cat, moreover, who shared his desire to get high from time to time.

Shaking his head, Quinn jerked the key out of the ignition and opened the door. His father wasn't cracking up, he was. He'd been talking to the damn cat too.

He took the elevator from the parking garage up to the main lobby where he transferred to another elevator that would take him to the floors used by the paper. The lobby was a pleasant, utilitarian space with granite floors, a reception console that could have been manned, but wasn't, and a listing of the floor on which each department was located.

Newspapers didn't spend a lot of money on fancy interiors or cushy office space. Not like the Jamieson Trust. Now there was an organization that saw interior decoration as an investment. They claimed it was because of the prominence of the Jamieson name. Quinn thought it was because the people who used the space liked to spend other people's money. That brought him back to the meeting three days before and Christy's reaction to it.

She hadn't spoken to him since she refused his help. That hurt. He didn't want to admit it did, but it did. Worse, when they were out on the sidewalk he'd asked her to share his car. She'd shaken her head, then driven home with his father. That was when she had announced she wanted the investigation to end. She'd told his father, not him. Why?

His father thought it was because telling him would be too difficult. What was that supposed to mean? Was he such a grouch that Christy couldn't talk to him? He thought they had something going, that when this was over they would see if sex was as good as it had promised to be on that beach in Mexico. Did he mean nothing to her?

That thought made him angry. She should have had the guts to talk to him directly, but she hadn't. When the chips were down she'd caved. He'd expected more of her. As he headed into the elevator, he pondered that. Why had he expected more? Was it because he was attracted to her? If he looked back, he could see that his relationships had been with women who were strong and independent, who fought for what they believed in, never allowing themselves to give up.

Women who would die for a cause.

He swallowed and pushed his thoughts away from that one. Christy was a stay-at-home mom, when all was said and done, despite the Jamieson name and the society page status that went with it. Why should he expect her to have the fierceness of a woman like Tamara, who had dedicated her life to tending the injured in the dangerous places of the world?

What burned him was that he'd misjudged Christy. Usually he was pretty good at reading people, but this time he'd created a character for her that didn't belong to her. That wasn't his style, so why had he done it? Because his desire for Christy was so strong he'd do anything to satisfy his needs? What did that say about him?

He should forget Frank Jamieson's disappearance and get on with the story he'd pitched over three months ago. There were plenty of candidates he could use as examples for an article on how inherited wealth shaped the lives of the children of the super rich. He didn't need Frank Jamieson, or Christy Jamieson, to be able to write the story.

So why was he here, chasing a paper trail, trying to find the killer of a man who was not officially dead?

The elevator reached his floor. He stepped out, moving quickly. At the door to the archives, he stopped. He was here because he had never run from a problem. Sooner or later he would have to face Christy, confront her with the issues between them. He wasn't ready to do that, not with the sharp pain of betrayal still fresh in his mind. He'd let it dull a bit before he talked to her. Otherwise, he might say something stupid in the heat of the moment.

Like something about commitment.

No way.

You're caving, babe.

"Shut up." Christy dug through Noelle's closet. There were built-in shelves for her casual clothes as well as a space to hang dresses. At the moment, Christy was looking at fall clothes like jeans, sweatshirts, and long-sleeved blouses to see what Noelle needed for the change of season.

You're letting them control you.

"Your trustees still hold the purse strings, Frank," she said crossly. "If I don't go along with what they want, I don't have grocery money until I get a job." Two pairs of jeans, a pair of sweats. She made a note on a piece of paper that she needed to look for another couple of pairs of pants.

Quinn and Roy say that you're too stubborn to let the trustees get away with pushing you around.

In the middle of stacking T-shirts, Christy stopped and briefly closed her eyes. "Quinn and Roy are wrong."

They made me look back at us. I didn't like what I saw. I wasn't much of a husband to you. There was a sigh in the words. *I blackmailed the trustees off and on for three years, Christy. You can't trust them. If you give in to them and stop the investigation, they'll just push you around on something else, later on.*

"I told Harry Endicott that I had enough information for now. I asked him to hold off on the audit." Two sweatshirts, three long-sleeved jerseys, four blouses, and a sweater. Not enough for a school that didn't require a uniform. She'd have to take Noelle shopping for clothes. How were her socks doing?

You can't hide in the cupboard, babe, the voice said gently. *My trustees are bad dudes. Hell, I should know. I grew up with them as my guardians. Aunt Ellen was always on my case for some stupid thing or another. 'Your father wouldn't have done that,' she used to say. 'He had ethics.*

He had morals. He was strong. Not like you. You're weak. You're not good enough.'"

Christy stopped her counting to look at the cat. It was prowling Noelle's bare, builder's white room, tail lashing, those thick tiger muscles bunching with each lithe movement. "Frank, I had no idea Ellen put you down that way."

Why should you? I never told you. Bidwell was just as bad, always carping. Nothing I did was ever good enough. Macklin simply told me I was stupid and left it at that. In a way, he was the best of them because he didn't bother with me much.

"What about Gerry?" Christy stacked fall clothes in the easy-to-reach spaces and put summer shorts and tees where the warmer clothes had been.

Gerry used to tell me I had to try, that I owed it to the family name to make something of myself. He was okay, I guess, except he was always after me to take up an internship at Jamieson. I felt guilty about blackmailing him. I never worried about the others, even Ellen who was my only blood relative.

Christy stopped, mid-stash. She hugged a pile of socks to her chest as she stared at the cat. "Gerry was one of the ones you were blackmailing? For heaven's sake, why? What on earth could he have done that was bad enough to give in to blackmail?"

The cat stopped moving. He stared at Christy silently, like an ordinary cat, as if Frank had suddenly abandoned Stormy's body. *He has affairs,* the voice said at last.

She laughed, relieved that the voice was back. "Get off it! Gerry is too much of a family man."

Ha! That's what he wants people to think, what he needs his wife to believe. Her father was one of his backers when he started Fisher Disposal and the old man still owns thirty percent of the company. Eve Fisher owns twenty. Gerry only owns forty percent. If his wife divorced him for adultery, he'd lose control of Fisher Disposal.

Christy closed the cupboard doors. "So why doesn't he stop, if he has that much to lose."

Again that hesitation, then the cynical tone. *Maybe he has. But do you think Eve would forgive him for the affairs he'd already had?*

"Good point." Christy glanced at her watch and headed down the stairs. "I have to pick up Noelle, then we're going to the mall."

The cat bolted past her. *Chris, you can't give in to them on this.*

At the bottom of the stairs, Christy stopped. She sat down on one of the steps. Stormy hopped onto her lap. She stroked his soft fur, soothing herself as much as her cat. "Frank, I don't have a choice. They threatened me, and they have all the power."

No one knows I'm dead but you and the Armstrongs. If you don't prove I'm gone you'll stay married to me, forever.

Christy sighed. "For years anyway. Yeah, I hear you, Frank. Eventually, when you never show up, I'll be able to have you declared legally dead. How long does that take? Seven years or something? By that time Noelle will be fifteen, almost ready to go out on her own."

That might be okay, the voice said thoughtfully. *It'll probably take Armstrong that long to sort through his issues.*

She stopped stroking the soft, silky fur. "What are you talking about?"

Quinn Armstrong, babe. He's got the hots for you.

CHAPTER 18

———◆———

Five days in the length of a life aren't much. Five days in the life of a child go on and on. Five days without contact with Quinn Armstrong were endless. Christy continued her usual routine. She bought groceries, cleaned the house, cooked the meals, washed the dishes. Each night before putting Noelle to bed she read her a story. She added a few new activities, like the mall visit to look for clothes and a Halloween costume for Noelle, and sorting through some boxes that hadn't been unpacked yet. Overall, though, her days were a dull, boring, repetition that made her wonder why she had been content to stay at home rather than go out and do something significant.

The cat didn't help. He kept telling her she had to take back her life, prove Frank was dead and, in the process, find out who killed him. Christy protested at first, then gave up and let him nag her. After a time nagging turned to sniping and Christy's mood went into the dumpster.

The five days ended when a courier truck pulled up in front of her house and her doorbell rang. Christy answered, wondering what was up now. She soon found out.

The courier handed her a single letter-sized envelope and had her sign for it. Turning the envelope over in her hand, Christy closed the door behind him. It was a thick, textured cream. On the upper left corner was a return address that sent a chill through her: McGrath, Johnson, and Bidwell, Barristers and Solicitors.

She shoved her thumb underneath the flap and ripped it open. Then she hesitated. She didn't want pull the single sheet of paper from the envelope. Instinct told her something was up, something she wouldn't like, otherwise, why would Edward Bidwell send her a letter by courier? Her hands began to sweat.

"Read it and get it done," she muttered. But she carefully closed the flap over that terrifying piece of paper before she ran up the stairs. She'd settle some place safe, then she'd read it.

She curled onto the sofa by the big picture window, took a deep breath, then finally pulled out the letter. She put off reading it for another moment or two by carefully smoothing the folds so the paper would lay flat. Then there were no more excuses, only necessity. And what a nasty necessity it was. The letter was stark and to the point. Written by Edward Bidwell on behalf of the Jamieson Trust, it stated that the trustees were no longer satisfied that Christy was the appropriate person to care for Noelle Jamieson. In the absence of Frank Jamieson and acting on his behalf, the trustees would be seeking court action to have Noelle removed from Christy's care. Further, they were asking for sole custody of the Jamieson heir, again on Frank Jamieson's behalf.

Horror engulfed Christy. She stared at the letter. Read it again, a third time and then a fourth, before she could accept the words written there. The trustees were following up on their threat to take Noelle. But why? She'd done what they asked.

The cat strolled into the living room. He stretched as if he'd just woken up. *Hey babe, how about a plateful of tuna? It's lunchtime and Stormy could use a little protein.*

Christy stared at him. "Can you talk to them?"

Hello? Talk to whom?

"The trustees. Did you tell them to send this?" Christy waved the letter at the cat.

He leapt up onto her lap. Claws out, he snagged the letter and pulled it down. *Stormy, stupid cat, can't read. Tell me what it says.*

"It says the trustees are seeking custody of Noelle on your behalf. Did you somehow ask for this?"

Hell, no!

Fury seeped into Christy's center. "He promised me they wouldn't do this if I stopped the investigation, if I did what they wanted. He promised!"

They're bad dudes, babe. You can't trust 'em.

Christy heard a smug 'I told you so' hidden beneath the words. "Shut up, Frank! Just shut up and let me think!"

Why? You haven't done a great job of thinking so far.

"And what is that supposed to mean?"

You know what it means. You let the trustees con you. They said what you wanted to hear and you believed them, when what you should have done was listen to me. But you never did, did you? You always believed the crap they told you. Took their word over mine.

"Not always!" Christy glared at the cat, who glared back. "Once I believed in you totally. I changed my life for you. I loved you! You were different in Kingston, Frank. You acted as if you cared, as if I was important to you. Then you came back here and you hung out with Aaron DeBolt and those other rich kids with too much money and not enough to do. They didn't like me. They put me down and you let them! Was I supposed to believe in you then?"

Aaron didn't mean half the stuff he said. I told you that, babe.

"Aaron DeBolt meant every word. Haven't you figured that out yet? He sold you drugs. He was your pusher. He didn't care about you! He used you. I found out what he was doing from Gerry Fisher, you know. He came to me, asking me to help get you into rehab, to straighten you out."

When?

"Two years before you disappeared. He cared about you, Frank. In their own ways I think all of your trustees cared about you."

You're wrong. They wanted you to think they cared about me. I was blackmailing Fisher by the time he came to you. He just wanted me put away so I wouldn't bother him anymore.

"Whatever." Still furious, she flounced into the kitchen, hauled out a can of tuna-flavored cat food, opened it, and set it in front of the cat.

Ugh! I was talking about real tuna, not this junk.

"Stormy likes tuna cat food," Christy said sweetly. "Enjoy."

You're still pissed at me, aren't you? the voice said mournfully, just before Stormy tucked into his tuna surprise lunch.

Christy laughed and returned to the living room. She re-read the letter. Anger, eased by her quarrel with Frank, simmered again. She'd been good. As little as she'd wanted to, she'd upheld her part of the agreement. She had stayed away from Quinn. She'd ordered the audit stopped. She'd dropped the pretense of seeking a divorce. So why this letter? Why this vicious, untrue accusation?

They were going to take Noelle away from her.

The horror of that slammed into her heart and it hurt. It hurt so badly that it stole her breath and shot pangs of anguish through her gut. She dropped the letter and collapsed onto the sofa. She clutched her stomach, holding herself tight as if that feeble comfort could ward off the anguish tearing her apart.

They were going to take Noelle away from her.

She rocked back and forth. A silent scream of denial rose in her throat, engulfed her, pounded through her brain. How could they do this? She'd been good. Why would they want to tear Noelle away from her? What had she done wrong? What had Noelle done wrong? She was eight years old. What would a custody battle do to her, hot on the heels of losing her daddy?

She would be terrified. The whole direction of her life would change. She would be at the mercy of four people who had hated her father. It must not happen. So how was she to make sure that no custody fight marred Noelle's life?

They want to get rid of you. The cat sauntered into the living room, licking his chops. The voice sounded grumpy. *If they control Noelle, they control the cash. She's not going to ask for audits or how they're spending her money.*

Very slowly Christy eased out of that protective hunch and sat up. Frank was right. For the trustees to cover up their embezzlement, they needed control. They had to be able to put their own spin on everything that happened and keep unanswerable questions from being asked. It was possible that one or all of them had already silenced Frank in the most final of ways. Now they planned to stop her by stealing away her daughter. She couldn't bear to think what they might be willing to do to Noelle.

Outrage swept through Christy, washing away the hurt, chasing away the fear. How dare they? How dare they think they could use her daughter to protect themselves?

Enough was enough. The deal was off. The investigation was on. She surged to her feet. She hoped that Quinn was home, because she needed to talk to him. Now.

Deliberately, fueled by fury and determination, she headed for the door. The cat bounded after her. *Wait up, babe! I'm coming too!*

Quinn scooped coffee into a filter and slipped it into the basket of the coffeemaker. "I tracked down Aaron DeBolt last night."

Sitting at the kitchen table, Roy paused, his hands poised above the laptop keyboard. "And?"

"He's not a very cooperative guy." Quinn added water, flicked the switch.

Roy observed him impatiently. "He's spoiled, self-absorbed, and not very bright either, but that doesn't tell us anything about Frank's murder."

Quinn grinned. He opened the fridge door and inspected the contents. "He claims there's nothing to tell. According to him, Frank is still alive and living it up in Mexico." Quinn reached for bread, cheese and ham. "Want a sandwich for lunch, Dad?"

"Sure." Roy saved, then shut down the computer. "Frank remembers Aaron guiding him over to the car then pushing him into the trunk. Even if Aaron wasn't actually there when Frank was killed, he is an accessory."

Quinn put the lunch fixings on the countertop. "DeBolt was with his friends last night. He wasn't going to admit to anything, but I think I shook him up. I'll catch him on his own and see what I can get out of him." The doorbell rang. Quinn put ham on bread and cocked his head. "Someone selling memberships to the new gym that opened up beside the furniture store?"

"They've already been," Roy said. "They won't send anyone back for another month or so."

A sharp, repeated pounding followed the bell. "Not a door-to-door salesman," Quinn said. He made a move.

Roy waved him back to his sandwich making. "I'll get it."

Quinn put the top piece of bread over the meat. He wasn't paying much attention to what he was doing so the top slice lay crooked over the bottom and the sliced ham dangled out over the edge of the bread. He listened to the dull murmur of voices from the doorway. He couldn't identify the words, but he thought he heard a woman's voice mixed with his father's deeper one.

His heart skipped a beat. Christy?

Hasty footsteps sounded on the stairs. Quinn sliced his sandwich in half as Christy stormed into the kitchen, a simmering cauldron of emotion about ready to overflow. She stopped abruptly in front of him, then slammed an envelope onto the counter beside his plate. "I want to crucify them," she said.

Quinn blinked. The Christy he knew was moderate, calm in her handling of situations, her emotions always under control. This woman was furious, fierce, even dangerous. His momentary flash of pity for the individuals who were the target of her rage disappeared as quickly as it came. He had a good idea who she was mad at and they deserved whatever she flung at them.

He picked up the envelope. Raising his brows in question, he waited until she nodded, then he pulled out the letter and quickly read the contents. No wonder Christy was so incensed. "This is crap."

"I won't let them take her," she said in a low, intense voice that was a promise and a plea at the same time.

No, she wouldn't. Christy's world was her daughter and from what Quinn could see she was doing an excellent job of raising the kid to be a bright, inquiring, loving person. This was a nuisance suit, the kind of thing unscrupulous lawyers used as a pressure tactic. The trustees represented wealth and respectability. Christy was the wife of a man who could easily be painted as a self-indulgent rich kid who thought nothing of stealing from his own trust fund. A descriptive touch here, a well-chosen phrase there, and Christy would be portrayed as being as dissolute as her husband. In the long run, he'd bet that any suit the trustees brought against her would fail, but she would have to prove herself. The result would be negative publicity and an emotional battering, while Noelle coped with the resulting lack of stability.

"What's up?" Roy said, entering with the cat. Quinn handed him the letter. He read it quickly. "We've touched a nerve."

Quinn cut his sandwich into quarters. Taking Christy's hand, he guided her to the table where she perched on a chair, edgy and tense. Sitting down adjacent to her, he put the plate between them, an open invitation to share. Roy sat opposite.

The cat hopped up on the table and eyeballed the plate.

"Quit complaining about your lunch, Frank." Christy said, glaring at the cat. "We've got bigger issues to deal with."

Quinn thought about kicking the cat off the table, then Christy said angrily, "They snowed me!"

Quinn waited for more. It wasn't forthcoming.

"Individuals relate to other individuals in different ways," Roy said. "Christy's experience wouldn't have trained her for dealing with the circles you moved in, Frank."

They were talking to the damn cat again, leaving him completely out. "Hey, people! Include me in the conversation, please!"

The cat stared at him. He had an unnerving sense of intelligence behind those wide, green eyes, an intelligence uncomfortably mixed with amused contempt. Then he told himself his imagination was running wild and cats always seemed to have a superior attitude when it came to humans.

"Frank figures you're un-evolved because you won't allow yourself to hear him," Roy said.

"Great," Quinn said, taking a sandwich quarter. "I'm being put down by a cat."

"And my daughter is in jeopardy of being snatched by a bunch of bad guys who don't want to play fair," Christy said. She had the letter in her hand again and waved it angrily. "They told me I had to stop the audit, so I did. They told me I should stay away from you and that I shouldn't divorce Frank, so I agreed, even though…even though I no longer love Frank." She glared at the cat. "And he's disappeared, leaving me destitute. I agreed! I did what they asked. Then this!" She tossed the letter down angrily.

Quinn looked at the paper. It lay on the table between them like a lethal weapon, a knife blade pointed toward Christy's heart. He hated that letter, the contents of it, the people who had written it. If ripping it into shreds and condemning the authors would do any good he'd have done it in a flash. But it wouldn't. The threat was there. It was real. It was dangerous. It needed to be dealt with.

He took a bite, then chewed as he fingered the letter meditatively. "I wonder whether Bidwell wrote this on his own or as a representative of the Trust."

Christy was staring at him curiously. "He was the one who signed it, but it's in all their names."

"Bidwell's not very bright then, is he?"

Christy frowned. Roy laughed. He'd caught the inference immediately, probably because he'd been the one who taught Quinn to think outside the box.

"I'm not sure I'm tracking this," Christy said.

"The threat worked. You were doing what the trustees wanted, or what they seemed to want. Then someone decided to act on the threat, to pressure you that much more."

"I'm with you so far, but I still don't understand what this has to do with intelligence."

"There's a fine art to intimidating someone. You can only force a person to accept so much before the strain becomes unendurable and the individual snaps. They reached your breaking point with this letter."

"Yes, they did," Christy said.

Quinn smiled. "Yes, and they didn't have to. What would you have done if this letter hadn't come?"

She had the grace to look shamefaced. "I would have done nothing."

"And now what are you going to do?"

Her jaw set and her eyes flashed. She was gorgeous.

"I am going to expose the embezzlement. I am going to prove that Frank couldn't have siphoned away half of his trust fund because he was dead before it happened. I am going to replace the Jamieson Trustees and I'm going to sue the bastards who stole Noelle's money. Shut up, Frank, you don't have to be sarcastic."

Quinn laughed. The cat hissed at him. "See what I mean? They've created a dangerous enemy, one with a strong motivation and not much to lose."

"And very little time to work with." Christy tapped the letter with her fingertip. "Quinn, I need your help."

"It's yours," he said. On impulse he caught her hand and lifted it to his lips.

Christy gasped, but she didn't pull her hand away. She did blush bright red.

Roy cleared his throat. "The cat says he wishes you well, but would you mind keeping the nooky for when he's not around." He helped himself to one of the sandwich quarters.

Quinn felt himself go red too. He dropped Christy's hand as if it was a white-hot brand. "For crying out loud," he muttered. The cat settled into a crouch. "You're welcome," Quinn said to it. Christy giggled.

"Do you think one of the trustees killed Frank?" Roy asked.

Quinn pushed his chair out and stood. Reaching across the counter, he picked up the coffee beaker and held it aloft in a question. Roy shook his head. Christy nodded. Quinn went for cups. As he poured he looked at Christy. He wondered how much the cat had told her of Frank's last minutes. "It's possible. This letter clearly indicates a desire to keep Christy from looking into trust business, but that may be because of the embezzlement."

Christy sipped from the pottery mug Quinn placed in front of her. "Frank says that Gerry Fisher was one of the ones he was blackmailing."

"I can believe that. His company cuts corners in the maintenance of their landfills." Sitting down, Quinn eyeballed the cat, then shifted his gaze to his father and Christy. "So what did Fisher do?"

"He had affairs," Roy said.

"Frank was blackmailing him over some affairs?" Quinn picked up another sandwich quarter. "And that's why Fisher was embezzling from the trust? That's not much of a reason for doing a criminal act. There's got to be something more."

The cat hissed as Roy said, "They weren't normal affairs. You know, two consenting adults looking for an adventure who happen to meet in the course of their work or social lives. Fisher apparently used a service."

"A service? Like an escort service?" Christy stared at the cat, frowning. "Frank, are you sure? This sounds so un-Gerry."

"Oh, yeah, he's sure," Roy said. He too was eying the cat, a skeptical expression on his face. "There's more, isn't there, Frank?"

"He says no." Christy tapped her fingers on the table. "Frank, you've been dishing information to us a little bit at a time. It's not good enough. This is about our daughter. This is important. If you're holding out on us, Frank, I swear…"

Christy and Roy stared at the cat, the expressions on their faces hostile. The cat's tail swished, its body tense. Evidence of a mental battle between Christy and Roy and the cat? Quinn swallowed hard. The sandwich went down in a painful lump. He was really losing it.

He chased the sandwich quarter down with a slug of coffee. Coffee helped him think and right now that was important. "Admitting to the use of an escort service can be embarrassing, especially for a guy in Fisher's position, but I wouldn't think it's something worth paying blackmail money over."

"Remember, though, he wasn't using his own money to pay off Frank's blackmail. He was using the trust's. Maybe he felt the same way Frank did, that the money was rightfully Frank's and so it was okay to give it to him." Roy held up his hands. "Look, don't shoot the messenger! We're brainstorming here. I'm just tossing out ideas. I'm not suggesting they're the answer."

Quinn decided that he could learn to hate Frank Jamieson, even if he was dead. "Who else was Frank blackmailing?"

"Bidwell and Macklin."

Christy's eyes opened wide. "I can't believe this. Frank says Bidwell is a bigamist! When he was at university he went to Mexico with a co-ed. They got drunk and they got married, but they never got a divorce. Instead, they just pretended their marriage hadn't happened. After graduation from law school he got a job at Greenham, McGrath, Johnson."

"A very conservative firm," Roy said. "Vivien came up against them a few times during her career. They represent the wealthy in this town. And the corporate welfare bums."

Christy's expression was horrified as she stared at the cat. Clearly she was having a hard time accepting what she was learning. "When he married the daughter of one of his clients, he couldn't afford to let anyone know that he already had a wife."

"That's a bit of a stretch," Roy said. "He didn't *want* to let anyone know he was married."

"And Macklin?" Quinn asked.

Christy dropped her head in her hands and shook it slowly. "This is unbelievable."

Roy said, "Macklin is a real winner. He's a partner in a national accounting firm where he's got a squeaky clean reputation. We know better, but you know what? He didn't start his embezzlement career with the Jamieson Trust. He began at university when he had a summer job as an accounting clerk with a small, local company."

Christy lifted her head. Her expression was bleak. "Frank says he didn't have much money, and university tuition was expensive. Samuel was brilliant, even then. He stole enough for a year's tuition and fiddled the books."

"A permanent employee of the firm was accused and convicted of the crime. Macklin never fessed up," Roy said angrily.

"Nice bunch of people," Quinn said. "What about the last of the trustees, Aunt Ellen?"

Christy laughed, rather grimly. "Frank says he wouldn't rule her out as a suspect because she's always hated him. She made it clear that she believed that her position as his custodial guardian eliminated her chances to marry." She looked at the cat. "You know, Frank, sometimes I think you're suffering from persecution delusions." She frowned. "Well, that's true, I suppose."

Sometimes this business of the cat talking to everyone but him was more than irritating. "What did he say?"

Sighing, Christy said, "Frank pointed out that he is dead, so maybe they aren't delusions at all."

Quinn hesitated, then said, "I have another suspect to toss into the pool."

"Who? Brianne Lymbourn?" Christy asked.

Quinn shot her a level look, wishing he didn't have to say what he was going to. "No. Aaron DeBolt."

"Aaron? Aaron's a jerk, but murder?"

"He was there when Frank was killed." Quinn watched Christy whiten and guessed that the cat was filling her in on the details of his final minutes. She swallowed hard. Quinn reached out, caught her hand, and squeezed it. He was rewarded with a smile that was wan, but there just the same. "I had another talk with Aaron, but I didn't get much out of him."

"When?" Christy demanded.

"Last night." He waited while she processed that, until he saw the bleakness in her eyes and he knew she understood what he'd guessed earlier. "Yeah, my meeting with Aaron may have been what caused the letter."

She stood up. Putting her hands in her pockets she went to the window to stare out to the street beyond. His father looked at him, his brows raised. Quinn shook his head. Though all three of the males in Christy's life had agreed that the investigation should go on, he couldn't hide behind the group decision. He'd done the legwork, and he'd kept the investigation alive. He bore the responsibility. "I took a chance and went to a club where I thought I might find some of Frank's crowd. DeBolt was there. We talked."

"I told you I didn't want to continue the investigation," Christy said, still staring out at the street.

His father watched him, his eyebrows still raised, waiting. Quinn knew that look. Roy was giving him space, offering support. All Quinn had to do was nod and his father would intervene. Until Quinn gave him the cue, though, Roy would keep out of the argument. The cat's tail flicked restlessly, but he too appeared to be staying silent. "Frank's murder was a deliberate act, followed by an elaborate cover up. Do you think whoever killed him would be willing to accept your word the investigation was over, then leave you alone?"

"No, I suppose not." She bent her head. Her hair swept over her cheeks, hiding her expression as she drew in a deep breath. When she turned, her expression was calm, remote. He preferred the fire. "You think Aaron contacted the killer after you talked to him, which makes one of the trustees the murderer." Quinn nodded. "You must have convinced him to tell you more than he should have. What did he say?"

"He was pretty cagey. He claims he left Frank passed out in the alley after shooting up. He figured Frank would sleep it off and go home. He went back into the club. He claims he can prove it." Quinn waited the space of a heartbeat, then added, "Brianne is his alibi."

"Frank says he's lying," Roy remarked, as if the exchange between Quinn and Christy hadn't happened. "I tend to believe Frank, even though I've never met this DeBolt guy."

"He's slimy," Christy said. She came back to the table and sat down. Slowly. Wearily. "He was Frank's best friend forever. They shared everything." She toyed with the handle of the coffee mug, then stiffened. Her eyes widened. "Oh man."

Roy whistled.

Again Quinn was reduced to demanding, "What?" He glared at the cat. "You're enjoying this, aren't you?"

Christy said, "They shared everything. Quinn, Frank and Aaron DeBolt shared *everything*—including stuff that was bothering them about their families."

Quinn frowned. "Like blackmail information?"

Christy nodded. "Frank says that they were drinking and doing drugs one night a few months before he was killed. They were talking about rich parents and trust funds and how difficult it was to get money out of them. He remembers bragging about his method, then he blacked out. He knows he mentioned he was blackmailing Gerry Fisher, but he's not sure if he told Aaron any of the details, or that he was blackmailing the others."

"Aaron DeBolt completely denies that he killed Frank," Quinn said. "But this puts a whole new look on his involvement."

Christy rubbed her palms on her jeans. "I think Aaron deserves another interview."

Roy nodded. Quinn frowned. The cat settled comfortably on his haunches and ate the last sandwich quarter.

CHAPTER 19

"Come on, kiddo. We don't want to be late," Christy said, urging Noelle out the front door.

While Christy locked up, Noelle shrugged on her backpack. "Aw, Mom. We've got lots of time." The school bell rang. Noelle's eyes opened wide and she bolted down the stairs. "Mom! We have to go!"

Christy laughed. "Hugs first!"

Noelle leaned into the hug in a wordless expression of affection, then she skipped away. Christy had to run to keep up.

After dropping Noelle at school, Christy hurried home. She had about six hours before she needed to pick up Noelle. She planned to use that time to interview Aaron DeBolt.

When she entered the house, she called the cat. After a minute there was a thump and the sound of a herd of elephants galloping across the top floor, then Stormy appeared on the staircase. "Come downstairs," she said.

Obediently, the cat trotted down the steps. *Breakfast time?*

Christy waited until he'd reached the bottom stair before she scooped him up, then she stuffed him into a canvas carryall, or tried to. As soon as Stormy realized what she was doing, he tensed every muscle. He stiffened his legs, shot out his claws, and fought the indignity of being dumped into a bag with the kind of passion cats bring to self-preservation. Christy cursed as she was scratched and bitten. "Frank, get in the bag, for heaven's sake! I need your help."

Why? But he calmed Stormy and the cat slid inside. She slipped the handle over her shoulder and tucked the bag securely under her arm.

"I'm going to see your old pal, Aaron DeBolt."

Stormy's head popped out of the top of the bag as she once again locked the front door. *Not a good idea, babe. It could be dangerous. Let Quinn do it.*

Christy set her mouth in a determined line. "No. Aaron will tell Quinn the bare bones. If I play it right, he'll give me the dirt."

There was no immediate response to this. She had a sense that the cat was searching for an answer, probably the right words to let her know just how wrong she was. She unlocked the passenger door and carefully put the bag on the front seat of the car. "Want a seatbelt, Frank?"

Very funny. Listen, babe, this is a mistake. Aaron isn't the nicest guy in the world. He can be pretty caustic...

"We've been through this. He's a complete jerk, full of snide comments about anyone and everyone. That includes me, big time." She slammed the door and came around to the driver side. Sliding inside, she shoved the key in the ignition. "And you probably, though I don't know that. Anyway, I'm well aware that Aaron is contemptuous of me. I can use that to my advantage, I think. At least, that's what I plan to do."

I haven't had breakfast.

Christy swept the cat a quick glance before she backed out of the garage. "Yeah, so? You look pretty well fed to me."

It's early. Aaron probably won't have had breakfast either. He may not even be up.

Christy showed her teeth and put her foot on the gas. "I'm counting on it."

Aaron DeBolt lived in the Yaletown area in a luxurious condominium high-rise. Within walking distance of clubs, restaurants, spas, and offices, it was miles to the nearest grocery store. People who lived at this sought-after address tended to use their apartments only to sleep, and often not even that.

The building rose tall and sleek. No ugly balconies or open windows marred the lean glass cladding. There was no need to draw the outside into this modern tower. Only the most effective air circulation and air conditioning systems had been used in its construction. The inhabitants were well-insulated, safe from the dangers of city smog and downtown pollution.

Just inside the front door a security guard sat at a waist-high console. Christy smiled at him as she entered. He stared back impassively. "May I help you, ma'am?"

"I'm here to see Aaron DeBolt."

"Do you have an appointment?"

I told you this was a mistake.

Christy's smile widened. "Call Aaron. Tell him I'm here. He'll see me."

The guard remained bored, his expression impassive. "Mr. DeBolt doesn't like to be disturbed before noon."

Christy laughed. "I know."

"I can take a message if you would like."

Christy moved closer to the desk. She put her hand on the smooth, dark wood. "I don't want to leave a message."

"I'm afraid—"

She made her voice rise, added an edge of urgency. "I need his help. I need *Aaron*. I don't *need* to leave a message." She slapped her other hand on the desk and let her body shake with tension as she leaned forward.

"Ma'am, I don't think—"

Hey! Watch it! You're squashing me, here.

The cat's protest almost made Christy laugh. She swallowed the amusement and managed to make the smile twitching her lips into a scowl. "I need a fix. I need it now. Aaron will get it for me. He won't be happy if you turn me away."

The guard stared at her a minute more. Christy glared back, but she made sure that her hands were twitching, as if her skin had a life of its own. A sneer curled the guard's lips and he waved her through even before he'd made his call.

In the elevator, Stormy's head popped out of the bag again. *Not bad. You sure snowed that guy.*

"Yeah. Now all I've got to do is snow Aaron."

Piece of cake. Stormy's head disappeared down into the bag again. Christy laughed, without amusement.

Aaron opened his door dressed in nothing but a pair of silk boxer shorts. His hair lay greasily against his head and his eyes were hooded.

"Good morning," Christy said cheerfully.

His eyes opened wide. The whites were bloodshot. "What the hell are you doing here?"

He didn't seem inclined to invite her in, so Christy simply stepped forward, forcing him to backtrack until they were inside his apartment. Then she took the initiative and shut the door. "I don't think we want to talk out in the hall."

"I don't think we want to talk at all."

There was a sneer on his mouth, but indignation in his voice. She smiled serenely. "The feeling is mutual, believe me."

He turned away from the door, heading deeper into the apartment. Christy followed him to the kitchen, where he hefted a bottle of cognac from the counter and filled a tumbler. Throwing back his head, he drank almost half in one long gulp. Then he turned to face her. Leaning against the counter, one arm crossed over his chest, the other propped on top of it, he played with the glass while he observed her. "Since I doubt that you've truly come to buy drugs, tell me what you want, then get lost."

"I want to know where Frank is."

"Gone."

The cat popped its head out of the bag. *That's an understatement.*

"Christ, you walk around with a cat! You always were totally weird." He tipped the tumbler, pouring the expensive brandy down his throat like water.

Christy smiled at him. "Frank says you killed him."

Aaron choked and went completely white before he began to cough. Cognac splashed on his chest and the floor. Christy watched him impassively.

Are you nuts?

"Jesus!" Aaron said when he was able to talk. "What kind of crazed accusation is that?" His eyes shifted, looking everywhere but into her face. "Frank is hiding out in Mexico with Brianne Lymbourn." He managed a sneer as he said the woman's name.

"I don't think so," Christy said. She moved closer to Aaron, invading his space now that she had him rattled. "Brianne was recently seen in town with a lowlife called Crack Graham. I think she came home to blackmail you, Aaron. I think she knows that you lured Frank into the alley behind the club and then you killed him."

Aaron took another slug of brandy, draining the glass. He turned, pouring himself a refill. "You think wrong."

Be careful, Chris!

"If that's true Brianne will confirm it. Tell me where she's staying."

After he'd drunk again, Aaron said, "What makes you think I know where Brianne is?"

Christy smiled at him without amusement. "Because she's your alibi. I figure you'd keep track of her, just in case whoever killed Frank decides to pin it on you."

"A minute ago you accused *me* of killing Frank."

"That was to shake you up and get your attention."

Aaron stared at her narrowly. Christy stared back. Finally he said, "Why should I help you?"

"Because you're Frank's best friend. Frank has disappeared. I think he's dead and Brianne knows who did it. I want to talk to her."

He'll never buy that.

Aaron drank while he considered. "I heard she was staying at a place a couple of blocks from here."

"I need an address."

He gave it to her, then shook his head. "You're right. She has hooked up with this guy, Crack Graham. If Frank is dead, it's because Brianne and Graham set him up."

"Why would they do that?"

Aaron laughed. "Frank was such an idiot, always wanting to do the right thing, figuring he was worth something more than his trust fund. Brianne was into him. She was going to convince him to dump you and marry her. Then she'd have great sex with Graham and all Frank's lovely money."

Inside the bag Stormy erupted into outraged violence, bucking and scratching for release. Christy shrieked, the bag fell open and the cat emerged, claws out and hissing. He leapt for Aaron's chest with a snarl that would have done a cougar proud. Aaron swore as Stormy made contact. The tumbler flew out of his hand, landed on the cold flagstone floor and shattered. Brandy splashed everywhere. Blood dripped from Aaron's chest where the cat's claws had caught and dug.

"Get this damn crazy animal off me!" Aaron screamed, flailing ineffectually against the furious cat.

"Frank, enough! Stop it!"

No! He's a jerk. He pretended to be my friend and he betrayed me! He knocked me on the head, then pushed me into that car. He sold me out and I'm going to make him pay.

There were months of pent-up feelings in that statement. Christy briefly considered letting the cat beat up on Aaron for as long as it took to satisfy Frank, but she figured that in the long run the cat was more likely to be seriously hurt than the human. Taking a deep breath she reached past Aaron's flailing hands to pluck the cat off him. Stormy's claws had sunk deep. Aaron screamed, then swore loudly as the sharp, curving talons ripped free. The cat twisted in Christy's hands, before he expressed his displeasure by hissing at Aaron.

"Take that effing rabid beast and get out of here!" Aaron dabbed at the wounds marring his torso.

"With pleasure!" Holding the still hissing cat, Christy made a hasty departure. In the elevator she stuffed Stormy into the canvas bag, despite his protests, then she walked from Aaron's building to the address he'd given her for Brianne Lymbourn. There her luck ran out. Brianne had indeed been staying at the apartment, but was no longer. The building superintendent told Christy she'd gone out around dinnertime, dressed in an expensive evening dress. That had been almost a week ago. He hadn't seen her since.

Christy left her name and telephone number and asked him to contact her if Brianne showed up. She reinforced this with a fifty-dollar bill as added incentive. The man pocked the money and nodded.

Christy doubted she'd hear from him again.

I'm not happy that Brianne is missing.

"She's probably gone off somewhere with Crack Graham," Christy said.

Could be. But the tone was dubious.

Christy checked her watch. She had about four hours before she had to pick up Noelle from school. Plenty of time to get back to her car and drive home. She walked quickly, thinking about what she'd learned this morning. "Aaron might have been involved in your disappearance, Frank, but he doesn't seem to be aware that Brianne hasn't been back to her apartment in a week. What do you think that tells us?"

I could say something rude about Aaron.

Christy laughed. She spied a sandwich shop and popped inside. "A coffee please," she said, smiling at the server behind the counter. "And a tuna sandwich to go, but hold the bread, hold the mayo, hold the lettuce."

The server stared at her in a bored way then he disappeared into the back. He returned with a can of tuna, the liquid drained away. "You want a fork with that?"

Yum.

"No need," Christy said. She carefully placed the can in the carryall, grabbed her coffee, and headed out. There were ecstatic sounds in her head, the most coherent of which sounded like, *finally!*

As Christy walked, she sipped her coffee and talked out loud, oblivious to the odd looks she was receiving. "When you disappeared, Frank, no one asked any questions because there were lots of reports that you had run off with Brianne Lymbourn. Brianne was a cover to make sure people didn't wonder about your disappearance. Now she's missing."

Not good.

"No, I agree."

Brianne hits on any guy she thinks is useful. Maybe she found someone new.

"Could be." Christy had almost reached Aaron's building, and with it her car. "Don't you think Aaron would know if she were with someone new?"

There was a sigh of satisfaction from the canvas bag, a mental smacking of lips. *Aaron's pretty self-centered. If Brianne wasn't hitting on him, he'd probably never notice.*

"That's not a lot of help."

The door to Aaron's building was thrust open. Quinn Armstrong strode out, a thunderous scowl on his face. He stopped when he saw Christy. The scowl turned to a smile that lit up his eyes, then darkened into a frown again. "I just talked to DeBolt."

Christy couldn't suppress a chuckle. "Is he still bleeding?"

Quinn grinned. "He said you were a nutcase who traveled with your familiar. What'd you do, bring Frank?" The cat popped its head out of the bag. "I might have known." There was resignation in Quinn's voice.

Christy laughed again as she set off for her car. "I just came from the place where Brianne was staying. She hasn't been seen in a week."

Quinn frowned as they walked. "You shouldn't have gone there on your own."

"Why not? Yaletown is a perfectly respectable neighborhood."

"Why not? Because Crack Graham might have been with her. Because both of them are involved in your husband's death and they're not likely to welcome questions from Frank Jamieson's wife."

Christy's car was across the street and down one block. She stopped at the light, waiting for it to change. "You're overreacting, Quinn. If Brianne had been there we'd have had a chat, but she wasn't. Get a grip!"

The guy's worried about you. Give him a break, Chris.

Quinn caught her arm as the light changed. He practically dragged her across the street. "You're lucky that she wasn't!"

On the far sidewalk, Christy stopped. She pulled her arm free, her temper simmering. "I wish she had been! I want to know what is going on, Quinn, and I think Brianne is a key. If I can find her, I'll learn who arranged for Crack Graham to use Frank's passport and for Brianne to go down to Mexico with him. I can find out who killed Frank."

Quinn glared at her. A muscle jumped in his cheek. "We."

"Excuse me?"

"We can find out who arranged all this. We, Christy, not I."

"It's my husband who's the victim. My life!"

"Not just your life," Quinn said, his tone gritty. The lights changed again. Pedestrians flowed around them. "Like it or not, I'm involved too."

So am I. Looks like we're a threesome.

"Shut up, Frank."

"Damn it, is that cat talking to you again?" Quinn drew a deep, annoyed breath.

The ringing of a cell phone interrupted them. He and Christy both automatically reached for their units, but it was Christy's that was ringing. She checked her watch as she answered, wondering if it was the school calling. "Yes?"

"Mrs. Jamieson, it's Detective Patterson here."

Christy frowned and glanced at Quinn. "Detective Patterson. This is unexpected." She began to walk. Quinn fell into step beside her. "What's up?"

"We have a report of a woman matching Brianne Lymbourn's description."

"Brianne?" Christy said eagerly. "Where is she? I've just come from the apartment where she was staying. No one there has seen her for at least a week."

"We believe she's in Kamloops, Mrs. Jamieson."

"Kamloops? Can't be. Kamloops isn't Brianne's style." Lying in the rain shadow of the Coast Mountains, Kamloops was a mid-sized city where two major highways met. It provided services to the ranchers who grazed cattle on the dry grasslands and accommodations for the tourists on their way somewhere else. It was a practical, working town without even a hint of glamour about it.

"We don't think she was in the area voluntarily." There was a second's hesitation before Patterson continued. "She's dead, Mrs. Jamieson."

Christy stopped short. She was vaguely aware that her car was parked two vehicles ahead and that Quinn was watching her with concern. "Would you repeat that, please?"

"Brianne Lymbourn is dead, Mrs. Jamieson. Murdered. In the Kamloops area."

CHAPTER 20

They flew to Kamloops.

Christy insisted on talking directly to the RCMP officer in charge of Brianne's case. Patterson had been reluctant, Quinn had protested, but Christy had been adamant. She said she needed closure.

Quinn's gut was sending out warning signals. Brianne's death had to be linked to Frank's, which meant that whoever had killed Frank was getting worried. Christy might want closure, but Quinn wanted out of the investigation, the sooner the better. If a trip to Kamloops and an interview with a cagey cop would help further that end, he was all for it.

There were no scheduled flights to Kamloops that left after school began and returned to Vancouver before it let out, so Quinn chartered a small plane to fly the three of them to Kamloops the next day.

Yeah, the three of them. That irked him. He hadn't wanted to bring the cat, but Christy insisted. The pilot wasn't too keen on flying an animal either, even one secured in a soft, onboard carrying case. He'd responded, though, when Christy raised her brows, her expression aloof, almost haughty, and became Mrs. Frank Jamieson, wife of wealth and privilege. The transformation was amazing. She'd gone from a worried, slightly harried woman to one who controlled the situation around her. He knew it wasn't natural, that it was a mask she assumed, but he found it damned sexy for all that.

The flight to Kamloops was short and uneventful. If Stormy was frightened at the noisy vibrations of the propellers, Frank kept him in line. The noise didn't allow for conversation, but flight was a visual treat as the low-flying plane soared over the tops of the magnificent Coast Mountains. By the time they were above Merritt, the green of the coastal rainforest had given way to the yellows and browns of the interior grasslands. High peaks were replaced by uplands and rolling hills. From there it wasn't long before they were above the Thompson River valley where Kamloops nestled.

An old railroad town, Kamloops was now home to British Columbia's newest regional university and an expanding ski resort, modeled after Whistler Village. The population topped eighty thousand, making it one of the bigger towns in the B.C. interior.

The police station was located in the downtown area where Kamloops had first been settled two centuries before. The detective who agreed to talk to them looked as hard and weathered as the old brick walls of the station building. His reluctance was obvious in the blank expression on his face and the shuttered one in his eyes. His name was Inspector Broadhurst. He was a senior man in the detachment.

"Detective Patterson e-mailed me you were coming," he said by way of greeting.

Christy smiled at him as they sat down in his office. She kept the bag containing the cat on her lap. "I hoped she would."

Broadhurst clasped his hands together on the blue blotter that covered the top of his battered wooden desk. "I am afraid you've wasted a trip. There's little I can tell you that you couldn't hear from Detective Patterson."

"Inspector, my husband has disappeared, and Brianne Lymbourn was the only link to his whereabouts. Quinn and I have been trying to locate her so we could ask her some questions. Before I give up my search for her I have to be certain that she's the person who is dead." Christy hesitated. Quinn noted that her hold on the bag tightened. "And if she is dead, I am hoping that the way in which she was killed might give us some clues that will lead us to Frank."

As she spoke Broadhurst's cold, blue eyes assessed her. Quinn knew he was seeing a woman trying very hard to hold it together, but whose emotions were close to the surface. He wondered if Broadhurst could see, as he could, the courage that had her sitting here prepared to look at photos of a grisly death, disturbing images that would remain in her mind's eye for an eternity, to provide proof and closure on another gruesome death.

Perhaps he did, for after a minute Broadhurst opened his hands, tapped them on the desktop and sat back. "Mrs. Jamieson, the woman's body was found at a private landfill near Merritt. She probably would never have been located, but there was a hole in the fencing around the site and a coyote got in." He raised his hand, palm up, a fatalistic gesture. "Dug up the body. Would have made a real mess of her if it hadn't been disturbed."

Out of the corner of his eye Quinn saw the pet carrier start to twitch. Broadhurst didn't know they'd brought a cat along to the meeting. He was relieved when Christy carefully placed the carrier on the floor. That feeling dissipated when she opened the zipper so the cat's head could pop out.

"A garbage dump? Brianne died in a garbage dump. Was that where she was killed? Or was her body moved there?"

"Killed there, definitely." Broadhurst shot her one of his assessing, cold-eyed looks. "Although why she was in the landfill raises questions. She was wearing the kind of clothes a woman chooses for an evening out—heels, a fancy dress, silk underpants, push up bra."

"Someone took her there to kill her and make her burial easier," Quinn said. He kept a wary eye on the restive package on the floor.

"Could be."

"Do you have any photographs of the body, Inspector?" Christy asked. She reached down to stroke the cat's head reassuringly.

"Mrs. Jamieson, I do not think that it is advisable for you to view the crime scene photos."

Christy's hand stopped. "Why?"

"The coyote was hungry."

Christy blanched.

With a sigh, the inspector continued, "And she'd been beaten."

"Is that how she died?" Christy asked in a soft voice.

"No, she was shot from behind."

The cat's head disappeared back inside the carrier. The zipper began to flex as the cat struggled to escape. "Please, Inspector. I need to see the photos."

Broadhurst's reluctance was obvious, but he opened a file folder, took some photos out, then spread them on the desk in front of Christy and Quinn.

The images were as bad as Quinn imagined. There were bruises on the woman's face and body, rope burns around her wrists. Christy stared at the photos for a moment, then picked up one that clearly showed Brianne's face and lowered the image so the cat could see it.

Quinn wasn't entirely sure that cats had the ability to read photos, but Christy was intent on giving Frank closure. Broadhurst frowned and seemed about to speak, but at that moment the cat began to howl.

"Think you can manage lunch?" Quinn asked.

They were out of the police station, into the sunlight of an arid fall day.

Christy breathed deep. "Yeah, sounds good."

How about shrimp this time? The cat likes tuna, but a little goes a long way, as far as I'm concerned.

"You don't deserve shrimp. Frank, how could you howl like that?"

Excuse me? I don't remember anyone asking me not to mourn a woman who died because she was involved with me.

"I did," Christy said, her temper heating. Arguments with Frank were always like this. She pointed out his shortcomings, and he avoided the issue. "In case you didn't notice, Broadhurst decided I was a total fruitcake when he found out I'd brought you with me."

And the point is?

"The point is that you blew it for us!"

Bull—!

"Don't swear at me!"

"You're talking to the cat again, aren't you?" Quinn said, guiding Christy across the street toward a sandwich shop.

"Yes, I am!"

"Are you having a marital spat?"

He sounded only mildly interested, but Christy had an immediate realization of what the conversation must sound like to someone else. She was, essentially, talking to herself. Arguments between a married couple were bad enough, but Quinn wouldn't hear Frank's annoying comments, only her increasingly irritated responses. "Yeah, I guess I am. Frank can be pretty infuriating when he wants to."

Thanks a lot!

She ignored him. Using the excuse that they were going into the sandwich shop, she zipped up the carrier, despite his protests. Quinn bought the sandwiches, splurging on a shrimp one for the cat, then they took them to a city park where they sat on a bench to eat.

Christy opened the bag and the cat popped out. As she laid out his sandwich, Frank said, *Shrimp! Babe, you're the best.*

"Thank Quinn. He bought it."

"What? Oh the sandwich. You're welcome, Frank."

"He hasn't thanked you yet."

"Figures." Quinn took a bite out of his turkey club. "I've been thinking about the information Broadhurst gave us. Brianne was found in a landfill."

Christy shuddered. "By coyotes."

"And the coyotes were noticed by a watchman, which means the dump was still being used."

Christy chewed on her veggie sub as she nodded. "Okay, so where does that get us?"

Nowhere. Brianne is dead.

Quinn said, "Remember the fundraiser? Gerry Fisher had us sitting on opposite sides of the table?"

"Sure. What about it?"

"I sat between two vice presidents who competed with each other by telling me stuff about Fisher Disposal, like where they had landfill sites. Guess what?"

Christy drew a deep hissing breath. "Fisher Disposal owns that landfill?"

"Bingo," Quinn said.

Can't we talk about something else?

"No, not when we're finally getting somewhere," Christy said heatedly.

"You're talking to the cat again. Share the wealth." Quinn took another bite of his turkey club.

"Sorry. Frank doesn't want to deal with this. He'd like to change the subject."

The look Quinn shot the cat was compassionate. "It can't be easy looking at a picture of a dead woman and wondering if your own body received the same treatment."

Tell him to stash his sympathy. I don't need it!

Christy sighed. "Or if your final resting place is a local landfill where your body will never be found."

"The thing is, did someone use Fisher's landfill to implicate him, or is he directly involved?" Quinn put the last of his sandwich into his mouth and chewed.

Christy shifted uneasily. "I can't believe Gerry would do something like this. He's not the type."

So what type of person commits murder?

"Good point," Christy muttered. Quinn cleared his throat. She took the hint and passed on what Frank had just said.

"I have to agree with the cat. We can't rule out Gerry Fisher, just because he is the least unpleasant of the trustees," Quinn said. "But Fisher Disposal's holdings are public knowledge. Anyone who wanted to implicate Gerry Fisher could find the location of his landfill and dump Brianne's body. The question is, who would know that Gerry Fisher was being blackmailed by Frank and so could be implicated in his death?"

My good buddy Aaron. The voice was filled with loathing.

"Frank thinks it's Aaron DeBolt," Christy said. She shoved the last of the sub into her mouth and chewed while Quinn considered that.

"If Gerry Fisher was arrested for the murder of Brianne Lymbourn, how would that benefit Aaron DeBolt? His source of income would be cut off."

"But not until Gerry was arrested," Christy said. "The person who put Brianne's body into the dump didn't expect the coyotes to dig up her grave."

Quinn said, "Good point. And if Brianne's body is found on a property owned by Gerry Fisher's company then he might be implicated. Okay, Aaron DeBolt as a suspect. Who else knew Frank was blackmailing Gerry Fisher?"

All of them.

Christy stared at the cat, who was now cleaning its whiskers with fastidious precision. "All of them? You mean all four of the trustees?"

Yup.

"Oh my."

The cat hopped onto Christy's lap. *They ganged up on me one day. I tried to play dumb, but they'd been talking amongst themselves. They knew it all, even old Aunt Ellen. They told me I had to stop.*

"And did you?"

No. I needed money, Chris. Aaron supplied prime stuff, but it was expensive.

"When did all this happen, Frank?" Christy's voice shook. Despite herself, she felt betrayed by the sham her marriage had become.

About a month before I got bashed in the alley.

Having finished off the turkey club, Quinn wiped his fingers with a paper napkin. "I'm taking a flying leap here and guessing that all of the trustees are still implicated, right?"

Christy nodded. "As well as Aaron DeBolt." She pushed the cat off her lap. "Frank, do you realize how this makes me feel? To know how empty our marriage had become? How could you?"

The cat hissed, then sat on the dry grass and licked first one paw then the other, a study in denial.

Quinn watched him moodily. "This situation is beginning to look pretty nasty to me. I want you out of it, Christy."

"All of this comes back to Frank and his blackmailing of his trustees. I'm involved, Quinn, I can't help it."

"Christy, as long as everyone accepted that Frank had run off with a woman and a fortune, his murder could be concealed. When we started to question his disappearance, the murderer began to feel insecure."

"So he—or she!—murdered Brianne. I get that. I just don't see how that puts me in more jeopardy than I was before."

"You're asking questions about Frank's whereabouts. You know about Brianne's death. You're too close."

She turned so she could look into his face. "So are you, Quinn. If I'm in danger, you are too." She touched his cheek.

He hesitated a moment, then he caught her head with his free hand and slowly covered her lips with his.

Christy closed her eyes, savoring the lovely sensation of his mouth over hers. If she could, she would make this moment last forever, preferably in a private place like their very own bedroom.

The kiss went on and on, creating wonderful sensations. When at last he pulled away, he said, "Promise me you won't be involved in this anymore."

"Only if you will promise me the same thing." Her voice was husky, charged with sensual promise.

"I can't," he said.

"There's your answer, then," she said, pulling his head down again. When his lips were a hair's breath away, she whispered, "We're in this together, Quinn. For better or worse."

CHAPTER 21

————◆————

The woman hosting the television show was perky. Her co-host was a dour fellow with big ears and a long, mournful face that reminded Roy of a basset hound. Together they were a popular combination. Roy munched healthy cereal that contained soy, flax, and oat bran as he tried to figure out why these two individuals had such popular appeal with the public.

As the two labored through an interview with a well-known actor shooting a movie in the area, Roy crunched the organic flakes. The questions were superficial, which allowed the actor to smile and smile and smile, while the girl bounced up and down, giggling. The male host glared at the actor as if he carried a contagious disease.

Roy found his head bobbing up and down in rhythm with the woman. Must be the breasts, he decided. She had huge boobs that flowed with her as she moved. Great enticement for men, but what about the female audience?

He munched more flakes, concentrating on the program. He had an interview on this show next week, and he wanted to know what he was getting into. Would they try to trip him up? Would they dote on his every word? Go for an intellectual discussion? The only way to figure out what kind of approach they'd take was to watch the show and hope the interviews he was seeing were representative.

After finishing up the flakes, he started on an organic apple. There was a howling sound in the studio. Odd that no one made any effort to fix the equipment causing it. That was disturbing. If the crew didn't have respect for the show, being interviewed would be a painful experience. He'd probably end up explaining proper procedures and doing his own interview himself.

That had happened once, years ago, in a small town in the American mid-west. His U.S. publisher had sent him on the granddaddy of all author tours, hitting not just the big cities, but also the small towns. If you had a bookstore, you could have Roy Armstrong visit it. The trip had taken weeks, Vivien had pretended she was going to divorce him, and he'd learned more about the book business than he'd ever wanted to know.

He got up to throw the apple core into the garbage. He wasn't happy about having gotten himself into this interview. He didn't have any books to sell at the moment and, while he didn't mind doing promotion, he didn't like to—

Old man, will you wake up? I need to talk to you!

"Frank?" There was no answer, of course. The cat wasn't in the house and so couldn't hear him. The cat was somewhere, though, and broadcasting loudly. He puzzled about it as he washed his hands, then returned to the living room. There the co-hosts were thanking the actor, the woman effusive, the man curt. The howling, he was thankful to note, had stopped.

The show's format was three interviews in each quarter hour, then ten minutes of news, weather, and sports. The first interview of this segment had been a city councilor, the second the actor. He'd just settled down to watch the third when the howling started again. This time it was accompanied by the thump of a body being thrown against a hard surface.

Roy frowned. The thump sounded as if it had come from the vicinity of his front door. He decided he'd better go down and investigate.

When he opened the door, the cat strutted inside. *Took you long enough!*

Roy shut the door and followed him up the stairs. He found the cat sitting on the sofa, tail lashing back and forth.

Your son is after my wife!

Roy considered that as he sat down in a chair that matched the oversized sofa. On the television, the guest was now a man who had invented a new form of lighting and was hawking it to the world, starting with local cable programming. The fellow was about as lively as a sloth in the sunshine, but concentrating on him had a lot more appeal than counseling a dead man who was mad at his son for taking away the man's woman.

The female host said something chipper and bounced in her seat. Inspiration hit Roy. "Would you look at that?" he said. "Isn't she something?"

She certainly is stacked.

They both contemplated the screen for a time. Roy began to hope that he'd successfully diverted the cat's attention away from thorny emotional problems. Then the inventor launched into a long-winded description of his wonderful new lighting system and the floodgates opened.

They did it in front of me.

Roy opened his eyes wide. "Really? My Quinn and your wife? You know, Frank, you're pushing your credibility with this one. They both know you're living in the cat. I can't see Quinn being that uninhibited."

They did it after we'd talked to the cop. I think Christy was mad at me. She probably believed all those rumors that Brianne and I were lovers.

"Could be," Roy said cautiously.

None of them were true. Not one. Yet they kept coming out. One of the trustees must have been feeding them to the press.

Roy looked at the cat. It crouched on the sofa, looking

dejected. "You really are in the dumps, aren't you?"

No one ever believed I was a decent guy at heart. They always looked at what was on the surface. The only one who cared was Christy, and now she's abandoned me.

On the TV screen the inventor had given way to a guy in a suit jacket doing the sports segment. Roy ignored him. "What happened to letting go and helping others to understand?"

It's harder than it looks.

"Well, yeah. I'm with you there." Roy almost felt sorry for the cat. Almost, but not quite. "So what's wrong with my Quinn as a mate for your Christy?"

He's a reporter.

"And a damn good one."

He's moving in on her too fast. She hasn't had time to mourn me yet.

"You've been gone for months, Frank. And it sounds like there wasn't much to your marriage for some time before that." The news headlines came on. The reader was a young woman with bright golden hair and an annoying voice that couldn't quite be tuned out.

I tried.

"Not hard enough," Roy said crisply.

I loved her.

"You loved drugs and partying more." Roy spared a brief moment of reflection for those years when partying and psychedelic drugs like LSD had been a prime focus of his own life. He'd dumped both when he met Vivien, and he didn't regret it, but he could still remember wild times when nothing seemed impossible and life was there to be lived.

I wasn't a bad guy.

There was a whine to the voice that matched the newsreader's nasal tones. Together they rose to an annoying crescendo. "Please, spare me," Roy muttered. More loudly he said, "Why don't you give Christy a break? Let her find her own way. Maybe she'll stick with Quinn, maybe not. It's up to her to decide, though, not you."

I'm not—

"In other news," the newsreader said, "the body of Brianne Lymbourn has been discovered near Kamloops. Lymbourn was the girlfriend of Frank Jamieson junior, son of ice cream entrepreneur Frank Jamieson. Jamieson and Lymbourn disappeared five months ago after Jamieson stole millions from his family trust. They were seen together in Mexico as recently as several days ago. Police are investigating."

"Well, hell," Roy said. "Quinn's been scooped by cable TV."

Christy knew that Quinn wanted her to stay out of the investigation. His reasons were logical, reasonable, maybe even correct. Her questions were drawing them closer to discovering who had killed Frank. That made her a problem. The more questions she asked, the more dangerous she became. Quinn wanted her to lie low. Let him do the legwork and take any flak that came their way.

She hadn't decided if she was going to go stay out of the active investigation yet, but she figured that checking facts was something she could do without arousing the suspicions of the killer, or worrying Quinn.

She began by doing a web search on local landfills. She discovered that most of the sites in the Lower Mainland area had been closed years ago. One had even become a housing development. But Fisher Disposal had one active site that was accepting deposits, and a second that had closed two years ago, both within easy driving distance of Vancouver.

As she saved the pages, she considered the possibility that Frank might be buried in one of the two Fisher sites. There was only one way to be sure. She'd have to visit each of them. The first would be the operational one, which happened to be the closest to Vancouver. She'd go there on her own, since Frank had avoided her ever since the kiss in Kamloops. She hoped he'd be over his snit by the time she went out to the second site.

* * *

The landfill was located in the Fraser Valley, a two-hour drive along the Trans Canada Highway and down a regional route that connected to a local road. The site was not what Christy expected. The access road was paved, the area around the fence was clean, and there was no obnoxious smell to contend with.

A chain link fence fifteen feet high surrounded the still operational site. At the wide, imposing gate was a booth where a man processed incoming traffic. All vehicles halted there, from massive trucks hauling loads of construction materials to insignificant little cars like Christy's.

"Hi," she said, after she'd rolled down her window.

The guard, burly and middle aged, said, "What have you got?" He was staring at her suspiciously, as if he didn't quite believe that she had anything to contribute to the dump.

Christy smiled. Smiles usually helped make people less grumpy, but this man's expression didn't change. "I don't have anything." That did get a reaction. His frown was something fearful to see. She hurried on. "At least, not yet. I'm planning a home reno project, though, and I want to know how to deal with the stuff I'm going to throw away. My local garbage pickup won't accept it. Is there someone I can talk to about bringing my old walls and, you know, that kind of stuff, here? Price and hours and how much makes up one load and all that?"

The guard studied her. His jaw worked. Christy couldn't be sure if he was chewing gum or tobacco. She wondered if he would spit out whatever was in his mouth if he found her wanting.

Finally he jerked his thumb in the direction of some trees. "Go park over there. The office is in the building beside the lot."

Christy parked where he'd told her, then she stood beside the car and assessed the set up. The site had a number of components. Foremost was the huge pit where most of the waste was accepted. However, there was also a center for material such as glass or plastic containers, newspapers, cardboard, and metal cans, which had to be recycled by law. Another area accepted hazardous wastes such as paints, household chemicals and engine oil. As well as the collection areas, there were a series of ponds and another hole that didn't appear to be used for garbage.

While she looked around the site, a massive truck, as big as a medium-sized dinosaur, stopped at the gate. Negotiations occurred between the driver of the leviathan and the grumpy guard, then the truck headed along the dirt road that led to the pit. Men sprang into action, directing the driver of the truck, helping him pull the bolts that secured the doors at the back, then they scuttled away. With slow precision, the container was lifted and the load slipped out. More action locking up, and the truck departed.

Christy thought about what she'd seen as she headed to the office. Nothing in the process was haphazard. The pit appeared to have been broken up into a grid, with the sections being used one at a time. The truck driver was directed to a specific part of the pit and he'd dumped the contents of his truck into a precise area.

She was also struck by the number of people working here. There was the guy at the gate, the men operating the dump area, the office staff. Now, most of them would be gone by the evening, but even so, the more people who were around the more likely it was that a body left here would be discovered.

The office was a large, prefab building that looked surprisingly clean and tidy for a dump site. The walls were fiberglass clapboard, painted a creamy yellow, the front door a warm chocolate brown. There were even curtains in the windows. Christy contemplated the door a moment, trying to make it fit into her preconceptions of what a dump site was all about, then gave up. She pushed it open and went inside.

A chest-high counter made of dark brown wood laminate graced the lobby. Behind it sat a woman working at a computer terminal. As Christy entered, the telephone rang. The receptionist smiled and waved Christy closer as she answered with practiced ease. While she talked, Christy looked around.

Opening off the lobby was a large room and a corridor. Four doors, possibly offices, opened off the narrow hallway, while the single large room appeared to be a staff room with a coffee maker set up on one counter. The beaker was half full, suggesting that the office staff wandered in and out when the urge took them.

The woman hung up the phone and smiled at Christy in a friendly way. "Sorry about that. What can I do for you?"

Christy explained about the mythical home reno once again, and the woman laughed. "So your hubby's leaving you to arrange the details while he has fun doing all the sawing and hammering. Typical. Do yourself a favor, honey, and call in a contractor. You won't be sorry."

Getting into the spirit of the charade, Christy sighed. "Not a chance. He's determined. For a long time he was satisfied with painting or hanging new doors—easy stuff. But he's been watching the decorating and home reno shows on TV. He feels empowered. He says he can do this."

The receptionist snorted. "If I were you, I'd have a contractor lined up for when the disasters start to happen and he loses interest. In the meantime, here are our rates." She set a folded brochure on the counter, then opened it. Pointing to the relevant areas, she said, "Hours of operation, rules and obligations—for both of us! Our landfill doesn't accept dangerous chemicals, banned substances, or other contaminates, although we have a recycling center for those kinds of wastes as a courtesy to our clients. Construction material only. This is a clean site. You want any more information, just give us a call or check out our website."

"What happens if my hubby gets here late? He has absolutely no sense of time. He's always trying to cram too much into the day."

The woman shook her head. "Aren't they the worst? Some guys just don't know when to quit. Well, you tell your man that our hours are firm. At closing time we lock those gates and don't let anyone in, no matter what. And just because you never know what people will do, we've got a posse of security guards watching the site." She jerked her head, indicating the corridor behind her desk. "There's a command center back there full of electronic gadgets that I couldn't tell you what they do, but there's always someone in there watching them, and others out prowling around the site. So your man better not even think about an illegal dump, because he'd be caught sure enough."

"Oh no! I didn't mean anything of the sort."

"Course you didn't, honey. I just wanted you to know that we are a safe, well-run operation here." She nodded, smiling as Christy thanked her and pocketed the brochure.

Outside, Christy walked to the edge of the parking lot. There she watched several more trucks follow the same process as the first one she'd seen. As the receptionist had said, the materials all appeared to be clean fill.

She wondered what Frank would have said if he'd come with her today.

CHAPTER 22

"Tell me what you remember just before you died."

I was blindfolded and someone hit me over the head. My hands were tied—like Brianne's. I couldn't see anything and my head hurt. I was not taking notes!

Christy resisted the urge to sigh. Frank was still not being any more cooperative and she wondered if it was because he was feeling edgy about going to the second Fisher Disposal landfill. "When did you regain consciousness?"

I was in the trunk of a car! How am I supposed to know?

"Frank, help me out here." She saw her turn and flicked on the indicator. This landfill was an older site, bought by Fisher Disposal in its early days of operation, not created from scratch as the one she'd visited earlier had been. The operation was closed now; in fact, it hadn't been accepting waste for nearly twenty years. Though located in the Fraser Valley as the newer Fisher site was, this landfill was much further from the Greater Vancouver area. The drive was three hours there and three back, a timing nightmare for Christy. She'd arranged to have Mary Petrofsky's mother pick Noelle up, just in case she didn't quite make it back during school hours.

"Brianne's body was found in a landfill site owned by Gerry Fisher. Maybe that's where they disposed of your body, too. In one of Gerry's landfill sites."

I don't like the way you said that.

"What?" Christy saw the marker for the local road she needed and turned off.

Disposed of your body, like you didn't care, or something. It sounds so cold.

From the highway, the site was another ten kilometers to a rather isolated location. The road curled past some houses and a farm or two. All were set well back from the pavement and shaded by large, old trees. "Is that it? What's got you so irritable? You're upset because you can't deal with your own death?"

Hey! There's no need to get personal.

Christy sighed. She'd been insensitive. She tried to imagine what it would be like to be Frank, a sexy, physical man, confident in his own body, now reduced to sharing his existence with a cat, but couldn't quite manage it. "You disappeared four months ago, Frank. By your own account, Aaron lured you into a situation where someone could hit you over the head, dump you in a car, and take you someplace to kill you. Since then you've been living in a cat, trying to figure out a way to make whoever murdered you pay so you can rest easy and go on to whatever."

Not quite.

"Not quite? What do you mean, not quite?"

I don't want to make anyone pay. And I'm not looking for peace. I wanted... Well, I wanted you to understand. I wanted Noelle to know that I didn't desert her. At least, not on purpose.

The smooth pavement had given way to rough, broken roadway. Christy slowed down in an effort to avoid, or at least minimize, the effects of the many potholes. The cat crouched on the passenger seat, claws dug into the upholstery, looking miserable.

She had a feeling that if a cat could cry, Stormy would be doing it right now. Or at least allowing an emotional sniff or two. She should be sympathetic. She should be supportive. Frank clearly hadn't adjusted to being dead. She snorted to herself. As if being dead was something you adjusted to. Give it a break, Christy! The man you lived with, loved with, was dead. He isn't the one who needs to adjust; it's you!

The car hit a particularly wide pothole, lurched, then bounced over another, smaller one. She swore to herself. "Frank, Noelle loves you. She will always love you. I'll make sure of that. When you disappeared, you and I weren't as close as we once were, but we were friends. I'm not angry with you, and I wouldn't ever say anything but the best about you to Noelle. I hope you know that."

I trust you, babe. I'm not so sure about your boyfriend.

"Boyfriend? What are you talking about?" The pavement was disintegrating badly on this part of the road. Not only were there big potholes, but there were lots of cracks and bumps. Some of the worst holes had been filled in with gravel, leaving a rough, uneven surface. Christy slowed again to avoid breaking an axel.

What will Armstrong say about me? He doesn't like me much.

"He doesn't know you. Frank, what's this got to do with Noelle?" She rounded a curve, then hit a series of holes that had the car bouncing along. The cat sat up. When they reached a smoother patch of road he stood up and put his paws on the dashboard. Ears pricked, he stared out the windshield. His tail danced from side to side in a silent expression of distress. "What are you doing, Frank?"

This is it, where I woke up. I remember those bumps. My head hurt so bad. I couldn't see. My hands were tied. I kept moving my head around, trying to find a comfortable position, but there wasn't much I could do to stop the hurting. I remember wishing I could die, just to stop the pain. A rueful note crept into the voice. *I guess it's true that you should be careful what you wish for.*

Christy had a vivid image of Frank's face, eyes dark with a kind of mournful humor, a half smile quirking his mouth. In that moment she thought her heart would break. This was it. This was real. Frank Jamieson was the man she'd loved and married, the man she'd made her beautiful daughter with. Even though she had a voice in her head, talking to her, and claiming to be Frank, somewhere deep in her heart she hadn't accepted that he could possibly be dead. In that instant, as the voice described what no one but Frank could know, she had to accept that it was true. The human form she'd loved and lain with was gone. The young man she saw in her mind's eye was as dead as last year's petunias. The essence of him might be sitting beside her in the family cat, but the physical reality of Frank was no more.

Her husband was dead. She had to move on.

She blinked rapidly to clear the tears that were threatening. It didn't work. She sniffed, loudly.

Christy...

"Frank!" She stopped the car, put her forehead on the steering wheel, and wept. The cat meowed. His paw tapped her arm gently, then he pushed his way onto her lap. She closed her arms around the warm, soft body, holding it close. Still sobbing, she laid her cheek against his. The cat purred, offering consolation. Occasionally he licked the tears from her cheek.

Around them were the quiet sounds of nature. Birds were singing, there was the rustle of trees, but no cars passed. The thin, fall sun beat down, warming the car, despite the crisp promise of winter in the air. Christy wept for her loss, wept for a life cut short and all that implied, wept for a little girl who would always miss the father she loved.

Gradually her tears slowed. The cat's rough tongue scratched across her cheek, the sun gave the promise of tomorrow, and the quiet somehow soothed.

Thank you.

She sat up and sniffed again. "For what?"

For caring enough for me to weep because I'm gone. The cat stood on its hind legs. With its paws on her shoulders it licked her cheeks clean. After a moment's hesitation, Christy stroked it, long gentle caresses from head to tail.

The cat gave her one final lick, then jumped over to the passenger seat. Christy started the car. The road became a series of curves, each filled with gaping potholes or ones that had been poorly filled. As the Coast Mountains loomed ahead, the well-tended farms gave way to shacks and tangled vegetation. The cat tensed. *We're nearly there.*

Christy's heart was beating hard and her hands clutched the wheel. The road widened, went round a turn, stopped at a chain link fence. A huge sign, with the words *Fisher Disposal* over the company logo, hung on the links. Though weathered, it looked remarkably like the sign outside of the active landfill site she had visited yesterday.

She turned off the engine. "We're here."

The cat stood with its front paws on the dash again, almost trembling with reaction. *Let me out!*

She opened the door. The cat bolted past her.

The chain link fencing was rusted and the great mesh doors looked as if they hadn't been open in forever. She glanced down, trying to see if there was any evidence of a car being driven through them within the last few months. Of course, there had been lots of weather since Frank had disappeared. Summer rains, drying, more rain, fall this time. Tire marks would disappear fast.

The cat was running along the fence, looking for a way in. *This is it. I'm in there. At least, my body's in there. This is where I was killed. Look at those gates. See the rust by the hinges? The car stopped, then there was a squeal, like metal rubbing on metal, before it started again. Then it bumped over rough ground before it stopped for the last time and they pulled me out. And it stank. Smell! This place reeks, doesn't it?*

It did smell. Like rotting garbage, in fact. Clearly this dump had accepted all kinds of refuse. It probably hadn't been capped off properly as well. Christy remembered Quinn talking about being part of a demonstration against Fisher Disposal when he was a teenager. They'd been protesting Fisher's poor environmental record. This site was the right age to have been one of those the dumps that had caused the problem. She put her hand over her nose to minimize the stench. If anyone ever made the effort to come up here they would never notice the stink of a decomposing body.

She looked around. The layout was much the same as the Fisher landfill she had visited yesterday, with the guard post by the gates and a parking lot to one side. The prefab house was gone, though, and there was no one around protecting the property. Only a chain with a padlock kept the gates locked.

And why should there be security? From what she could see, earth covered the refuse beneath. Natural decomposition was causing the escaping gas, which was more than enough to keep sightseers away. Landfills were supposed to be monitored to ensure that no contaminates escaped into the ground water, but monitoring didn't mean checking on a minute-by-minute basis. A Fisher employee could come up once a week, or once-a-day, whatever the law required, take a sample, and leave. They wouldn't be expected to remain here.

The cat was howling now. She scooped him up, held him close. Once again she rubbed her cheek against his. "I'm so sorry, Frank."

He licked her cheek. *Me too, babe. Me too.*

They reached home mid-afternoon. When contacted, Noelle opted to stay at Mary Petrofsky's house until dinnertime. The cat disappeared into some private safety zone. Frank had been silent and miserable on the return drive, and Christy respected his need to be alone. She suspected that knowing he was dead was one thing, but coming face-to-face with the reality of it was another, quite different, one. A period of quiet reflection would certainly be called for.

Christy wondered if she should contact Detective Patterson and ask to have the landfill searched. She could imagine the conversation. Patterson would ask how she'd concluded that the landfill was where Frank had been killed. Christy would respond that she'd visited the site and her cat had identified it. She could already hear the annoyed click of the phone as Patterson hung up. Even if she could convince Patterson—a big if—the landfill was out of the detective's jurisdiction. She'd have to organize the operation with other police forces, and for that she'd need hard evidence.

What Christy really wanted to do was to talk to Quinn, about the landfill and what it meant to their case, but more importantly, so she could share her feelings with him about the discovery. But when she knocked on his door there was no answer. With a resigned sigh, Christy went home to start dinner.

By the time Noelle came home, the cat had emerged from his hiding place. He was curled up on the sofa, saying little, participating not at all. He even ignored the shrimp Christy gave him for dinner.

"What's the matter with Daddy?" Noelle said as she dug into the spaghetti Christy had prepared.

Christy dropped her loaded fork. "Pardon me?"

"Come on, Mom. You know Dad's come back to us in Stormy. He says you can hear him like I can."

"You can hear Dad talking?"

"Sure." Noelle scooped up spaghetti. A noodle slithered through her teeth into her mouth like a thin, pale worm.

Christy picked up her fork again. "What do you talk about?"

"All kinds of stuff. I tell him what I do in school and he tells me about when he was a kid. I think I've got a better school than he did."

"Not necessarily better, honey, just different," Christy said automatically. Noelle was eating with great enthusiasm, no evidence of distress as she talked about her father. "It doesn't bother you that Daddy is a cat?"

Noelle cocked her head and screwed up her face as she thought about that. "Maybe. I'd like Daddy to be Daddy again, you know, so he could hug me and stuff, but he cuddles in my lap and purrs and that's cool too. And he spends more time with me now. I like that. So what's wrong with him? He didn't even say hi when I came in."

Christy ate some spaghetti and wondered how to tell Noelle that her father had just found the place his body was buried. "Dad's had an upsetting day. He needs to deal with some big problems. He'll be okay."

Noelle slithered more noodles through her teeth. As Christy was trying to decide if it was worth chastising her about her table manners, the girl said, "It must be tough living in a cat. I bet there are lots of things you want to do, but can't. Can I go outside after dinner, Mom?"

Christy needed some time to deal with her daughter's revelations. "Okay, but not for long. It gets dark early at this time of year. I don't want you out after dusk."

Noelle polished off the last of her supper, downed a full glass of milk in one gulp, and departed before her mother could change her mind. Christy finished her dinner more slowly, then she cleared the table and loaded the dishwasher. Finally, she could put off a conversation with the cat no longer.

"Frank," she said, going into the living room.

The cat opened wary eyes. *Yes?*

"How long have you been talking to Noelle?"

Since the beginning.

"Does she…I mean…" Christy couldn't quite bring herself to ask the main question, not yet. "What do you talk about?"

Her experiences, her fears, what my life was like when I was a kid, what I remember of my parents. Personal things. Why? Is she upset about something?

"No! No, she's fine. It's just that I had no idea you could talk to her, so when she told me tonight it came as a surprise."

The voice grunted. The cat stood up, stretched, then jumped off the couch, heading for the bowl of shrimp.

Christy followed. "Frank, have you, well, told her that you're dead?"

The voice sighed. *Yes.*

"And...did she accept that?"

I think so. I told her God had sent me back to help her understand why I was gone, because he knew I loved her and because God loved her. I think she liked that. It was a comfort for her.

Christy leaned against the counter as the cat devoured the shrimp with obvious enjoyment. "Do I need to worry about emotional scarring because of this?"

Why?

"Not every little girl has a father who lives in a cat and talks to her telepathically."

The cat paused to digest before consuming the rest of the bowl. *Good point. Look at it this way, though. This experience will broaden her mind and encourage her creativity. You're not going to tell me to stop talking to her, are you?*

"No." No, she couldn't do that to either of them. She hoped that Noelle would have the sense not to blurt out the secret to her teacher or one of the trustees. No one would believe she was speaking the literal truth. "Frank, she's worried about you, so don't clam up on her because of today, okay?"

The last of the shrimp disappeared into the cat's mouth. *I won't. Thanks for the supper, babe. Shrimp are the best.*

Christy sighed. "You're welcome."

When she dropped Noelle at school on Monday morning Mrs. Norton eyed her strangely. Christy told herself that she was being paranoid, but as she hugged Noelle good-bye, she whispered, "Have you told anybody that Daddy lives inside Stormy the Cat?"

Noelle drew away, looking at her mother with a disconcertingly adult expression. "No, of course not! Who'd believe me?"

Who indeed? Then why had the teacher avoided her gaze, while staring at her when she thought Christy wasn't looking? Something had happened. If it wasn't the story about Daddy being a cat, then what was it?

She found out when she opened the morning paper. There, on page three, was an old picture of her holding a glass of wine and staring goofily into the camera. It had been taken not long after she miscarried the baby that had been the incentive Frank needed to ask her to marry him. It had been a bleak time for Christy. They hadn't been in Vancouver very long, the trustees thought she was a gold digger, and Frank's Aunt Ellen had told her it was a good thing she lost the baby, because Frank wasn't ready to be a father and Christy wasn't capable of raising a Jamieson on her own. Lost and hurting, Christy had drunk too much and partied too hard.

The dark period had only lasted a few months, but it never seemed to go away. The press liked to use pictures of her from those days, when her hair was long, blond and tousled, holding a glass, laughing as if nothing was wrong in her life. They always referred to her as a party girl or blond fluff, or a hot chick. Throughout the summer, whenever the embezzlement of the trust was mentioned, so was her party girl image. Now, here it was again, with a massive headline that screamed, *Wife of Ice Cream King Heir Gone to Dogs—Or Cats?*

Brianne Lymbourn's death had already been in the news, but until this article Christy's name hadn't been linked with the death. The reporter who wrote this piece had not only made the connection, but he had also interviewed Aaron DeBolt. The way Aaron told it, Christy had barged into his apartment, carrying a manic cat in a shopping bag. Christy, he said, had been obsessed with finding Brianne so she could have it out with the woman who had stolen her husband. Aaron claimed he had been polite, supportive and helpful, but Christy was so far gone in her hatred that she had screamed obscenities at him, setting off the cat, which had jumped out of the bag and lacerated Aaron so badly he had to go to a hospital emergency room.

If the interview with Aaron wasn't bad enough, the reporter had also learned of Christy's visit to the Kamloops police detachment. The police declined to comment, so the reporter was free to suggest that Christy was being interviewed as a suspect in Brianne's death.

By the time Christy finished the article she was shaking. There was no byline attached to the story, just the awful headline and the enormous, out-of-date picture. So who had provided the info? And who wrote it?

Anger began to seep through the shock. Anger at having her life judged and found wanting. Anger that no one had asked her for her side. Anger that someone believed she could be libeled without fear of repercussion.

She busied herself making a pot of coffee. "Damn reporters," she muttered as she poured coffee into a mug with a picture of Noelle on the front. She read the article again, felt the anger grow, let it simmer. She wanted to be angry. She had a right to be angry. The article had violated her privacy. Someone had betrayed her trust. She wanted to know who so she could tell them exactly what she thought of them in the rudest way possible.

The doorbell rang.

It was Quinn. Her heart leapt at the sight of him, then sank when she saw the paper he held. "Come in," she said, stepping away from the door. "I've just made a pot of coffee."

He lifted his hand. "Christy—"

She turned her back and headed up the stairs. He followed.

In the kitchen his eyes flicked over the open paper, then back up to Christy's face. "You've seen the article."

She made an abrupt slashing motion with her hand. "Quinn, how could someone write something like this?"

He put his paper by hers. "The facts are essentially correct."

She glared at him, then turned to a cupboard to haul out a mug. Her hand was shaking as she poured. "The spin isn't.

And the spin distorts the facts." She thrust the cup at him.

"Perhaps." He accepted the mug and sipped, watching her over the rim.

"Perhaps! You're defending him?"

"Or her—"

"Then you know who the author is? I can't believe it's a woman. It sounds so much like a man!"

He put the mug down then held out his hand, palm forward. "Whoa! I don't know who wrote this. I can guess, and I can find out, but at this moment I don't know for sure."

She glared at him, her temper steaming full blast. She wanted clear, defined answers. She wanted a name and a person she could rail at, someone to vent her anger on, someone to hand her pain to. Right now reporters were about the lowest creatures on this earth, as far as she was concerned. They were all equally unethical, all equally relentless.

She wanted a reporter to wale on. Luckily, one was standing right in front of her. "I suppose you're the one who leaked the details about our Kamloops visit."

She thought he paled. "What?" Then his eyes narrowed as anger rushed in to rescue him. "Say that again. I dare you to say that again and mean it."

She thrust out her chin, balled her fists. "Someone betrayed me. Someone close to me."

"And you think it was me?"

She raised a brow, saying nothing, letting her expression speak for her.

"Why?"

"You're a reporter, Quinn. I don't trust reporters."

He was white now, his eyes ice-blue chips of fury. He dumped his coffee into the sink and slammed the cup onto the counter in a savage gesture. "Fine. Hear this, lady. I didn't betray you. I didn't write this article. I don't know who did, but I'll find out, and when I do I'll make you take back those words."

He didn't slam out of the room. He walked quickly and lightly, closing the front door behind him with nothing more than an ordinary snap.

Christy slowly released her balled fists. She turned to the counter and put her elbows on the granite surface, then she dropped her head into her hands and began to sob.

CHAPTER 23

When she went to pick up Noelle after school, Christy was ready to deal with the teacher. She planned to explain that the reporter had not interviewed her and so most of the story had been based on old information and speculation. She hoped Mrs. Morton would buy it.

She reached the school a few minutes after the bell had rung. Usually Noelle was waiting at the door, chatting with those of her classmates who were also waiting for a parent to arrive. She'd run to Christy then leap into her arms and give her mom a big hug in greeting.

Today the usual crowd hung around the doorway, but Noelle was nowhere in sight. When Christy neared, Mary Petrofsky pointed to the classroom. "She's in there. With the lady who came to see her today."

"What lady?"

"The one from Social Services," Mary said. Her eyes gleamed with excitement. "We had the principal as our teacher all afternoon so she could talk to Mrs. Morton and Noelle."

Christy stared at the little girl in horror. "The lady from Social Services spent the afternoon talking to Mrs. Morton and Noelle?"

Mary nodded. She was clearly enjoying the importance of being the bearer of news.

Christy looked at the door. It gaped open, a dark, dangerous cavity leading into a cave full of danger. She didn't want to go through that door, to face the possibility that the unnamed Lady From Social Services might take her daughter away from her. She wanted to turn around and walk away, to go back to her townhouse and hide inside, as if that would somehow eliminate this problem, as if it had never happened.

She smiled at Mary, thanked her, and then walked through the door as if it was a perfectly normal day. Inside she found Noelle sitting at her desk looking mutinous. Her hands were linked together in front of her and she was saying hotly, "Of course my mommy will be here. She picks me up every day!"

Anger flooded Christy. How dare they pressure her daughter that way! At the same time pride brought a bright shine to the dark emotion. Noelle's defense of her in the face of two powerful, adult authority figures showed just how much the girl trusted and believed in her. Her daughter's courage steadied Christy for what was to come.

She walked straight to Noelle's desk without acknowledging either the teacher or the social worker. "Hi, kiddo," she said, bending down for a hug and a kiss. "I was talking to Mary Petrofsky outside. How come you're sitting in here instead of waiting in the schoolyard as usual?"

Noelle hugged Christy tight. "Mrs. Morton said I had to wait here. She doesn't believe that you pick me up every day."

Christy looked over Noelle's head. She raised her brows, shooting the teacher a haughty look. "Mrs. Morton doesn't come outside to watch you guys until you leave, so she doesn't always know which child is picked up by a mom or a dad and which ones go to daycare or home on their own."

"These children are not in kindergarten!" Mrs. Morton said. "We teach them independence. They are old enough to wait outside on their own."

"Exactly." Christy allowed a small, humorless smile. "Noelle knows I will be there to pick her up every day. I may occasionally be a few minutes late, but I'll always be here. I believe she was trying to explain that to you."

Mrs. Morton had the grace to color. "After reading that article, I did wonder if perhaps...I was going to watch today and for the next little while, to see if, well, everything was all right."

I'll bet you were, Christy thought. She let it go, though. Getting into a fight with her child's teacher wouldn't help. Instead, she looked at the woman beside Mrs. Morton. She appeared ordinary. She was, perhaps, overweight, but not excessively so. Her hair was short, cut so that it could be cared for easily and her clothes were practical—shoes that were well broken in and had flat heels, inexpensive slacks and a polyester shell beneath a tailored jacket. Her purse was a briefcase made of some man-made faux leather product. In her hand was a clipboard, stacked with papers. Christy glanced at Mrs. Morton again. "Will you introduce us?"

Mrs. Morton flushed. "This is Joan Shively. She's from the Ministry of Children and the Family."

"She's been asking me questions, Mom." Noelle sniffed, tears very close.

Christy hugged her. "What kind of questions, kiddo?"

"About what it's like living at home. The kind of stuff you do. How you look after me. I didn't like it."

"Ms. Shively is trying to make sure that you're treated the best you can be," Christy said, giving Noelle another hug. She looked at Joan Shively over the top of her daughter's head. "Don't worry about it."

Joan Shively said briskly, "Your mother is right, Noelle. We only have your best interests at heart. Mrs. Jamieson, I would like to see where Noelle lives. If you show me your car, I'll follow you back."

Christy allowed herself a thin smile, although she was seething inside. "That would be rather difficult, as I walked over. It's not far, and I don't believe in driving kids when it's possible to walk."

Joan Shively shuffled through the papers on the clipboard, then wrote something down. "What about security measures?"

Truly baffled, Christy said, "What security?"

Shively pointed to Noelle, who was still huddled against Christy. "For your daughter, Mrs. Jamieson. I gather she's heir to a fortune. There's always the possibility of kidnapping."

Christy frowned. "She was heir to a fortune, until embezzlement and debts turned it into nothing more than a nice little nest egg for her university tuition."

Pursing her lips in an expression of disbelief, Joan Shively said, "So you have no security measures in place."

Christy hung on to her temper. "Ms. Shively, I walk my daughter to school every day and make sure she is safely in her classroom. At the end of the day I pick her up, again at her classroom. I cannot control what happens while she is in the care of the school, but I trust her teacher and the administration of this institution." She took Noelle's hand. "Come on, kiddo, we're heading home. Ms. Shively can meet us there."

"Good-bye, Mrs. Morton," Noelle said politely. "See you tomorrow."

"See you tomorrow," Mrs. Morton said. As they went out the door, Christy heard her add, "She really is a very well-mannered child."

Mary Petrofsky and the other kids had all gone on their way, so the schoolyard was empty. "Mom," Noelle said. Christy looked at her. "Dad says he didn't steal all our money. He says someone else did it. Is that true?"

"Yes." Panic surged through Christy. She crouched down so she and her daughter were eye to eye. "Noelle, you didn't mention Daddy to Mrs. Morton or Ms. Shively, did you?"

Noelle shook her head.

"Good. Now look, if Ms. Shively—"

"I thought I would walk home with you, rather than

driving. That way I can get a good feel for Noelle's lifestyle."

"Great." Christy straightened slowly. Noelle clutched her hand tightly.

Throughout the walk home the social worker bombarded Noelle with questions about her friends, what they were like, what kind of games they played. Then she asked Christy about the neighbors and why she'd chosen this area to relocate to when she'd decided to sell the mansion.

"I didn't decide, Ms. Shively. The mansion was sold by the person who embezzled my husband's trust fund."

"Nonsense," Joan Shively said. "I have documents proving you arranged the sale. When the Jamieson trustees protested, believing the Jamieson mansion was part of Noelle's heritage, you insisted that it was nothing more than an expensive, difficult-to-maintain, house."

Christy stared at her. "You have letters from me demanding the house be sold because it was expensive to run?"

"No. I have copies of letters from the Trust pleading with you to reconsider. I believe the mansion sold for a considerable amount of money. I understand you used a small portion to buy the townhouse you now live in and that you have squandered the rest on expensive clothes, jewels, and social events."

Noelle tugged at her hand. "Can I see your jewels when you show them to Ms. Shively, Mom? I've never seen them before. Are they pretty?"

"Where are you getting all this stuff?" Christy said. She knew though. Joan Shively was getting her info from the same person who had been feeding lies to the press.

"I know you've got that pretty dress you wore when you went to the party with Quinn, but where are the rest?" Noelle said. "Usually you just wear jeans."

"I can't divulge my sources," Joan Shively said. She was frowning at Noelle. "Who is Quinn, dear?"

"He's Mom's friend. He lives with his dad two doors

down. Roy is a good friend of mine. He babysits me sometimes."

"I see," Shively said.

Christy almost groaned. She said hastily, "I had an audit of the Jamieson Trust done a few weeks ago. It proved that substantial funds have been embezzled from the trust. I also have letters proving that the mansion was sold as part of the same embezzlement scheme. Someone has supplied you with a lot of misinformation, Ms. Shively."

"The documentation is comprehensive," Shively said.

"So is mine," Christy retorted. "I keep all of my correspondence with the Trust. I have their letters, as well as copies of my responses." They had reached the edge of the townhouse complex. Christy pointed to a street. "My townhouse is just over there."

"I'd like to see those letters," Shively said.

"I'll make copies and send them to you."

"No. I want the originals."

They reached Christy's walk. She said, "Hey, Noelle, is this one of Mary Petrofsky's daycare days?"

Noelle looked warily from her mother to the social worker. "No, she's home today."

Christy hugged her daughter tightly. "Then why don't you guys play while I talk to Ms. Shively?"

Noelle nodded. "Okay, Mom."

Christy watched her daughter dart up the street to Mary's house before she turned back to Shively. "The file is packed away in a box. I'll have to dig it up first."

"You haven't finished unpacking from the move yet?"

Christy sighed. "Look, come inside. I'll find the file and you can take a look at it. I'm not going to give you the originals though. They're the only proof I have that someone is deliberately trying to blacken my name."

Joan Shively stared at her for a minute, then she nodded. "I will need to inspect your home, in any case."

It was unnerving, searching for a file in the basement while a stranger wandered freely through her house. Christy tried not to imagine Shively picking up cushions to look underneath, or opening cupboards to view their contents. With each passing moment her anger at the trustees grew. She was sure that Joan Shively was here as a result of their petition to have custody of Noelle given to them. That one of them had forged documents so that Christy appeared to be interested in her daughter only for the money she could wring from the Jamieson estate was a despicable, perhaps desperate, ploy.

Christy found the file she needed with others in the bottom of a cabinet in the basement. The files were bunched together in no sort of order. She made a mental note to organize them if her life ever got back to normal, then she yanked out the folder and ran upstairs. Shively might feel she had the right to look through Noelle's home, but she could do it with Christy tagging along, monitoring her. She found the social worker in Noelle's bedroom.

"Your daughter has a great many stuffed toys."

"She likes animals," Christy said. She thrust the file at Shively. "Take a look at this. I'm sure you'll find the documents quite different from the ones you received."

As Joan Shively read the letters, she frowned. "I would have to study these letters in more depth, but they seem to indicate that what you say is true." She closed the file, then opened her briefcase.

Christy held out her hand. "I'll keep the file, as I said. I'll provide you with photocopies."

"I can copy these in office and return the originals to you."

There was no reason to believe Joan Shively was not an honest woman caught in a web of lies, but caution kept Christy's hand out in silent demand. "I'll bring the file to your office. For now it stays with me."

The social worker pursed her lips in annoyance, but she handed over the folder. She pulled out an appointment book, thick with notes paper-clipped to the pages, checked it and said, "I'm available between two and three on Wednesday."

"And I will be picking up my daughter from school about that time. How about Thursday?" The woman's eyes flickered. Christy realized that she'd used the time as a sort of test. They agreed to meet mid-morning. Shively pushed her planner into her briefcase and hefted it as she prepared to leave.

Christy followed her down the stairs and out onto the porch.

"Thank you for your time, Mrs. Jamieson," Shively said formally.

The cat bounded up the stairs, a maimed, half-dead mouse clutched in his jaws. He spat the creature out at Christy's feet.

Shively screamed. The mouse twitched, then lay still.

The cat thought you deserved a treat. I couldn't persuade him you'd rather have chocolate. He doesn't always listen to me. Who the hell is this?

Without thinking, Christy said, "This is Joan Shively. She's a social worker. She's here to see if I'm abusing Noelle."

What?!

Shively had stopped screaming. Christy looked over to see that the woman was staring at her in a peculiar way. "You do talk to cats."

"Mommy, what's wrong?" Noelle had come running over as a result of Shively's scream. She saw the mouse. "Yuck." She turned to the cat. Shaking her finger, she said, "Stormy, you shouldn't do that. It's not right. The little mouse was your friend."

Hey kiddo, I'm with you. The cat, on the other hand, enjoys a mouse or two at mealtimes.

"Ew," Noelle said.

Shively frowned.

Down the street a door opened, then slammed shut. "Roy!" Noelle shouted and bounded over to the porch where Roy Armstrong was standing, stretching luxuriously, his arms outstretched, his head thrown back.

He looked as if he'd just woken up after sleeping off a bender. His clothes were rumpled, while his long hair was escaping from its ponytail, giving him a wild, manic appearance. When Noelle reached his porch he scooped her up, gave her a big hug, then they ambled back to Christy's place hand in hand.

As he neared he looked even worse, if that was possible. His face was drawn, his eyes bloodshot. Christy could see Joan Shively making mental notes. She wondered if the woman was sniffing the air to see if she could smell booze on his breath.

When he reached Christy he shot her a weary, but contented smile. "It's done," he said by way of greeting.

Shively tilted her head and looked at him sideways.

"What's done?" Noelle asked.

Roy smiled and ruffled her hair. "What—Oh. Don't mind me if I sound a little vague. I haven't had any sleep in a couple of days. I had to get it finished, you see. The murder. There was more to do than I'd expected. Clues and stuff. But it's done. Over. Completed."

"Murder?" Shively said, frowning.

A car appeared at the top of the street, moving too quickly. "Let's step back a bit, until the car passes," Christy drew Noelle out of harm's way.

Roy looked around. "Oh, that's okay. It's only Quinn. He'll park at our place."

Shively raised her brows. "This is the Quinn Noelle spoke about?"

"Probably," Roy said cheerfully. "My son, Quinn Armstrong." Apparently just noticing he was talking to someone he didn't know, he added, "I'm Roy Armstrong, by the way. Who are you?"

"Joan Shively." She did not hold out her hand.

She's a social worker.

"A social worker!" Roy said, narrowing his bloodshot eyes.

"I don't believe I mentioned that," Shively said.

"He probably heard us talking," Christy said, casting her eyes heavenward.

Roy stared at Shively for a minute. Christy could see the wheels working in his head as he searched for an explanation. "Noelle mentioned it as we walked over."

Since they'd all heard every word the child had said, this wasn't the greatest of lies. Shively frowned some more and this time she pursed her lips.

The car door slammed. Quinn marched purposefully over to the little crowd on Christy's doorstep. "I'm glad you're here," he said, planting himself foursquare in front of Christy.

"Quinn, this is—"

"Joan Shively." This time the social worker held out her hand and waited, her head cocked.

Quinn ignored her. He said to Christy, "The guy who wrote that story was the same little weasel who was pumping out lies about you before."

Shively lowered her hand. "You have proof that the story in the paper is untrue?"

Quinn continued on, focused on Christy. "It was one of the trustees who fed him the stuff. I forced the little worm to show me the press release he used when he wrote the article. It was on the Trust's letterhead."

"How did you *force* this individual to share his information?" Shively demanded, her voice rising with disapproval.

Quinn seemed to notice her for the first time. "Who are you?"

"She's a social worker, here to snatch Noelle," Roy said.

"Now just a minute—"

"She wants to take me away from you, Mommy?" Noelle asked, then started to cry.

Christy caught her up in a hug. "Don't worry, honey. No one's going to take you away from me."

Damn right.

Noelle looked at the cat, then she sniffed and pulled away from Christy. Facing the social worker, she said with great dignity, "This is my family. I don't ever want to go away from them. Leave me alone."

"You know, I don't think we ever properly introduced ourselves. As I mentioned, I'm Roy Armstrong. I'm a writer. Ten books published, a million copies in print. Two Governor General's Awards. This is my son, Quinn Armstrong. He's a prize-winning journalist."

Joan Shively glared at Roy and Quinn. Roy smiled serenely. Quinn glared back. "I think I understand your meaning, Mr. Armstrong, and I do not appreciate it." She turned to Christy and said crisply, "Mrs. Jamieson, I will see you in my office on Thursday."

As she marched away, Christy sat down on the porch steps. "I'm toast."

CHAPTER 24

R oy looked at his son. "What exactly *did* you mean by 'forced' him to show you his data?"

Quinn frowned. Noelle had thrown her arms around Christy's neck and buried her cheek against her mother's. The child was crying. Christy offered wordless sounds of comfort. "I had no idea that woman was a social worker."

"Of course you didn't," Roy said. "The thing is, if you forced someone to divulge information by roughing them up, that woman can use it against Christy, because of her association with you. So did you?"

"Come on, Dad! What do you think?"

"I think you're worried about Christy and that you'd do whatever needed to be done. So what needed to be done?"

"I threatened him."

Roy shot him an impatient look. "We got that. What did you threaten him with?"

"Professional exposé. I told him I had proof that everything he'd written was untrue and that I would make sure all the news outlets in town knew he was submitting fictionalized reports. He'd never sell another piece again."

"Shively thought you'd beaten him up," Christy said, looking over the head of her clinging daughter.

Her eyes were red, her expression bleak. His gut clenched as he looked at her. He might not have caused all of this, but he'd been part of it. He'd been so full of anger that he'd wanted to prove to her he was not the cause of her problems. He'd rushed home to confront her without pausing to consider.

"It's just an expression." He went over to the porch. A mouse lay unmoving. If Noelle raised her head from her mother's neck, the mouse would be right in her field of vision. "Cat," he said, pointing. "Deal with this." He nodded in Noelle's direction. If Frank did live inside the cat, he should act without the need for further explanation.

Stormy put his paw on the mouse and glared at Quinn. Roy laughed. Christy made a watery sound that might have been a chuckle and said, "Tell Stormy thank you very much, but you're right, chocolate is more what I need right now."

The cat picked up the mouse in its mouth. Noelle sat up, rubbing her eyes. She laughed and hiccupped at the same time as the cat slowly, with great dignity, descended the stairs.

Quinn stared. "What is so funny?"

"Stormy and Frank had an argument about the mouse. Stormy brought it as a present for Christy and he apparently was hard to convince that it should be taken away," Roy said. "We only heard Frank's side, so it was a little goofy."

"You okay, Noelle?" Christy's eyes searched her daughter's face.

Noelle nodded.

"All of you can hear the da—the cat talking?" Quinn demanded incredulously.

Christy nodded, but stayed focused on her daughter. "Do you want to stay here? Or play with Mary?"

Noelle sniffed. "If I play with Mary will you sit here, where I can see you?"

Christy's jaw hardened for a minute, then she smiled and nodded. "You bet, kiddo."

"Okay. I'll see if Mary still wants to come out." Noelle gave Christy a kiss and a hug, then she ran off, looking back several times along the way. Just before she reached Mary Petrofsky's house, the cat appeared from some bushes. She stopped to give it a pat as it twined about her legs. Then she ran on while the cat trotted back to Christy's walkway.

"This has got to end," Christy said, watching her daughter. "I don't care what it takes. Whoever killed Frank and embezzled from the trust must be exposed. Now."

Quinn sat down beside her on the steps. He wished she'd lean against him and let him comfort her, but she was sitting with her arms around her knees, contained within herself. Her features were set in an expression that was not angry, but determined. "Christy—"

She shook her head. "Tell me what you know, Quinn. Frank," she said to the cat, now sauntering up the walk, "don't hold anything back. We need everything you remember. I will not let these people take our daughter."

"Clearly it's one of the trustees," Roy said. He ran his fingers through his hair, dislodging more graying locks from his ponytail in the process.

For the first time since he'd arrived home Quinn took a good look at his father. "Have you had any sleep in the last twenty-four hours, Dad?"

"No," Roy said simply. "I was on a roll. I finished my rough draft." He grinned. "I've never tried a murder mystery before, and it's harder than it looks, but Frank's been helping me."

"You mean the cat's been feeding you information and keeping it from the rest of us?" Quinn asked, absolutely furious.

Roy stared at him, aghast. "No! Not at all. Frank has been talking to me about what happened and I've been…speculating. Plotting. Building scenarios. I don't know if I'm right or not, but I have a heck of a good story."

"Dad!"

"So who do you think did it, Roy?" Christy asked.

"In my story Edward Bidwell, the lawyer, did it. I didn't call him by name, of course, because he'd sue me, but he's the one."

"Why?" she said, her voice flat, her eyes hard.

"Well, lots of reasons, actually. Frank was blackmailing him because he's a bigamist, so not only was his marriage on the line, but so was his professional reputation. Through his wife, Bidwell has had access to clients with money and status. It's his client list that has provided him with a partnership in one of the city's oldest and most prestigious law firms. If his wife ever found out that he was already married when she married him she'd be furious. If she discovered the marriage had never ended, well…So even though neither he, nor the girl he married down in Mexico, want to acknowledge their marriage, he'd still have much to lose if it ever came out."

"I don't know, Dad. What about Aaron DeBolt? How would he tie into Bidwell? The only trustee he knew about was Gerry Fisher."

"Ah," Roy said, waving his forefinger, "that's the kicker. Frank doesn't know whether he told DeBolt about Bidwell or not. The night he blurted out the details of his blackmail scheme, he and Aaron were drinking and doing dope. They got mellow. He was bragging. He remembers talking about Fisher, then nothing. Frank could have spilled the goods about what he had on each of the trustees. He doesn't know. If DeBolt was a little less stoned than Frank was, he might have remembered everything."

"Then that means any one of the trustees could be behind this," Christy said.

"I still like Bidwell," Roy said. "He's got a lot to lose."

"They've all got a lot to lose," Quinn said. "But you're right. Marriage, social standing, career, money, Edward Bidwell would lose it all if it came out that he was a bigamist."

"It's not just Frank, anymore," Christy said. "Someone killed Brianne. Is there any way of connecting Edward Bidwell to her death?"

"Bidwell has a client with a property about thirty miles from Kamloops. He flew there for a meeting around that time. He rented a car and put way more miles on it than a round trip to the client's estate would account for." Quinn felt himself coloring as Christy looked at him with surprise. "Look, I didn't spend the day just verbally abusing other reporters. I also did some digging."

Christy smiled faintly. "What else did you find out?"

Heartened by this evidence of thawing, Quinn said, "Ellen Jamieson was in the area too. She's on the board of a charity that funds halfway houses for women. One opened in Kamloops about the time Brianne was killed. Ellen was there for the official ceremony. Gerry Fisher was looking at a new site for a newspaper recycling plant. He flew to the city, then was escorted from location to location by the mayor and the town council. There was a civic dinner and a public meeting before he flew back to Vancouver."

"Frank just pointed out that none of them could have taken Brianne there," Christy said. "So who did?"

"Crack Graham," Roy said. "Obviously. She must have met him somewhere near her apartment, in Yaletown probably, expecting that they were going out for the evening. He may have killed her here in Vancouver, or at the landfill. But I'll bet he's the one who did it."

"So the trustee who is behind all this didn't necessarily have to be in the area where Brianne's body turned up." Christy sighed. "We're really no further ahead."

"I still vote for Bidwell," Roy said.

"He's not a bad choice," Quinn said.

"Frank agrees," Christy said. She shook her head. "But Bidwell is only a guess. We need proof."

"When the police find Graham, they'll get the proof we need," Roy said.

Christy shook her head. "I can't wait. I need to know now. I have a meeting with that social worker on Thursday morning. Until then I think Noelle is safe, but who knows what is going to happen next? And on Thursday I'm going to have to work real hard to convince Joan Shively that somebody is setting me up. I need proof that somebody is one of the trustees. So, I am going to get that proof."

"How?" Quinn said. Alarm bells were going off in his head.

"I'm going to talk to each of them about Frank's blackmailing. I'm going to let them know that their secret isn't safe, not any more.

She started with Ellen Jamieson. The three males in her life had all argued that she shouldn't do this alone, but Christy had been adamant. She knew the trustees better than anyone, other than Frank. Since Frank only seemed able to communicate with certain people, he couldn't talk to them directly, so that meant Christy was the one to do it.

She brushed aside Quinn's claim that his interview skills would serve the purpose better. This was her show. She had to do it herself.

Ellen agreed to meet her that evening in the lobby bar of the venerable Hotel Vancouver. Christy rushed through dinner and didn't bother changing from her jeans and plain white shirt, so she arrived first. She found a table with a good view of the entryway and sat with her back to the wall.

Then she waited for half an hour.

When Ellen arrived, she made a grand entrance. Dressed in a sumptuous evening gown that sparkled in the light, she swept up the low staircase into the bar area. Pausing, she glanced at a jeweled watch on her wrist before she scanned the tables. In that moment her resemblance to Frank was so strong that raw emotion squeezed Christy's heart. Along with grief was pity for a family so dysfunctional that she was actually considering her husband's aunt might also be his murderer.

Ellen's gaze flicked over Christy, then moved on. Christy didn't wave to catch her attention. She knew Ellen had seen her. The woman was just making a statement about how unimportant this meeting was to her. *Well, let her play her little games.* Ellen Jamieson was in for a shock.

Ellen tossed her blond head, and glided over to the table where Christy sat. "I'm running late, and I'm the guest of honor at private function. Say what you have to quickly. I have no time for this."

"I'm looking for a murderer, Ellen, and you're on my list."

For a moment she stared wordlessly at Christy, her expression blank, then she laughed and shook her head. "What nonsense!"

Christy's heart was pounding and her hands were sweating with nerves, but she was outwardly cool. She'd learned how to be a Jamieson. "Someone killed Brianne Lymbourn outside of Kamloops, where you opened a women's shelter about the same time."

Ellen gasped. "Are you accusing me of killing Frank's girlfriend? How dare you! You're only doing this to shift suspicion away from yourself. You have good reason to be jealous of Brianne."

"No, I don't, Ellen."

"Of course you do. After all, Brianne has been living with the husband who abandoned you. Even if you didn't love Frank—and I've always doubted that you did—pride would provide a good reason for resenting Brianne."

"Frank was never in Mexico with Brianne," Christy said steadily.

Ellen laughed. "Lord, I thought you were more of a realist than that. Frank was never the man my brother was. He was weak. He didn't deserve that beautiful little girl you gave him. Look how he treated her, abandoning her for a money and a gold digger like Brianne Lymbourn."

"Frank didn't abandon us, Ellen. He was murdered, like Brianne. Both his body and Brianne's were buried in Gerry Fisher's dump sites."

Ellen jerked in her seat and her face paled as the impact of Christy's statement shook her composure, but she recovered quickly. "Christy, what nonsense is this? My nephew is one of those people who always gets what he wants. He's good to look at and fun to be around. No one takes him seriously, and no one would bother killing him. He's just not worth it."

Samuel Macklin saw Christy in his office at the national accounting firm where he was a partner. The firm's offices were twenty floors up in a modern tower on West Georgia, but Macklin's office was paneled in dark wood that harkened back to the decorating style of a century earlier.

He shut the door behind her with a decided click. "I suppose you've come to beg," he said.

Christy walked to the windows. Though they stretched from floor to ceiling, the dark wood had been used to frame the panes so there appeared to be three separate windows along the wall. Silk curtains draped the glass, adding to the illusion, but the view of the very modern Vancouver harbor, with the North Shore mountains beyond, broke it.

Christy turned her back on the faux windows and real view. "Are you gloating, Samuel?"

He laughed. "If I am, are you surprised? Your auditor made allegations against me I didn't like. Now you're the one facing accusations. How's it feel?"

"Not good," she said evenly. "You know, Samuel, Frank blackmailed you for money. I have proof of that."

"So? He forced me to provide him with some extra funds from the trust. So what?"

"What did he blackmail you with, Samuel?"

Macklin threw back his head and laughed. "You expect *me* to confide in *you*?"

Christy smiled faintly. "Put that way it sounds pretty stupid, doesn't it? Almost as stupid as the actions you took when you were a university student. Remember that summer you worked for a small company in Victoria? The responsibility they gave you, the trust? How you responded to that trust? Let me see now…" Christy tapped her chin as she stared up at the ceiling, noting the ordinary ceiling tiles, drawing out the moment. "Didn't you fiddle the books and steal thousands of dollars? Enough cash to ensure your university fees were paid for? And how about responsibility? When the loss was discovered it was blamed on a permanent employee. That man went to prison. You continued on at university and built a career based on your complete honesty."

Macklin stood very still while she spoke. "You can't prove any of that."

"I can use the same method Frank did."

Sweat broke out on Macklin's forehead. "The diary was stolen from the mansion after Frank took off. You can't have seen it."

"Who says I didn't see it before Frank disappeared?"

"I don't believe you." Macklin's eyes narrowed. His face was twisted with rage. "If you'd known about the diary you would have said something."

Christy took an involuntary step backward. "I can prove that you've embezzled from the trust."

"I did that because your husband blackmailed me!" Macklin shouted. He took a step toward Christy.

"Were you being blackmailed by Aaron DeBolt as well?"

That stopped Macklin. "Who? DeBolt? That friend of Frank's?"

Macklin's frown indicated he really didn't know that Aaron had been blackmailing at least some of the trustees. Christy wondered what else Samuel Macklin didn't know about. "Someone sent the bulk of the funds in the trust to a bank in Indonesia then on to a numbered account in Brazil. I'm betting that someone was you."

"Well, you'd be wrong. I wasn't involved. One of the others did it."

"You knew that the other trustees were being blackmailed?"

"Of course. I supervise the accounting at the Jamieson Trust. When the first irregularities appeared I knew immediately a person on the inside was stealing from the trust."

"You mean someone other than yourself."

His jaw hardened dangerously before he continued.

"Your husband wasn't blackmailing me then. I looked into irregularities and found out about the diary Frank senior kept while we were in university together. We all knew what the others had done, but my pal Frank was the only one stupid enough to write it down. I was furious when I discovered that his son was using the diary against one of us, but I never imagined the little upstart would blackmail *me*! When I think of all we did for that kid and how he's paid us back it makes me furious." He put his hand on the doorknob. "Your husband deserves whatever hassles he gets." Opening the door, he added, "And you do too."

Hell of a way to start off the day, Christy thought, as she rode down the elevator. She had rushed straight from dropping Noelle at school to her appointment with Samuel Macklin. She had two days left before she saw Joan Shively again and she was not really any further ahead.

She had arranged to meet Gerry Fisher at eleven o'clock in his office at Fisher Disposal. She didn't expect much from that interview either. The really tough one would be Edward Bidwell, tomorrow at ten o'clock.

The Fisher Disposal building was located in an industrial park in Richmond. Traffic was good, so she arrived about fifteen minutes early. She had her first inkling that the circle was closing her out when the receptionist told her that Gerry Fisher's secretary had no record of a meeting with her. Not only that, but when contacted, the secretary announced that Gerry had said he didn't have time to see Christy this week.

The same thing happened the next morning. She had dressed carefully for her appointment with Edward Bidwell in a tailored, teal-blue suit and black pumps. Beneath the jacket she was wearing a simple white silk shell. A string of pink pearls completed the outfit, providing a timeless look of understated wealth. When Christy arrived at Bidwell's office, the receptionist announced she had no record of an appointment, and that

Mr. Bidwell had left a message that he had no time for a discussion now, or in the future.

Christy smiled and thanked the receptionist, then she walked out of the office. After Gerry's refusal to see her she'd expected Bidwell to do the same thing and she'd worked out a strategy. Standing in the reception area making a scene wouldn't work—they'd just throw her out. No, she'd catch Bidwell where he was vulnerable, in a public place where he couldn't avoid her.

After being turned away at Bidwell's office, she bided her time until twelve thirty, then she went to a restaurant she knew to be one of his favorite haunts.

She stood for a moment allowing her eyes to adjust to the muted lighting. The décor was old-fashioned: dark wood, dark carpets, heavy furniture. She'd been here before, with Frank and the trustees. The food was mainly beef and lots of it. The prices were astronomical. She remembered one evening when Frank had complained, saying he hated the place, claiming the food gave him indigestion. Edward Bidwell had jeered at him, calling him a wimp who didn't understand the good life. She shuddered at the memory now that she was seeing Frank's relations with his trustees in a new light.

The maître d' noticed her immediately. She smiled at him and said, "I'm meeting Edward Bidwell for lunch. Has he arrived yet?"

At Bidwell's name the man smiled. "Of course! He did not tell me he was expecting another guest, but I will take you to his table."

Great. What if he was with a client? "Oh! Edward didn't mention that we would have company."

The maître d' hesitated. "It is Mr. Fisher, an old friend."

Christy smiled and allowed herself to gush. "Gerry's here? How wonderful. I haven't seen him in ages."

A smile broke over the maître d's stiff features. "It is a family party then, Madam?" he said, as he led her to Bidwell's table.

Christy crossed her fingers and breathed deeply to quell the butterflies in her stomach. "That's exactly what it is." Seeing both Fisher and Bidwell together would save time, but they would have each other as allies. She had no illusion that this would be easy.

They were sitting at a table for four next to the wall at the far end of the room. Both men had drinks in front of them. Gerry was just raising his to his lips when he caught sight of Christy. She saw him put his glass down as he spoke to Edward Bidwell, who swiveled in his seat to take a look.

The maître d' hesitated. Christy brushed past him, marched up to the table. "Gentlemen, how nice to see you both together."

The maître d' rushed up. "Mr. Bidwell, is everything all right? Madam Jamieson said you expected her…"

Christy sat in a chair between the two men. Bidwell shot her a sardonic look. His jowls quivered a little, but he said calmly, "Everything is fine."

Clearly relieved that there wouldn't be a scene, the restaurateur left. Christy smiled at Bidwell. "It would have been easier if you'd seen me in your office."

"I don't have time to waste on unimportant matters," Bidwell said. He sipped from his glass, watching her warily over the rim.

"That was rude, Edward," Christy said. "But I have to agree. I don't have time to waste either. Tomorrow I have to meet with a social worker who believes I owned the mansion outright and that I sold it against the wishes of the Trust. How do you think she got that idea?"

"I wouldn't know," Edward said.

"Gerry, can you guess?"

Fisher frowned at her. "Don't drag me into this, Christy. It's your mess."

"Not really," she said. "You guys made it for me. One of Frank's trustees killed him, ripped off all his money, and now that person is using the trust to punish me by stealing my daughter. I'm here to tell you that you won't get away with it."

Edward Bidwell's lip curled and he said, "You are an unfit mother and we can prove it."

"With forged documents? I keep records of all our correspondence, Edward. Letters and e-mails from the Trust, my letters and e-mails back. I can prove those letters Ms. Shively has are forged documents. She won't tell me who in the Trust provided them to her, but she knows, and once she sees my documents she'll wonder if she's being set up. I don't think she'll like that, do you?"

Gerry Fisher slanted a glance at Bidwell, whose cheeks were bright with anger. "No one in the Trust has done anything wrong, Christy, except Frank, who began this whole thing by blackmailing a trustee."

"Please, Gerry! He used his father's diary to blackmail three of you!"

Fisher toyed with his glass. The liquor inside swirled back and forth with increasing force. "That diary no longer exists."

"So *you* burgled the mansion? Samuel Macklin thought Frank senior's diary had been stolen then, but he wasn't sure. Did you steal Frank's passport too? Then give it to a lookalike so people would think Frank had taken off to Mexico?"

"This is ridiculous," Edward Bidwell said, curtly. "Why would anyone bother to impersonate Frank? He was a worthless addict who stole from his trust fund so he would have more money to waste on drugs and fast living."

Christy looked from Bidwell to Gerry Fisher, then back to Bidwell again. "Frank was murdered by one of the people he was blackmailing."

"You've gone too far this time, Christy." Gerry Fisher sounded indignant. "I will not sit here and allow you to accuse me of murdering Frank. Or of being blackmailed by him."

"Gerry's right. Bad enough that you're claiming we have secrets that merit blackmail, but there's a big step between paying blackmail and murder."

Christy drew a deep breath. "Maybe the step isn't so big when a second blackmailer is involved."

Bidwell frowned. "What do you mean?"

"I mean Frank told his secrets to Aaron DeBolt and Aaron promptly started his own little blackmail business. Didn't you know, Edward?" She looked from Bidwell to Fisher. "Or was it only Gerry's secrets Aaron discovered?"

White with fury, Fisher said, "These are lies."

Bidwell said calmly, "I knew. Now I'm going to ask you, Christy, how much do you intend to reveal to your boyfriend?"

That surprised her. "What boyfriend?"

"That reporter fellow, Quinn Armstrong, the one who is using you to further his career."

"He already knows all the sordid details."

Gerry had been staring at his glass while Edward spoke. Now he looked up, his features twisted. "I suppose you've been fool enough to trust him. Did you ever wonder if he was the one responsible for that awful story about you in the paper, the one that convinced the Ministry of Children and Families that you weren't a suitable guardian for Noelle? The one that made them take our petition for custody seriously?"

Christy glared at Fisher. "If I had any doubts, you just washed them away, Gerry. I know Quinn wouldn't do that to me."

Bidwell laughed mockingly. "You sound like a lovesick female."

"You don't know what you're talking about." But did he?

"Predictable answer, Christy. I'd have thought better of you."

Fisher's smile was closer to a sneer. It flicked her on the raw. "It's the killer who's been feeding stories about the Jamieson Trust to the media, not Quinn. Maybe that's you,

Gerry. Or maybe it's you, Edward. Or maybe all of you are involved."

She pushed her chair out, then stood up. "The police are hunting for Brianne's Lymbourn's killer. Tomorrow Joan Shively will have proof that whoever tipped her off lied and provided her with false documents. She's going to be asking questions that will probably end up with the police. The net is closing. Which one of you will be caught inside?"

CHAPTER 25

"Come on, kiddo, let's go out to dinner tonight."
Christy ruffled her daughter's hair. It was five thirty and she and Noelle had just seen Mary Petrofsky back to her house. Having the girls playing in the family room on this rainy fall afternoon had forced Christy to keep herself together, but she freely admitted that she was exhausted after the emotional meeting with Gerry Fisher and Edward Bidwell earlier in the day. The thought of making dinner was more than she could manage.

Noelle shot her a calculating look. "Can we go to the barbecue chicken place?"

Christy laughed. "Your favorite. Yes, we can go there."

Noelle grinned, then pouted. "Daddy can't come though."

"Nope, they don't appreciate cats in restaurants."

The cat sauntered up the stairs from the family room. *Bring me home some takeout.* He stretched and yawned. *You and Mary tuckered me out, kiddo. I think I'll have a nap until you get back.* As the cat rubbed against her legs, Noelle picked him up and cuddled him against her chest. Stormy purred loudly.

After a minute, Noelle carefully placed the cat in the center of the most comfortable chair in the room. Frank sighed and the cat rubbed his cheek against Noelle's hand. She scratched his ear, then danced back to her mother. "Since Daddy can't come with us, why don't we invite Roy and Quinn?"

That was a good question. Why not invite the Armstrongs? Maybe because she'd been avoiding Quinn since the day she'd accused him of being the cause of all her problems simply because he was a reporter. They'd gone from there to his demanding that she let him do the interviewing of the trustees, which led to her refusal. That had been two days ago and, though he'd called a half-a-dozen times since, she hadn't responded to his messages.

Call him, Chris. You need to touch base and let him know what you've found out. The cat's voice was half asleep. She could hear the yawn in it. *Roy says Quinn's pretty worried. You guys need to work it out between you.*

"So how about it, Mom?" Noelle said, "Dad's right. You don't want Quinn to be upset, do you?"

Christy wagged her finger at her daughter and tried to look stern. "You shouldn't be listening to conversations between your father and me."

Noelle grinned, not in the least intimidated. "Is that a yes?"

Christy sighed. "Let's do it."

Dinner was fun, but it didn't solve anything. Christy briefly described the meetings she'd had, trying not to go into too much detail because she was aware of Noelle's listening ears. Roy talked enthusiastically about his agent's reaction to his new manuscript and entertained Noelle with stories about book tours packed with disasters. Christy and Quinn danced around the arguments they'd had, leaving Christy relieved. She didn't have the energy to deal with emotional issues tonight.

By the time they were finished coffee and dessert, it was Noelle's bedtime, so they said good night to Quinn and Roy at Christy's front door. It was Roy who suggested a strategy session after Noelle went to school in the morning.

Christy agreed, but she wished that Quinn had been the one to propose the meeting. He'd been strangely silent since they'd reached her doorstep.

She was in bed by ten o'clock, asleep by half past, then suddenly awake again. The room was very dark. She blinked sleepily and yawned, wondering what had roused her. Rolling on her side, she punched her pillow, determined to go back to sleep. She wanted to be rested for her meeting with Joan Shively the next day.

She was drifting off again when a sound made her open her eyes. Suddenly alert, she looked at the bedside clock. One in the morning. She listened intently, waiting to hear a toilet flush, or the cat thumping around as it prowled through the house chasing imaginary mice and snacking on leftover dinner.

Her straining ears caught the sound again. What was it? The creak of a floorboard, then the muffled click of a drawer being closed somewhere below. Cats didn't close drawers and Noelle wasn't likely to be downstairs checking out her toys at this hour of the night. Christy slipped out of bed. She pulled on her dressing gown for warmth and comfort, then went into her daughter's room.

Noelle was fast asleep, oblivious to what was happening below. The cat, who usually slept with his head on her knee, was sitting up in bed, staring alertly at the door.

"Frank, do you hear that? Is there someone here?" Christy asked in a whisper. Her skin was beginning to prickle as her stomach knotted.

I hear it. There was a grim note to the voice. *I'm going to go check out what's happening.*

"Thanks. I'll—" The stealthy sounds increased. Christy was sure she heard footsteps from the direction of the staircase. Fear clutched at her insides, real, primal fear that verged on panic. The cat dashed out. Christy remained by Noelle's bed, torn between standing guard over her daughter and going for help in the form of the telephone on her bedside table in the other room.

Call the cops! The mental command was followed by an angry, vocal hiss.

The footsteps hesitated. Christy whimpered. She had that feeling of dream inertia, where limbs are weighted, unable to move, even though danger approaches. Maybe this was a nightmare she'd wake up from in a couple of minutes, sweating and anxious, but blessedly safe.

The deep nasal yowl of a furious cat broke through her frozen panic.

This was real and she had to do something. She looked at Noelle. Her daughter was still asleep, moving a little restlessly, but so far not aware of the danger that surrounded them. A man's deep voice shouted with sudden pain and Christy heard Frank's voice grunt in her head.

She looked about the room, desperately seeking a weapon of some kind. The lamp on the table beside Noelle's bed was a possibility. To get to it she'd have to go to away from the door, deeper into the room, but that would put Noelle between her and the intruder, exactly the opposite of what Christy wanted to achieve.

The footsteps were louder now, making no attempt at quiet after the battle between cat and man. There was no chance now to bolt into her bedroom and call the police. The intruder would be upon them before she'd ever make it to the phone.

She had a wistful thought of her cell phone, downstairs, tucked securely into a pocket in her purse. From now on she'd bring it upstairs. She'd put it in her dressing gown pocket. She needed a weapon.

The footsteps sounded so close now, dragging her jumbled thoughts into focus. What could she use as a weapon?

She looked wildly around the room. There were toys, six-inch dolls made of hard plastic, and some stuffies on the end of Noelle's bed. Her duvet was half on, half off the bed, as usual, along with her second pillow, which had made it to the floor almost at Christy's feet. Not one thing close to hand looked remotely like a weapon.

Christy whimpered, desperately aware of the intruder who might be anywhere by now, and who could be on top of her in seconds. What could she use for a weapon?

A floorboard creaked. Christy knew that sound. She cursed it every night when she came up to bed because she worried the noise would wake Noelle. The board was right at the top of the stairs, impossible to miss.

The intruder was close. A few footsteps and he would walk into this room and do whatever horrendous act he wished. The danger to Noelle was acute. The time to act was now.

Christy grabbed the pillow and bolted from the room. She closed the door behind her in a vain attempt to protect Noelle from whatever happened in the hallway.

Christy's townhouse was a roomy one, but it was tall and narrow. The boxed-in staircase led up to a narrow hallway from which three bedrooms opened. The first was at the top of the stairs and looked over the back of the house; the second, where Noelle slept, was at the end of the hallway; while the third, the master suite, was on the front side of the house. The hallway itself was only twenty feet long from staircase to Noelle's bedroom door.

As the intruder crested the top of the stairs, moonlight shone in through the window in the first bedroom, highlighting the man. He was dressed in dark clothes that included tailored slacks and a black turtleneck sweater under a bulky down vest. His body was long, though well-fleshed, whether from muscles or good food, Christy didn't know and didn't want to find out. Leather gloves protected his hands, the kind used to ward off winter cold. A thick black stocking covered his head, obscuring his features. She guessed that his skin was white, but more than that she couldn't have said.

They stood for a moment, assessing each other. Christy knew she had a certain advantage. The drapes in the master bedroom were lined, limiting the amount of light that spilled over her, so the intruder would see little more than her shadow against the white of Noelle's bedroom door.

She held the pillow close to her body, desperately hoping the man would go away and leave them in peace.

Chris! Did you call the cops? The voice was thick as if the owner had been out of it for the past few minutes and was only just coming to. There was an urgency there too, a desperation born of an inability to act.

"No! There was no time!"

Her voice broke that fragile moment of assessment. The intruder launched himself down the hallway. Christy leapt forward, screaming madly, raising the pillow as she went, then she swung with all her strength. As he raised his arm to deflect the blow, she saw the black cloth was ripped. Large red scratches, deep enough to still be bleeding, showed where the cat had torn his skin. The pillow hit the wound with a solid thump. The intruder cried out. Christy raised the pillow again, slamming it against his head this time.

Made of feathers, the stuffing had bunched down at the base of the pillow as Christy swung it. The blow might shock and sting, but feathers did not have the impact of a more solid substance like a wooden baseball bat, a metal poker, or a glass vase. There was no way she would ever be able to deliver a knockout blow. The best she could hope for was that her resistance would convince the man that staying was too much trouble.

The intruder swore and grabbed at the pillow as Christy raised it again.

His flailing hands connected with the pillowcase and pulled. It slipped off. He stumbled backward, leaving Christy still in possession of her weapon and with a momentary advantage. She brought the pillow down on his face in an overhead blow that had her bent double with the effort. He snatched again, but she danced back, out of his reach.

She was breathing hard, but so was he. She had retreated as far back as the doorway to her room, but she dared not go inside, leaving Noelle's door unguarded and her daughter vulnerable to the intruder.

The attacker had her measure now. He knew her weapon was nothing more than a feather pillow that he could grab and tear from her grasp. He approached carefully, not running at her, but judging his timing so he could disarm her then grapple with her, using his superior strength to overwhelm her.

Christy choked back a sob. This was it. This unequal contest would soon be ended, but she was determined that even if she lost the battle she would not give up now, before it was over. She raised the pillow to bring it down in a stinging blow. The intruder reached up, caught the cloth, closed his fingers over the ticking, and pulled.

The pillow was wrenched from Christy's grasp. She heard him grunt with success, then he tossed the pillow behind him, far away from Christy's reaching fingers.

"Noooooo!" The word wrenched from her heart was a wail of despair and frustration. Over the intruder's shoulder, illuminated by the moonlight, she saw the cat at the top of the stairs. He was moving slowly, favoring the leg that had been injured weeks before.

The intruder's hand curled around her forearm. Christy struggled and screamed, "Frank, help me!"

The intruder froze. His hesitation gave her a sudden, not to be repeated, opportunity. She jerked backward at the same moment as the cat uttered one of its blood-stopping howls and sprang.

The intruder half turned at the cat's battle cry, then swore as the animal landed on his shoulder, front claws digging deep into his flesh, hind feet raking viciously. Christy broke his hold on her arm. Or perhaps the intruder let her go as he tried to shake the cat off his body. Their battle was short and vicious. At the end, the intruder's sweater was torn in a dozen places where blood seeped from nasty gashes caused by razor sharp cat claws, but the cat's lithe body was limp. The intruder shrugged off the cat and stumbled backward.

Horrified, Christy watched Stormy fall. All she could think was that once again Frank had been murdered, this time in the defense of his wife and daughter. No matter

what he had done in his life, after his death he had been her
friend and Noelle's confidante. She had a brief mental
image of her daughter mourning her beloved father/cat as it
lay limp on the hallway floor and was so filled with fury
that she rushed the shaken intruder. Her body landed hard
against his, pushing him backwards so that he hit the wall
at the top of the stairs. His cat-scratched shoulder took the
brunt of impact and he howled with pain. Still, one hand
closed over her shoulder, seeking control.

Christy struggled. She raised her elbow and rammed it
hard into his ribcage. He grunted and swore in her ear, his
voice hauntingly familiar.

Christy knew nothing about proper self-defense
techniques. She'd never taken a course and she could no
more toss someone over her hip than she could swim the
English Channel. But long ago her mother had taught her
that a man's most sensitive spot was also his weakest and
that a woman's knee rammed into a man's groin was an
effective way of proving no meant no. Christy used that
method now, putting all her fear and outrage into the blow.

The intruder screamed and fell to the ground, clutching
his groin.

Christy backed away. She noticed the pillow, forgotten
on the floor where the intruder had thrown it, and picked it
up. She raised it again, preparing for another energetic
whack.

The intruder looked up, raised his hands to ward off the
blow, and then threw himself down the stairs in what was
half stumble, half tumble to the landing. There he dragged
himself to his knees and crawled to the next set of stairs.
Christy heard him thump down them, then clatter down the
flight that led to the front door. She didn't follow. She
stood trembling at the top of the stairs, holding the pillow
aloft, listening. It was not until the front door slammed
against the inside wall as it was flung open that she
accepted the intruder had gone.

Reaction flooded through her. Her heart pounded. She
shivered as the sweat drying on her body caught every

small draft. Carefully, she lowered the pillow to the floor. It seemed important to place it in just the right position, for some reason that she couldn't fathom, but she didn't fight the urge. Doing what seemed right had allowed her to survive this ordeal.

She knelt in front of the cat. "Frank, oh Frank, what has he done to you?" She stroked the animal's soft fur, seeking life, giving comfort.

The door to Noelle's room opened. "Mommy?"

Christy gave the cat one last stroke, then she was up, gathering her daughter into her arms. "Sweetheart, it's okay. It's okay now."

"I heard noises. Thumping and a man's voice swearing. Daddy told me to stay in my room and not to come out until he said it was okay. Then it was quiet for so long. I was scared. I had to come out. I'm sorry, Mommy."

"Sh. Don't be scared, Noelle. It's over now. You did exactly right."

"Is Daddy mad at me? He isn't talking to me anymore."

Christy shuddered, her eyes automatically going to the body of the cat. Its ribcage rose and fell with shallow breaths, but she was afraid it had been badly injured. She stroked her daughter's hair. "No, Daddy's not mad at you. He was hurt in the fight, and he's taking a nap now."

Noelle accepted that. She cuddled against her mother, seeking comfort and security. Christy held her tight. The warmth of her daughter's body chased away the cold; the strength of her arms wrapped around Christy's neck provided a need for calm in a world gone crazy. Christy rocked gently, muttering nonsense that soothed them both.

Down below came the sound of entry. Christy's rocking froze in place. Her head came up. She stared through the darkness. Panic hammered in her chest. She should have used these last moments to call the police! Why had she knelt holding her daughter and mourning the death of a man already dead? How could she have been so stupid? Now she had put Noelle in danger again! What should she do?

"Mommy?" Noelle said, confusion in her voice.

The clatter of footsteps was followed by a bellow. "Christy!"

Her body sagged. She hugged Noelle more tightly than before. "It's okay, honey. Everything's okay now. Quinn's here."

She was crouched in the hallway, her arms wrapped tightly around her daughter, her head buried in the little girl's shoulder. Quinn had charged up the stairs, switching on lights as he went, but when he saw Christy she looked so fragile that he approached her cautiously, the way he would a wild animal that had been injured and needed help.

She looked up. Her face was white, her eyes huge. "Frank is hurt."

He crouched down beside her. She seemed to expect him to do something about the cat, so he touched it gently. It was warm, its chest rising and falling in a steady motion. "Frank will be fine," he said. He had no idea if that was true or not, but it seemed to be the right thing to say. "Dad's phoning the police right now. When he's through he'll come over. He can take the cat to the vet."

Christy nodded. "Hear that, kiddo?" she said to the child in her arms. "Daddy will be okay."

Noelle sniffed. Christy began to rock again. "I didn't know vets stayed open in the middle of the night."

"There's a twenty-four hour emergency hospital on Boundary." Quinn touched her cheek gently with his knuckles. "Christy, what happened?"

"There was a man—" She gulped and shuddered. "He was masked. It was dark. He came up. I hit him, but he kept on coming. Frank jumped on him. Then Frank was hurt and he ran away." She was shaking when she finished her broken recital and Noelle was crying. "Oh, baby, don't cry. Don't cry, baby."

Quinn sat down. His back was against the wall, the injured cat on one side of him. He stretched his legs across the narrow hallway, then he tugged Christy down against him. He helped her settle Noelle on her lap before he wrapped his arm around Christy and pulled her close. He was crooning soft words of comfort when he heard his father shout his name. "Up here, Dad!"

Roy made no attempt to be quiet. "Quinn! The cops will be here any time. They said we shouldn't…" He reached the top of the stairs, took in the vision of his son snuggling both Jamieson females, and finished with just the barest hesitation, "…take any chances."

Christy lifted her head from Quinn's shoulder. "Roy, Frank's hurt. Help him. Please."

Quinn leaned his head against the wall. "Can you get him to the vet, Dad? Both Noelle and Christy are worried about him." He shot his father a look that he hoped Roy would understand. The cat hadn't moved since he'd reached the scene and he feared the animal would not survive.

Roy crouched beside the cat and stroked the soft tiger striped fur. He nodded at Christy and Noelle. "What happened?"

"There seems to have been an intruder," Quinn said. His gut clenched as he thought of Christy in danger.

"As in a burglar or a home invader?" Roy asked.

"He wore a mask," Christy said.

Roy looked around the scene. He pointed to the wall where there were dark red smudges. "Frank's work?"

Christy nodded. "Frank jumped him once downstairs, then he followed him up. I was hitting him with the pillow—"

"You mean the one Quinn's sitting on?" Roy said, a laugh in his voice.

"Yes," Christy said. "He caught it and pulled it away from me. Frank jumped on him and dug in his claws. The intruder shook him off, but not before Frank raked him pretty badly."

"Yea, Daddy," Noelle said.

Quinn laughed. "You're a bloodthirsty pair."

Noelle giggled. Christy cuddled closer. Quinn thought how much he liked that.

"Okay," Roy said. "I think I've got at least some of the

picture." He gently scooped up the cat. "I'll take care of Frank."

The police arrived a few minutes after Roy had left. Quinn heard the sirens and then the officers entering, but he didn't move. He called out, "We're upstairs!" and let the policemen work out the details for themselves.

There were two cops and their visit lasted about an hour. They took statements from Christy and from Noelle. When she told them she had stayed hidden in her room while the altercation went on outside her door they praised her, telling her she'd done exactly as she should. They eyed Christy dubiously as she described the battle with the pillow.

"Have you ever been given a real good whack with a pillow, officer? It hurts," she said with as much dignity as a woman wearing her dressing gown in the middle of a crowd of strange men could possibly have. "I didn't have many options. I used what I could."

After the police had finished taking statements, Christy and Noelle went to bed, leaving Quinn to deal with locking up. That done, he went upstairs and found Christy cuddled with Noelle, sound asleep in her double bed. He stood looking at them for a time, feeling the shock of the evening settle over him.

He'd been asleep when Roy had burst into his room, shaking him roughly awake with the news that he'd seen someone stumble out of Christy's house and stagger down their quiet street toward the main road. He was calling the police, Roy had said. Quinn needed to go to Christy.

Taking only enough time to pull on a pair of jeans, he'd rushed to her house. He would never forget the empty feeling in the pit of his stomach as he stared at her open doorway, uncertain what he would find inside, desperately afraid that whatever it was would include blood and broken bodies. He'd seen that kind of carnage all too often and raged helplessly against the mindless violence of it, then done what he could to describe it to the world.

This time he had no plans to describe what he saw. He

stepped back, out of Christy's room, and closed the door behind him. He'd already decided not to do an interview with Christy or write the story of Frank Jamieson's disappearance and the embezzlement of the Jamieson Trust. She deserved her privacy. He could not steal it from her.

He was in the living room, brooding about the night's events and women who took on impossible situations, when the doorbell rang. He checked his watch. It was three a.m.

At the door he looked through the spyhole. His father stood there, grinning widely and holding the cat.

Relief flooded Quinn as he let Roy inside. They took the cat up to the living room and laid it on an armchair. Then they both sat on the sofa and watched the animal sleep.

"So is he going to be okay?" Quinn asked.

Roy nodded. "One of his back legs is hurt. The vet couldn't find any break, so he figures it's bruising and maybe a pulled tendon. He's got a concussion as well. I'm supposed to wake him every so often to test his reactions and make sure there's no swelling in the brain."

Quinn looked at his father suspiciously. "Dad, you didn't tell the vet you could talk to the cat, did you?"

"It made things simpler," Roy said. "He thought I was drunk at first, but he couldn't smell any booze on my breath, so I expect he decided I was stoned. Once I'd convinced him that I was harmless, he accepted my descriptions of the cat's symptoms. We got on pretty well in the end."

Quinn yawned. "What a family."

Roy laughed softly. "Works for me."

CHAPTER 26

Thursday morning brought the locksmith and an argument about whether Noelle should go to school or not. Christy wanted to keep Noelle home, Roy thought she should go if she felt up to it, while Quinn offered the suggestion that kids are resilient and that he'd seen them cope in worse situations. It was Frank who decided the issue. He limped off to spend some quiet time with Noelle, and when he came back he told them she was okay with going to school. It was tonight that had her worried.

When it came time to walk to school, they all went, including the cat who made the journey nestled securely in Noelle's backpack. Mrs. Morton, the teacher, was immediately concerned about security for Noelle. After some discussion, it was decided that Noelle would stay in at recess, along with her best friends, and that she would have lunch with Christy.

It wasn't until Christy and the Armstrongs were halfway home that Christy realized that the cat was still in Noelle's backpack at school. There was nothing she could do about it, however, as she had just enough time to gather the papers she needed then get to Joan Shively's office in time for their meeting.

"This is very serious." Shively was frowning as she read document after document. "Edward Bidwell assured me that the Trust was disclosing all papers relevant to this case."

Christy's breath caught. "Edward was the one who made the accusations against me?"

Shively looked up from the papers, then resumed reading without answering. Evidently the mention of Bidwell's name had been an accidental slip. "Edward Bidwell is not above lying in order to achieve the goals he's set for himself."

Shively straightened. She drew a deep breath, puffing up her torso. Her mouth was a hard, annoyed line. "One of the reasons we do not disclose the identities of those who report the mistreatment of a child is the name calling and retaliatory accusations by the accused parent in an effort to turn the investigation away from them."

Christy flushed. Battle, she thought, was fairly joined. Exhilaration shot through her. Last night when she'd faced an intruder who was bigger and stronger, she'd held her ground and forced him to flee. Joan Shively personified danger of another kind, but hers was no less real. "I believe you will find that I am not simply name calling, Ms. Shively. I suggest you talk to Detective Billie Patterson of the Vancouver police, who is investigating the Jamieson Trust and the trustees for embezzlement and worse crimes. I might add that Edward Bidwell has a past that is not above reproach."

Joan Shively frowned. Indecision dawned on her face, followed by curiosity.

Satisfied that she'd won this little skirmish, Christy added, "I won't gossip over the details. Should it be necessary to disclose them, I will. However, I believe the documents you have in front of you will be enough to prove that the allegations against me are untrue."

"This case may take some time to conclude," the social worker said, fingering the paper beneath her hand. It happened to be a letter from the Trust to Christy stating that

they had purchased a townhouse in Burnaby for Christy
and Noelle to live in since the mansion had been sold by
Frank Jamieson Jr. It directly contradicted the letter
supplied by Edward Bidwell.

Christy said, "I'll ask Detective Patterson to contact you.
Perhaps that will help move things along."

Shively flushed. "I have a heavy case load, Mrs.
Jamieson—"

Christy glanced at her watch. "And I have to pick up my
daughter for lunch. Will you photocopy the documents,
please? I have just enough time to get back."

At the school, she found Noelle holding her backpack,
ready to go. She had a big grin on her face. Christy's heart
lightened. One of her lingering terrors was that the danger
they'd been through would scar Noelle. She knew it was
early days yet, but she figured the big grin was a good sign.

By way of greeting, Noelle said, "Mrs. Morton thinks
Stormy should come home with me at lunch."

The teacher said, "I gather the cat is something of a hero,
Mrs. Jamieson. One who was wounded as a result of its
bravery."

The voice said sleepily, *She's got that right. I'm not sure
about the stuff she's teaching my kid, though. Have you
ever heard of a planet out beyond Pluto?*

"Stormy was very helpful," Christy said, on tenterhooks
whenever Noelle talked about the cat, in case she
mentioned his special qualities. "I hope Stormy wasn't a
problem. Noelle wanted to bring him along this morning,
but we didn't intend to leave him behind."

Mrs. Morton said with a sniff, "He caused a sensation
when his head popped out of her backpack just after recess.
However, it gave Noelle the chance to describe the events
of the night and the rest of the class the opportunity to
discuss them. It was very healthy for all of us."

*They didn't do this kind of stuff where I went to school.
You should have seen these kids. Hugging each other.
Telling Noelle how brave she was. Talking about what you
should do if you're in danger. Amazing.*

Christy agreed with Frank. The response to the incident had been amazing. "Okay, kiddo. Let's have lunch. We'll see you later, Mrs. Morton."

Once Noelle was back at school that afternoon, this time without the cat, Christy had her first opportunity of the day to simply sit. Doubts crept in, concerns that she hadn't handled the situation with Shively in the best way possible, worry that Noelle was in danger, fear that she couldn't keep her daughter safe.

Roy arrived with his laptop and said that he was going to babysit Frank, then Quinn showed up with an extra set of keys for the new locks that had been installed. Christy realized they were giving her space, but they weren't going to let her brood. She smiled gratefully as she took the keys from Quinn's hand. He smiled back, caught her hand in his, and raised it to his lips.

The doorbell rang. They all froze. Finally Frank said, *So who's going to answer it?*

Christy stood at the top of the stairs, looking down, but it was Quinn who went to the door. He put his body squarely in front of the opening, his feet planted wide apart, ready for anything. From Christy's vantage point he looked big, strong, and tough. His presence was reassuring.

The woman at the door flashed a badge. Quinn stepped back. "Detective Patterson, come in."

Billie Patterson had come to gather further information about the break-in with the hopes of linking it to Frank's disappearance. She looked curiously around the living room. "Doesn't look like anything much was taken. Or did you spend the morning cleaning up the mess?" She sat on the sofa opposite the chair where the cat was resting. There was a clear view of Roy working at the kitchen table, but it was the cat that her eyes rested on for a thoughtful minute.

Billie's lips twitched as Quinn parked himself on the arm of the cat's chair. She turned to Christy, who had settled beside her. "I can see that you've surrounded yourself with friends, Mrs. Jamieson. This is good."

Christy flashed Quinn a quick, intimate smile, then she identified Roy, who paid no attention to the group in the living room. Christy said, "Nothing was taken, Detective Patterson. I think I surprised the intruder when I woke up."

"The uniforms who responded to the call mentioned that the locks weren't broken. Does this suggest anything to you?"

Christy's lips tightened. "I didn't realize that. Quinn, did you notice?"

"Yeah," he said.

She frowned. "Is that why you stayed over last night?"

"I didn't see any reason to take chances. I didn't think the guy would be back, but you never know."

Christy shivered. "We had the locks replaced this morning."

"Who has keys to this house, Mrs. Jamieson?"

"I do. And the Trust. The house belongs to the Trust, you see, so they have to have a set of keys." She set her jaw. "Or they did. They won't now."

Billie made a note. "Where would those keys be kept?"

"At Jamieson Ice Cream, where the Trust has offices, I suppose. The staff or any of the trustees could have had access to them."

Billie tapped her notebook with her pen. "We picked up Crack Graham yesterday evening on suspicion of the murder of Brianne Lymbourn. He's got a lawyer and he's not talking. Yet. We can link him to Aaron DeBolt though, through Ms. Lymbourn. We detained DeBolt this morning. He claims he doesn't know anything about Lymbourn's death and he denies being involved in your husband's death. He also has a lawyer, but he's scared."

I'm not surprised. Aaron never did believe he'd get caught.

"I want to hit him with everything I can," Billie said, unaware that there'd been any kind of interruption. "Is there any possibility that DeBolt was your intruder?"

Aaron? He doesn't have the guts.

"I don't think so. The body shape was wrong. The intruder was bigger, broader, and heavier, than Aaron. But there's one way to find out for sure."

Billie snapped her notebook closed. "The cat scratches. Unfortunately, he doesn't have any." She moved the book thoughtfully as she stood up. "Well, it was a long shot. We'll speak to the trustees and maybe DeBolt will give us something substantial. In the meantime, Mrs. Jamieson, don't open the door until you're sure you know who it is."

"That won't be a problem," Quinn said. "I'm not about to leave her on her own."

Christy kept seeing the intruder in her mind's eye as her subconscious played with information her conscious mind refused to contemplate. After Noelle went to sleep in the big master bed, with Stormy curled protectively against her, Christy sat on the living room couch with Quinn, reviewing all that had happened. Roy worked at the kitchen table, revising his current work-in-progress with a focus that blocked out the activities of those around him.

"If the police picked up Crack Graham last night, the intruder couldn't have been him. And Aaron DeBolt is the wrong body type. So that means that the intruder was one of the trustees," Christy said, thinking aloud.

"Not necessarily." Quinn slipped his arm around her waist, holding her securely against him. "You're assuming the intruder is somehow associated with Frank's disappearance and Brianne's death. It could have been an ordinary break and enter."

Christy laid her head on his shoulder. "But the lock wasn't broken, Quinn. The door was opened with a key. A burglar wouldn't have access to the house key. It's got to be one of the trustees." She swallowed hard. "But which one, and why?"

"Dad still thinks it's Bidwell." He shifted her so that she was on his lap and they could maintain eye contact as well as stay close.

With her head resting on his shoulder, Christy reached up and shaped Quinn's face with her fingertip. His short, dark hair was silky to her touch, his skin warm. "Edward appears to be the one who forged the documents that Joan Shively has. He wasn't the one who entered my house, though. He's too fat and he's out of shape." Her finger trailed down Quinn's jawline to the tip of his chin. "I can't imagine Bidwell creeping into my house in the middle of the night to do—what?"

Quinn nipped her fingertip. Christy laughed.

"If it wasn't Bidwell then it must have been Macklin or Fisher," Quinn said. "Or someone the killer hired. Which would mean it could have been any of them."

Christy moved restlessly. "I don't think he was a professional thief. He wasn't wearing the right clothes."

Quinn laughed. "So what kind of clothes does the well-dressed criminal wear these days?"

Christy shot him a 'well-duh' look. "Jeans, cargo pants, casual stuff. This man was wearing trousers with a knife-edge crease and the gloves he had on were hand-sewn, supple leather."

"Old guy establishment clothes," Quinn said slowly. He stared at her. "Definitely one of the trustees."

"Yeah." That made it very personal. "So what was he after?"

They each considered that in silence, then Quinn tipped her chin toward him with one finger. "This will be over soon. The cops have accepted that Frank was murdered. They've identified Graham and DeBolt as accomplices. It's only a matter of time and due process before the killer is caught."

"And in the meantime?"

He smiled, then touched her lips with his. "I'll keep you safe."

She put her hands on his shoulders. "Thank you." Her voice was husky.

Quinn took advantage of the invitation in the sound to catch her mouth in a long, passionate kiss that involved nips and tongues. The caress shoved the mystery into the background and put Quinn squarely in the forefront.

"When my dad woke me up last night and told me that some man had just come out of your house and scuttled down the street like an injured crab, I thought my world was about to end. Then I saw you kneeling in the hallway weeping. All I could think was that as long as you were alive we could work things out." His mouth played with hers again, while his hands eased under her shirt. "Can we work things out, Christy?"

She wasn't sure what he was asking for, but she did know that whatever it was, she was ready to agree. "I'm open to suggestion, provided you kiss me again."

He laughed.

Quinn and Roy both stayed the night. Roy had apparently forgotten that he was in Christy's house. He accessed her coffee pot, made occasional visits to the bathroom, which was in exactly the same place as it was in his house, and typed furiously during those times when he wasn't staring into space, lost in some parallel universe. Quinn sprawled on the sofa with the television on, a blanket over his legs and a pillow behind his head. There was no way any burglar would bother this house tonight. If one bolder or stupider than the rest did try, Christy knew she was well protected.

That didn't stop her imagination from working overtime. She lay in the big bed beside Noelle, playing with information, trying to decide what was fact and what was illusion. The key was whatever the intruder had been trying to find. Was it the diary kept by Frank Jamieson senior? But the diary had been stolen from the mansion at the time of Frank's disappearance, and all of the trustees seemed to believe it had been destroyed.

Perhaps it was the documents proving she didn't instigate the sale of the mansion. That would mean that it was either Fisher or Bidwell, as both were involved in the effort to blacken her name. There was always the possibility that it was Noelle that they were after, whether for ransom or simply to prove to Joan Shively that Christy didn't have the security arrangements in place to adequately care for her daughter.

Her mind shied away from that frightening possibility. Instead, it replayed the fight with the intruder. She saw the man's hands close over the pillow, her only weapon. She saw his eyes gleaming behind the stocking mask, heard his curse of pain mix with the cat's howl of outrage as Stormy landed on his shoulder and dug in.

The scene was in her mind as she drifted off to sleep. Her dreams brought it alive, magnifying each movement, emphasizing the shape of the intruder's body, his hands, his head. Remembered terror made her shift restlessly. Then, in the middle of the skirmish, as she fought for her survival and her daughter's safety, the black stocking-mask dissolved and she looked into the eyes of the killer.

CHAPTER 27

——◆——

"Sleep well?" Quinn asked after he had kissed her awake. Christy sat up groggily. He handed her a cup of coffee.

She drank deep, savoring the first hit of caffeine in freshly brewed coffee. Then she yawned and rubbed her eyes with her free hand. "Not particularly." She looked at the clock, which read seven fifteen. She reached over and shook the still-sleeping Noelle. "Hey, kiddo. Look lively, time to get up."

Noelle grunted and burrowed deeper.

Quinn let her enjoy another jolt of coffee, then he took the cup, put it on the bedside table, and caught her chin in his hand. Christy stared up at him, surprised. He bent to kiss her. She murmured deep in her throat, a sound that was part giggle, part moan, as his mouth covered hers. When he pulled away she sighed.

He grinned and touched the tip of her nose with a careless finger before he replaced the coffee mug in her hand. "Breakfast will be ready in fifteen minutes. I'll see you downstairs."

"Hmm, right," Christy said. He sauntered out, looking pleased with himself. Christy sipped more coffee and gathered her scattered wits about her. "Okay, kiddo, it really is time to motor." She put the cup on her bedside table then looked over at Noelle and saw the cat wide awake and staring at her.

She blushed. "How much did you see?"

Everything. There was a sigh in the word. *The guy's crazy for you, Chris.*

"Frank, I—I didn't know you were awake, or I wouldn't have kissed Quinn that way. In front of you, I mean."

But you would have kissed him.

"Yes."

Are you in love with him?

"I—"

Wait, don't answer that! It's doesn't matter. The voice was gloomy. *I don't do sex anymore. The cat does, from time to time. I think he's got at least a half-a-dozen families out there. He doesn't seem to care though.*

"I don't think I want to know this, Frank."

I was trying to explain to you that I'm not jealous. Much. I've been working on this, so don't go thinking about the other day when I got mad about it. We had something special once, a long time ago. I'd like to see you have that again.

Christy stared at the cat. The cat stared back, unblinking. Finally, she stroked his back, then scratched him behind the ears. "Thank you, Frank." The cat began to purr. Christy patted him a while longer then she threw off the covers and shook Noelle. "Sleepy time's over, sweetheart. You need to get up." Noelle didn't stir.

Let me. The cat nudged the child's cheek with his head, then licked her nose. Noelle sat straight up, brushing at her nose at the same time.

The radio was on when Christy came downstairs, leaving Noelle in the shower. Along with the traffic report, the stock market report, the sports report, and a few lively quips between the host and the various contributors, was the main morning news, which covered everything not dealt with elsewhere. Quinn was flipping eggs onto plates already heaped with bacon and ham, Roy was packing up his laptop, and Christy was setting the table when one news item stopped them all.

"The police have detained Thaddeus Graham, also known as Crack Graham, in the death of local socialite, Brianne Lymbourn. Graham has a previous record for distribution of drugs. Ms. Lymbourn is known to be involved with Frank Jamieson Jr., whose disappearance several months ago has been linked to embezzlement from his trust fund. The police are also looking into this and have asked for assistance from Jamieson's friend, Aaron DeBolt. In other news…"

Christy was the first to react. "Uh–oh."

"I wonder who leaked that information," Roy said. He snapped his laptop shut and moved it out of the way so Christy could lay down a place setting. "One of the lawyers, I'll bet. Sounds like a strategic news release."

"Could be worse." Quinn brought plates over and set them on the table. "It could have said that the police are seeking Frank's murderer."

Christy looked down at the cutlery still in her hand. "All the same," she said, "this will be all over the city. There may be more details in the paper. There may even be a clip on the morning TV news. The killer knows now that the police are this close to him." She held up her hand, forefinger and thumb a scant distance apart. "He's bound to act."

"Yes, but how?" Roy asked. He'd already sat down and was digging into his bacon and eggs.

Quinn brought another two plates and nudged Christy into a seat. "Eat. I'll get Noelle going." He flicked off the radio as he headed out of the kitchen. She heard him shout, "Hey, Noelle, breakfast! Come on down."

There was no more talk of murderers. The cat went to school with Noelle and Christy again. This time he was rousted from Noelle's backpack and sent home with Christy, despite the protest of the twenty-four eight-year-olds who wanted to adopt him as the class mascot.

The house was empty when Christy unlocked the door. There was a note on the fridge from Quinn saying he'd

gone to the bank and another from Roy saying he'd gone
for a jog and would be back by the time she returned from
school. Christy laughed a little at that. Roy's sense of time
was more than a little off.

As she did morning chores the telephone rang. "Mrs.
Jamieson? This is Harry Endicott, the auditor."

Christy made a polite reply, frowning as she tried to
figure out why Endicott was calling. As far as she knew the
audit was on permanent hold.

Endicott wasted no time coming to the point. "Mrs.
Jamieson, when I first began the audit I asked a friend of
mine in the banking business to make some enquiries into
any significant financial transactions which might relate to
the Jamieson Trust. He discovered something rather
interesting."

"He knows where the embezzled money is?"

Endicott hesitated. "In a way."

Christy resisted the urge to sigh. Instead, she poured
herself a cup of coffee and settled on the sofa in the living
room. She had a feeling this conversation would take a
while. "Okay, Mr. Endicott. You've got my attention.
What's up?"

"The embezzled money was used to buy the Fisher
Disposal shares sold by the Trust to finance the purchase of
your present home."

In the middle of taking a sip of coffee, Christy choked.
"What! How can this be?"

"Interesting, isn't it?" Endicott said, with considerable
relish. "The Fisher Disposal shares owned by the Jamieson
Trust were sold to Snowcap Investment, a venture capital
company in Toronto. The company is a legitimate business,
with an excellent reputation. My friend is one of the
shareholders. Snowcap recently received a large influx of
cash, from a numbered company, which is privately held,
so ownership is not public information. The deal was
arranged by a gentleman with South American
connections."

"Oh, my," Christy said.

"Yes, indeed," Endicott said enthusiastically. "Snowcap used part of the new funds to purchase the Jamieson Trust's ten percent share of Fisher Disposal."

"They used Frank's money to buy the stock he already owned?"

"Among other investments," Endicott said. He sounded dazzled by this latest twist in the serpentine travels of the Jamieson fortune. "Not only that…"

He paused, waited for Christy to prod him. "Yes?"

"Gerry Fisher has been appointed to the Snowcap Board."

A minute later Harry Endicott was saying good-bye and Christy was hanging up the phone. She sat for a moment, holding her coffee cup in both hands, staring over the top.

As a member of the board at Snowcap Investments, Gerry Fisher would be able to influence how the company voted its ten percent share of Fisher Disposal. That meant he controlled fifty percent of Fisher Disposal. He didn't have to worry about his wife learning he used an escort service so he was no longer vulnerable to blackmail.

Still, murdering a man, embezzling from his trust fund, then buying back stock as the result of a series of convoluted financial transactions seemed like a lot of work just to cover up a few sexual indiscretions.

"Frank?" she said to the cat, who was finishing off his breakfast after his jaunt to the school. "Was there anything weird about Gerry Fisher's affairs? Something that would make him really anxious not to have them exposed?"

You're kidding, right?

Christy felt herself go cold. "No. I'm not kidding."

You mean you didn't know? Gerry is a pervert. He likes underage girls, the younger the better. It started with an affair he had in college. He was twenty and the girl was fourteen. When he married Eve it was for money and social position. He always figured affairs were okay. His problem was and is that he can't get young girls just anywhere, so he uses a pimp who supplies him with street kids, no questions asked.

"He's the one," she said.

Gerry? Could be.

"He's the right build, and his voice…" The vivid dream of the night before came back to her. She heard the intruder's voice and visualized the shape of the face behind the stocking mask. Oh, yes, the intruder was Gerry Fisher all right. "I have to call Detective Patterson."

Patterson wasn't answering her cell phone. Christy left a voicemail, then hung up, wondering what to do. On impulse, she called Fisher Disposal and asked for Gerry Fisher.

"I'm sorry. He's not in the office today, Mrs. Jamieson, and I don't expect him in until next week. Would you like me to schedule an appointment for you on Tuesday or Wednesday?" his secretary said.

"Don't bother." Christy hung up. She stared at the cat. "Frank, he's going to run. He's probably got money—your money!—tucked away somewhere. If he leaves we'll never find him again. And this will remain unresolved. I have to stop him."

Chris! Don't do anything hasty—

Christy ignored him. As she shoved her arms into a jacket she said, "I'll keep my cell on, Frank. If Quinn or Roy comes home tell them I've gone to Gerry's house."

Why are you going to Fisher's place?

She slung her purse over her shoulder. "Just in case he hasn't gone yet. The news report only came out this morning. He may not have had time to make his travel arrangements. If I can catch him at home maybe I can stall him long enough for the cops to get to him."

This is crazy, babe! Forget it! Let the cops deal with Fisher. He's dangerous.

She opened the door. "I'll leave a message for Quinn on his voicemail. If he gets home before Roy you need to make sure he checks his messages. Now shoo!"

* * *

Gerry Fisher's home was large, modern, and not particularly tasteful. It was crowded onto a lot with a great view of English Bay, but not much land. Christy parked on the street a few doors down. She took a moment to phone Billie Patterson, but once again all she got was a request to leave a message. This time, she identified where she was. As she climbed from the car she felt alone and vulnerable.

Eve Fisher smiled as she answered the bell. "Why, Christy! What brings you here?" She opened the door wide and stepped back, inviting Christy in.

"Hi, Eve. How are you doing? I need to see Gerry. I called the office, but his secretary said he was going out of town. I thought I'd try to catch him before he left."

"Not a problem." Eve gestured toward the back of the house as she closed the door. "He's in his study, gathering up the papers he needs for the trip. His plane leaves at eleven thirty, but it's only a local flight, so he doesn't have to be at the airport too early." As she and Christy approached the study they could hear the whining crunch of a paper shredder at work. Eve pushed open the door. "Gerry, look who's here to see you."

He turned with a start. Morning sunlight and pale blue walls made the room bright and fresh. The man who stood by a pile of papers, shoving them into the shredder with single-minded intensity, was gray and rumpled by comparison. He glared at his wife and at Christy. "Why did you let *her* in?"

Eve's face tensed. She looked like a woman who was biting her tongue to keep from settling into a good old-fashioned domestic squabble in front of a guest. "I'll leave you two to discuss whatever it is Christy wants to discuss."

Eve left the room with a quiet dignity that Christy found quite disturbing. She hesitated, not sure where to begin now that she was standing in front of a man she thought was a killer.

Gerry Fisher continued to feed the shredder. "Well?"

She cleared her throat. If she was right, this was the man she'd beaten off with nothing more substantial than a pillow. "Two nights ago a man came into my house. He was looking for something that he didn't find."

The shredder whirred. "So?"

Christy eyed the shredder, wondering what it was Gerry was destroying. Evidence of his embezzlement? "I wish you'd stop doing that, it makes my skin cringe, like nails on a blackboard."

"You think I care?" More paper went in.

That made Christy mad. "You're a jerk, Fisher, you know that? I think you killed my husband and Brianne Lymbourn, and I think that you invaded my house two nights ago."

She had his attention now. He stopped feeding the machine and straightened. "That's nonsense."

"Yeah? What if I asked your wife where you were on Wednesday night? Would she tell me you were in her bed, fast asleep?"

Fisher's face paled, then reddened. "You wouldn't dare!"

Christy stepped into the doorway. She angled her head so she could keep Fisher in view. "Eve, have you got a moment?"

"Now listen here—"

Eve came into the room. She looked uneasily from Christy's set features to her husband's red face. "Is there a problem?"

"Was Gerry home on Wednesday night, Eve?"

"Don't answer her, Eve!"

"What is going on here? Christy, why are you asking about Gerry's whereabouts?"

"Because I think your husband broke into my house on Wednesday night to steal some documents."

"That's ridiculous!" Eve said. "Gerry would never do such a thing. You've said enough, Christy. I think you'd better leave."

"You haven't answered me," Christy said, not moving. "Ask your husband where the scratches on his arm and shoulder came from."

Eve colored.

"So you've noticed them," Christy said. "He got them from a cat."

"Was that it?" Eve smiled. Her voice sounded relieved. "I thought it was from one of his wo—for another reason."

"No, it was a cat. My cat. A man broke into my house two nights ago. That man also murdered my husband."

"Gerry!"

"You can't prove any of this," Fisher said, narrowing his eyes.

What he said was true, but Christy didn't have a single doubt that she might be wrong. "I can't, but the police can. There were bits of the home invader's blood clinging to the cat's claws. The police took samples for DNA testing. I bet the DNA will match yours."

"I can't be forced to supply my DNA," He circled around the shredder. "You haven't got a case."

"That's not what the police are saying."

"Gerry! Is all this true?"

He looked at his wife impatiently as she advanced toward him. "Use your head for once, Eve! I won't admit anything, to you or to Jamieson's wife."

Eve reached for him. "Gerry, what has happened to us? What's happened to you?"

"Oh for heaven's sake, Eve! There's never been an 'us.' Our marriage is a business arrangement. Haven't you figured that out yet?" He glanced at his watch. "Now get out of my way. I've got to get going or I'll miss my plane."

Eve slapped him across the face. The blow landed with a resounding smack and left a red handprint on his cheek. No one expected the attack. Christy certainly didn't and Gerry Fisher was staring at his wife as if she had just morphed into Hades' three-headed dog. Even Eve had a horrified expression on her face.

"You bitch!" Fisher said, then he hit her with a backhanded blow that had blood spurting from her nose as she staggered backward. Her arms windmilled before she lost her balance and crashed to the floor. Her head hit the edge of the desk with a thud that sounded, to Christy's ears, as if it included the crunch of breaking bone.

"Oh, my God," she whispered, staring horrified at the still form of Eve Fisher. A whisper of sound made her look up, just in time to see Fisher pick up a letter opener from his desk. "Oh, my God," she said again as he advanced upon her.

CHAPTER 28

Quinn glanced at his watch as he parked the car. He'd taken longer than he expected to do his little errand. Christy was probably fine, but he was willing to bet his father was prowling around her house like a caged lion. He'd seen the signs before he'd left. Sitting at the computer for long periods gave Roy the fidgets. His muscles would cramp or begin to twitch, and the only way he could work out the problem was with exercise. Roy had been working flat out for days now. *He must be badly in need of a run.*

Quinn grabbed his package, a soft, butter-leather bag, from the trunk of the car then headed up the walk to his front door.

There he found the cat, sitting like a sentinel at the top of the steps. His stomach knotted. "What are you doing here?"

Stormy didn't answer him, of course. Cats don't really talk to people.

He ran lightly up the stairs, then stopped abruptly as the cat hissed at him. His stomach knotted again. The cat might not fire words into his head, but its body language was clear. "Something's up."

The cat bounded down the stairs, running off in the direction of Christy's townhouse. Relief flooded through Quinn. The damn animal was locked out and it wanted to get inside. He headed to his own front door. Well, it could wait until he'd put his package inside. He'd be going over Christy's in a minute, anyway...

The cat appeared at his feet again, this time standing on its hind legs so it could paw his leg. Its claws caught in the fabric of his jeans. He frowned down at it. "What's going on here?"

The cat abandoned his pants to race down the steps again, then off to Christy's house.

Quinn sighed. "All right, all right." He unlocked his front door, put the leather bag on the stairs, and came back outside.

The cat was waiting for him. "Okay. I'll go over and get Christy to let you in. Will that satisfy you?" He could have sworn the cat shook its head. What *was* going on here?

At Christy's house he pushed the doorbell and waited, uneasily. "I suppose you want your breakfast." The cat danced around his feet, clearly upset. Quinn frowned, thinking back. "Wait a minute, we fed you when the rest of us had breakfast." No one had answered the bell so he rang again, and then a minute later, a third time.

The cat was now pacing the porch like a tiger trapped in a tiny cage. Quinn swallowed hard. "She went out for a walk," he said. The pacing continued, accompanied by a low growl of what might have been frustration, but which certainly indicated some strong cat emotion. "Okay, no walk. Where the hell is she?"

The cat shot him an annoyed look, then jumped off the porch, heading back to Quinn's place. Quinn followed. He found the cat at his door, clearly waiting to get in. "You know, you've got me baffled, cat. What do you want? To get into Christy's place, or mine?"

The cat stood on its hind legs and pawed the door.

Oh, man, Quinn thought. He opened the door then watched the cat bound inside. He was about to follow when he heard a shout. He turned with some relief to see his father jogging up the street toward him.

"You're here," Roy said, puffing a little as he wiped his sweating forehead.

"So are you. Where's Christy?"

Roy looked surprised. "Isn't she back from school yet? I left for my run when she and Noelle headed off. I figured I'd be home before she was, but I went further than I intended. Oh, well, I guess it all worked out."

"Dad! It's nine thirty. It takes five minutes to walk back from the school."

"Maybe she stopped to talk to the teacher again, or stayed in the classroom with Noelle. Man, I need a shower," Roy added, as he headed into the house.

Christy was fine, Quinn told himself. All those warning instincts that had kicked in as the cat danced around him like a mad creature were just nerves activated by the events of the past few days.

He followed his father inside, then stopped. Roy was standing halfway up the stairs, his body tense and still, while the cat stood at the top, staring fixedly at him. Its tail lashed from side to side and its back was arched. It was the picture of feline outrage.

Slowly, Roy turned. His face was white. "Frank says Christy pinpointed Gerry Fisher as the murderer. She's gone to his house to keep him from leaving."

"What?" Quinn whispered, then added in a bellow, "Is she crazy? Never mind. Dad, ask Frank when she left."

There was more silent communication as he picked up the leather bag on the stairs.

Roy said, "Fifteen minutes ago, maybe less. He said she left us a phone message."

Still holding the bag, Quinn ran up the stairs. "The message should be time stamped."

It was and the cat was right. Christy had left the message less than a quarter of an hour before. "Maybe I can catch her. I can try, anyway." He opened the bag, checked the contents. "Dad, you call the cops—Billie Patterson. Tell her to rush a squad car to Fisher's address."

"What's Fisher's address? Christ, Quinn, is that a handgun?"

"Yup." Quinn weighed the pistol in his hand.

"Do you know how to use that thing?"

"I do." He loaded bullets into the chamber. "I learned in the Boy Scouts, Dad. Remember? I took a marksmanship badge."

"That was a long time ago, boy."

"Came in handy when I was in Afghanistan."

"You bought it there?" Roy held out his hand. Quinn put the gun into it.

As Roy turned the weapon in his hand with a kind of morbid fascination, Quinn said, "When I went into the back country one of the soldiers suggested I'd be smart to go armed. He wanted me to carry a semi-automatic rifle. I figured that would ruin my credibility as a journalist, so I opted for something that would fit in a pocket."

Roy offered him the gun back. "You brought it with you when you returned from Afghanistan."

"Yeah. I didn't have to use it and I thought..." He shrugged. "It was a sort of reminder of what I shouldn't do if I wanted to maintain my journalistic credibility. I put it in the safety deposit box for safekeeping."

Roy shook his head. "The safety deposit box? Does the bank know?"

Quinn laughed shortly as he slipped the loaded gun into the pocket of his windbreaker. He added bleakly, "I left it here when I went to Africa."

"Having a weapon wouldn't have helped Tamara." Roy followed his son to the doorway.

"I know." Quinn ran down the stairs to his car. "But this time I'm not going to take the chance."

The blade of the letter opener shone in the sunlight streaming through the window beside the desk. Shocked by the violence Fisher had shown to his wife, Christy stared at the shiny, lethal weapon with a horrified fascination. Above the glittering blade, the hilt was ebony, inlayed with ivory. The contrast of creamy white and gleaming black drew the eye and made the decoration leap out. Designed by a master craftsman, the piece was an effective example of the decorative arts.

Fisher smiled. Christy dragged her thoughts back to the matter at hand. What the hell was she doing?

She'd come here to keep Gerry Fisher from leaving town, but at this moment letting him go wherever he wanted seemed like a very good idea indeed. He could hop on that plane and fly to the moon for all she cared.

He took a step toward her, still smiling that warm, kindly smile. Still holding the letter opener like a dagger.

Christy stared at him. She had an awful feeling that the moment she moved he'd be upon her, but if she stayed where she was he'd creep toward her until he was close enough to lunge. Either way she was toast. What to do?

Think. Squash panic like a pesky mosquito and use her intellect to plot and plan.

He took another cautious step toward her.

He hadn't yet figured out that she'd pulled herself out of shock and was in active survival mode. That was good. When she moved she'd be able to make the most of this small advantage.

So what to do?

Get out of the house. Plant herself on the sidewalk where there were people. Find somewhere she could use her cell phone to call 911.

The key was to get out of the house.

How?

Run!

And she did.

She pivoted on the toes of one foot and took off the way she used to when Noelle was a toddler and had wandered where she wasn't supposed to, unaware of the danger she was putting herself in. Then Christy had run with the recklessness of love; now she added the desperation of utter terror to her sprint.

She was out of the room and into the hallway before Fisher realized what she intended. She reached the front door as he roared with fury. The knowledge that he was now on the move, only seconds away from capturing her, made her fingers clumsy. As she fumbled with the unfamiliar door locks she muttered, "Do it, do it, do it! Come on, Christy, you can do it. Come on!"

Behind her she heard the thud of his footsteps, and then, chillingly, his laughter.

Her voice rose to cover the sound. "Do it. Do it! Now!" The lock clicked. The latch gave under her hand.

With a little sob, Christy flung the door wide and leapt out. The cool fall air caressed her skin, promised safety, filled her with hope. Two steps and she'd be across the porch. Take the stairs two at a time and in another three she'd be on the walk. A dozen more and she'd be at the sidewalk.

She took the first of those steps. And the second. Then, as she was poised to rush down the stairs, Fisher reached the doorway.

Using his six-foot plus height he dove, grabbing for her.

Alerted by the sound of his footsteps and the delicate shift of the air around her, Christy glanced over her shoulder in time to see Fisher's attempt to tackle her. She screamed as she twisted to one side, trying to avoid him.

The porch was about twelve feet wide and six feet deep, enough room to grapple, not enough to maneuver. Christy lost her balance. To her horror, Fisher's hands closed around the loose cloth at the back of her open jacket.

Instinct kicked in. As he tugged at the fabric, she flexed her shoulders and let the garment slide down and off. She put her hand on the railing that edged the porch to help regain her balance. Fisher flung her jacket away with a savage gesture.

Too late, she remembered that her cell phone was in the pocket. Her link with the rest of the world, with the police. She grabbed for the garment. Fisher lunged for her.

She screamed again. He was inches away now. His eyes were wild, gleaming with a rage that made fury seem a moderate emotion. He had bared his teeth in a snarl that evoked primal terror. In seconds his reaching hands would touch her, then they would tear her apart while he howled his pleasure to the four winds.

He would kill her, here on his front porch in this oh so very respectable part of town. He would kill her and he would enjoy killing her. With her gone, Noelle would be an orphan. Who would care for her child then? Her cold, pitiless great aunt, Ellen Jamieson, who had ruined Frank's childhood?

The thought brought out a primitive savagery of Christy's own. She would not let this man steal her life, ruin her daughter's future. With a shriek, she curled her fingers into a fist, then she punched him with all her strength.

Fisticuffs and self-defense were not skills Christy had ever learned. Her blow may have had surprise and the weight of her body behind it, but her aim was off. She didn't connect with his nose, or the tip of his chin. There was no satisfying crunch of cartilage or the snap of his head. There was just the dull thump of bone on muscle.

Arm muscle.

Arm muscle recently clawed by one furious cat.

Fisher howled with pain and redoubled his efforts to secure Christy. He grabbed her, wrapping his arms around hers to pinion her. She writhed in his hold, kicking at his shins, twisting, pushing, pinching, doing whatever it took to make him release her.

Tightening his hold, Fisher snarled, "Stop! You can't win."

"Go to hell!" Christy threw her weight forward in a blind attempt to unbalance him. She did. They hovered there, on the edge of the porch, teetering dangerously.

"You bitch. You stupid bitch," Fisher said, then they tumbled down the stairs.

There were six steps from the top of the porch to the concrete walk below. They missed the first stair, but hit the second. Christy's knee snapped against the wooden tread, but she felt no pain. Even as they flew downward, she was trying to fight off Fisher's lethal embrace.

On the forth step they bounced, their hips hitting the painted wood. Christy was sobbing now. This was it, her last chance at life. If she landed on the bottom Gerry Fisher would be able to do whatever he wanted to her. She jabbed at his rib cage, using her fingers like pokers. Fisher grunted, shifted, and landed flat on his back on the concrete walk with Christy on top of him.

Hope welled up in her. She fought and struggled. Her thrashing legs connected with Fisher's flesh. Already winded by the fall, he grunted and his hold around her torso loosened. Christy redoubled her effort, using her arms now as she writhed and twisted.

His hold broke. She sobbed as she scrambled to her feet and took those first staggering steps toward the street and freedom. Behind her she heard him swear. Worse she heard the scraping sounds of movement. He was after her again.

"No!" Not now, not when she was so close to escape. Gasping, sobbing, she pushed herself to run. She counted the steps to the safety of the sidewalk.

One.

Two. He was on his feet now. Roaring his fury.

Three. He was moving. After her. She couldn't make it.

Four. She could do it. She just had to hang on.

Five. He was so close she could hear his breathing. He would grab her again. One more step. That was it, all she needed. Once they were on the sidewalk she would be safe. There were people there. There was freedom.

Six.

She hit a wall, a solid, warm, human wall. An arm wrapped around her, pulling her hard against that wall. Holding her close. She screamed and struggled.

Behind her she heard Fisher laugh. It was a gloating laugh that rubbed her on the raw. It told her he wanted her to fight her captor.

It told her it was time to stop and take stock.

She looked up into Quinn's face, and she stilled.

"Back off, Fisher," he said. "The cops are on the way."

Gerry Fisher wasn't about to listen to anyone, certainly

not to a man with his arm full of terrified woman. He laughed, that sneering, arrogant laugh. As Christy turned in Quinn's embrace to face her assailant, Fisher took a menacing step forward.

Christy cried out, then covered her mouth with her hand in a frightened gesture. Quinn put his hand in his pocket and pulled out a gun. He pointed it at Gerry Fisher with a calm that astounded Christy.

"Like I said, Fisher, the cops are on the way, so you just stay where you are until they get here."

Fisher stood poised. He stared at the gun, then at Quinn, that wild look still in his eyes. A siren sounded, coming close. Fisher's gaze shifted. His body tensed.

"Watch out," Christy cried. "He's going to pounce!"

"I don't think so," Quinn said. Then, as Fisher made a move, he fired.

CHAPTER 29

The bullet went nowhere near Fisher, but it shocked him into stillness. He froze in place, poised to run, but motionless. That was the way the police found him.

The cops relieved Quinn of the gun, put handcuffs on Fisher and called for an ambulance for Eve Fisher. They bore Christy's angry denunciation when they patted down Quinn, then let him hold her as she gave her explanation of the morning's events. Billie Patterson arrived at the same time as the paramedics. As a stretcher was wheeled up the Fishers' walkway, she told Quinn to take Christy home.

Outside the police perimeter, a crowd had gathered. Christy could see camera crews from the local television stations and photographers toting still cameras with enormous lenses and heavy bags of accessories. Reporters were less easy to pick out, but she knew they would be there, working with the cameramen, holding microphones, ready to thrust them into her face.

She watched Billie Patterson read Gerry Fisher his rights, then nudge him into a squad car. Cameras clicked madly, capturing the scene. They were focused on Fisher's arrest right now, but when she appeared they'd swarm her in exactly the same way. She swallowed hard. "I'm not ready to face the gauntlet."

Quinn understood immediately. He smiled at her and rubbed her cheek with his knuckle. "So you won't. We'll figure out a way of getting you out of here incognito."

She sighed and nodded. Reaction set in and along with it came the chill of a brisk morning. She shivered. "Gerry pulled off my jacket when we were fighting. It must be over by the porch somewhere. I'd better find it. It's got my cell phone and wallet in the pocket." She headed back toward the porch. Every step was an effort as her body began to ache in more and more places.

"Christy."

She turned to see Quinn frowning at her. "What's up?"

"You're limping."

"I am?" She looked down. Her pants were filthy, but otherwise okay. Now that Quinn mentioned it, though, one leg was beginning to throb. She wondered how that happened and thought about it for a minute. "Oh, yeah. I hit my knee when Gerry and I tumbled down the stairs."

He made a sound that was half laughing, half disapproving, then said, "Stay put."

She blinked. It was such an odd thing to say, particularly when she should be looking for her jacket—

He scooped her up, carrying her over to the porch steps where he set her down. After retrieving her jacket, he raised her pant leg so he could take a look at her knee. It was swollen and reddened. He probed gently.

In the act of thrusting an arm into her coat, Christy froze. "Ouch!"

"I think we should have the paramedics take you along with them."

"To the hospital?" She finished putting on the jacket. "It's not that bad, Quinn." Her knee hurt like hell, but she wasn't prepared to admit it. She crossed her arms over her chest and hunched her shoulders, trying to banish the cold.

"Maybe not, but I'd like to have you checked out anyway."

The paramedics came out, carefully maneuvering the stretcher down the stairs from the porch to the walk. Eve's form lay still and pale on the white surface. Christy had a vivid visual image of her crashing against the desk as her body absorbed Gerry's vicious blow. She must have made a sound of distress, for the paramedics paused and one detached herself from her place at the end of the stretcher. Quinn spoke to her, then she crouched beside Christy. She examined Christy's knee, then suggested she ride with them to the hospital.

"I'm okay. Really."

The paramedic looked at Quinn, who was now sitting beside Christy on the stairs, holding her hand. He said, "It's a good idea, Chris."

She frowned, feeling mutinous.

Quinn smiled and rubbed her knuckles with his thumb. "There is an added benefit, you know."

Figuring out what that cryptic comment meant was way beyond her. Right now she had more important things to think about. She reached in her pocket and pulled out her cell phone. "I wonder if it still works?"

He gently turned her face toward him with his fingertips on her cheek. His smile was warm, kind of amused, but there was concern in his eyes. She wasn't sure why.

"If you go to the hospital in the ambulance, we can get you out of here without facing the press."

"Oh." She stared at him. "Oh! I hadn't thought." She pondered the idea for a moment, without making much headway.

"Say yes," Quinn said, smiling at her.

Put that way, it seemed like a good idea. "Yeah, okay. I'll go."

"I'll meet you there."

She looked at him and smiled. "Yes, please."

The arrest of Gerry Fisher for the murder of Brianne Lymbourn and Frank Jamieson produced a media frenzy. The details of Frank's disappearance were hauled out and re-examined. Christy became a heroine, a loving wife desperately trying to find her husband, then courageously facing a murderer to reveal the truth.

Within a week the media had moved on to other stories, but the arrest of Gerry Fisher, occurring the day before Halloween, meant that Noelle spent the thirty-first inside, away from prying eyes. Christy regretted that. She'd always enjoyed trick or treating and Noelle's experience as the Jamieson heir had been sedate, well managed parties. Noelle didn't seem to mind missing the new experience, though, so Christy told herself not to worry.

Though much ink had been used and videotape wasted on the Jamieson-Lymbourn murders, no one had put the whole story together. Elements were missing. Elements Christy knew. Elements Quinn knew.

Of all of the stories that were filed about Gerry Fisher's crime, not one was by Quinn Armstrong. Weeks ago they had made a deal: when the mystery was solved, Christy would provide Quinn with an interview and he would write his article. Somewhere along the way he'd come to understand why she avoided media attention. Now, even though he was part of the biggest story the area had seen for months, he hadn't used his insider information. He wouldn't write his account because he cared about her, and he didn't want to hurt her.

Because he loved her.

All Christy had to do was to get him to admit it.

She chose her timing carefully. On a Saturday evening she waited until Noelle was in bed, with the cat asleep beside her, then she carefully shut the door to her daughter's room. She changed from the sweatshirt she'd worn all day into a silk shirt that slithered over her skin and emphasized the shape of her breasts. She paired that with form-fitting jeans that clung to her hips.

Then she called Quinn. "Hi. Have you got a few minutes? Can you come over?"

There was a slight hesitation before he said, "Sure."

Christy hardly had time to dim the lights and touch a match to the candles she had arranged in the living room before she heard the bell.

He paused at the top of the stairs. "This looks like a seduction."

Christy smiled a slow, pleased smile. "Would it be so bad if it was?"

The intensity in his eyes made her heart thump. "You don't have to seduce me, Christy."

"No." She gestured toward the living room. "It's not really a seduction. The candles are for...tenderness. Mellowness anyway." He sat on the couch. As she sank down beside him, she said, "I asked you over, Quinn, because I want to give you a gift."

He reached over to draw her close. "Your body?"

She laughed at his half-teasing suggestion and leaned her cheek on his shoulder. He was wearing a v-necked sweater that was scratchy under her skin. "You wish."

He laughed too, then bent his head. He kissed her slowly, thoroughly, until she was pliant against him. When he drew away she wanted more.

It would have to wait. She cleared her throat. "Quinn, I need to know. Are you writing an article about Frank's life? About his murder?"

His fingers fiddled with her hair. "Christy," he began. Then he shook his head and said simply, "There won't be a story."

"Why not?"

"I couldn't put you through that."

Catching his hand, she raised it to her lips. "Thank you."

He smiled.

"But not telling the story isn't an option."

He sat up. "Hold on a second—"

She was shaking her head before he had even finished. "No. Listen to me, Quinn. You're the only journalist who knows the full story. I want you to write it. I don't care whether it's an article, or a documentary, or a book. I just want you to do it. And I'll provide you with whatever details you need, no strings attached."

He stared at her, frowning. "What happened to your dislike of the media and your desire for privacy?"

She laid her hand against his cheek. "Nothing's changed, Quinn, except my feelings for you. I trust you to tell my story. I also know that you won't write it unless I ask you to. So I'm asking you now, please write the story, Quinn. For Frank, for Noelle, but mainly for me."

Quinn stared at her. She was smiling at him in a way that was almost mischievous, as if she knew how shocked he was. The gift she had given him was incredible. The potential in the story of the Jamieson Trust was massive. There would be articles, a book, a television documentary, perhaps a movie deal. The story could fuel his creative energies for months. Afterward he would be able to pick any assignment he wanted, anywhere in the world.

Anywhere in the world sounded pretty bleak without family around him.

He looked at Christy consideringly. "Before I accept your gift, I need the answer to a question."

"Okay." She sounded cautious. That was good. He wanted her to think carefully about this.

"Your gift may be given out of trust, but I think it was also given with love. Am I right?"

She traced the shape of his mouth with her finger. "Yes."

He raised his brows. "That's it? Just yes?"

She laughed, a light-hearted sound that filled him with joy. "I love you, Quinn. How's that?"

She would not be an easy woman to be with. She was headstrong, independent, and managing. She didn't hide away from problems. Instead, she faced them down, not always in the most sensible of ways. She would be far more inclined to chase after a threat than to try to avoid it. "Sounds pretty good to me." He cupped her cheek with his hand. "You scared the hell out of me last week, running off to Fisher's place. Promise me you won't do anything like that again."

"I promise." She crossed her heart solemnly.

"Okay. Since you promised, can I kiss you now?"

She laughed. "Sounds good to me."

*Turn the page for an
excerpt from*

THE
CAT'S PAW

The 9 Lives Cozy Mystery Series

Book Two

◆

Louise Clark

——◆——

"So you're a friend of Brit's," Lorne Cossi said. He looked her over, from the top of her head to her feet, his gaze lingering too long on her breasts and then—disconcertingly—on her groin. When his gaze drifted back to her face there was something unnerving in the depths of his dark blue eyes. "Frankly, you don't seem her type."

Christy flushed. She'd met guys like Cossi before. Arrogant, self-absorbed jerks who assumed every female in sight was a sexual plaything, there for a man's enjoyment. "And what was her 'type'?"

Cossi smiled slowly. It wasn't a nice smile. "Silly women who'll do anything for a lay. Especially if they can get high at the same time." He cocked his head. "You now, you look disturbingly sober."

Christy figured he'd meant that as an insult. She thought it was actually a compliment, given who it came from. "If you'd bothered to listen, you'd find that people act out of 'type' all the time."

Cossi raised his brows. There was a contemptuous curl to his upper lip that said he didn't like backtalk from uppity women.

Christy allowed herself a small smile. "Take Brittany, for example. Here she was, grad student, privileged daughter of a wealthy Calgary family, and a party girl, with the likes of Aaron DeBolt, a man whose reputation doesn't bear scrutiny. Now tell me, Mr. Cossi, what exactly was Brittany's 'type'?"

His eyes lit with temper before he said mildly, "Brittany Day was a nasty little tease who came on to every man she met."

"Including you?"

"Including me."

"Did you take her up on her offer?" Christy could hardly believe she'd asked that, but she had.

His mouth quirked up into a very real smile and he laughed. "What do you think?"

"I think you did."

"And you'd be right." He took a threatening step forward.

Christy didn't move. But she wanted to. Oh, how much she wanted to.

"If a sexy piece like Brittany Day offers me her body, who am I to refuse?"

Another step. At this rate he'd cross the small space in another couple of moments and he'd be right in front of her. In her space. Intimidating her. Maybe even taking it further. The desire to flee was strong.

She glared at him, sending him a message. "That's pretty cold."

He shrugged, but he stopped. "There was something dark in Brit and she pulled it out in other people too. She liked Ecstasy and Meth. She tried to get me hooked on the stuff."

"Did she?"

This time he shook his head. "No. No way am I polluting my brain with that kind of junk."

The answer sounded honest to Christy. Lorne Cossi probably had aspirations of entering the academic world as a professor. Frying his brain wouldn't help him achieve his goal.

"Have you shared this office space with Brittany since she started?"

The question didn't fit with the previous ones. Cossi eyed her thoughtfully and paused to think before he answered. Why? It wasn't a hard question. It was a yes or no answer.

"Yes," he said, finally. "Rochelle and I set up the office the year we both began. Brad came next, then Brittany."

"It's a small space. An easy place for everyday habits to become irritating. Tempers tend to flare when people have to share limited resources."

His expression hardened and anger glinted in his eyes. "Are you accusing me of Brit's murder?"

Was she? Until he reacted with such heat she hadn't actually thought of it. She shrugged, but didn't confirm or deny.

Lorne Cossi chose to take her shrug as acknowledgement. His temper flared hotter. "Brittany Day was a lazy bitch who used her body and her family connections to smooth her path. She was entitled and manipulative. Worse, from my point of view, she wasn't even all that good as a mathematician."

"Then why was she here?" Christy wasn't sure she believed Cossi, though he sounded genuinely annoyed.

He flung himself away, turning toward the window. "Don't you get it?" he said. "She was sleeping with our fearless leader, the good Dr. Peiling. Why else?"

------◆------

The Cat's Paw

available in print and ebook

THE
9 LIVES COZY MYSTERY
SERIES

The Cat Came Back
The Cat's Paw
(More to follow)

Louise Clark is the author of cozy mysteries and contemporary and historical romance novels. She holds a BA in History from Queen's University.

For more information, please visit her at www.louiseclarkauthor.com or on Facebook at www.facebook.com/LouiseClarkAuthor.

LOUISE CLARK

9 Lives Cozy Mystery 🐾 Book 1

Stormy the Cat, rescued by journalist Quinn Armstrong, is not what he seems.

Young mother, Christy Jamieson, just learned her husband, Frank, embezzled his trust fund, sold their Vancouver mansion, and ran off with a socialite. Worse, Frank's trustees are telling Christy to let them handle it. But they aren't doing anything, and Frank's enemies are coming after her and her daughter.

Desperate to find Frank and fend off his enemies, Christy asks Quinn for help. His price: the dirt on Frank. But the closer Christy and Quinn get to the dangerous truth, the more convinced they become that the only one who knows where Frank is at, is Stormy the Cat.

THE CAT CAME BACK

ISBN 978-1-61417-858-3

90000

9 781614 178583